DIVA

Diva

Barrett Magill

SAPPHIRE BOOKS

SALINAS, CALIFORNIA

Diva

Copyright © 2020 by Barrett Magill. All rights reserved.

ISBN - 978-1-952270-10-9

This is a work of fiction - names, characters, places, and incidents are the product of the author's imagination or are used fictitiously. Any resemblance to actual persons living or dead, business, events or locales is entirely coincidental.

All rights reserved. No part of this publication may be reproduced, distributed, or transmitted in any form or by any means, including photocopying, recording, or other electronic or mechanical methods, without written permission of the publisher.

Editor - Heather Flournoy
Book Design - LJ Reynolds
Cover Design - TreeHouse Studio

Sapphire Books Publishing, LLC
P.O. Box 8142
Salinas, CA 93912
www.sapphirebooks.com

Printed in the United States of America
First Edition – October 2020

This and other Sapphire Books titles can be found at
www.sapphirebooks.com

Dedication

To all of the souls we have lost in 2020, for those lost to senseless violence and so many gone from an insidious virus that wasn't stopped in time. R.I.P.

Acknowledgments

First, I would like to thank one of my oldest friends, Annie Waterman, for her generous gift of sharing music. I learned about the classics from her (Erik Satie, Bach, Darius Milhaud). She taught me about 12-bar blues after we saw Muddy Waters in Old Town, Chicago. And opera, she took me to see Birgit Nielsen in Aida.

When I moved to New Mexico, she invited me to join her at the Santa Fe Opera where they had season tickets. It was breathtaking! (And inspired this book.) Well trained in French, she also reviewed an early version of the book. Thank you, Annie!

When the Golden Crown Literary Society began a mentoring program, I was fortunate to have KG MacGregor review and provide her suggestions. Thanks, KG. It finally got published.

Many thanks to my friend and beta reader, MaryAnn Bosworth, for always supporting me and my work.

This book might never have seen the light of day had it not been for L.J. Reynolds, who read an early version nine years ago and pestered me relentlessly to submit it. L.J., I hope you enjoy this—and thank you.

I'm grateful to Chris Svendsen, my publisher and friend for supporting my vision and providing so many learning opportunities. I'm delighted my books have found a home with Sapphire Books Publishing.

The story you are reading is the polished version that comes from a good editor. Heather Flournoy, I am so grateful to have you by my side for this journey .

As always, F.O.W.H. #251 and my Lodge sisters have continued to buoy me up during rough seas and cheer me through good times.

TreeHouse Studio and Ann McMan are the creative force behind the inspirational book covers and the Push I frequently need. Salem is my gentle nudge.

Finally, I'd like to thank my brother, John, for his company, loving support, and enormous help the past four months of this endless *Pandemic. The perfect roommate.*

To my readers. Always, I write for you. Your kind words are the fuel for my engine. Thank you.

Act I Scene 1

"Bravo!" The movie theater audience erupted in applause as the last chords of Bellini's *La Sonnambula* faded. My heart pounded in rhythm with the clapping hands. My throat constricted and my eyes burned as a rush of emotions welled up inside me—not all of them good. *That could have been me singing just as we did when Nicole performed it with us in Santa Fe.*

Again, the nagging reminder of what might have been.

Some kinds of music bypassed all my safety valves and tore me open. This particular performance and Nicole Bernard seared my senses. Judging by the enthusiastic energy around me, I wasn't alone.

My friend Liz let go of my arm. "I have never seen anything so incredible! It was wonderful—the music, the costumes, all of it. Thank you so much. Meg Ellis, you are just the best friend for making me come along. And wasn't Amina amazing? Her voice is mesmerizing."

"I know, this is the same show we did together when I was apprenticing in Santa Fe with different staging. I loved it then. Nicole Bernard is by far the most amazing performer around—singer, actor, and dancer."

"Really? Now I see why you were so smitten. No wonder you loved working with her." She grinned slyly.

Jeez. That's an understatement. "True. She's so gifted and generous with new young singers. Whenever we had some extra time she would help us individually, or even give small master classes."

We trailed along with the slow-moving crowd exiting the theater. Liz engaged a woman behind her in the rapture of the moment. I felt relieved and excited because one of my closest friends had finally attended one of the Met HD performances with me. Plus, the experience evoked some warm memories. The HD series was new but incredibly popular with opera lovers and regular moviegoers. Live broadcasts from the Metropolitan Opera for twenty bucks were hard to beat.

It took about fifteen minutes to exit the multiplex, and Liz and I agreed it was too late to stop anywhere for a bite to eat. It was after eleven and Liz had to work in the morning.

"I'm glad we had a chance to get together," I said as we embraced.

"Me too. It's always good to see you, Meg. Be careful driving back to Santa Fe."

"I'm going to stay at my folks' house tonight. I'll head back to Santa Fe in the morning. Take care, Liz."

It was less than a mile to my parents' house, and I parked on the street so they could get out in the morning. The back door was unlocked for me and I could hear Murphy's tail wagging before I was halfway in the door.

"Hi, girl," I whispered as she nuzzled me. "I know, I'm glad to see you too. Let's go upstairs."

After getting ready for bed, I slipped between the soft, clean-smelling sheets as Murphy jumped up in front of me and curled up. I wrapped one arm around her and rubbed her belly. My meager energy stores faded as I stroked the dog's silky fur and thought back to when we got her.

While going through cancer treatment two years earlier, I had stayed with my parents. Since they both worked, they wanted me to have a companion. The three-year-old Labrador retriever became more than a companion. She was my best friend during one of the most horrible periods of my life.

Moonlight danced across my heavy eyelids and Murphy's breathing became slower and deeper. The fur on her neck carried the scent of freshly cut grass, and my breathing began to match hers.

When I awoke, the bed was empty and the house smelled like cinnamon. I dressed and went downstairs to find a note:

Good morning sweetie. I'm sorry I couldn't stay to visit with you but I had an early student.
I made your favorite cinnamon rolls and there is fresh coffee in the carafe.
Call me later and tell me what you thought about the opera. The New York Times raved!
I love you,
Mom

The phone was ringing when I unlocked my front door, and I tripped over my tote bag reaching for the phone. *Shit.* "Hello?" I said, juggling the receiver. Pearson, my cat, took the phone call as a cue and began to rub against my knees, meowing.

"Hello, this is Thad Allen from the Santa Fe Opera. May I speak with Margaret Ellis?"

"This is she."

"Ms. Ellis, I'm calling you because of your previous association with our apprentice program. Something new came up this summer—a kind of situation—and we started brainstorming...well, your name came up. If you're available, we might be able to use your help."

My imagination went wild trying to imagine why this venerated opera company would want to talk to me. "Gosh, I'm flattered. What kind of situation is it and what would it entail?"

The young man at the other end of the phone laughed a little nervously. "I don't want to sound like this is all cloak and dagger, but it is a rather sensitive matter and...it would be better to speak with you in person. Is there any chance you could come for a meeting?"

"I think so, when did you want to do this?"

"Would tomorrow afternoon be too early? Maybe come around three or four?"

I sat down hard on the stool at the counter. What could possibly be so important that he needed to see me immediately? I was intrigued. "That would work."

Memories flooded back of the two years I worked as an apprentice. Some of my happiest memories remained linked to the people I met and the friendships I formed during that time. It was during those two summers that my dream of becoming an opera singer was born, I met the woman who would become my partner, and I studied with a remarkable singer who would become my idol—the same one I watched perform last night.

Just getting the phone call brought back a rush of emotions. In all honesty, there was nothing wrong with my job as a school nurse; I loved the kids, I had the summers off, and it paid decently. It just hadn't been my dream. I studied nursing as a means to my goal of a reliable career. "Guess I'll find out tomorrow. Right, Pearson?" I reached down and stroked his back.

Then the overfilled laundry basket got my attention. "Pearson, weren't you going to handle this?"

After I started the first load, I tackled the stack of mail and unpaid bills on my kitchen counter.

"Of what possible interest could I be to the Santa Fe Opera all these years later?" I asked my disinterested cat who was lying comfortably on the newspapers strewn artistically on the table.

※※※※

The drive north from Santa Fe to Tesuque, home of the fabled Santa Fe Opera, went quickly as my brain conjured dozens of different scenarios from grand theft—for taking part of my costume, a rehearsal skirt—to offering me a job because of the superb work I did as an apprentice. But surely they had notes in their records about why I left the company, so that couldn't be it.

The name Thad Allen didn't ring a bell. He must be one of the new underlings in Creative Services. I didn't keep up with many of the people I knew and it'd been more than three years since I worked there. Of course there would be changes in personnel.

I drove slowly through the upper parking lot toward the pavilion and stopped, putting the car in Park as memories flooded back. I smiled. This parking lot had been the site of my first make-out session with a girl. A girl I went home with after our second date. *How long were we necking like teenagers in that Chevy Blazer the first night? Long enough, I guess.*

The trees on either side of the parking lot were beginning to bud out because of the warm spring weather. The groundskeepers were repairing the damage from the winter snows and brutal winds, which ripped across the mesa. The beautiful sail-shaped roof panels on the pavilion not only lent a dramatic air to the mesa-topped theater, they also collected rainwater that the crew used in the landscaping.

The scene felt almost subdued today. It was as though a dead calm enveloped the large sailing ship and stranded her in a windless sea. In a short time, this whole area would be bustling with activity and sound. I felt a small ripple of energy run through me remembering the excitement.

I'd been so happy during those summers, and it was where I met Bekka, my first serious relationship. I swallowed hard as my chest tightened recalling our ugly breakup. I quickly put the car in Drive, steered around the east side and down the hill to the offices.

Parking the car in front, I found the handsome Mr. Allen waving from the door waiting for me. He couldn't have been more than twenty-three years old with blond, gelled hair combed back and a gold stud in his left ear. His sharp navy blue slacks and crisp pink oxford shirt made me feel sloppy. He had just the right combination of sculpted good looks and boyish enthusiasm.

His neat appearance made me glad I had my hair cut recently, but my khaki pants and short-sleeved black shirt looked somewhat casual compared to Thad. He ignored my outfit and enthusiastically reached for my hand. I liked him immediately.

"I'm so glad you could make it." He pumped my hand briskly.

"I'm glad to be here, and a little surprised that I've been asked."

He held the door open and waved me in. "Please come in. May I offer you some iced tea or water?" He ushered me into a small conference room with a round cherry table and leather chairs. I sat in one of the armchairs near the window and tried to inhale a few deep breaths. *You are not in trouble, they only want to talk to you, and you don't have to do anything.*

"Iced tea would be lovely, thank you."

Thad returned with a small tray containing a pitcher and several glasses, followed by a tall woman with curly brown hair pulled back in a twist. She looked imperious as she walked in, but her soft gray eyes sparkled with warmth.

"Mrs. Mueller, may I introduce Ms. Margaret Ellis, who has graciously driven up here from Santa Fe to meet with us."

The formalities were short lived. Turned out, Mrs. Mueller's title was "Guest Artist Liaison," and she was much less formal than her initial appearance. I vaguely remembered her from a couple of meetings while I was apprenticing. Her face flushed pink with warmth, and she removed her jacket and then sat down next to me.

"Please call me Greta. I'm delighted you were able to come on short notice. Now if I may, let me cut to the chase." She sighed loudly. "There is a very delicate issue I'd like to discuss and would rather it did not leave this room. Ms. Ellis, we would be very grateful if you could help us with this, but if not I'll certainly understand. I had Thad call you because you worked in our apprentice program, but also because your background is in nursing."

She took a deep breath and a large swallow of iced tea, and put the glass down in front of her but held it with both hands. Her facial expression turned serious. I said nothing, but she had my full attention.

"You are probably aware this summer's repertoire includes a new production of *La Traviata* with Nicole Bernard. We're all very excited about this new production, especially since Lars Logan will be guest directing."

"Yes, I was thrilled when I read about it, probably the biggest draw of the season." At least it would be for me. "I love that opera, and there is no singer I admire more than Nicole Bernard."

"I believe it will be, judging by early ticket sales. And since you are already familiar with Madame, well…here's the dilemma. Madame Bernard generally travels with her family because they use this engagement as a kind of vacation. This year however, her husband is unable to be with her. And her parents won't be here until later. We feel it's possible that she might need some assistance, though, as you might guess, she is not convinced of that.

"The second part of the dilemma is medical. She has developed a slight health problem. I don't need to tell you these items are strictly confidential. It seems her blood sugar fluctuates unpredictably, and she has experienced several episodes where she collapses unexpectedly."

I didn't know what they thought I could do about either of those problems.

Greta stood up, walked over to a desk in the corner, and returned with a file folder, which contained several legal-looking forms. "'We'd like to offer you, with Madame Bernard's tacit agreement, a job working as her personal assistant for the duration of the show. The Santa Fe Opera would technically handle the paperwork, and we would pay you. Of course, she will set the terms according to her needs. Your obligation to the company is to provide the support service, which will enable her to perform consistently and safely. Of course, we understand you cannot guarantee that. We would also expect you to sign a confidentiality agreement. If you're interested in this position, Thad will take you over to meet with her to be sure you're both in agreement. Would you like to look over the forms?"

Are you kidding me? A chance to work with Nicole Bernard...every day. This would be a dream come true. My heart thudded so loudly I was sure they could hear it up in the pavilion. "I'm flattered and completely at a loss. This is an incredible opportunity, but I have to be honest. I really have no experience being anyone's assistant, and my nursing experience has been primarily with schoolchildren. If she has a serious medical problem—"

"Yes, we understand, it's for safety. We know you worked with her when she did *La Sonnambula* several years ago, so you have the advantage of knowing how our programs work."

This got better and better. They wanted to pay me money to spend three months with Nicole Bernard. I thought my head would explode. "Well if Madame is agreeable, I would love the opportunity."

Greta sighed loudly and slumped back in her

chair. "Right now nothing is more important than the safety of my biggest star. Her happiness and well-being are paramount, and you will earn my undying gratitude."

Thad beamed at both of us. "Shall I'd take her over to see Ms. Bernard?"

"By all means. Let me call her to make sure it's all right. Will that work for you, Margaret?"

"Sure. I only wish I had time to go and buy a new outfit."

"Don't worry about that. It's more important you both feel comfortable."

⁂

Thad jabbered as he navigated an all-terrain vehicle up through the back lot to the main road and then turned west into a nearby gated community. "One of our biggest benefactors owns a home in this community and he makes it available for Ms. Bernard and her family whenever they come to New Mexico."

"The streets, they're all named after musical things," I said. The first street sign read *La Scala*, the next *La Traviata*. "What fun names." During my two years as an apprentice, I never saw this little gem.

He turned right onto *Camino Caruso*, which wound up into the hills overlooking vast open areas surrounded by majestic mountain peaks. The view amazed me. At the end of a cul-de-sac sat a very large modern adobe home. He parked and we started walking up the concrete squares curving to the entrance. I marveled at the hand-carved wooden door and heavy iron fittings. Thad lifted the knocker once and dropped it with a resounding clank.

The large door swung open to reveal the amazing Nicole Bernard. She smiled warmly and nodded as she listened to Thad's introduction. She laughed as Thad regaled her with the story of finding me. More than once, she touched his arm as though they were lifelong friends. No wonder people loved her. I stood stock-still and stared with a stupid grin on my face.

She looked wonderful. It had been years since I had seen her in person. Her light blond hair was shorter and pulled back in a loose ponytail. I had forgotten she was a couple inches shorter than I, probably five foot five, and slim. Perhaps she had lost weight? She had on white cotton drawstring pants and a tight white tank top. Her eyes had not changed a bit. They were still large, intense, peacock blue gems looking directly at me.

Thad put his hand on my elbow and moved me closer as Nicole carefully took my hand and held it.

"I think I remember you, you were in *La Sonnambula* with me, the lovely mezzo soprano. But there was something else…ah, it was so long ago, such a nice surprise to see you again. Please come and sit down." Her soft French accent turned words into silky syllables.

She led me by the hand to a large seating area in what must have been the main living area. The walls were off-white plaster with a couple of large windows overlooking the mountains. I quickly scanned the open space with the kitchen off to the right. The back of my bare knees brushed the front of the plush leather sofa that faced the fireplace.

Open your mouth, Ellis. You need to respond or she will think you are retarded.

"Madame Bernard, I can't tell you how thrilled I am to see you again and to be offered an opportunity to work with you. This is something many people would love to do…It's a privilege…" *Shut up, Ellis. You're blithering.*

Fortunately, Thad intervened so I didn't have to kill myself. They were discussing Greta's earlier phone call and the fact I had agreed to take the position, if Madame was agreeable.

"Thad, is it possible for you to leave us for an hour, so I can talk more with Ms. Ellis?" Nicole's soft voice and delicious accent would render almost any human being helpless, doubly so her biggest fan.

"Of course, Madame. I have some things to check on and will return in an hour, unless you call." Before I could take a breath, she had escorted him to the door and was standing in front of me.

"Would you care for something to drink? I am supposed to drink juice at regular intervals, but I'm sure they told you all about my spells."

"No, thank you, Madame. I've just finished some iced tea." I hoped she didn't notice my perspiration.

"I think, if we work together, you should please call me Nicole." She was already in the kitchen pouring something from the refrigerator.

"Thank you, yes, of course. I will. My friends call me Meg." I took another breath and shook my tingling arms and fingers to loosen them. My God, I was stammering.

Nicole returned to the sofa with a tall glass and a file folder, both of which she placed on the glass coffee table. The sofa cushions sank slightly as she sat down next to me. I could smell the faintest hint of lilies of the valley. Without makeup, she looked even younger than her forty years. Once again, she was staring at me.

"You are so familiar." She smiled again. "I must tell you this whole idea of hiring an assistant is rather silly. I am perfectly capable of taking care of myself. I understand the concern because of liability problems, but I am not certain I need a babysitter."

She reached for the file folder and pulled out several papers. "Greta told me you are a nurse, so I think these papers from my doctor will mean more to you than to me. You may take them with you to read." She leaned back. "What happens is I get very lightheaded and sometimes faint." She laughed. "It is amusing to see everyone running around like chickens. It would not be so funny if it would happen during a performance, I think." Nicole stood up and walked over to the wide fireplace. Her manner changed as though some grave thought intruded.

"Greta believes we can avoid this if I have someone help me monitor my blood sugar and remind me to drink. Perhaps so, I am not convinced. Do you think she is right, Meg? Is this an important problem? Is it something you could do?"

. Nothing brought me back to my comfort level better than talking about my profession or music. Of course, I needed to read her doctor's explanation, but if this were straightforward hypoglycemia, no problem. "Yes, I'm quite sure I could help, and it might take a worry off your mind so you could concentrate on your job and give us another brilliant performance."

The cloud seemed to vanish. "All right. I suppose there is no harm, and I certainly could use reminding." The relief faded slightly. She was leaning back against the low mantel on both elbows and it was impossible not to notice the absence of a bra. I tried hard to focus on her eyes, which looked worried and darker suddenly.

"There is another matter, which you must know about if you work with me. It is private and serious. I need to know you will not talk about this with anyone."

"Nicole, since I will be working for you, anything you tell me is confidential except those things your doctor needs to know."

She returned to the seating area and sat in a companion chair to my left. She tucked her legs beneath her and fidgeted with the drawstring on her pants. I waited.

"For several years, my husband Mario and I have arranged our travels schedule in order to help one another for performances."

I had heard this from more than one source. Her husband, the rising new tenor Mario De Luca, accompanied her whenever she traveled, and she returned the favor. Greta had just told me he would not be joining her.

"Mario is not able to be here this year because he has chosen other…obligations. Mario would normally help me to rehearse. This year is different, as he has more important things to occupy him," she said with a clear note of bitterness.

Nicole didn't look at me but clenched her hands in her lap. "You know, one of my favorite reasons for coming to Santa Fe is all the time I am allowed to create the role while working with the director and this wonderful company."

She looked up at me but she wasn't quick enough to hide the sadness I saw in her eyes. "That is another reason they wanted to choose a former apprentice, because you understand the rehearsal schedule and the demands of a new role. Greta told me you also can play piano."

I wanted to laugh, but settled for a polite smile. "She was being kind. I can read music, but I'm not a pianist. I can certainly help you rehearse and I would enjoy it. Working with you would be an honor, Nicole."

Her face broke into a smile, and mine did the same.

"Well then, Meg, I think we will work together. Tell me, do you live far away?"

"No, actually. I live on the west side of Santa Fe so it doesn't take very long to get here. Do you have any idea of what kind of a schedule you'd like me to work?"

She draped her right arm across the back of the chair and cocked her head to one side. "I suppose you do need some sort of plan, don't you? I did not think too far ahead. We start rehearsal Monday. I have been working a little with Lars, our incredible director. You know, I don't really have a daily schedule yet. Generally I do my yoga first thing in the morning, then I run for a short while." Her laugh bubbled up like water in a brook rippling over stones. "In spite of what the interviewers tell you, it takes me a long time to get used to the altitude here. I run to increase my stamina, not for any athletic reason."

The sun returned to her bright eyes and I could tell I was going to be in a lot of trouble working so closely with this beautiful woman. *Stamina.* I swallowed and tried to keep my mind on the subject of her well-being and not my juvenile fantasies. Her public persona blossomed when she spoke with such joy and animation.

Act I Scene 2

My weekend plans changed in a hurry. Originally, I had planned some lazy self-indulgence as a reward for completing another busy school year. Instead, I decided I'd better concentrate on laundry, house cleaning, and grocery shopping, as well as boning up on the treatment of hypoglycemia.

For my musical homework, I chose two different recordings of *La Traviata* from my growing CD collection. I wanted to be ready. Shortly after listening to Anna Netrebko sing the first aria, the exquisite music permeated me. Just thinking about Nicole singing that aria and being in such close proximity gave me goose bumps. I uttered a silent prayer I'd be able to hold it together during rehearsals so I could get my job done without behaving foolishly. More than once in my life, I'd embarrassed myself with an overly emotional public display.

My cell phone chirped from under a pile on the kitchen counter, and I scrambled to check the caller ID since I gave the number to Nicole. In fact, it wasn't Nicole, and I tried to keep any hint of disappointment out of my voice when I answered.

"Hi, Liz. How are you?"

"I got your message, but I couldn't call you back because we had company. What's up?"

I could hear her stereo in the background. "Are you sitting down?"

"Yes…oh my God! You found someone special and fell in love?" Liz's voice went up an octave, indicating her excitement.

"Not exactly, but maybe the next best thing. Do you remember us talking about Nicole Bernard after seeing the opera?"

"Sure, the one who made the big impression, with the incredible voice?"

"The same. Well, when I got home on Thursday, the Santa Fe Opera called wanting to talk to me, in person. I drove up there and met with some of the staff, and they offered me a part-time job—are you ready for this? As Nicole Bernard's personal assistant." As I said the words, I could feel fluttering in my chest. I'd been so busy taking care of chores and preparing I hadn't allowed the full impact to hit me.

"Shut up. How in the hell did that happen? You haven't worked there for years—suddenly, bang!" Liz said. She knew what this meant to me.

"I guess they went through the files to find a former apprentice with some medical experience, and I fit the bill. I'm starting on Monday."

"Oh Meg, that's so exciting. What will your job entail?"

"I'm not sure. There's no real job description because they've never needed it. I guess I'll improvise. I did have to sign a confidentiality agreement."

"Meg, is this going to be hard for you? I know you were majorly crushing on this woman and you've been alone awhile…"

I was embarrassed when she reminded me of my crush. It was true, but I didn't want to let it interfere with my job because this was too big an opportunity to blow. "When I first saw her it was incredibly awkward, but after we talked for a while it was fine. She's a professional and a very kind person, and I think it will work out fine. She really needs some assistance, and honestly, I love being there with all the people and the music. I've missed it."

"It sounds like a wonderful opportunity, and I know you'll do a great job," Liz said.

"Thanks a lot, I appreciate it. I had better get back to my chores. I have a ton of stuff to do before I head up there tomorrow morning. Don't worry, I'll keep you in the loop. Send me good thoughts."

"You know I will, hon. Take care."

There was another car in the driveway when I arrived at Nicole's summer residence, a late-model Honda. I rechecked my watch to make sure I wasn't arriving at the wrong time. Nope, right on time. As I approached the front door, I could hear music through the open windows, and I paused before knocking. It was a piano, and it would run for a few bars then stop as two people started talking. When there was another pause, I knocked on the door.

"Come in," Nicole called from somewhere back in the house. Nervous energy fluttered through me.

I entered cautiously, put my backpack near the door, and followed the sound of the voices to a sunny den off the kitchen containing a grand piano at one end and a couch and some chairs at the other. I saw a man seated at the piano marking up the score while Nicole stood next to him pointing out changes. Today she was wearing leggings and a soft brown smock.

She looked up at me and smiled. "Good morning, Meg. Please come in. I'd like you to meet Carl, my accompanist. This is my personal assistant, Meg Ellis."

Carl stood and offered his hand, while Nicole gave me a quick hug. "We will finish in a few moments. You may sit with us, or perhaps you would like to make yourself some tea or coffee?"

"Thank you, I'll leave you two alone and make myself busy."

I slipped out and found my way to an enormous country kitchen. I could hear her singing softly as they reworked several phrases from the opening scenes. Her voice was soothing and velvety. I stood mesmerized. I really was in Nicole Bernard's house listening to her singing. I wanted to pinch myself. Instead, I set about investigating the kitchen.

The refrigerator held a fair amount of fresh produce, fruit juice, bottled water, and a large pitcher of iced tea. I made a mental note to talk with her about what she liked and what kinds of products might affect her voice. Some singers were careful to avoid dairy products and some were careful about hot or cold beverages. I filled a teakettle on the stove, then started looking for tea or coffee.

I found myself enjoying the familiar melodies listening to Nicole sing as I quietly went through the kitchen cupboards. *Nothing like making yourself at home, is there?* I set out three mugs, tea, sugar, and milk just as Nicole and Carl walked through to the living room and the front door. She returned to the kitchen while I poured the hot water.

"What a lovely treat. Too bad Carl had to rush off. I am delighted you made yourself at home instead of waiting for me." She reached for the sugar, brushing against my arm and setting off a small tingle effect up to my neck. "Shall we sit at the table?"

"I'm glad you don't mind," I said with a nervous laugh. "I'd hate to get fired my first day." A blush rose up my neck, furthering my embarrassment.

She laughed and shook her head. "Were the doctor's notes any help for you?" Thank God, a medical topic. She tucked one leg under her, leaning across the table until we were only a foot or two apart. "If they were, maybe you could explain it to me."

I prayed she wouldn't notice the beads of perspiration across my hairline. "Actually, the notes were clear," I said, leaning back in my chair because her closeness was unsettling. "Of course, I don't have all the history. It looks like there's a problem with the way you burn calories. Maybe you just have a fast metabolism. From the doctor's orders it looks like he wants your blood sugar tested daily, and whenever you get light-headed, if ever."

We both sipped our tea as I tried to stay focused. I explained the rationale for eating frequent protein snacks because they metabolized slower. She nodded at appropriate intervals, watching me intently. I tried to remember that English was not her first language and my high school French was pathetic.

After some discussion, we agreed to go through her appointment book so I could get an idea of her plans. She hopped out of her chair and riffled through a large briefcase near the couch to retrieve it. The number of social events required of her surprised me. There were several cocktail parties and interviews in addition to rehearsals and vocal coaching. I saw a scratched-out notation that her husband had been scheduled to visit in two weeks.

"Would you like to take a walk and I will show you around?" Nicole picked up both of our cups and took them to the kitchen sink. "Every Friday the housekeeper comes and she will manage the routine maintenance. The Goddard family lives here only part of the year but they have full-time help."

The layout was very open and sunny; in addition to the clerestory windows there were dozens of skylights spaced between the large wooden vigas in the flat ceiling. At the end of the hall was the master suite, which was spacious and warm. French doors lead to a private balcony. The master bath contained a square sunken tub, glass shower stall, double sinks, and stone floors.

The French doors off the living room opened onto a large covered patio with outdoor wet bar and a built-in grill. Beyond the adobe wall, a path of cement block led to a small walled patio containing a hot tub. The path continued to a charming adobe guesthouse containing a living room, two bedrooms, bath, and a full kitchen.

She locked up the guesthouse and we walked back to the main house, which looked even more majestic against the bright blue sky from the lower vantage point.

"This home is breathtaking. Doesn't it make you feel like a princess living here?" *Lord, I sound like a country bumpkin.* I stammered and said, "I'm sorry, that sounded so stupid. It's just, well, I've seen houses like this, but I never really imagined people lived in them." *Damn.*

Nicole took my arm as we rounded the corner of the patio. She patted my arm. "Do not be embarrassed. I must tell you I do not live like this at home. I have a very small house in the countryside and I have no servants. This does feel very special and I so appreciate their generosity. I hope that is not uncomfortable for you."

"I promise you I will try very hard to get used to it, for your sake." We both laughed.

≈≈≈≈

The next four days were busy for both of us. We had to arrange appointments with the costume department, the music director, the vocal coach, her accompanist, and the PR department. As things seemed to smooth out and the weekend neared, she asked me if I would be willing to accompany her to a special luncheon on Saturday given in her honor by one of the benefactors. Attending fancy black-tie social events was not something I felt comfortable doing. Even though I was so shy, there was no way I could say no to her polite request.

That evening I hurried home to rummage through my closet, hoping to find something that was suitable for the luncheon. After years in the school system, I had virtually given up on owning nice clothes. Common wisdom will tell you nurses don't dress up much after work, at least the nurses I know. Even though I worked in the schools, there was the ever-present danger of infectious bodily fluids from the children, aka Tiny Vectors of Disease.

When my closet failed to deliver, I gave up and went to the mall. I hate going to the mall as much as I hate shopping. Reluctantly, I parked the car a block from an entrance and schlepped back to the J. Crew store.

At least there were a few summer dresses left on the rack, surprising me since it was only the end of May. I hastily picked three to take into the dressing room. Two fit decently so I picked both, figuring I might need to attend some kind of formal function during my three-month tenure. The multicolored sleeveless sundress looked appropriate and actually flattered my figure. The black sheath would be useful with a scarf or sweater. They were both, pleasantly, a size smaller than usual.

A long overdue soaking in the tub Friday night with a glass of wine had me feeling incredulous at how the past week had just flown by. Spending so much time with Nicole was like being in high school again. Even though I'd acted nervous, silly, and awkward, I'd never felt more alive. I had to pinch myself ten times a day. The woman was not only beautiful and talented, but also so very kind to everyone with whom she worked. At every opportunity, she would hug and kiss all of us. Frequently she'd take my hand or put her arm around me at unexpected moments. It was thrilling and a little unnerving.

I wanted to call Liz. I wanted to tell someone how my feelings were growing, but I resisted. A thirty-two-year-old professional woman needed to act with a little decorum. In spite of my best efforts, the long-held attraction was flourishing.

Act I Scene 3

I arrived on time Saturday morning with my dress on a hanger and everything else in my bag. There was a note on the front door.

Come in, Meg. I'll be right back. N

I took down the note and stared at it. *My first personal communication.* I folded it carefully and put it in my pocket. Her delicate handwriting was small and flowery.

The house was quiet, so I took the opportunity to wander around a little. I stopped at her bedroom door and turned back. It just seemed more appropriate than going through her closet, which was what my devilish imp urged me to do. I wanted to discover more about the enchanting creature that had captivated my imagination for so many years.

The living room was almost too big to be comfortable. A warmly colored adobe wall beside the stairs contained a wide fireplace and divided the entryway from the living room.

I nestled into an overstuffed chair and looked around. It was kind of fun to pretend that I temporarily lived in this sumptuous residence. Made me glad there was help because I'd sure hate to clean it. I had no sooner opened a magazine when I heard the front door and watched as Nicole made her entrance. She had evidently been running, judging by a black jog bra and tight shorts. She smiled immediately when she saw me. My heart skipped a beat—or ten—and I almost dropped the magazine.

"*Bonjour, mon amie.*"

"Hi, Nicole," I managed to reply.

She leaned over at the top of the steps, her hands on her knees. A sheen of perspiration glistened on her creamy white shoulders. She was petite but well-toned, and looked good.

"I must take a shower, I will be right back." She disappeared down the hall to the master suite and I exhaled the breath I held. *Wow*.

I made my way to the kitchen and managed to pour some iced tea, thinking we could both use a cool drink. The woman captivated my imagination and set free a flock of butterflies in my chest every time she walked into the room. I left the glasses on the counter while I checked the refrigerator. I had a hunch that she hadn't eaten and would probably be hungry after her run. I pulled out the carton of eggs and some sliced melon.

The kitchen island was immense and contained a multi-burner stovetop beneath a large exhaust hood in the ceiling. It made me wish I knew how to cook.

I closed my eyes and imagined myself in a professional chef's outfit, starched white apron and a tall white hat, wielding razor-sharp knives with great skill, moving fluidly between steaming pots and sizzling sauté pans. I would also oversee an oven filled with delicate pastries. When all was in readiness, I would pull off my chef costume and be dressed in a fabulous formal black ensemble, and pick up two beautiful plates and carry them to the adjoining dining room.

The unique round dining area sat at the east end of the kitchen. Three double-hung windows and a patio door covered the curved outside wall. Carefully formed and intricate concentric circular patterns of wood pieces created the wood floor and ceiling. An outsized oak pedestal table added a warm sturdy presence, which complemented the beamed ceiling in the kitchen.

I looked up to find Nicole standing near the entrance watching me.

"You look very far away," she said with a bemused smile, towel drying her hair. She wore a dusty-rose silk robe over bare legs that were lovely.

"I'm sorry. I guess I was daydreaming," I said, feeling my face grow hot. "Would you like some iced tea?"

When I looked more closely, her flushed cheeks had turned pale and her eyes unfocused. "Nicole?" I quickly moved toward her just as her knees began to buckle. Fortunately, she fell forward and I was able to catch her. I managed to get her into the adjacent den and into a large chair with an ottoman. Her breathing was slow and regular, but she was frightfully pale, probably the result of overexertion and a hot shower. I hurried to the kitchen for some water and a damp cloth.

Returning to the den, I sat next to her on the footstool and gently wiped her face. Even in a dead faint, she was beautiful. Her features were delicate, and her relaxed posture gave her lips a rosebud appearance. I was holding my breath again, unable to believe she was so close. Her eyes fluttered.

"Nicole, you're all right. You just fainted," I whispered as gently as possible.

Her eyes tried to focus on me and as they sharpened. "Meg? What happened?"

"It's all right. Just rest a minute. Take a drink of water—easy now. I'm not sure, but I'd guess you didn't have breakfast, and then you exercised and took a hot shower…" I placed the damp towel on the back of her neck and took her hand automatically.

She drank a little more of the water and held tightly to my hand. *"Je suis gênée."*

"No need to feel embarrassed Remember, that's why I'm here. No harm done and you weren't hurt. I think it would be a good idea for me to check your blood sugar again. Is the testing kit still in your bathroom?"

"It's on the counter just inside the door."

I jogged to the other end of the house and found the kit, opening it on the way back to the den. I found Nicole sitting up with a bit more color in her face.

"Have you tried this on your own yet?" I pointed to the lancet.

"I tried once but could not stick my finger." She smiled weakly.

"No problem." I pulled on the disposable gloves, swabbed the side of her ring finger, and quickly pushed the button on the lancet.

She jerked slightly, then smiled. "That was not awful. You are so quick."

I scooped a drop of blood into the center of the test stick, placed it in the meter, and held the tip of Nicole's finger tightly with a tissue.

"The test strip reads fifty-six and that's too low. It should come in at between seventy and one hundred. Just sit here while I get you some juice, and I'd like you to eat some eggs if you're able."

"I will try."

"Do you feel up to attending the party this afternoon? Because I can call and cancel," I offered, thinking it might be wiser to stay home.

"Oh, I must attend. Mrs. Carlisle would be so disappointed, and she is such a lovely woman," Nicole said emphatically.

"Okay, you rest a minute."

After handing her a small glass of juice, I melted some butter in the skillet and added the eggs. We still had several hours before the luncheon, and if she rested she would probably be fine. With two slices of melon already on board, I added the scrambled eggs to the plate and delivered it to my charge. I spread the napkin and handed her the plate.

Nicole's eyes lit up. "Thank you, this looks delicious. You were right. I did not think to eat. It is so easy to forget with so many things on my mind."

"I'll let you eat in peace while I clean up," I said, moving to the kitchen.

"Would you stay? I enjoy your conversation. While I eat this lovely meal maybe you could tell me about why you chose not to continue your singing career. I seem to remember you as very enthusiastic."

"Oh, I was. It's sort of a long story and not a happy one. I don't want to unload on you."

"You are not required to tell me anything, but I am interested. You might have been very successful and you seemed to want to continue. Please...I have shared my awful story with you."

I felt the familiar tightness in my chest. I seldom discussed that chapter of my life because so few of my friends understood how much singing meant to me.

I pulled out the oak desk chair and sat down.

I didn't know where to begin. I hadn't talked about it for years, but I knew Nicole, of all people, would understand. After summoning some courage, I said, "Shortly after we did *Sonnambula*, I noticed some problems with hoarseness. That was unusual for me. My partner commented that I was constantly clearing my throat and sounded raspy. I eventually gave in and made an appointment. My doctor sent me to an ear, nose, and throat specialist. He found a small lesion and suggested a microlaryngoscopy."

I pulled at the neck of my T-shirt, which suddenly felt constricting. I could remember that moment as if it were yesterday. The foreboding and dread. That kind of fear was new to me.

Nicole, who had finished eating, was watching me and nodding her head. I read somewhere that she'd had a similar procedure, so I figured she understood what I was saying. Once I started, the unshared words poured out.

"He removed the lesion, but the biopsy indicated a malignancy." My voice cracked as I said the word. "And I required radiation to be sure that it hadn't metastasized. I still have it checked twice a year and there's been no recurrence." My throat was tight and burning with unshared grief.

I continued with some difficulty as the memory came into sharper focus. "I couldn't speak for months, and I've never really tried to sing since then." Tears stung my eyes and I could feel them spill over. I swiped at them and coughed, hoping to avoid a full-scale meltdown.

Nicole sat very still. The compassion radiating from her face was enough to undo my self-control. After what seemed like an interminable silence, I stood up suddenly and went to pick up her dish, hoping to mask the discomfort I felt. When I reached for the plate, Nicole took my hand and pulled me to sit beside her.

"*Chérie, c'est tragique.* Of course, I understand, I have had the same operation. But you must not be afraid, not if you really wish to sing." She smiled gently and put her hand on my cheek.

I swallowed hard and fought the surge of emotion but couldn't stem the sobs shaking within me. I began to cry, and it was all I could do to keep from falling into her lap. She pulled the napkin and wiped my face. The pain and grief tore at me. Being so close to her and sharing this hidden sadness made my heart ache. I wanted to be in her arms.

I took the napkin and plate, then stood up. "I'm sorry. I think hearing the music and being back here stirred things up."

She followed me to the kitchen and watched me as I busied myself with tasks.

"Are you all right?"

I nodded.

"I am better now, too. Perhaps I will start getting ready. I do not know how long we must drive to get to the luncheon. I only know her house is in Santa Fe, Thad gave me directions. Do you feel able to go with me?" she asked, standing at the end of the counter watching me.

"Of course I do. I brought some clothes with me so I don't embarrass you by looking like a ragamuffin." I tried to sound chipper. My puffy red face would surely make me an attractive companion.

"Ragamuffin? What is this?"

I laughed. "A raggedy street urchin."

Nicole looked very confused. "But that is not true. You are a very beautiful woman. I thought that when I met you years ago." She blushed.

Aw, crap.

"Thank you. I'm not sure that's true, but I do clean up pretty well."

※ ※ ※ ※

I splashed my face with cold water at the bathroom sink. I put on eye makeup then applied some mousse to tame my unruly black waves. Surveying myself in the mirror, I decided that I didn't look half bad despite the crying jag. My eyes were still puffy, but the sink splashing helped. My dress fit well and looked nice with the white sandals. A spritz or two of CK One and I was ready for Nicole's public.

Nicole was ready within five minutes of me, and when she walked down the steps into the living room, my breath caught in my chest. She looked amazing. She had chosen a black silk sleeveless top with flowing satin pants paired with expensive high-heeled shoes. Her makeup was perfect and her eyes glowed. She had on a turquoise squash-blossom necklace with matching earrings that accentuated her eyes. Around her waist was a silver Concho belt.

"You look stunning," I croaked, my voice cracking. "Very New Mexico."

"*Merci.* And you were correct, you clean up well. The dress is perfect for you and you look nothing like a raggedy muffin."

We arrived precisely at one o'clock and a valet parked the car. I snuck some of the emergency snacks into my purse and followed Nicole as she strode confidently through the opulent home. Mrs. Carlisle was waiting for us on the large brick patio behind the home. There were half a dozen round tables set up with umbrellas, and a staircase opening up to a spacious lawn with an in-ground pool.

"Oh, Madame Bernard it is such an honor to have you in my home. Thank you so much for joining us today." I watched the perfunctory double-cheek kiss. "And this must be your guest, Margaret Ellis. Welcome." I shook her hand.

Our host spirited Nicole away and I slipped over to a bar where a uniformed server was pouring champagne. "Would you care for a champagne cocktail?"

"Thank you. Think you could make it without the champagne?" He substituted ginger ale and it looked equally bubbly and refreshing for a warm afternoon. There was an unoccupied table nearby, and I chose a seat in the shade.

On the way to Santa Fe, I had suggested Nicole eat one of the energy bars and drink a bottle of water. I didn't know how her body might react to this kind of situation, so I kept an eye on her. The little episode in the morning had demonstrated how quickly she could move from alert to unconscious.

Being somewhat introverted, I was perfectly comfortable to sitting and sipping my drink while Nicole worked the room, so to speak. Every single woman at the luncheon enjoyed a gracious smile, handshake, and a few kind words. Nicole treated everyone she met with respect and interest. *The Opera should be paying her more for this kind of goodwill.* I couldn't be happier or prouder being in the company of the most interesting and amazing woman I had ever known.

Two or three times I saw her look around until she found me staring back. We both smiled and lifted our glasses in mock salute.

After half an hour or so of mingling, I was feeling pleasantly relaxed and enchanted by the half dozen hummingbirds at a nearby feeder. I felt cool fingers on the back of my neck and looked up to see Nicole slip behind me and pull out the chair next to me. I shivered at the touch.

"This is very beautiful, *n'est-ce pas*? I hope you are not too bored. I tried several times to get over here and talk with you, but someone always comes with a question. *C'est la vie.*" She removed her dark glasses, unleashing the blue eyes. "Are you all right? You seem so quiet."

I snapped out of my trance. "Yes. I'm fine, please don't worry. I'm having a wonderful time. I'm not much of a talker—in groups. This is a beautiful home and garden, I'm just enjoying the out of doors and the birds." I winked.

Her eyes started to twinkle first, and then she laughed out loud. "You are full of surprises. I would think you would be very outgoing. I'm delighted that you are enjoying yourself. We will leave shortly after lunch is finished, I think." She leaned a little closer and whispered, "I can only do so much talking." Her warm breath caressed my neck.

On the ride back, she kicked off her shoes and turned on the radio, flipping stations until she settled on some rock music. I looked at her with raised eyebrows.

"What? There is more in life than opera," she said with pursed lips.

"Yes indeed, Madame, and you may do as you choose since this is your car."

She poked me in the arm just as her cell phone rang. Quiet curses filled the air as she sorted the large purse to find the cell phone. "*Alo? Attendez, s'il vous plaît...* I must take this call, please excuse me."

I concentrated on driving and listening to the radio, although I couldn't help but hear how angry she became. The conversation was in French with what seemed like a few Italian phrases, so I deduced her husband was the male voice I could hear shouting on the other end of the line. It made me uncomfortable, but there was nowhere to go. Her voice was cold and hard. That surprised me. There was little doubt about another side of Nicole Bernard I had yet to meet. I hoped I'd never be on the other end of a conversation like this.

She hung up and threw the phone into her purse. The rest of the ride was quiet except for an occasional sigh. From the corner of my eye, I could see Nicole folding and unfolding the strap on her purse as she stared out the side window. The garage door opened, filling me with a great sense of relief.

As soon as we got into the house, I set her keys on the counter. "I'll just get my things from the guestroom and be on my way, unless there is something you need me to do?"

She just stood there in the middle of the living room looking even smaller. She shook her head. "No, there's nothing. Enjoy the rest of your weekend, Meg."

"Nicole." She looked up at me with the saddest eyes I'd ever seen. "Please remember to eat, and call me if you need anything."

She hugged her arms and nodded slowly with a

half smile.

Act I Scene 4

"Hey, Mom, I'm home." I closed the patio door and put the beer on the kitchen table. I tried to get home to Sunday dinner as often as possible. Sadly, I only made it once or twice a month. It wasn't as if it was too far—my folks lived in Albuquerque. My mom didn't push it, but my dad never missed a chance to tell me how much my visits meant to her.

"Hi, honey. I was so glad when you called this morning, especially since we didn't get to talk when you stayed over." I got a warm Mom-hug and kiss. "That's a cute shirt, is it new? Turquoise is a good color on you."

"Thanks. No, I got it before school let out. I just haven't had much of a chance to wear it. Where's Dad?" I put the beer in the refrigerator and sat down at the table. I could smell something baking.

"He'll be right back, he just ran out to get some more propane for his grill. Did you get your grandma's letter? I sent it last week."

"You know, I haven't even looked. The mail's all sitting on my kitchen counter. I hope to get to it tonight."

"Hi, Meggy. It's good to see you, sweetie." Dad came through the back door, walked over, and gave me a big bear hug the way he always did. "So where have you been keeping yourself? Once school was out, I thought you'd be down here all the time eating us out of house and home."

He joined me at the kitchen table while my mother continued chopping vegetables. "As a matter of fact, I've been busy."

My mother looked up, surprised. "Really, have you started dating someone?"

"No, Mom, I got a part-time job."

"Honey, if you need money all you have to do is ask—"

"No, I don't need money, Dad. It was a great opportunity, and I couldn't pass it up." When I explained my job responsibility—and for whom I was working—they smiled at each other. My dad taught music theory at the University of New Mexico and my mom taught at the Apple Mountain Music Center. Music was an integral piece of my life until a few years ago. It seemed that I always got involved in some kind of music in school. Whether it was the choir in grammar school, touring with a theater group in high school, or studying voice in college, participating in music was the driving force in my life. My parents loved music and encouraged me to pursue my dream. Neither one asked about my singing anymore. My cancer scare knocked back any more talk about my music career. They both understood how much this job meant to me.

I relayed the story of my hire and first week on the job. There was no need to tell them how much I admired Nicole Bernard; we all felt the same way about her role in modern opera. Well, almost. I had a little different interest. Oddly, talking about Nicole to my parents made me realize I missed her a little. We had been together every day, and it felt funny not to be there.

"Meg, that sounds wonderful. Her English seems quite good, is that true? And is she really as petite as everyone says she is?" Mom stopped her chopping.

"Yes, Mom." *Oh brother.* "We actually communicate in English because, as you know, I don't speak another language. Of course, she speaks French, Italian, and German, as well." I got up and took a beer from the refrigerator. "Nicole is probably a couple of inches shorter than I am. But listen, guys, I don't want to be gossiping about my employer. She's terrific, and I think I will be able to help her out a little in preparing for this performance."

"Where is her husband? I understand they usually travel together. He's a wonderful young tenor. I think he's going to mature into some nice roles," my mom said, resuming her chopping.

Uh-oh, not going there. "He stayed in New York. He had a conflict with his schedule, that's one of the reasons they wanted some extra help. What time is dinner?"

"It will be about an hour. Why?" Mom said.

"I just wanted to give Liz a call while I was here."

"Okay, honey."

I walked back to my former bedroom and closed the door. I hit speed dial.

"Hey, Liz, did I catch you at a bad time?"

"No, it's a good time. I just threw a load of laundry in the dryer. What's up? How's the new job?"

"So far, so good. Nicole has been nice and we've been working with her schedule. It's really kind of crazy. I think she has more public appearances than she does performances, but that's part of the job," I said, stretching out on the bed.

"What's it like being with your *idol* every single

day?" She laughed.

"My arms are black and blue from pinching myself. Actually, it's kind of a weird experience, Liz. It's been busy and I don't really know exactly what I'm supposed to be doing. We talk about everything like the opera, her job, her travel schedule, and she's been interested in my school-nursing job. She actually asks my opinion on things and she's been so…genuine."

I got up and walked to the window where the sun's rays peeked between the evergreen boughs. "It's hard sometimes because I find myself just staring at her as if she weren't real. I feel like I'm with two people—a beautiful talented opera diva and a friend you want to sit with and have coffee. Mostly, I can't believe my luck."

"I'm so glad. It must be incredible. Are you flirting with her?"

"Oh, Lord, no. I wish I could, but I can't. She's a married woman, and I'm her employee. It's hard sometimes because she's real touchy-feely, you know, that European hugging, kissing, and touching business."

"I never thought of that. I guess I'd have trouble, too. I'll bet you have some sweet dreams though." I could hear her laughing.

"It's not funny. A girl can fantasize… But, I just try not to lose track of reality. This is only a few months, and then it will be over. I'd rather not get invested in something that will rip my heart out."

"I know, Meg, but it's been years since you've been with anybody—I refuse to consider Tina was ever a serious girlfriend. It's only natural to be thinking about it."

"You're right, it has been a long time. For the

record, Tina wasn't a girlfriend, she was just, I don't know, a fill-in. A friend with benefits, and there sure wasn't an emotional connection with her. The book is closed on that one."

"I'm glad. She kind of worried me."

"I know, me too. Listen, I had better get back downstairs. My folks think I came to see them. Thanks for listening."

"Thanks for calling. I'm glad the new gig is working out. Keep me posted, sweetie." Liz clicked off.

It was after six by the time I got back on the highway. My dad was a world-class grill master and he had once again outdone himself. He marinated chicken and pork chunks and then grilled them alongside skewers of fresh vegetables. My mom added a beautiful pasta salad and a freshly baked chocolate cake. I groaned just thinking about how good it was and glanced over at Tupperware containers on the seat beside me. I unbuttoned my cargo shorts and settled in for the long drive.

My relationship with my parents had always been close, and I was grateful that they had been so wonderfully supportive over the last few years. Coming out to them ten years ago was a little rocky, especially for my dad. He eventually rallied and turned into an amazingly supportive parent. My dear mother reacted much the same as she had when I told her at the age of six that I wanted to be Prince Charming in the school play. "If that's what you want to do, honey, then do your very best."

The chirping of my cell phone interrupted my

trip down memory lane. I flipped it open but couldn't recognize the number. "Hello?"

"Meg? It is Nicole. I do not wish to interrupt you…"

My heart began to pound. "It's no bother. I'm on the way home from my folks' house. Is everything all right?"

"Yes, of course, I did not mean to alarm you. I just wanted to let you know that I got a call for a fitting tomorrow morning. The costume designer has some things ready for me. I did not want you to worry if you showed up and I was not here."

"Thank you, that was very thoughtful. Do you want me to come early to drive you?"

"That is not necessary. I can drive over to the theater. You can either wait for me here or come and meet me if you feel like you want to hang around until I finish."

"I'd enjoy that. I'll swing over if your car's not at home." There was a pause.

"That would be good. I am glad I caught you, so you would not be worried. I guess I will see you soon."

"Thanks, Nicole. I'm glad you called. Enjoy your evening."

"*Au revoir, amie.*"

"Good night." The line went dead and I released a sigh. Just her voice alone caused tingling. All over. Nicole Bernard just called me on my cell phone. Incredible.

Act I Scene 5

I followed Opera Road and stopped before the turnoff into the gated community. On impulse, I decided to go by the theater first in case she was already in wardrobe. As soon as I got out of the car, I marveled at the sounds of a piano tuning up, hammering and sawing, and the voices of the men calling out lighting cues. There was so much more behind the scenes than most people ever knew, and at one time it was the most important thing in the world to me. I loved the energy of theater and the way people worked together to create magic. I reluctantly walked away from all that and chose a career in nursing instead. It was a good fit for me because it allowed me to work with people, but I'd be lying if I said I didn't miss the rush of live theater.

The costume department seemed larger than I remembered, and as soon as I turned a corner I could hear Nicole's lilting French accent in conversation. I stopped for a moment just to listen.

Nicole enjoyed a reputation as being a singing actor and not a diva. I remembered how cast and crew alike always enjoyed working with her in spite of her perfectionism. She demanded the best from herself and those around her—but she did it respectfully. By raising the bar, everyone performed just a little better. It was true for me. Just being part of the ensemble made me want to put in longer hours, do extra voice work, and be willing to try just a little harder. We were all proud of the productions we did together, and I always believe it was because of Nicole's example. Her example wasn't easy to follow, but it was worth it.

There were a few chairs in the back of the room. I chose one and put down my cooler. On Saturday, I had gone to the health food store and picked out a few different items that might help maintain Nicole's blood sugar levels. The early morning protein and frequent use of fruit juice and energy bars was a good start. However, the rigorous demands of performance or intense rehearsals might change the picture. I also brought along my blood pressure cuff and stethoscope, just in case.

Nicole emerged from around the corner in a stunning ruby red ball gown that was low cut and very sexy, and I gasped. She was surprised to see me sitting there, but evidently pleased.

"Meg, I'm so delighted. Come and meet with Louise." She reached out her hand to me, pulled me to her for a quick embrace, and then dragged me around the corner.

"This is the amazing Louise Roussard, who makes me look beautiful. Louise, I wanted you to meet Meg, who's my very own personal assistant."

We shook hands. "It's my pleasure." The older woman smiled and nodded in a perfunctory sort of French way, and stabbed a few pins into her wrist pincushion as she looked me over carefully.

I returned to my chair and watched as Nicole put on two more dresses. They pulled, pinned, and further adjusted the costumes. It was time consuming but important. When the wardrobe mistress left for a moment to find additional material, I quickly grabbed a bottle of juice and took it over to Nicole. Her face showed signs of fatigue, but I decided not to mention it. When the last simple white nightgown was hemmed, the ordeal ended. I suggested we go back to the house for a rest, and she offered no argument.

    Nicole pulled into the garage as the automatic door creaked open. I parked in the drive and followed her in. She was reviewing aloud her morning's events.
    "The early call surprised me, I thought we were scheduled for later. But it is good, now it is done." She tossed her bag on a chair near the door and carried her music into the den, still talking about the afternoon rehearsal. "I brought you a copy of the score in case you wanted to write notes in it. It would certainly make things easier for me if you were able to write down directions on the score as we rehearse, that way I can concentrate a little easier. If I need to go through it again at home, you'll be there to help me."
    I'd only been gone for twenty-four hours but I still felt a rush just being in the same house with her. The first week was so busy trying to remember everything that I barely had time to think about myself. The more familiar we became, the more conflicted I was about working for her. She was beautiful, talented, and in very close proximity. Once again, I reminded myself that my wounded libido had lain dormant behind a heavy self-constructed door for several years, and every moment I spent with Nicole scratched at the door.
    "Would you like to sit out on the deck with me for a while? I really need to rest. Lars wants to stage the first scene, which is a huge party. It may take all afternoon."

"Sure. Let me get you something to drink, and I'll join you. Have you eaten lately?"

"I just had a protein bar and some juice before I left this morning."

I snooped around the refrigerator until I found some boiled ham and some hard rolls. After loading a small tray with the sandwich, some orange slices, and a large glass of ice water, I grabbed the glucometer and headed out to the very large patio off the den and dining room. There was a low adobe privacy wall, which provided shelter from the wind, and a slatted vigas and latilla cover that allowed some sun, but not too much.

Nicole was dozing on a large padded chaise lounge, arms crossed behind her head making her look longer and leaner. My breath caught at her vulnerable appearance. I cleared my throat so I wouldn't startle her. She opened one eye partially, and smiled.

"I brought a little lunch if you're hungry, but I'd like to check your blood sugar since I didn't do it earlier." I sat down next to her and placed the tray on the table.

"I should not be such a baby, but I just hate waiting for that sharp thing to poke into my finger." She blushed and laughed.

"It's not a big deal, and I don't mind doing it." I enjoyed holding her hand even if it was testing her blood sugar. "It's much better today, it's eighty-five."

"Remind me again where it's supposed to be."

"Anywhere between seventy and one hundred is within normal range." I reluctantly let go of the gauze pad on her finger. "All set. Now you can eat and take a nap if you feel like it."

She sat up, stretched, and crossed her legs. I

handed her the plate.

"This looks wonderful. I feel so spoiled. I'm not helpless, you know." She grabbed the sandwich as though she hadn't eaten for days.

I got up and sat in the chair next to her, trying to create a little space. It was a beautiful afternoon, and because of the altitude it still was relatively comfortable. It would get warmer as the day went on. The view from the patio was breathtaking. The distant mountains formed an impressive backdrop for this beautiful setting. The high desert hills extended for miles, speckled with cholla and juniper.

"Why did you choose to do *La Traviata* right now?" I asked.

Nicole wiped her fingers with the napkin, then folded it and put it on her plate. She smiled a little wistfully. "You know, I think it was just time. Of course, I have always loved this opera. The music is magnificent and Violetta is a wonderful character to play. Frankly, I wasn't sure if I was ready to do it. When they approached me and then told me Lars would be directing, I did not say no. And most importantly, if I chose to do it here in Santa Fe, I would have plenty of time to rehearse such a difficult role."

"I'm not familiar with the tenor. Have you worked with him before?"

"Actually, I have not. He has a lovely voice and good range but he's quite young. He will arrive at the end of the week and I think we will have some time together to be acquainted. Lars, of course, is very excited because the young man is also Swedish."

"In his pictures, he looks very attractive." I noticed her eyes were becoming heavy lidded. "Why don't you nap a little bit while I get a few things together for this afternoon's rehearsal?"

"I think I will. Thank you, Meg. You are a darling."

After rinsing off the dishes, I put them in the dishwasher. I felt a strange sadness lurking around me. I missed the fun times I had as an apprentice because we all felt so important and so lucky to be working with a great company of artists. Life gets busy, I suppose, and that time is gone. The other side was that even though I was not going to be in the opera, I was spending every single day with a woman who captured my imagination and burrowed into my heart. Nicole was warm, kind, and funny. She treated me like a peer and appreciated my help. What more could I ask?

The afternoon rehearsal ran long. The director was infinitely patient while the large chorus bumbled around backstage. I found myself smiling on more than one occasion because the apprentices looked so young and they were giggling amongst themselves at their good fortune and embarrassment. I remembered. Mostly, I hung around the sidelines taking every opportunity to provide water or juice when it seemed appropriate. Since my only responsibility was to keep an eye on Nicole, her body language and gestures relayed more information. I could even tell when she was frustrated or irritated, although she never said a word.

Mr. Larson asked for quiet and then signaled Nicole to sing through the opening aria. The accompanist paced the music exactly as he and Nicole had worked out. I followed the lyrics in the score and listened enthralled as the inspired notes and heartfelt lyrics filled the air. *"Amore misterioso, misterioso alter, croce, croce delizia, delizia al cor."* Mysterious love—a joyous burden.

She sang with passion and moved with purpose. Nicole seemed incapable of standing in one place and singing; she paced, and she sang, *"D'amarmi dite ancora."* Tell me again, you love me. My throat constricted as I listened to her plea.

"Excellent. I think that's enough for today. Please work on that chorus, ladies and gentlemen. Act Two tomorrow." Bodies scattered in all directions and I quickly wiped at my moist eyes as Nicole approached.

She narrowed her gaze. "Is something wrong?"

"No, of course not. I was just so caught up in the music—we should probably go." I scrambled to pack up the music, the libretto, and the other paraphernalia I dragged along. It still took several minutes as one person after another wanted to ask her one more question.

I started the car and Nicole put her hand on my arm. "I am grateful for your support, but I would like to ask you to be very honest with me. I am singing this part for the first time and I would very much like to make it special. Normally, my husband would tell me about weak places or a wrong interpretation, but as you know he is not here. If you have suggestions or ideas, would you feel comfortable enough to tell me?"

"Thank you. I hardly think I'm the person to ask. I'm really not that familiar with the opera." I was stunned and flattered by her request. I turned the car into the subdivision and up to the house.

"Something upset you and I would hate to think that you could not tell me."

When we were in the garage, I shut off the car. I was embarrassed but figured it was likely to happen again so I might as well own it. "Because I don't want to embarrass you unnecessarily, I should tell you that I get pretty emotional with some music and certain singers, and you're one of them. I'm just completely undone by your voice, every single time. So, I wasn't upset, just sort of overcome. Do you understand?"

She was leaning back against the car door looking at me as though I were speaking Greek. "Undone? I do not think I understand this."

Great, how the hell do I explain it without sounding like this is my first crush? "Emotionally unraveled, overwhelmed, you know, because of the beauty of the music. Pavarotti does the same thing to me. It goes beyond words. It's just intense emotion."

"I think I understand." Her eyes twinkled, and she grinned. "I think I am a little bit surprised. You are always so professional, and I wasn't sure whether you enjoyed working with me or were just being so very responsible. I am pleased you are moved by my work."

I knew I was blushing and scrambled to get out of the car. I wanted to blurt out how much working with her meant to me. However, if she looked at me as a professional I'd better act that way. "You are an absolute joy to work with, I'm just not sure how qualified I am to help with your…work. This is a tremendous opportunity for me, and I guess I'm still a little nervous." I put the cooler on the counter and began to unpack it.

Nicole came around the counter and put her arms around my waist, which caused my breathing to stop. "Oh Meg, please do not feel nervous. I want you to feel comfortable. I suppose I would feel the same way, but I want you to think of me as a friend, not an unapproachable diva, because that is not who I am. Maybe you would like a hug." *Jesus save me.*

I turned and she pulled me into her arms. Seconds lasted a lifetime as our bodies melded together, and I was aware of her hands on my shoulder and waist, the softness of her cotton T-shirt, the scent of lilies, and her warm breath on my neck. Every nerve in my body was tingling, and I wanted the moment to go on forever.

She pulled back slightly with her hands on my elbows. "You are better? And maybe you can trust me a little more?"

I nodded like a bobblehead doll. "Yes, of course I trust you."

"Since it's so late, why don't you stay and have dinner with me?"

There was nothing in the world I would have rather done, but it might be dangerous. "I wish I could, but I have a couple of errands I need to run before I get home. But I'll see you tomorrow morning."

"*Bonsoir*, Meg."

I was on the highway before my breathing slowed. Thin ice was not even a good enough analogy. I was knocking on the door of my limits of self-control. My adolescent infatuation was reaching grown-up proportions rapidly, and it only been a couple of weeks. Ten more weeks might prove impossible.

I put in the earpiece and picked up the phone. "Call Liz," I instructed and drummed my fingers on the steering wheel for the interminable ten seconds it took her to answer.

"Hi, Meg. What's cooking?"

"I'm driving back from work, thought I'd call you and let off a little steam."

"Are you angry about something?"

"No, I mean steam literally." I closed both car windows and turned on the air conditioner. I could hear Liz chuckling.

"Is the venerable Ms. Bernard shaking your resolve?"

"Boy, is she ever." I recounted what happened after rehearsal. "She's so incredible and so married. I'm not sure how to create space between us because she's so physical. And I don't want to, but it's really hard."

"Talk about a rock and a hard place, you've gotten into one. I don't know what to tell you. Be careful," Liz said with a sympathetic tone.

"Tell me. Maybe things will ease up as the rehearsals get busier. We won't have as much time hanging around her house. I'm almost home and ready for a shower. Let's hook up soon so you can fill me in on the latest gossip."

Act II Scene 1

My morning commute consisted of self-talk about professionalism and self-control. After all, I was an adult and I was certainly capable of behaving like one instead of an adolescent. Nicole Bernard was a beautiful, talented woman who was not looking for a quickie with her assistant. Right? Right.

I parked in my usual spot next to the garage and let myself in the front door. It was beginning to feel like home, sort of. The house was unusually quiet. I checked my watch and it was 10:00 a.m. Her yoga and morning run would be completed. I called her name and then began to look around. The living room, kitchen area, and patio were empty, so I headed down the main hall to the master bedroom. I knocked, and when I got no answer I cracked open the door. "Nicole?"

The bathroom was empty but the door to her balcony was open, and that's where I found her stretched out on the chaise lounge in a very small bikini. She was breathing, so I cleared my throat and said, "Good morning." She turned her head and face toward me and smiled a very sleepy smile.

"I won't interrupt you, just wanted to remind you that Carl will be here in about forty-five minutes," I said and started to leave.

"No, do not leave yet. Would you mind helping me with the sunscreen? I did the front and want to get a little sun on my back." She rolled over on her stomach after she untied the top of the suit.

"Sure. You have to be careful of this New Mexico sun. It can sneak up on you and cause some serious damage. I know I've been burned on more than one occasion." I was blithering and I knew it. A bottle of sunscreen sat on the side table. I poured a liberal amount in my hand and sat on the edge of the lounge. I rubbed my hands together to warm it a little bit and took a deep breath. With long strokes, I spread coconut-scented lotion up her back and across her shoulders, down to her small waist up the sides, and then the back of her arms. I was afraid she could feel my hands trembling.

"Don't forget the backs of my legs," she mumbled.

I was perspiring and blushing. Fortunately, she couldn't see me. I continued until the lotion was absorbed, then stood up. "I'll bring you something to drink. Did you eat this morning?"

"Yes, I had cereal and fruit."

"Excellent, I'll be right back." I almost ran to get back to the kitchen. *God, why are you doing this to me? It's not funny and I'm not made of steel.* I washed my hands for several minutes but could still feel the touch of her skin on my fingers, soft and silky over a smooth frame of muscle. My vision prickled with little lights and I felt a burning ache in my pelvis. I let go of the refrigerator door handle and slid to the floor. The Saltillo tile was cool, and within a few minutes I thought I could stand without fainting.

I carried a small tray with lemonade and a couple of energy bars. Nicole told me early on she needed to avoid any kind of dairy products before singing, which eliminated a good source of protein. As I approached the balcony, I had to caution myself to stay present. I set the tray down on the nearby table.

"I thought lemonade might be in order. It's getting really hot out here." No kidding. Her skin was glistening with the sheen of perspiration, and already turning pink.

She sat up, naked from the waist up, and reached for a towel. My sunglasses covered my surprise and reaction. So, modesty was as optional as clothing.

"It's amazing how quickly it gets hot out here. When I came out it was almost too cool." She draped the towel around her shoulders and picked up the lemonade, drinking heartily.

The doorbell chimed and I immediately offered to get it. "I'll go, it's probably Carl."

There was a man at the door, but it was not Carl. "May I help you?"

The attractive stranger stuck out his hand. "Hello, my name is Mario De Luca. I'm looking for Nicole." Her husband. *Wow.* I had to hand it to her, she had good taste—this guy was very attractive. He had a lean frame that stood close to six feet tall, with longish dark brown hair and a gleaming white smile. He wore linen slacks, a pale silk shirt with a cliché gold neck chain, and Italian loafers. Plus, he gave off the scent of citrus and sandalwood mixed with leather.

"Of course, please come in. My name is Meg, her assistant. Why don't you have a seat and I'll go get her?" He set a suitcase inside the door and I ushered him into the living room. "Would you like some lemonade?"

"Yes, that would be wonderful. I always forget how dry it is in New Mexico."

He walked around the living room, clearly comfortable in his surroundings. I handed him a glass. "I'll go get Nicole."

"Thank you." His smile was dazzling. I could certainly see why she was attracted to him.

Nicole was in the shower when I returned to her room. The bathroom door was open and I could hear her vocalizing in the steamy shower. I wasn't sure how she'd take this announcement. In the original plan, he wasn't expected for another week, but Nicole had told me he wasn't coming at all.

"Nicole, it's not Carl. It's your husband."

The water shut off in a hurry. "What?" She stepped out of the shower dripping wet and grabbed a towel. I averted my eyes.

"Your husband is here, in the living room. Would you like me to send him back?"

Her face paled slightly. "Yes."

"Are you okay?" I asked.

"Yes, I'll be fine." Her words were even, but I saw that she clenched her jaw.

I walked back to the living room slowly to give Nicole a little time to absorb the news about her husband's unexpected arrival. Maybe he felt guilty about not accompanying her and decided to come early. Maybe this was their normal high-intensity relationship, not for me to judge.

"Nicole said to go on back. She's just getting ready for her accompanist." I was quite sure he knew where the bedroom was. After all, he had been here the previous year. I also wanted him to know that she had an appointment. I made myself busy moving the musical scores and libretto from the rehearsal bag to the den adjacent to the kitchen, which had become the de facto music room during her stay. I wasn't sure if Mario would be attending her practice time.

The sunny kitchen had become my little office. I used a corner desk to keep my things during the day. It also held the large calendar that Nicole and I both used to keep track of her schedule. In case of schedule changes, I had posted a list of important phone numbers.

On more than one occasion, I found it prudent to make myself scarce when Nicole had phone calls or visitors. This morning, I suspected that the unannounced visit from her husband would be one of those times to disappear.

My suspicions were confirmed within ten minutes. Voices from the bedroom were getting louder and sharper. Just about the time I decided to make an excuse to go somewhere, the doorbell rang. Today, I was especially glad to see Carl. His wild, birds-nest gray hair offset by twinkling brown eyes and the bushy silver beard lent an air of quirkiness to this normally sedate musician. I watched him work with Nicole on several occasions and he had a wonderful understanding of the way singers worked. He was intuitive. It was almost as though he knew in advance how she would interpret phrases and lines. It was magical to watch them work.

"Good morning, Carl. Please come in. I'm sure Nicole will be ready in a few minutes."

"Meg, how are you on this beautiful morning?"

I closed the door behind him and was about to reply when angry voices interrupted me. Nicole and Mario were coming down the hall.

"My dear Carl, I'm so glad to see you," Nicole said, kissing him warmly and taking his arm. "You remember Mario?"

"Of course, of course. Good to see you, my boy. I thought I heard somewhere you weren't going to make it out here this year."

"I wasn't sure I could because I have several other obligations this summer, but I had a few days free and needed to see my beautiful wife." He gazed adoringly at Nicole, who did not return the favor.

She shot a look at me that I couldn't quite describe. Annoyance, irritation? I shrugged. The three of them moved toward the den and I set out three glasses of lemonade for them, then escaped to the kitchen. I thought I should remain close by and decided to spend some time trolling the Internet. My email account was jammed with unanswered messages, and I wished I brought along some of the bills I needed to pay. Every few minutes I stopped to listen to snatches of conversation. I had a niggling fear that Mario might be here to stay. If that was the case, there went my job.

Ellis, you might want to get your head out of the clouds once in a while. Her husband is back, got it?

I tried to refocus and sent off my responses to the many questions asking where I'd been for the last few weeks. My friends knew I had no social life during the school year but always made it up to them by planning events during the summer. To date, I'd done nothing. This job with the Santa Fe Opera required a certain amount of discretion, so I hadn't told very many people. I figured I wouldn't have to lie as much if I just kept it to myself. Maybe that was a mistake. After all, without hearing from me they were probably making up heinous stories.

In the background, Nicole had finished vocalizing and started working on one of her arias. Her voice instantly permeated my entire being with twinkling light. I closed my eyes and listened as she effortlessly caressed Verdi's music. I could feel the hair on my arms stand up as she glided into her upper range. The sound alone made me feel like my heart was swelling. I should have been paying them for this exquisite experience.

I heard Carl make a few comments and then Nicole started another duet, but this time Mario joined her. I stopped what I was doing and walked over to the door. They were standing together reading from the score in front of them. It was the aria from the first act, and their voices blended perfectly. She stopped them and asked Carl to go back to the previous line. Her eyes closed and her arms moved as though she were directing herself.

My Italian and my memory of the lyrics weren't perfect, but this first duet beautifully described Alfredo's unrequited love for Violetta. He tells her how he's pined for her love for over a year. His desire for her exquisite love became a cross he gladly bears. Ironically, Violetta tells him she was not a good choice; he should go and find another. I almost laughed.

As I watched, I had to admit they were a handsome couple and sounded wonderful together. The Norman Rockwell painting didn't last long. Nicole moved to another section of the score while Mario excused himself. He slid past me, nodding as he moved to the living room. In a minute, he was talking softly and laughing on his cell phone. There was nothing to do in the kitchen, or anywhere else, so I went into the den to listen to the music.

Carl and Nicole skipped through several spots in

the score that she wanted to work on and finished with the finale, which was tricky. Dying characters belting out a final aria are sometimes less than believable. In this particular opera, Violetta has been slowly deteriorating throughout the piece. Just when she's about to give up the ghost, she rereads the letter promising her Alfredo will return to beg her forgiveness. She rallies when he arrives, then fades again. Finally, she has the last rally, which many people experience in the end.

It's a vocal roller coaster, and while Nicole did not possess a gigantic voice, she had an innate power behind it that was palpable. Even when she sang very softly, the emotion was unmistakable. I sat across the room riveted by the grief-laced phrases wrapped in a tender melody.

When she finished, I noticed the tears on my face at the same moment she turned and looked at me. In an instant, I think she understood what I meant when I told her that her voice stirred me. She nodded and winked at me.

She walked Carl to the door while I cleaned up the glasses and packed up her music. All the while I was in the den, Mario continued to talk on his cell. I could hear a few words from the living room and an occasional French phrase thrown out with more than a little vehemence.

I was feeling more and more uncomfortable being under the same roof and needed to find some way to escape. Rehearsal would start in less than two hours and I could only imagine that Mario would accompany her just to put on a good face.

Tricky bit to juggle, huh, Ellis? I was feeling a little awkward as there were no directions for this in the Personal Assistant handbook.

Nicole returned to the kitchen alone and sat down at the table but said nothing. My move, I guessed. I had no idea what to say so I went to nurse fallback, retrieving her glucose meter from the cupboard.

"Do you suppose we should check your blood sugar? We didn't get a chance to do it when I got here this morning."

"Yes, that's probably a good idea." She sighed heavily and reached her arm across the table toward me.

I gently took her hand and swabbed one finger. One poke and I collected the blood drop and then inserted the test strip into the meter. I held pressure on her finger while I waited. I wasn't exactly holding her hand, but it was close enough. The current passed between us and I could feel her relax.

"Pretty good. It wouldn't hurt to eat something before you go to rehearsal." I folded her fingers and squeezed her hand a little before letting go. Instinct told me to just sit there and be quiet, which I did.

Nicole leaned heavily on the table with her arms crossed and her head down.

I sat with one arm resting on the table and just watched her. Something happened, but I wasn't sure what.

"Meg—" She started, and then stopped.

"I'm a pretty good listener."

"This is very difficult for me. I have chosen to do a role that is unfamiliar and very demanding, and after making that decision, my husband decided he did not have time to help me. Now he is here making promises that I know are false." Her eyes glistened with sadness and I could see her set her jaw to contain her frustration.

I bit my tongue because I wanted to give her platitudes assuring her everything would be all right. I wanted to put my arms around her and promise to stand by her side. I said nothing.

"My friends call me from New York and they tell me that Mario is seen all over the city with a very young woman." She looked up and two streams of tears rolled down her cheeks. "He swears he is faithful only to me, there is no other. But his eyes are dead to me, and I think it is only his reputation he thinks of."

I retrieved the tissue box from the counter, handed it to her, and took my seat. I was not the right person to be asking about cheating lovers; that train had left the station two years ago with Bekka. Yet I could still feel a tiny kernel of my simmering rage, not fully extinguished. I knew what was going on in Nicole's heart. It was hard, but I needed to remember I was her assistant and not her shrink.

"I wish I had a magical answer for you, but I don't. Listen to your heart. Maybe it's not the right time to try to solve this while you have so much on your mind. Or maybe you just need some privacy to talk this through."

Nicole could only nod her head and wipe the tears from her eyes.

I took a deep breath. "Tell you what. I've packed up the cooler, and I have your music ready. Perhaps I should leave you two alone for a while. Mario can take you to the rehearsal and then maybe you could have a nice dinner together. I'll have my cell phone with me in case you need anything. Then I'll come back tomorrow, if that's all right?"

She seemed a little frightened for an instant,

then nodded. "Of course. This must be very uncomfortable for you. I did not mean to burden you with my personal problems. I am just too embarrassed to talk to anyone."

I instinctively reached over and grabbed her hand. "Please, I'm not leaving because I'm uncomfortable or because I don't want to be here. I just thought you and Mario might be able to talk more easily. Nicole, I'm here for you. I'm not going anywhere. I'm just giving you a breather. If you'd rather I'd stay…"

"No, you are right, we should talk. You go and enjoy yourself. It is not for you to worry."

"You're sure?"

"Yes, dear Meg."

I gathered up my things and she walked me to the door. "*Adieu, chère amie.*" She wrapped both arms around my neck then released me.

Act II Scene 2

I drove up through the patron parking lot and down the hill to The Ranch, where the offices were located. Although I had not called ahead, I was pretty sure someone would be in the office. After all, it was the beginning of a new season and it was much busier than it had been two weeks earlier. More traffic, more noise, and more excitement.

I stood and waited, as Thad was busy on the phone. He smiled when he saw me and motioned me over. "How great to see you. I've wanted to call you to see how you're doing but it's just crazy over here. Is everything okay? What's it like working for our fabulous Nicole? Come sit down and tell me everything."

I had to laugh at his enthusiasm. Who wouldn't love this guy? "Everything is going fine, and she's a joy to work with. Very courteous and very gracious, just as you'd imagine. I just stopped by because I never asked anybody about recordkeeping or timesheets. I don't even know how often you do payroll."

"Oh my gosh, I can't believe I forgot that! Greta will kill me." He began to rifle through his desk looking for something.

"Is she busy right now? I'd love to ask her a question."

"I don't think so. Just poke your head in and see if she's on the phone."

I tapped lightly on the partially open door just

as Greta sat down at her desk. "Is this a good time?"

She looked up and smiled. "Margaret, how nice to see you. Why don't you come in and shut the door? I've been meaning to check in to find out how you were managing."

"Ms. Bernard has been very welcoming, and I think we have a pretty good working relationship. We've worked out a basic schedule to accommodate her daily routine as well as some vocal work. And this week we've added rehearsals. Medically she's doing quite well, and very agreeable to my intrusions and suggestions. I'm getting pretty good at reading her energy level so I can intervene if necessary."

"Excellent, that's exactly what I was hoping for. Everything is on schedule except for a few delays in the scenery department, but I'm looking forward to a fabulous production. What brought you over here this afternoon?"

I tried to formulate my words very carefully. "Well, first, I needed to find out what I'm supposed to do for payroll, but Thad is working on that. I also wanted to let you know that Señor De Luca arrived this morning unexpectedly, and I...thought it prudent to leave them alone for a bit. I asked Nicole if that would be all right, and that I would be back tomorrow morning. She was agreeable."

Greta tented her fingers several times, looking rather pensive. "I think that was probably wise. I hope it won't prove to be a problem. I want her to be able to focus and not have, shall we say, unpleasant distractions. We're certainly in no position to be managing her personal life, but I would hope she could give as much energy as possible to the role without having her loyalties tested."

I knew what she was saying and agreed wholeheartedly. There wasn't much anyone could do unless she asked.

Timesheets in hand, I headed for home. I felt relieved to be out of the conflict, but a little disloyal as well. Some personal assistant, fleeing at the first sign of trouble. I opened the car windows, inhaled deeply, and turned up the radio.

Spring in New Mexico was wild and unpredictable, usually bright blue skies with a large warm sun promising wildflowers regaling the high desert. Suddenly the temps could drop from the fifties to the twenties with unrelenting and powerful winds.

I had made last-minute plans to meet up with some friends for Happy Hour in Santa Fe. I'd have just enough time to pick up some cat food, coffee, and hair gel. Pearson, my tortoiseshell kitty, was quite content to spend his days out in the fenced-in kitty habitat outside, but he still needed feeding. Good thing he understood about my erratic schedule.

The days were longer now as we approached the summer equinox, and the sun was overhead. Our hottest days would soon be wilting people and pets. Santa Fe was abounding with flower boxes and gardens filled with brightly colored blooms, accentuating the warm hues of adobe walls. Tourists daily filled the plaza with cameras and traffic. Santa Fe bloomed in the summer.

I generally avoided downtown, if possible. My friends lived farther out on the fringe of popular, and we generally hung out at some local dive.

Once Pearson was content and stretched out on the balcony, I proceeded with my shower. The tepid water felt good cascading across my back. I took my time shampooing my hair thinking about a haircut appointment. Shorter was better when it got too hot. As I rinsed off, I remembered Nicole stepping out of her shower. She had a beautiful body for a forty-year-old woman. Yoga and her active metabolism served her well. A laugh bubbled up at the thought.

Clearly, I was fond of my employer. I even missed her a little. I hoped that they could reconcile so Nicole could focus on her work and not feel so unhappy. Remembering her tears brought an ache to my heart.

It was still early when I parked at TGIFridays. Lena and Brenda beat me; I spotted their gigantic red pickup parked at the rear of the lot. Lena worried about damage to her precious baby and took excellent care of it. She and Brenda had been together for over twenty-five years. They owned a nice ranch southeast of Santa Fe, closer to Cerrillos. They boarded several horses, and Lena managed the ranch while Brenda worked as an executive vice president at one of the larger banks.

Lena and I had known each other since high school, so they were like family to me. It didn't take long to spot them when I entered the bar. They had chosen a table in front of the big-screen TV and started on a pitcher of beer and a basket of peanuts. Their haircuts were similar as was their dress. After so many years, they were looking more and more alike, and that was a good thing, even though it was cliché. I smiled watching how they both hoisted a beer glass the same way. Lena was the taller of the two, probably three or four inches above my five foot seven. Brenda was closer to my height, or maybe slightly shorter, with a great curvaceous figure—nobody did jeans better than Brenda. Lena was lean, strong, and without curves. Years of hard ranch work had toned her better than any gym. Brenda sported what used to be called a Wedge haircut for her thick salt-and-pepper hair. It was really short at the neck, longer on top, and looked professional. Lena had a very utilitarian cut that I was sure she trimmed regularly with the horse trimmers, but with her sun-bleached blond hair, it always looked flattering

"Hey, you two. Couldn't wait?"

"Ellis! Long time no see." Lena jumped up and gave me a bear hug. Brenda stood up and did the same. "Beer okay with you?"

"Thanks, looks good." She poured, then called for another pitcher.

"Keely called about five minutes ago, caught in traffic, should be here soon."

Keely Jarrett was a transplant from the west coast who came with a film company eight years earlier and liked it here. She briefly dated my ex, Bekka. Fine with me; she could have her.

"Brenda, I saw the blurb in the paper. Congrats on the promotion at the bank. I hope that comes with more time off," I said.

She laughed. "Oh, sure. Less actually, more damn meetings. How've you been? We haven't seen hide nor hair of you for a long time."

I took another swallow of beer. "It's turning out to be a busy summer, and I apologize for not getting in touch with you guys. Time just seems to evaporate."

"I hear ya," Lena mumbled.

I would have told them the story except the giant TV had captured Lena's attention for the moment with a crucial play and we might not get her back. I decided to wait. Keely showed up looking like Hollywood gone bead-and-feather Santa Fe—big hair, too much makeup, fringed leather vest, and a cotton broom skirt. That meant another round of greetings. We agreed on some appetizers to absorb the beer.

Feeling sated, the conversation stalled until Keely cleared her throat. "Brenda, would you mind if I asked you for some investment advice?"

"Of course not. I'm no expert, but I can find you one if I can't help."

"Come on, Meg. Why don't we excuse ourselves and play a little pool," Lena said as a declarative sentence.

Seeing it was not a question, I decided to join her at the pool table.

"You seemed a little preoccupied. What's going on that you're not talkin' about?" Lena asked, racking up the balls.

I chalked the tip of my cue. I never could fool Lena, not since high school. She read me like the Sunday Funnies. "Go ahead and break first."

She did, and immediately sank a solid in the corner.

"I got a summer job offer from the Santa Fe Opera as a personal assistant to a guest artist."

Her head shot up. "Seriously? Who?"

"Nicole Bernard."

"*The* Nicole Bernard? The beautiful French singer?" She pulled her cue back.

It always caught me off guard when my old buddy in Wranglers and boots said something about opera or fine art. Those were sources of joy for her, but she seldom discussed them in public.

"One and the same."

"Well, damn, girl. Isn't she the same one you were crushing on a few years ago when you worked with her?" Lena moved around the table, sinking one ball after another, then scratched. "Your turn."

"Yes, and she's even more amazing off stage. It's a dream job, for sure."

"Is it hard to keep your mind on business?"

"It's getting that way, more every day." I was hopeless, couldn't sink another ball no matter how hard I tried. All I could think about was what Nicole was doing—with Mario. I stood and watched as Lena cleared every ball from the table then sank the eight ball.

I put the cue back on the rack. "Okay, let me buy you a drink." We each ordered a shot of Cuervo Silver and stood at the bar.

"Meg, are you sure you're okay? You seem kinda off."

"Well, the job was going okay until recently. Her husband showed up unexpectedly and I was surprised that I felt jealous of him. It's crazy, I mean she's married and straight…it's just that she's very physical and affectionate—with everyone, not just me. But the other day she wanted to hug me and I felt something from her. I can't swear it wasn't my imagination, but it was more than a buddy hug."

"None of my business, but it sounds like a recipe for heartbreak. You sure you wanna go there? I remember trying to get you through the last one."

"Of course not. I think I can stay objective and help her out. I was just a bit surprised how easy it is to care."

Lena turned to face me. "Just be careful. I'm not

sure you're over Bekka yet."

I laughed. "I must be transparent."

"Just to me, darlin', otherwise you're rock solid," Lena said, winking.

We returned to the table as Brenda headed to the bar with the pitcher.

I raised my hand. "No more for me."

Keely was in the middle of a dramatic tale of deceit and denial with her current paramour. I smiled and nodded appropriately. More dyke drama—God save us all. Fortunately, Brenda returned and Lena changed the subject.

"Hey, you guys, we're thinking about another big Fourth of July barbecue at the ranch, real country style. What do you think?"

"That sounds great, can we bring dates?" Keely asked.

I chuckled. "The one last year was wonderful. Will you roast a pig again?"

Lena poked me in the shoulder. "Just for you, buddy."

"I'll check the schedule and let you know," I said.

Brenda started making a flow chart on the paper table cover of what they needed for the event and by which dates. She ticked off a mental list of necessities. After a dozen items, I asked if she'd please just email the list, providing a grateful laugh from all.

Mentally, I was trying to recall performance dates to be sure I would be available. *Traviata's* schedule was about three times a week, so I would technically be off the other nights. That fact meant I might not see Nicole during off times. I wonder if she had planned other events like appearances. Would she want me to hang around?

"Ellis. Are you listening?"

"What?"

"Keely asked if we wanted to run over to the Cold Stone Creamery for ice cream."

"Oh, sorry. I was thinking about that weekend. I think I'll pass on ice cream. I'm beat."

We divvied up the bill and I walked out with Lena and Brenda. "I'm glad we could do this on short notice. I promise I'll try to be more connected."

"Good. We miss you, you know." Brenda hugged me.

"Give me a call and let me know how you're doing, and be careful," Lena said, winking.

I pulled her close. "Thanks."

❦❦❦❦

Pearson meowed when I put the key in the lock. "I know I've been a rotten mother. Let's see if I can make amends and find one of your little balls under the sofa." I put down my keys and moved the sofa away from the wall, revealing nine tiny yarn balls and one with bells. I tossed them all out in the center of my living room and Pearson dove after them.

I sat and watched him, thinking that this was the first time I'd been able to just "be" for several weeks. A good night's sleep, breakfast with Pearson, and I should be ready for duty. In truth, I'd be glad to see her again.

Act II Scene 3

I slept like a baby. Well, except those dreams were a little R rated, but very pleasant. The images remained pleasurable and quite vivid as I showered. The sound of my cell phone on the bedside table broke the mood. I wiped water out of my eyes and craned my neck to see the Caller ID display. *Nicole. Crap!*

I tripped lunging out of the shower, smacked into the vanity, then reached around and picked up the phone. "Hello, I'm here."

"Meg, I didn't mean to disturb you. I just wanted to know what time you might be here." Her normally smooth voice sounded tight and a little shaky.

"I was just getting ready to go. Is everything all right?" I knew it wasn't. But I didn't know how worried I should be.

"Yes. It is good, I just…we can talk when you get here."

"It'll be okay. I'll be there soon, I promise."

My mind was racing in a dozen different directions. I grabbed the clothes I'd laid out the night before. I pulled on the khaki shorts and buttoned the navy blue shirt. My sandals sat by the front door. What could have happened overnight that had her so shaken? I couldn't picture that another argument would upset her; after all, their relationship was already volatile. *God, I hope he didn't hit her.*

I poured a large quantity of dry food for Pearson

and refilled his water dish. "You guard the house, bud. I'll be back as soon as I can."

The original plan was to stop and get some coffee and something to eat, but now all I could think about was getting there as quickly as possible. I was worried, even though she said she was all right. Her voice told me something else, but what?

Fortunately, traffic was light going north. This was a good time, I thought when I looked at the dashboard clock as I turned off on the Tesuque exit. Maybe I shouldn't have taken off yesterday afternoon. I had cleared it with Greta. Maybe it was nothing. Maybe there'd been a change in the rehearsal schedule. However, I wouldn't count on it by the way Nicole sounded.

I glanced at the mirror when I got out of the car and almost laughed. My hair was in complete disorder just the way it was when I got out of the shower. *Deep breath, Ellis.* I exhaled.

The front door was unlatched, and I pushed it open. Nicole was in the living room, sitting in the corner of the sofa with her knees tucked up in front of her. She didn't look good. Her face was puffy and red, her lips swollen. Her clothes suggested she had been jogging, but I couldn't be sure. The room was in disarray—rearranged furniture, things knocked over, dishes strewn across the top of the kitchen island. Did she have a party? It certainly looked like the morning after.

I dropped my bag, closed the door, and walked down the steps toward Nicole. She still hadn't spoken. "Nicole?" I said softly. "Are you all right?" She nodded. I wasn't sure what to do, so I knelt in front of her and waited. Her eyes were focused but indiscernible. There was no evidence of injury, and all I could do was hope she would tell me.

After several moments, I tried to engage her. "Would you like me to make you some tea?"

"Yes, please."

I went out to the kitchen, heated some water, and set up two cups with milk and sugar—just the way she liked it. When I returned to the living room, she was still sitting in the same position but had her head back, eyes closed. There were red flags, telling me something was wrong. I looked around, suddenly worried that someone else was in the house. I set my tea on the table and handed Nicole her cup. "Where is Mario?"

"He's gone." There was a note of finality in her voice. Her body was tense.

I sat down near her and picked up my cup. "Nicole, can you please tell me what's going on? I'm really worried."

Because of a slight tremor, she held the cup with both hands and sipped the tea. "It was a very bad fight and I made him leave." A deep breath. "He tried to tell me that I was wrong, that there was no other woman. He lied, and I knew he lied. Now I think maybe he was always lying. I told him I knew about the woman in New York. He only laughed and said I did not know what I was talking about."

The tears started first, then came the sobbing from deep inside her. I reached over, took her cup and put it on the table, and handed her a half-empty box of tissue. "I'm so sorry, Nicole." All I could do was watch helplessly as my pain-filled memories threatened to surface.

"Please, can you just hold me?"

My heart ached as I slid closer and wrapped my arms around her quaking form. She turned toward me and clung to my shirt with her head tucked under my chin. I held on and she sobbed, deeply. My throat constricted with my grief because I knew how she felt. I pressed my lips into the top of her head to keep from crying myself.

She cried for a long time and then shifted slightly. After untucking her legs, she draped them across my lap and nestled comfortably into me. I wrapped both arms around her warm body and I could feel the tension dissipate. Sometimes it feels safe to be wrapped in a warm embrace.

Within minutes, her breathing slowed, and she became limp as she dozed off. There was no reason in the world to move. I tilted my head back, laced my fingers around her small waist, and matched the pattern of her breathing. Her situation was horrible, but I could not remember the last time I felt so content. Nicole was asleep in my arms, and this moment might never happen again.

Sometime later, maybe half an hour, she began to stir. I was half afraid she would jump up and scream, but she didn't. She looked up at me, and those beautiful blue eyes looked a little more peaceful and less frightened. Then she smiled.

"Thank you for being here. What would I do without you? Did you think that this would be part of your job description?"

Dear Lord, no. I never would've asked for a paycheck. I chuckled. "Mrs. Mueller never mentioned it," I said, but did not release my hold. Nor did she.

"Does this make you uncomfortable?" Nicole asked seriously.

"Not in the least," I said, and noted my voice sounded a little husky.

She tilted her head and looked at me. "You like

women, I think, yes?"

Oh, fuck. I am such dead meat. I wasn't sure I could make my voice work, but I was certainly in no position to be lying to a woman inches from my face. "Yes, I like women. Very much." Then I swallowed hard.

There was a very long pause. A quirky little smile crept across her face. "I like them, too." A sigh escaped her lips and she stroked the back of my wrist. "My very first lover was a woman. A girl, actually, we were only fifteen. I have never forgotten." She looked back at me. "The redheaded woman on the stage crew from *Sonnambula*, are you together?"

"How in the world would you... No, not now. We were." What an amazing memory.

"I thought so. You both looked so very happy, and I was a little jealous. Where is she now?"

Now I was uncomfortable. I sat up a little straighter and relaxed my arms. "I don't know. We broke up two years ago. She...she had been cheating on me."

Nicole touched my face with her fingertips. "Ah, maybe this is the reason you are here, because you understand. Thank you for telling me."

Every fiber in me screamed to kiss her while the cautionary voice warned against it. "I...er, I'm supposed to be working for you—"

"I understand, and I take advantage of you. I am so sorry. Please forgive me." She pulled away and stood up.

"No, no, there's nothing to forgive. That's not what I meant. I want to be here for you and support you. I'm just afraid of getting too close."

She smiled warmly. "I understand, and I am very glad you are here. I think maybe you could call Lars and Carl to explain that I am not able to work today. Maybe tell them my throat is a little sore, because it is true."

"Good idea, I'll call them right now. Why don't you go lie down and I'll get you something to eat if you like?" She simply nodded and headed down the hallway to her room. I collapsed on the couch with my arms around my head. *God help me. This situation just keeps getting worse. And so much better.*

Her scent and her touch lingered long after she left the room.

❧❧❧❧

Right after I made the phone calls, I threw together a peanut butter sandwich and poured a large glass of orange juice. Neither Lars nor Carl had posed any questions but asked me to send their regards. It was almost noon when I carried the tray down the hall to the master bedroom. Nicole had showered and was dressed in a comfortable T-shirt and shorts. I thought she was asleep at first when I saw her curled on her side. I carefully set the tray at the foot of the bed and turned to leave.

"Can you stay for a minute?"

"Sure, are you okay?" I came back and sat at the foot of the bed. When I did, I noticed some bruises on her right forearm but decided not to ask. I felt a brief surge of anger. There could be no other explanation for four round impressions.

"Yes, I feel much better, but I wanted to explain a little bit." She picked up the sandwich and started to eat. "Thank you, this is good."

I smiled, proud of my culinary skills. "Oh. It's

an old family recipe. Lars sends his regards and says to baby The Voice. Carl will call later."

Nicole wiped peanut butter off her chin. "I'm sure your mother is very proud of your cooking skills." She smiled. "I have been doing a lot of thinking since Mario left in the middle of the night. I think I must divorce him quickly. I think it is unwise for me to allow him to use my name. You see, much of his success has been because of our relationship. Maybe that was the only reason he was attracted to me." Her voice cracked and tears threatened. She clenched her jaw and continued. "I will call my agent to make arrangements. She knows lawyers to handle this."

She stood up and walked into the bathroom. After rinsing her hands and face, she came back and sat on the bed with her legs crossed. "Meg, I think I will need help, out here in New Mexico as well. I'm not sure what to do first. I do not want any publicity. That will affect the show. I want to make sure that he does not come to the opening and bring his girlfriend."

I hadn't thought of that, but this kind of domestic discord was like raw meat to the press. I was quite sure that the Santa Fe Opera would not like that kind of publicity. This was the very definition of a rock and a hard place, and beyond my expertise.

After a little more discussion, Nicole agreed that Greta Mueller should be involved, and that she would nap a bit more. I offered to arrange a meeting for later.

༄༅༄༅

I drove slowly to The Ranch and hoped I could catch Greta alone to talk about a delicate matter. This had nothing to do with me, but here I was being messenger—those individuals notoriously blamed for carrying bad news. I wished I had taken two minutes to comb my hair this morning.

Thad was on the phone and waved me in when I pointed at Greta's door. She, too, was in the middle of a phone conversation, but indicated a chair. I sat patiently for less than a minute and she joined me.

"Nice to see you again, Margaret." It was too late to correct her or suggest Meg. The woman seemed comfortable and relieved to have someone handle one of her problem areas. Now, here I was with un-glad tidings.

"Thanks, but it may not be. Your delicate situation with Nicole has gotten a tiny bit more complicated. Nicole agreed it would be best to discuss it with you, and I'm hoping you might have time to come over and talk with her."

"Please don't tell me she's sick." A panic-stricken look blossomed on her face.

"No, she's all right, it's about her husband, but I think it would be better for you to hear it from her." I wanted to stay as far from this issue as possible. I pushed back in the chair and crossed my legs.

She turned back to her computer for a minute. "I've got a meeting in twenty minutes, but would three o'clock work?"

"I'm sure that would be fine, thanks. I'll get back to work now," I said, anxious to be done with this unpleasant task.

I took my leave and drove over to the rehearsal hall to talk to the director.

The job of my dreams morphed subtly into a very serious responsibility. It was no one's fault, but the simple notion of checking Nicole's blood sugar and helping her rehearse was now layered with some rather intense distractions. Her emotional state would have a direct bearing on her hypoglycemia. That meant I needed to be a little more vigilant and a little less distracted.

The rational mind argued: *Her flirting is probably just more to do with her wounded pride rather than an attraction to me. Right? That must be it.* The fantasy kept clouding my judgment. Nicole Bernard and me, wow. My brain always wanted to go back to those brief physical encounters because of the heart-pounding yearning I felt at that time. I wasn't sure if she suspected my feelings, and I didn't think I wanted her to because it felt just too dangerous. But having her in my arms carried me aloft to some ethereal plane. It was divine.

I almost missed the turnoff to her house.

Ellis, you have to get a grip. First, because it's your job. And second, because she's counting on you to help her get through this. So suck it up and stop daydreaming.

It was already two thirty when I came in the front door. I heard music and headed back to the den, where I found Nicole at the piano singing an aria from one of her scenes quietly. My feet stopped before I could enter the room. I leaned against the doorjamb and listened for several minutes, allowing my soul to soar to the same heights. Each phrase twirled around inside of me like spun glass reflecting a million different beams of light. It was like a drug.

Years before when a vocal career consumed my heart and soul, I experienced the most amazing moments of vocal purity, so pure that I truly believed angels channeled the sounds. They were rare occurrences, but powerful enough to keep the dream alive and to continue to practice my craft, still waiting for the moment when the angel's voice would appear.

Cancer killed that dream.

To be in the presence of a voice that divine was pure pleasure to me. Nicole sang the final aria from the opera, "Addio del passato." Goodbye to the past, to the dreams, and the love. The sadness in her voice tore at my heart. I knew how she felt, and I recognized the sound of anguish. When she finished, I stepped into the room and applauded. "*Brava, signora.*"

She looked up, surprised, while a crimson tint crept up her neck. "I did not hear you come in."

"That was beautiful. I hope I didn't startle you." I walked over closer and leaned on the piano. "Did you have a chance to sleep a little?"

"I slept like a rock until a little while ago. The music was in my head, so I had to get up and work. Were you able to speak with Mrs. Mueller?"

I glanced at my wristwatch. "Yes. As a matter of fact, she should be here in about half an hour, if that's okay."

Nicole stood up and stretched. "That's fine. I suppose I should change my clothes and look a little more professional." I thought she looked just fine in the shorts and T-shirt, but I might be a little more casual than most.

I pulled out the notes from the director and laid them in front of her. "Lars sent you a few notes about the next rehearsal."

She read the notes and smiled. "As soon as we block the final act, he wants to do a complete run-through. It's probably a good idea, to see how long this will run, and to see if I can manage for that long."

I followed her out through the kitchen. "When I read through the score, I noticed you were on stage almost the whole time. We are going to have to find a way to get you something to drink whenever possible. Either that, or I hope the scene changes are long ones."

She paused and turned to look at me. "I hadn't thought about that. The time, I mean, how demanding it would be. Do you think it's a concern?"

"I'm not sure. You haven't had to work that many hours without a break. I guess we'll find out. It's nothing to worry about now because I'm sure there's a way around it." I smiled as reassuringly as possible. "I'll just need to keep a closer check on your blood sugar for the next few days."

Nicole responded by flopping her arm onto the counter with a dramatic sigh. I laughed. I pulled out the supplies and muttered, "You're a remarkable actress." That earned me a glare from the diva.

"Fifty-eight, that's borderline. How are you feeling?" Her face was a little pale. I attributed that to the lack of sleep and stress.

"I think I have better days than this," she said with wry humor.

I let go of her finger and proceeded to wash my hands again. "I guess I'll make some iced tea while you get ready." She trotted across the living room and down the hall. I watched her for a minute thinking about how we all take people for granted. We never really understand what goes on behind the scenes, especially those celebrity types. All we have are glimpses. Nicole Bernard was a woman, just like me, with problems and concerns and her share of demons. I was fortunate to have a brief peek into the life of someone I admired so much.

The tea was ready, so I took a few moments to straighten up the living room. Although it wasn't part of my job to pick up her house, I didn't want Nicole to be embarrassed. Call me crazy. It took only minutes. I replaced fallen objects, rearranged the furniture, straightened up the shelves, and emptied the basket of used tissues. No wonder her face was puffy; that poor woman shed some serious tears over a man who, in my humble opinion, was not worth one of them.

I heard Greta's car before the door knock and went to meet her. I did a quick look around and ran my fingers hastily through my pokey hair. "Hi, Greta. Please come in. Nicole will be right out."

Greta looked around and nodded. "This certainly is a beautiful home. I'm grateful whenever I don't have to find acceptable lodging. The Goddards have been very generous. Hmm, it looks like they bought some new furniture since last year." She ran her hand across the back of the leather sofa and then sat down.

"If you excuse me a minute, I'll tell Nicole you're here and get the iced tea."

Nicole had changed into a pair of straight-legged jeans and a purple V-neck T-shirt. With a final change to her makeup, she looked up at me in the mirror and winked. "Do I look presentable?"

"Utterly. Greta's waiting in the living room. I'll get the tea." The jeans fit her like a glove, and I hurried out of the room to the cooler air of the kitchen. After I poured two glasses and put them on the coffee table, I added a dash of lemon and some sugar.

Nicole made an appropriate entrance down the steps and enthusiastically greeted her guest. "I am so grateful you would take time to come over and talk with me. I do not wish to be any more of an inconvenience than I already am." She waved toward me, smiling. "Meg has just been a godsend."

They embraced and sat down, Greta on one couch, Nicole on the other. I chose the kitchen counter and worked busily on the calendar with the rehearsal schedule. The small talk lasted sixty-four seconds. Greta was more of a get-to-the-point kind of gal.

"Margaret said you wanted to talk to me about a problem with Mario."

Nicole sputtered a little and set her glass down abruptly. She glanced at me and I nodded supportively. I think most Europeans are accustomed to more of the social niceties in conversation. "Well, yes. I do not want to waste your time with a long story, and I would prefer it not go much farther." She tucked her legs under her and sat up a little straighter. "Mario showed up unexpectedly yesterday morning. He attended a rehearsal with me and we had dinner with Lars and his wife. When we got back here I confronted him with numerous rumors I was receiving. Well, it was a heated discussion and not the first time or even the second we have argued."

She was sounding agitated and I wanted to go to her, but didn't.

Greta nodded solemnly and said nothing. Even from a distance, I could see the calculating in her eyes. She was working on a cover story.

"I told him to leave and then I insisted on telling him I would be asking for a divorce. I have notified my agent to start the papers. Greta, I am so sorry that this has happened now, but I could no longer keep closed my eyes. It is betrayal. I do not want him to come back here and I do not want publicity about this if we can help it. I want to work and concentrate on my performance."

The tears were very close, but she was holding it together. I felt immense admiration for her.

"Nicole, please don't worry about a thing. Of course, we'll honor your wishes and I will contact our attorney. I'm afraid I did hear rumors that you were having some domestic problems but didn't want to pry. No one needs to know anything about this. However, you might want to say something to Lars. But that's up to you." She stood up. "I'll leave you to your work, but if there is anything you need, please don't hesitate to ask. Margaret, whatever you can do to support Nicole, please feel free."

Nicole stood up and walked Greta to the door. A quick hug and Greta left. Nicole leaned heavily against the door and her shoulders began to shake. *Oh, crap.* I hurried over and put one arm around her shoulder, moving her back to the couch. Tears streaked her face.

"Bastard!" she yelled. "He has ruined my life and I would like to kill him." I would, too. We sat together and Nicole railed the indignity and loss. The arranged marriage, the way he used her celebrity, and his verbal abuse. The creep snuck around behind her back humiliating her for no reason except vanity and ego. Well, that and a younger woman. Still, her rage surprised me.

When the fury subsided, I tried a diversion. "Nicole, what would you say to busting out of here and playing hooky?"

That took her by surprise. "Hooky?"

"Let's just get in the car without the cell phone and get away for a couple of hours."

"Where could we go?"

"Anywhere you like, but I thought we could take a drive and get something to eat. We're not going to get any work done anyway. We may as well enjoy a nice evening."

I backed the Infinity out of the garage. The car was a rich mink color with a large sunroof and a great stereo. The sun moved slowly toward the horizon, leaving several hours of June sun to enjoy. The temperature was in the mid-eighties and comfortable. I took the service road out to the highway and headed north intending to backtrack to Highway 592 and head east to the Encantado Resort and Spa. My parents' friends offered good reviews and I thought it might be a safe getaway where Nicole was unlikely to be recognized. No one would expect the jean-clad, T-shirt-wearing woman with windblown blond waves to be a renowned opera singer, especially when she's hanging out with a very unglamorous school nurse. I chuckled a little while Nicole fiddled with the radio, when she suddenly said, "No, no music."

She settled back and let the wind and the sun wash over her. "I think maybe we have spent too much time talking all about me. Tell me about you, Meg. Please."

I didn't expect that request. "What exactly would you like to know?"

"You could tell me about your family."

I flipped on the cruise control. "My folks live in Albuquerque and have for forty years. My dad teaches music theory at the University of New Mexico and my mom teaches piano and voice. I was born and raised here, graduated from Eastern New Mexico University with a nursing degree and a minor in music. After two years at the University of New Mexico Hospital working in pediatrics, I applied for the program at the Opera. I apprenticed for two years up here, then took a job with the Santa Fe school system."

I couldn't see her eyes behind the dark glasses, but her small mouth curved in a grin.

"Do you see your parents often?"

"Not as much as my mom would like, but at least once a month."

"Will they come to the opera so I can meet them?"

"I'm sure they will. They love *La Traviata* and are huge fans of yours. They usually attend one or two each summer," I said, knowing they wouldn't miss this opportunity.

"I'd like to meet them. Maybe they would like to see a performance and have dinner?"

"Seriously? They'd be thrilled."

"Of course. We must plan it," she said with conviction.

We rode in silence for several minutes. We were off the main road and just wandering through the high desert, mostly scrub, cactus, and juniper. I loved the stark beauty of the unadorned or un-landscaped desert. Many visitors were put off. "What do people see here? It's brown and so desolate." I loved the stillness and hidden attractions, like the tiny wildflowers, intricate cactus, and wildlife. It was warm and pleasant, and the wide-open spaces seemed to dwarf the recent drama. I felt relaxed and very content.

"Meg, are you happy?"

This woman was full of surprises. "Do you mean in life, or at this moment?"

"Both."

"At this moment I feel content, relaxed, and

very happy. In my life...that's a little more complex."

Nicole looked out the passenger window for a while. Without turning, she said, "Is it difficult to be alone?"

Aw, damn. The pensiveness. I get it now. "Yeah, sometimes it is. I have supportive parents and some very loyal friends. I have a good job and I can travel when I want. Then unexpectedly, I get a chance to work with you and the opera company. What's not to like?"

"Do you miss having a lover?"

I glanced over to see if she was joking. She wasn't. *Crap on a cracker. How do I answer that one?* "Of course I do."

"Enough that you would choose to make love with a married woman?" I heard the sharp edge in her voice before the question was out of her mouth. She was asking about Mario now.

"No, Nicole. I would never do that with someone in a committed relationship."

It was quiet again. I saw the sign for the resort, but it was still ten minutes before we arrived. From a distance, it looked like a miniaturized, modern Xanadu stuck out in the middle of the desert. The heat waves rising off the ground lent a mystical kind of appearance. As we followed the long driveway, the main building appeared to be primarily a spa. The small rental units were hidden from view. When I inquired, the concierge assured us that we were welcome to enjoy a cocktail and light meal at the bar. Dinner would require a reservation. We both nodded.

The brochure indicated accommodations in sixty-five casitas, a dining room, meeting rooms, and a fully equipped spa. It seemed like an elegant retreat, beautifully appointed and hidden in the desert. He directed us to the bar, and we opted to sit outside and watch the sunset.

Each comfortable seating group had an umbrella and thick white cushions. We were at a slightly higher altitude and it was noticeably cooler, still nice as the sun inched closer to the distant horizon leaving long shadows.

Nicole sat back and smiled broadly. "This was a brilliant idea, Meg. I feel better already."

Looking at her relaxed face, I did too. "This is a pretty neat place, kind of hidden away."

A handsome young server arrived and asked if we'd like to order something to drink.

"What would you suggest, do you have specials?"

"Would you be interested in a classic margarita or our house special?"

"What's the special?" Nicole asked.

"The Terra Special is a Ketel One Citroen martini, with freshly squeezed blood-red orange juice and a hint of lime."

"That sounds perfect."

I smiled at her enthusiastic reply and said, "Make it two."

We sipped the tasty drinks and watched the sky go from lustrous blue to pale, and gradually a few cirrus clouds formed on the horizon, transforming the evening sky with hints of pink and orange—the same colors as the cocktails.

"Excuse me, I don't mean to intrude." An older woman came up to the table. "Are you Nicole Bernard?"

Nicole smiled graciously and took off her sunglasses. "Yes, although I am surprised you could even recognize me looking so casual."

"I told my husband it was you—we are just your biggest fans—but he said no. He said you wouldn't be out here without all kinds of people with you."

"Well, I am afraid I do not have so many people, but this is my wonderful assistant, Meg Ellis."

The woman shook hands with both of us. "This is such a treat. We have tickets to *La Traviata* in a couple of weeks and I just can't wait."

"That is wonderful. You must come back afterward and tell me what you thought of it."

"That is just so sweet of you. We will, you just look for Harold and Elvira Carlson. It was such a pleasure to meet you. I'll let you get back to your dinner."

I leaned over. "You just made her day. That was nice of you."

Nicole smiled and looked surprised. "But it was she who made my day."

The server left a menu and we each picked an entrée. Nicole opted for Chimayo—blackened cod salad with grilled corn, black beans, Espanola red onion stack with chili-lime vinaigrette.

I ordered the New Mexico style shepherd's pie with cumin-ground Colorado lamb and local beef, green chili, and mashed potatoes.

There was little conversation as we watched the sun move slowly behind the horizon.

This lovely evening was one I would treasure for the rest of my life.

We passed on dessert and walked slowly back to the car. Nicole paused as we got to the car and looked at me. "This was wonderful. It is exactly what I needed."

"I've enjoyed it, too. It was like a mini-vacation." After unlocking the doors, we both climbed in and buckled up. The sky was fading from pale lavender to deep purple, and without the moon there were pinpricks of light from a profusion of stars visible in the Eastern sky.

"I appreciate your driving. I am a capable driver but must confess I enjoy riding and sightseeing." Her face looked tranquil and that made me happy.

"It's the least I could do when we used your car and you insisted on paying for dinner. I do have an income, even if I dress like I'm destitute."

"*Mon amie*, it is the least I can do to repay you for your patience." She paused and looked me over slowly, causing little goose bumps. "I like the way you dress. You look quite fetching."

I had no smart-aleck remark for that. I just glanced over and smiled stupidly, even as my face glowed.

Although it had only been several weeks, I was beginning to feel that Nicole and I had a comfortable relationship. It was more than I ever dreamed of, and I hoped it was comfortable for her as well.

"I think we've pretty well covered my history, what about you?" I asked.

"I still have a small home outside of Paris because most of my engagements are in Europe. Since there are now more in the United States, Mario and I bought an apartment in New York City a few years ago. I guess I should say I bought it." The bitterness returned to her voice.

Damn. I wished I hadn't said anything. "You do have a very large following in the United States, you know."

"Yes, people have been wonderful. I am very flattered by all of the attention I get. This reminds me, I will have a few publicity events as soon as the show opens. Some of them are fundraisers, but most are just interviews. I hope you will be available to help me. It is so much disorder when I'm by myself. Between you and me, sometimes I get lost." She chuckled.

The ride seemed much faster on the way home, and before I knew it the garage door was opening. A beautiful day ended too soon. As soon as we got into the house, Nicole stopped and looked at me. "Meg, I would feel much better if you did not have to drive home so late. Of course, it is up to you. There's certainly more than enough space here, and even a guesthouse. Would you consider staying?"

Oh my God, would I consider staying overnight? The sound I heard was like the tin man beating on his metal chest. In reality, it was my heart thundering audibly. "That's kind of you, but not necessary. It's not too far." I spoke but didn't move.

"Still, we have rehearsal in the morning. It would save you travel time." She took a step toward me. "To be honest, I would feel better if you were here."

That's all I needed. "Of course I will. I didn't think about that—well, I don't mind."

We walked down the hall toward the guest rooms. She stopped and pointed at the one close to her room. "This one has a private bath and the much more comfortable bed." She opened the wardrobe and pointed at two bathrobes hanging there. Then she went into the bathroom and checked the drawers where she found extra toothbrushes, mouthwash, and lotion.

I was amazed. "Do the Goddards think you have

dozens of visitors?"

She laughed. "No, but often my family comes at some point during the run of the show. I never know how many will come. I think you'll find everything you need here, and I can find you a clean shirt for tomorrow if you like." She started to leave, then turned back and put her arms around me. "I am really glad you are here." Then she was gone.

It had been a long and wondrous day. I pulled out my cell phone and made a quick call to ask my neighbor to feed Pearson. I mustered enough energy to wash up, strip out of my clothes, and climb between the sheets of the queen bed that was only ten or fifteen feet away from the bed in which Nicole Bernard was sleeping. *Sweet dreams, Ellis.*

ACT II SCENE 4

Sunlight peeked over the Sangre de Cristo Mountains, lighting up the guestroom. Like the others in the house, this room had beamed ceilings and adobe walls painted a goldenrod color. The furniture was Mission style in a light pine. It was a large, comfortable room.

The gradual awareness of my surroundings increased a warm spot that glowed in the middle of my body. The fact that I was naked added to the pleasant sensation of the cool, soft sheet brushing against me. I could lie there and fantasize about another way to start this day, or I could get up and do something productive. Enticing as the fantasy was, I opted for the latter.

Showered and dressed, I made my way out to the kitchen and started a pot of coffee. Sunlight bathed the east-facing dining room and patio. It was a beautifully designed home, and I enjoyed being there. While the coffee brewed, I looked over the calendar.

The schedule would get busier now, as we drew closer to opening night. The opera would not open until the second weekend in July, and today would be Nicole's first opportunity to work with Stefan Eriksson, the young tenor. An attractive young blond, he and Nicole would make a handsome couple.

I poured a cup of coffee and walked to the patio. The temperature was probably in the low sixties, but it was warm in the sun. I relaxed into a comfortable chair and tried to focus on my responsibilities instead of my desires. This week would be a good sample of how well Nicole could endure the demanding schedule, and I would need to stay on top of her blood sugar and stamina.

The sound of the cupboard door alerted me to the fact that Nicole was up. Instantly, my heart rate increased. She appeared in the doorway, a steaming coffee cup in her hands, wearing loose-fitting cotton pants and a tank top. An older navy blue sweatshirt was draped over her shoulders, and her sleepy expression made her all the more adorable.

"Good morning."

"*Bonjour.* Thanks for making coffee, it is very good." She wandered over and stretched out on the lounge chair next to me. "Did you sleep well?"

"Like a baby. I wasn't sure I could get to sleep right away, but within two minutes of hitting the pillow, I was out. I guess I was more tired than I thought. How about you?"

"Pretty well." She smiled. "I was a little restless, but eventually I slept. Would you like to take a walk with me?"

"That's a good idea, too much sitting lately. We need to check your sugar before we go."

Her blood sugar was low normal, which I expected considering she hadn't eaten. "I'll check it again when we return to see what exercise will do." The walk took us up to the west end of the subdivision and back, which was almost two miles. We saw very few neighbors, but two jackrabbits, a family of quail, and a lonesome meadowlark serenading us. The entire area was formally landscaped—or rather, xeriscaped—to maintain the southwestern atmosphere. The homes were adobe, each with a different design but all huge.

For someone as petite as Nicole was, she set a blistering pace. My legs were longer, and I still had to work to keep up with her. School nursing had its demands, but since the surgery I had not been good about exercising. Mercifully, it was downhill on the way back, and halfway she began to slow.

"The next few weeks will be busier. In addition to the rehearsals with the entire cast, I will need to work with Stefan and with my coach. There will also be public relations events," said Nicole.

"Are you concerned about the schedule? If you are, I'm sure Lars would work with you."

She looked over at me and grinned. "Actually, I was thinking about you. The hours will not be the same, and sometimes they change during the day. You might find it easier to stay up here, and I would enjoy the company."

I didn't expect that invitation. On the surface, the idea made good sense. It would also mean we would be in even closer proximity, and I wasn't sure I could handle that. "It's probably a good idea. However, I think we should talk about it. We both may need some…private time. I don't want to be intrusive."

When we were back in the house, each of us grabbed a bottle of water.

"Meg, does this idea make you uncomfortable?" Nicole asked, finishing her water.

"A little bit. Please understand that you've been incredible to work with. I have no complaints."

"I see, but maybe you have other feelings? It might be easier if you tell me."

I pulled out a stool and sat down. Exactly what other feelings did I have? "Nicole, you've had a very unpleasant emotional experience and you're about to open in a brand-new production. I don't want to be a complicating factor."

"That is all true, and it is a little scary. You did not answer my question, though."

Shit. "I have tremendous admiration for you as an artist and as a woman. You're vibrant, attractive, and exciting. Under different circumstances, I might have difficulty…not being attracted to you." Did I just say that aloud?

Her eyes locked on mine, but they gave nothing away about her feelings. She sat down and folded her hands on the counter. "I think I understand. You are not completely sure you trust yourself, or me, if you stay here."

I looked up, surprised. "It has nothing to do with trusting you. I do. My concern is your vulnerability after this breakup with Mario. I understand what that feels like and how easy it is to…misinterpret emotions. I just think we have to be very careful."

"I am sure you are right. It is good you are honest with me. Perhaps I am selfish, then. I am used to depending on you, and I would rather not be alone right now."

That didn't make this any easier. "Okay, how would this be? I'll bring some things up here and stay in your guesthouse. We'll try it for a couple of weeks and then reevaluate. Does that sound fair?"

She cocked her head to one side and nodded. "That is reasonable."

We shook hands, and she said, "Good, we will have breakfast and then go to rehearsal. I need to meet my costar, and he definitely needs to meet me." She winked.

※※※※

The rehearsal buzzed with excitement as the chorus and principals mingled. Lars Logan was at the center of a small group of people, waving his arms and pointing in different directions. Several members of the chorus were in various locations, walking back and forth and vocalizing while others were scribbling notes on their scores.

As soon as we arrived at the theater, Nicole visibly lit up; this was her element. I took her belongings to a row of chairs while she flitted around exchanging warm greetings with many of the cast. As soon as the director saw her he motioned her over, and I could see her shaking hands with an attractive young man, who smiled and kissed her hand with great finesse. Soon they were talking together amicably. They moved to the other side of the room to begin reviewing some notes.

I had mixed emotions about returning to the world of opera. I missed being a part of the company, the memories, and the attendant excitement, but I also enjoyed being an observer—especially Nicole's observer. It was my job to watch her every minute of the day, working, playing, flirting, or grieving. No one could accuse me of stalking Nicole Bernard, because I was her personal assistant.

When I visited the set earlier, I spoke with the director about my responsibility to check her energy level discreetly. I assured him that once we had a stable regimen she would be fine. My only lingering concern was not a question of her stamina, it was more about whether or not she recognized her own limitations. That seemed to be the only weak area. She didn't know soon enough that she was running out of gas, and it would be up to me to recognize those subtle changes.

Lars Logan supported his diva and gave me carte blanche. We agreed that if I stood up and brought a bottle of water or juice, he would break the rehearsal for a couple of minutes. I didn't want to embarrass Nicole, but I needed to be able to keep her hydrated without drawing attention.

The morning went smoothly, and they managed to run through the first two acts without major interruptions. I was enthralled with the music and the energy of the cast. Nicole and Stefan struggled a bit with their duet, but this was the first time singing together. Their voices matched well. His sound was not overpowering but a good range, and to his credit he had already memorized his part. Nicole was very patient with him and held back just enough to save her voice. She was much better at pacing herself vocally than she was physically.

It was nearly one o'clock when Lars broke for lunch. He asked everyone to be back at two thirty, which would allow enough time for rest, hydration, and nourishment. After a brief conversation with the accompanist, Nicole found me and asked if we could run home.

"I am exhausted and would like to rest a little while," she said as we walked out into the bright sun on the way to the car.

"It's a perfect idea. I made some tuna salad before we left. You can have something to eat and then take a nap if you like," I said, sticking the cooler in the backseat.

"That sounds lovely. How do you think the rehearsal went?" We both got in and I started the car.

"Very well, considering it's the first run-through. I know you and Stefan will probably do some work together, but your voices sound good. I'm not sold on the two guys you came in with during the first entrance. Both of them are a little mousy for such a grand opening. Just my opinion."

She turned and looked at me. "My, you are observant, and I completely agree with you. I think Lars will talk to me about that later. You are also a little bit psychic. The two times I felt like I was getting dizzy you magically showed up with fruit juice. It is a mystery how you do it, but I'm certainly grateful." She reached over and squeezed my arm.

"I just had an idea. While you eat and nap, would you mind if I run home and pick up some things I need? I'm not sure how late this afternoon will run, and I may not feel like doing it later. If I'm not back in time, I'll meet you over there."

"So you have not changed your mind?" Her smile was heartwarming.

"No, I'm willing if that's what you want. It's a good suggestion. Now you go eat, and I'll be back as quickly as I can." We got out of the car and Nicole headed into the house. I jumped in my car and backed out, intent on getting to Santa Fe and back in the next ninety minutes.

For the first time outside of the air-conditioned rehearsal space, I noticed the oppressive heat. My car was a toaster oven. I powered down the windows and headed south trying to wrap my brain around the wisdom of staying with Nicole. Part of me was ecstatic at the prospect, but the inner critics were telling me I was out of my frigging mind to believe I could rationally and platonically live with this woman.

You are walking a very thin line. This woman has been through an emotional wringer and she is extremely vulnerable. You, on the other hand, have had a crush on her for years and you've been alone for over two years. Ergo, your needs and her needs are likely to crash into one another for entirely different reasons with the force of a Category 5 hurricane. Just think about it, Ellis.

"What is this with the last name? Damn it."

Sometimes it was as though I had two brains: one between my ears and another seated squarely between my atrium and ventricles. I hit speed dial and left Liz a message.

Okay, this is not insurmountable. I will stay in the guesthouse and only provide those services for which I am paid. Oh, hell. It's only for two weeks, and I'm sure she'll get tired of me hanging around all the time and tell me to go home. On the other hand, maybe she'll turn out to be moody and temperamental. Why not just take it one day at a time and see how it goes?

The parking lot was empty at this time of day because most of my neighbors were nine-to-fivers.

I picked up some clean clothes, toiletries, my iPad, a laptop, and downloaded three audio books. I also selected two dressy outfits and some nice shoes in case I had to do something fancy. Fortunately, I'd already cleaned my apartment, so it would be all right for a couple of weeks. Especially since I wouldn't be there to mess it up.

I went next door to explain to Mrs. Cochran that

I had a part-time job and needed to stay away for a couple of weeks. It wasn't the first time I'd asked her to babysit for Pearson. She was more than agreeable, and I thought Pearson liked her better anyway.

My cell phone rang as I loaded the bags into the trunk. "Hello."

"Hi, Meg, it's Liz. Got your message and I wanted to see how you were doing with your new job."

I plugged in my earbuds and started my car. "So far, so good. We haven't killed each other. I think she appreciates the help. Since the rehearsals are just starting to kick into high gear, Nicole suggested I stay up there while it's so busy. It's probably a good idea because I don't know what time things will be starting and stopping. We're going to give it a two-week trial. I was just at home to get some of my things." I turned on to the expressway and looked at my watch.

"So, you're moving in with Nicole Bernard?"

"No, it's not like that. I'll be staying in a guesthouse." I hope that sounded more nonchalant to her than it did to me.

"So what's it like, being a personal assistant?"

"Well, I don't know how to compare it to anything since I've never done it before, but I'm getting the hang of it. We have a practical daily regimen. Of course, it changes with her schedule. I have to say I enjoy being with the theater company again. It's a great bunch of people full of energy and fun."

"You sound happy. When do you think you'll be in Albuquerque again?"

That was a good question, as was when I would see my parents. "I'm not sure, but I promise to call you."

"Okay, I'll let you go and I've got to run too.

Take care, Meg."

I hadn't even thought about my parents for two weeks, but I was surprised my mom hadn't called. *I should call her tonight. I also need to let Lena know about the barbecue. Boy, have I been remiss.*

When I turned into Nicole's driveway, I noticed the car was still there. I grabbed my things and took them into the house. I could hear Nicole vocalizing, so I followed the sound just like the RCA Victor dog.

She stopped singing. "You made a very quick trip."

"Don't stop on my account. I'll just throw these things in the guesthouse if the door's unlocked."

"I left the keys on the counter."

I grabbed them and headed out across the patio. The brick walk curved down the hill about one hundred feet, just barely visible from the back patio. Inside the little casita it was still cool, even without the swamp cooler. I tossed my things on the couch and hung up my dress clothes. I flipped on the cooler anyway, because it was getting hotter by the minute and by five o'clock it might be uncomfortable. I glanced in the two bedrooms and both beds were made up, so I had my choice. This would be nice. It was my own little space, but it was close by if Nicole needed me. That thought sent tiny electrical sparks shooting through my nerves. What about my needs?

I shut the door and jogged up the path to the patio.

"Ready when you are," I said, closing the door behind me. "Did you get a chance to nap?"

She folded up her music and followed me into the kitchen. "Yes. After a delicious lunch, I curled up on the couch and slept for at least half an hour. Did you eat anything?"

"No. Too busy. I'll get an energy bar to take with me."

※ ※ ※ ※

The afternoon session started more slowly. The third act party scene included some major drama between the three major characters as well as a big dance number. I settled in, eager to watch an entertaining performance, but the afternoon chorus performance was a tad lackluster. Everyone was hot, tired, and a little bit cranky, so Lars had to interrupt several times to have them do it again.

Nicole and Stefan had an emotional scene to play where he humiliates her in front of her friends by throwing money at her. The character's father intervenes and admonishes him for treating her so badly.

They took a break, and I hustled over with a bottle of juice and a damp hand towel. The entire cast was sweating because of sheer exertion, and I was more concerned with Nicole overheating. She understood my concerned look and patted my arm when she returned the towel. "I am all right, thank you."

After a few comments, Lars dismissed the chorus so he and the principals could work on the fourth and final act. This required only five major characters: Violetta—the dying heroine; Alfredo—her lover; Germont—his father; Annina—Violetta's maid; and the doctor. The whole scene rested on Nicole's ability to make the audience suspend its disbelief. Her ability to capture and hold our imagination made it possible to forget the absurd premise of the woman singing as she expired. It was a testament to the talent of this artist.

Lars walked through the scene explaining what he wanted out of each of them, then we all sat back and watched the magic. I had seen Nicole rehearse this particular number countless times, and yet I was transported. The rehearsal space fell away and all I could see were the two young lovers hanging on to their last moments together. In the instant when Violetta is between life and death, she feels a surge of joy. Her pain is gone and she feels hopeful, if only for a moment.

Nicole's voice faded, her eyes closed, and tears ran unabated down my face. No one noticed me as Lars moved onto the set to make comments. I was glad everyone else had left. Not that anyone would care, but I felt embarrassed by my emotional display.

I began to pack up the cooler when I felt a hand on my back. "Is it so horrible that this performance makes you weep?"

I looked up and saw she was smiling. "This is what undone looks like, and I'm afraid it will continue to look this way as long as your voice holds awe-inspiring powers."

She stroked my cheek, brushing away a tear with her thumb. "You are so very sweet."

※ ※ ※ ※

We both stood in the kitchen as I unpacked my backpack. It was nearly 7:00 p.m. and I was starving. Nicole set her music on the island and plunked down on one of the stools. Her color was a little pale and I knew she was tired.

"I'm thinking that pizza in the freezer might taste pretty good right now. How about you?"

She looked up at me and nodded. "I would like that, and I have no energy for much else."

I turned the oven on to preheat and got testing equipment out. "Since you are too weak to resist, let me check your sugar." I took her small hand and swabbed the side of her finger. I could feel her watching me and turned my head to meet her gaze. Her glistening eyes held mysteries, some of which I wanted to know. I didn't pull away. The glucometer beeped. "Looks okay, but I think you need to eat something."

She rubbed her fingers through her hair and shook her head. "I think I'd feel better if I took a quick shower. Do I have time?"

"Sure, I won't put it in till you're ready." I looked through the refrigerator while I waited and spotted a few things to throw into a salad and a chilled bottle of Pinot Grigio. I knew I still had to unpack, but that wouldn't take long. The patio glowed in golden light from the setting sun. The mountain range to the east still had sunlight on the peaks.

I stretched out on one of the comfortable lounge chairs and took a deep breath. Sometimes, I had to pinch myself to realize how lucky I was. There was no way on my salary that I would ever be able to live in a home like this. It was spacious, well designed, and beautifully decorated. Every detail provided either beauty or comfort.

My mind drifted aimlessly until it stopped on a vision of Nicole in the shower. *Just stop it.* My fantasy world was beginning to encroach on reality, and it was dangerous. It was so hard because Nicole was everything I could imagine and more. *Meg, you need to be very careful or you will be jobless and humiliated.* I heard the oven timer ring, which meant it was preheated.

Nicole and I both entered the kitchen at the same moment and stopped. Her face was pink and her hair still wet. She wore shorts and a tank top.

I swallowed hard and smiled. "You look all fresh and clean, do you feel better?"

"*Mais oui. Je suis merveilleux.*"

Oh, yes, ma'am. You are marvelous. The time she had spent in the sun was providing a little bit of a tan, which looked healthy and very attractive. "Would you like a glass of wine? There's a cold bottle in the refrigerator, and I thought I'd make a salad while we waited for the pizza."

She nodded, and I pulled out the bottle.

"You know, while I was in the shower I was thinking. It is not your job to cook for me, even though it is a nice treat. I would like it though, and since you will be staying here, to eat together and not alone. It might be easier for both of us. If that is agreeable, I think we should both go to the store to get some food. After all, I have no idea what you like to eat."

That was something else I hadn't thought of, but I certainly didn't want to have to cook for her and myself. I knew my job did not include cooking, but I was responsible for her energy and therefore her calories. Here was another gentle entanglement that brought us closer together. Another push-pull.

We took food and wine to the table on the patio and dined al fresco while enjoying one of the longest days of the year. The temperatures had dipped into the seventies and it was a perfect summer evening. A crescent moon was just rising and the whole mesa had gone very still. I remained unsure if anyone lived in houses around us because I hadn't seen or heard anyone. It was nice, thinking we were alone.

Nicole sipped her wine and said, "When I was a little girl, we were allowed to play outdoors on summer nights until it became dark. I can still remember running to the fields behind our homes chasing *lucioles*, or as you say, fireflies. It was a happy time with no worries. We could swim in the pond in the daytime or ride our bicycles." She pulled her feet up onto the chair and rested her chin on her knee. "What about you? Tell me about little Meg."

"It seems so long ago. I suppose it wasn't very different. Of course, I grew up in Albuquerque so we didn't have a pond, and we didn't have a field to play in. However, we all had yards, bicycles, and long summer evenings. Sometimes we would take a vacation to the Midwest—my grandparents lived in northern Wisconsin. I loved those trips. We would drive for days and days, and suddenly be in a place that was so cool and green. They owned a cottage on a small lake, and my dad taught me to fish and row a boat. My grandfather taught me to swim off the pier. Man, that water was cold!" I laughed at the memory of my blue lips and feet.

"You had no brothers or sisters?"

"I had a brother, who was two years younger than me, and he died when he was three of a congenital heart problem." I hadn't thought about Sammy for years. Nevertheless, somewhere inside, I always missed him.

"How tragic. That must have been very difficult."

"What about you, do you have brothers or sisters?"

"I have a sister who is ten years older and is a

nun, a Franciscan. My parents are very proud of her, but we seldom see her since she works with the poor in India." Sadness reappeared on her face.

"We should probably call it a night. I still need to do a little unpacking, and I'm sure you're exhausted. What is the plan for tomorrow morning?"

"I asked Carl if he would work with Stefan and me for a little while. I would like you to help if you would because we both have to practice the staging. I think you might remember it better than we do."

We cleared the table and cleaned up together until the awkward moment when we had to say goodnight. I started toward the patio door with Nicole right behind me. We stopped at the door.

"I will leave the door open in case you need to come back," she said softly.

The lights were off in the kitchen, and it was dark except for a small night-light in the hallway. She stood an arm's length away in the dark with just a faint hint of moonlight reflecting off her pale skin.

I didn't want to say goodnight, and I didn't want to leave. Any minute she was going to hug me or kiss me on the cheek and I had to resist the overwhelming desire to pull her into my arms. I couldn't make words come out of my mouth, and somehow she knew this. She just stood there waiting for me to make a move. Finally, I pulled myself together, leaned forward, and kissed her cheek. "All right, I'm off. Sleep well, and I'll see you in the morning."

I jogged down the walk to the safety of the guesthouse and a cold shower.

Act II Scene 5

I awoke with a start, sat up, and looked around the room. For an instant, I had no idea where I was. Oh yes, Nicole's guesthouse. I flopped back on the pillows and reached for my watch; it was only 7:00 a.m. Sunlight bathed the room, reflecting off the white plaster walls, a stunning departure from the goldenrod adobe of the walls in the main house. The large bed was extremely comfortable, and I wasn't sure I wanted to get out of it.

It had only taken me a short time to put away my meager belongings and set up my computer the night before. Not surprisingly, Wi-Fi was available so I had Internet access—another plus. I enjoyed a long luxurious shower, along with the use of some extraordinarily thick towels. I began to think I could get used to this lifestyle.

Just before I'd gotten into bed, I'd walked out on the small front patio, which had a nice view up to the main house. From where I stood, I could see a single light burning in the master bedroom. Nicole had still been up. I stood for a few minutes in the cool night air, thinking about our proximity and wondering where all this would lead.

By the time I shook loose the cobwebs, got ready, and came up to the house, Nicole was already up and cooking breakfast. She was humming and looked chipper. "*Bonjour,*" she said, sounding a little like Julia Child.

"Good morning. You're up early and looking well rested." I poured a cup of coffee and enjoyed the rich aroma.

"I feel quite well and am making some eggs, if you would like."

They looked wonderful and smelled even better. I grabbed a couple of plates and silverware, then set them on the counter. I went over and stood behind her as she mixed eggs with cream, then added cheese and chives to the mix. She slowly poured the combination in the pan with some cooked, crumbled bacon. I was surprised to find my mouth watering, literally.

We sat at the counter drinking coffee and orange juice and eating delicious eggs. I decided I wouldn't be doing all the cooking. "I think these are the best eggs I've ever eaten. They are so light and flavorful."

Nicole winked at me. "An old family recipe." We both laughed at what was beginning to become an inside joke. This kind of familiarity felt good and I had missed it. I'd be guessing, but I think Nicole missed it, too.

We were almost finished when her cell phone rang. She went to retrieve it and soon began speaking French. I took that as a good signal to start cleaning up the kitchen. Within five minutes, her tone became angry and agitated. It must've been Mario. *Mind your own business, Ellis.* Nicole paced in the living room and finally disappeared down the hall to her room.

I had a bad feeling about this. She'd gone several days without mentioning him. It was not for me to judge, because maybe she really was happy with him, but it sure didn't seem like a good pairing. The clock on the microwave showed eight forty, and I guessed that Carl would be arriving around nine.

Another ten minutes passed, and I made my way down the hall, listening. She was no longer talking so I tapped lightly on the bedroom door, which was ajar. "Nicole, are you okay?"

She was sitting cross-legged on the bed, hugging one of her pillows with tissues tucked in one hand. I walked closer and sat on the foot of the bed without saying anything. What was there to say? We both knew what had just happened.

"The lawyer called him and he's angry because he does not want a divorce, he wants to reconcile."

My heart sank a little bit, dreading the thought of either a protracted court case or a difficult reconciliation. It was not what she needed right now. Selfishly, it was not what I wanted.

She blew her nose, took a deep breath, and stood up. "I told him no. I no longer trusted him." With that, she walked into the bathroom and ran the water. When she returned, she was calmer and more focused. She handed me her cell phone. "We must get ready to sing. I want you to hold this for me, because I don't want to talk to him anymore."

I was surprised. A mere forty-eight hours earlier she had been devastated by the demise of her marriage. Today, I watched her pull herself together and shake it off. Every day this woman showed me something new, another piece of the puzzle.

Nicole went directly to the den and began to warm up. I followed her as far as the kitchen and then thought that perhaps another pot of coffee might be in order. This might be a long morning. I no sooner flipped on the coffee maker than there was a knock at the door. The ever-cheerful Carl greeted me warmly, and we both joined Nicole in the den.

"Good morning, Madame. You look ravishing." He kissed her cheeks and proceeded to lay out his music. "I received a call from Stefan a few moments ago, and he has been unavoidably detained but will get here as soon as possible."

"We can start anyway. I want to include the movement. Meg, will you help us?"

"Sure, what would you like me to do?" I couldn't imagine what help I could possibly be.

She handed me the score. "Would you just read Alfredo's part starting here?" she said, pointing to a line halfway down the page.

I took the score and could feel my heart begin to pound. Dear God, she didn't expect me to sing, did she? "Nicole, I can't—"

She saw the panic and touched my hand. "It's all right. Just read his lines. I need to get the timing." She looked me in the eye to confirm her intent, then patted my hand and turned back to her accompanist.

"Carl, let's begin here at where everyone goes to dance and Violetta suddenly becomes faint, *usciamo dunque*." Walking toward me, she sang the line then swayed as though she might faint.

I remembered the scene and moved toward her, taking her arm and reading the next line. Suddenly, in my mind, we are the characters, we are the scene. She pushes away, singing that she's all right and grabs for the back of a chair and sits down. I ask her if she's in pain, but she denies it and encourages everyone to leave.

The scene continues as Alfredo tries to convince Violetta of his devotion. He tells her of the love he has carried silently for over a year while she teasingly disbelieves him. His poignant aria about the mysteries and pain of love win her over.

Nicole remembered her blocking and moved away, and I pursued her reading his beautiful entreaties, finally kneeling to profess his love. It was slightly embarrassing and strangely real to be kneeling before her reading poetry of love. My heart surged with fullness as she looked me in the eye and sang the beautiful response. The song ends with an embrace. I stood up and she put her arms around my waist, singing—no more about love, you must go. She gives Alfredo a flower and tells him to come back when it has wilted. He leaves joyfully, while she asks him if he really loves her. He replies: You have no idea how much I love you. He leaves and returns to kiss her hand—which I did with surprising ease.

Together they sing, "*Addio, addio.*"

Our eyes locked as Carl finished the final notes. We were standing facing one another and breathing hard. Her eyes were dark and unreadable. She spun away and went to the piano.

"Anyone for coffee?" I said as I hurried to the kitchen. They both said yes.

Once there, I ran cold water on my hands and splashed my face. I quickly played through the scene and realized how realistic it was for me. I meant every word I said to her. If she could see through me, I was in deep trouble. I hoped she would believe my great acting skills.

I put two cups of coffee on a tray with cream and sugar and carried it out to the den as the door knocker sounded.

Stefan Eriksson stood bouncing on the balls of his feet when I opened the door. He looked young, and he looked nervous. I would be too if I had kept Nicole Bernard and her accompanist waiting. "Please come in, Mr. Eriksson. Ms. Bernard is waiting for you." He followed me back to the den.

"This is a very beautiful house, and so large." He looked around as though he had never seen anything like this. Of course, maybe he hadn't. He didn't look like he was older than thirty and had a real baby face with pale skin, natural blond hair, and blue eyes. Stefan was the stereotypical Scandinavian. I overheard someone say that he had studied at Juilliard, which would explain his excellent English.

"Madame, I am so terribly sorry to keep you waiting. The wardrobe mistress had many things to change." He laughed. "I think they were expecting a much bigger man." He kissed her on both cheeks and stretched across to shake hands with Carl.

"It is no problem. I wanted to work on the first scene anyway. We were just having coffee, would you like some?"

"Oh, that sounds wonderful, yes, please."

Nicole came up to the kitchen for another cup. "I'm glad you thought to make coffee, it seems to be very popular." I poured a cup and handed it to her. "Thank you for helping me with the first scene. Remind me to ask you a question later."

As they ran through plans to work on the third act, I snuck out and went to the guest cottage. It was cool and quiet, and I sank into one part of the large pit sofa. It was a soft orange fabric with several brightly colored throw pillows. The ceiling and walls were white and the wood floors covered with Native American rugs. There was a small fireplace facing the sofa. I closed my eyes.

I still felt a little shaky from the scene with Nicole and needed to regroup. I was comfortable with the notion of staying there and enjoying my private retreat. I was less comfortable about the possibility of any more rehearsing.

With a little distance, I realized that when I told Nicole how her voice affected me, I should have been listening. Rehearsing the blocking or staging might've been okay, but having her sing to me was a whole other thing. When she put her arms around me and sang the final lines, my knees nearly buckled. I would have been mortified. Yet, I was totally powerless to tell her to stop.

When I looked at my watch, an hour had passed. I stood up and slipped my feet into my sandals, then walked outside. The heat enveloped me like an electric blanket. It was midday and the sun was directly overhead, heating the cement pathway and adobe walls. I listened for a minute, and even with the doors closed I could hear Nicole and Stefan singing. Their rehearsal time was unscheduled so I imagined they would sing until one of them got tired.

I went back inside and decided to put on a cooler shirt and shorts. I stuck a book in my back pocket and headed up to the big house. Whatever was going on, Nicole probably needed to take a break. I carefully opened the patio door and slipped in. They were standing at the piano, talking with Carl. Nicole turned around, sensing a presence, and just smiled. I walked through into the kitchen and tried to guess from their conversation what section it was. From the sounds of it, they were not in complete agreement about some part of the third act. Carl's voice interrupted, correctly suggesting they let Lars decide. If anyone had asked,

I agreed. A few minutes later, they were all trooping through the house to the front door, thanking me on the way.

When Nicole returned, I could tell she was flagging. The early morning chipper-ness had faded. I handed her a bottle of fruit juice, and she nodded. "Come sit down with me, please. I am exhausted."

We sat in the den. She chose the overstuffed chair and pointed at the ottoman for me. She put her head back but in the sunlight I could see the fatigue. After drinking a large quantity of the juice, she opened her eyes and gave me a mischievous look. "How much would you charge me to massage my feet?"

I adopted a very serious expression, but I was laughing on the inside. How was it possible that she could not know by now that I would pay to rub her feet—or any other part of her for that matter? "Well, I'd have to think about whether I would charge by the toe or by the time. Either way, I think it would be pretty expensive. I'm not sure you can afford it."

She laughed loudly, and the sound floated into my chest. "You are probably right. I am just a poor singer. What if I would barter with you?"

I looked up, taken aback by that comment. "What do you mean?"

Her look turned serious. "Meg, I was watching today and I see how moved you are by music and I know how good your voice is—or was. If you wanted to, I would help you sing again."

She was serious, and I was overwhelmed. It was an unvoiced dream I had held on to for many years. I never told anyone how badly I wanted to sing again. And I was so afraid I couldn't that I never tried. Ever. I never even sang in the shower or in the car. I believed that the radiation had completely taken away my ability to sing. Now, Nicole Bernard was cracking open a shell. I didn't know what to say, and I must have looked like an idiot with my mouth open and no sounds coming out.

    Nicole reached out and put her hand on my leg. "I am only offering if you want to. I think you are afraid that you have no voice, and that is not true. Your speaking voice is rich and resonant. I don't hear strain or hoarseness. I am not a doctor, but I know about the voice, and I think I can help you."

    I could feel tears brimming and wiped furiously at my eyes. "I don't know what to say."

    "Tell me you'll think about it, and maybe consider my sore feet," she said pleadingly.

    In spite of my emotional state, I laughed. "Okay, you win. I'll think about it while I massage your poor feet." She sat back and lifted her legs into my lap. *You are dead meat, Ellis.*

    I started with the sole of one foot with both thumbs in a circular pattern at her heel, working toward her toes. She groaned appreciatively as I worked the small muscles between the dozen small bones of her foot. Like the rest of her, her feet were narrow and delicate.

    During my nurses training, I had learned a bit about reflexology and had many opportunities to practice with my partner for three brief years. That was a long time ago, but the moves came back as if I'd done them every day. I continued the alternating pressure along the sides of her foot and up her ankle. I rotated the foot and then massaged her calf.

    The softness of her skin and the long limb draped across my lap were slowly increasing the temperature in the room and in my body. Nicole lay immobilized by the sensations she was experiencing. This could so easily get out of hand. I had to be careful. I switched to her other foot and focused on the muscle groups and not the increasing heat in my hands. I would gladly have gone on for hours, except the heat in my pelvis was threatening to consume me.

She must have sensed it too, because when I stopped, she pulled her legs into the chair with her. This time, her smile held a different message. It was pleasure mixed with desire, and I was sure of that.

In a husky voice, she said, "If Greta knew of your other talents, she would be paying you a great deal more money."

"If she knew what I was bartering for, she might think it was a good deal."

"Would this be what you call a win-win?" She grinned lasciviously.

"It would be for me, but I guess you'd have to answer for you."

It was all I could do to stay seated. The longing in her eyes was unmistakable, but I couldn't take the chance. Verbal sparring was one thing; making a move on her would be something entirely different.

"Yes, I think it would be a win-win." She slowly reached out her right hand.

I slid my fingers along her palm before grasping it gently. "Deal."

"Will you tell me something?" she asked sincerely. "Tell me why you have not tried to sing."

I turned on the footstool to face her and clasped my hands tightly between my knees. I wasn't sure where to begin, or how. This might be the darkest part of my soul, the one little secret never shared. It was difficult, but I couldn't hold on to it. Of all the people on earth, Nicole might be the one person who could understand, and maybe even help. I dared not hope too much, as the thought of losing the dream again was almost more than I could bear. Yet, if a tiny glimmer of hope survived, I would have to try. What she just offered me was like a thousand Christmases.

I had always placed Nicole on a pedestal of sorts, but if it were within her power to help me sing again, I would have to believe this was some kind of miracle that our two paths crossed at this time. I looked up at her infinitely kind expression and took a deep breath.

"The lesion they removed from my vocal cord was very small, but because it was malignant the doctor strongly recommended radiation. Another oncologist suggested both chemo and radiation. I didn't want either and certainly not both. After hours of research and discussion, I opted for the radiation, and it was horrible. It was painful but the radiation burns on my neck were worse. At first, the skin turned red and hurt. After a couple of weeks, the pain prevented me from sleeping and a small sore opened up into a hole on the side of my neck. Even narcotic pain meds didn't help. I couldn't talk for weeks. And when I did, it hurt. I couldn't swallow, I lost twenty pounds, and I was depressed."

My chest and throat were burning with the memory, a combination of hurt, anger, and shame. Nicole handed me the juice bottle, and I took a swallow. My hands shook.

"I had to work with a speech therapist three times a week, and also see a psychologist. That was when I found out that my partner was seeing someone else. She later claimed she couldn't deal with cancer, the treatment, or my depression, and she didn't have the guts to tell me directly. I wouldn't have known except she left a letter from her new lover where I could find it." Tears were streaming down my face, but I didn't care. I had never shared this with anyone, and I had just opened a part of myself which I'd been careful to seal. The pain poured out of me like toxic fluid. I wanted to scream and yell and hit something. However, I just kept talking, letting it all explode out of me.

Nicole said nothing, just let me talk. At one point, she got up to get the tissues, handed them to me, and resumed her seat.

I don't know how long I talked, just long enough to get rid of all the words I'd never shared. When I finished, I knew I would never have to say those words again. They were gone, out of the dark space and into the open.

"Meg, would you like a glass of wine? Because I would." All I could do was nod. She climbed out of the chair and went out to the kitchen, returning in a few minutes with two glasses of wine. I took a swallow and realized that I had never felt so drained in my whole life, yet I felt a kind of lightness inside as though a space had opened up. I couldn't describe it except to say I felt glad and very relieved.

"I'm sorry, that was probably a little more information than you asked for. It was certainly more than I thought I had to say," I said.

"Well, it would explain why you did not want to sing, or even try. Your experience was dreadful, and I am so very sorry. It is an honor you feel to trust me with your pain. I will always be respectful of that."

I sipped the wine and began to feel self-conscious. "I felt safe telling you, because I knew you'd understand, because you had the same scare. It feels so much better to talk about this after keeping it secret for so long. Now I'm a little embarrassed. Do you think we could talk about something else?"

"I have an idea. Let's make up a list and go grocery shopping. There is an Act Two rehearsal tomorrow morning for the principals, but nothing for tonight, and I'd really like to get out of the house. If you feel too tired, I can just go to the store."

I was tired, but I was afraid if I stayed in the house alone my mind might slip back into a dark place. I certainly didn't want that. The distraction of shopping would probably be a good idea. At the moment I felt very close to Nicole, and very safe.

Act II Scene 6

Faint morning light caught my eye and I rolled over reviewing the previous day's events. The topic of our bartered agreement did not come up again for several days. The closer we got to opening night, the more frenetic days became. At some point when the five operas were selected, the board made a decision about which order the operas would premiere in. *La Traviata* would premiere on the second weekend in July. Two other operas, *The Marriage of Figaro* and *Madama Butterfly* would open the season. That meant that rehearsal space went to those two operas first. It also meant Nicole had a little extra time to prepare.

Lars was feeling the pressure and had been irritable with the cast. Stefan was overly sensitive, and Nicole was frustrated with him. One of the secondary characters developed a serious throat problem, which took him out completely, and an understudy had to be prepared quickly.

I took the opportunity to lie low and do my job unobtrusively. Nicole was more tense than usual, and I was getting better at reading her moods and heading off crises. The better prepared I was, the easier the day would go.

Watching dark clouds rolling on the horizon suggested a summer storm was threatening. I enjoyed storms, particularly electrical energy, but also because three-hundred-sixty-degree vistas allowed for spectacular viewing.

It was still quite early when I quietly entered the house to make coffee, well before Nicole was up. She was sleeping later each day, because of exhaustion, and I felt the rest was important. The house was quiet and peaceful. Everything was shining due to the recent visit of the housekeeper. Maria had been with the family for years and took great pride in shining and polishing every surface. I was grateful that I didn't have to do it and that others took such great pride in their work. My small contribution was to make sure I put our things away before she showed up.

As soon as the coffee was ready, I poured a cup and went out to the patio to watch the clouds. Storms made me feel re-energized and a little reflective. As I looked around the arroyos and hills, I couldn't help but think about the direction of my life.

Four weeks ago, I would've said that I was content and happy with the choices in my life, but after spending those weeks working with Nicole and living in this very elegant home, I began to wonder if I'd set the bar too low for myself. Perhaps I didn't expect enough of myself. Becoming a personal assistant was not my new life goal, but realizing how adaptable I was gave me pause. I wouldn't have considered this job had it not been for Nicole, and yet I had rearranged my life in a matter of days and created a job description that seemed to be very successful.

Then there was Nicole: elusive, enigmatic, and endearing. She no longer dwelled on her make-believe pedestal, and yet had even more power. If possible, I was even more captivated by her presence and happier than I'd ever been.

The sound of the sliding patio door drew me back into the moment and I turned as Nicole came out carrying her own coffee. She had on a long cardinal red caftan that ruffled with the breeze. My breath caught for a moment. It reminded me of one of the gorgeous dresses she wore in the first act.

"*Bonjour, chère amie.* Were you unable to sleep?"

"I slept well, but I love thunderstorms, and got up early to watch. I didn't mean to wake you."

She walked over and stood very close to me, just tempting me to put my arm around her. I resisted. I could smell shampoo and body lotion. The hardest part of every day was keeping my hands in my pockets. Nicole was demonstrative and affectionate. She never missed an opportunity to touch not only me, but also everyone else she worked closely with. Her touch was gentle and caressing. She never grabbed but trailed her fingers and allowed her hand to light wherever it chose.

Being demonstrative wasn't limited to Nicole. It seemed the other European cast members, including the director and a couple of other actors, all shared this sense of relatedness. Maybe it was just theater people, but it made me realize the difference between therapeutic touch, which I used in my work, and relational touch—the way Nicole used it. It also reminded me how long it had been since I had been touched personally with meaning and caring.

As if she read my mind, Nicole looped her free hand through my arm and held on to me. My heart fluttered and I sighed deeply. The comfort of her closeness and casual touches felt loving and also stirred desire in me. We stood silently, watching the clouds for several minutes until a few raindrops blew in from far away, sending us both indoors.

"Since we don't have to rehearse until later, would you mind helping me with some vocal work here? And maybe if you feel like it you could join me." She set her cup on the counter and turned to face me with an expression of pure expectation.

I felt both charmed and apprehensive. "Does that mean your feet hurt?" I said suggestively.

"Maybe a little. Would you join me?"

Oh, Nicole, I would join you anywhere, anytime, to do anything. Why do you play with me so? "I'll give it a try."

She giggled with delight, pulled me by the hand into the den, and plunked down at the piano. I turned on a light by the piano because of the darkness outside. She played a few scales, then said, "I'll start, and you just listen."

I felt my chest tighten as I heard the familiar sounds and remembered the first sensation of singing scales, and then the memory of the pain. She started slowly with the lower register and gradually moved higher.

"Come and sit beside me and just try a few notes." She started with middle C and put her left hand in the middle of my back. "Take a deep breath and just allow the sound to come out."

I was afraid I would hyperventilate, but did as she asked. Surprisingly, a weak but not altogether unpleasant sound emerged. She immediately hit the next note and so did I. By the time I'd sung all five notes, I turned to face her in utter disbelief. She only smiled proudly.

"All right, let's try this." She played another series of notes and sang them for me. I copied her and was amazed at the sound and the freedom. There was no pain or even strain; it flowed effortlessly. It wasn't pretty, but it wasn't bad.

We continued singing simple exercises for the next half hour. Then she raised it an octave and we tried it again. I certainly had lost some of my higher register, but that might come back with practice. When we stopped for a break, I began to giggle uncontrollably. "Nicole, I'm absolutely stunned."

She was giggling, too. "It's good, Meg. There is more to do, but I think your voice is fine."

I jumped off the piano bench and whooped. "I did it. Oh my God, I sang!" She stood up, and without thinking I pulled her into my arms in a great bear hug and swung her around. "Nicole, you were right. It's not gone. My voice is not gone." I was ecstatic. It was a dream come true and the goddess in my arms made it happen. This time it was tears of joy running down my face.

She held on to me even as I set her down. "This is wonderful. It is what I hoped for you. That you have your instrument and you can use it however you choose." Nicole took my face gently in both her hands and looked into my heart. Again without thinking, I leaned forward and she touched my lips with hers, sweetly and carefully. The soft pressure sent an electrical current shooting through my nervous system awakening every single pathway. My eyes closed and my hands slid to her waist. I wasn't breathing. I was afraid to. She pulled back slightly and smiled. "Do you want to kiss me back?" she whispered with more than a little urgency.

"More than anything in this world." The fluttering in my chest had become a raging inferno threatening to consume not only me but her as well. I looked into her eyes and saw her desire. The voices were screaming in my head to stop and move away, however my own desire surged. Her warm breath on my face, the lingering smell of her perfume, and the burning fingers caressing my face overwhelmed my senses. My legs began to tremble, and I pulled her closer to keep from falling. When her breasts and belly pressed against my body, I thought the aching between my legs would cause me to faint.

"Please, Meg..."

I moved one hand to the back of her neck and leaned down to her parted lips. I pressed gently as her lips parted further and I tasted her for the first time. I swooned and felt the tip of her tongue press between my lips. I captured her mouth and returned the invitation.

Time stopped for me as I lost myself in Nicole. The room may have been spinning, or maybe it was me. I was dizzy and lightheaded. My mouth was hot and wet, and so was hers. Her arms were around my neck and her strong fingers pulled me in tightly. I leaned into her trying to get closer, trying to feel every curve of her body while I explored her yielding mouth and velvet tongue. I could feel the heat between us, and I wanted to feel her skin but I couldn't stop kissing her. I never wanted to stop.

The phone rang, and we both jumped. *Fuck!*

We stood breathless and flushed, still clinging to each other. The sight of raw passion on her face stopped me cold. *She wants this as badly as I do. What do we do now?*

"God, I'm sorry, Nicole. I never meant—"

"Shh, no, I was just happy for you."

We were both trying to make excuses but knew that it was mutual. "We can't do this, it's not okay. You're married, and we don't want to jeopardize your—"

She pulled away and stepped back. "It is true. It would not work, for you would get in trouble." She said it too quickly.

"I'm not worried about me, it's you." The phone continued to ring. "I'll get it." I ran for the kitchen phone and left her by the piano with her fingers touching her lips. The ache was not gone.

"Hello? Hello?" Dead air. Sonofabitch. My hands were sweating and I felt prickly as though lightning had hit me. It must have. I pushed on my chest, hoping to quiet the pounding. *She wanted me to kiss her—Nicole wanted me. She still does. This is so wrong.* I paced across the floor, hoping to be able to focus but my body still tingled from her touch. We needed to talk.

She wasn't in the den when I returned, but the patio door was open and rain blew in on the wood floor. She was standing near the low wall, drenched. The red silk caftan clung to every inch of her body like a sculpture, eliciting another jolt. I wanted her so badly.

It was hard to tell what she was doing because of the pouring rain, and as I came closer, I could see she was smiling. "Are you okay, Nicole?"

"*Mais oui*, and you?"

"I'm not sure. Can we go inside and talk?"

She turned and preceded me into the house.

I closed the door. "You're soaked. Would you like me to get you a towel?"

She looked down as if she was surprised, then

smiled softly. When she looked up at me, she had the self-conscious kind of expression of a child caught in her mother's makeup. "I'll go and change."

    I used a kitchen towel to dry my hair and face. Then I dried the rain from the den floor. Why was she just standing out in the rain? Although, it must have felt refreshing if she was as hot as I was, I mused. Standing in the den, I looked at the piano and the flood of adrenaline returned when I thought about singing with her. I never believed I would ever utter a note, and with Nicole's help, I did. I sang. It was glorious.

    "Yes, you did it."

    I turned at the sound of her voice. She stood behind me in long pants and a cotton sweater. I smiled. "Yes, I did, and I will be forever grateful to you."

    "You are not finished, maybe just for today. I think you could warm up each day with me and maybe we could work on the score a little." Evidently, she had put some thought into this.

    I put my hand out. "Can we please talk?" I led her to the chair and I took the ottoman, facing her. I continued to hold her hand. "The kiss—"

    "Meg, I know what you worry about. We must be honest. I wanted you to kiss me very badly, and I have for some time. Maybe it was improper, but I think you felt the same way. You look at me with desire in your eyes. It has been a very long time, but I always remember the exquisite beauty of a woman's kiss. It is still the same for me."

    I tried to pull my trembling hand away, but she held fast. I couldn't look her in the eye. "You're right, I did want to kiss you desperately, and I'm glad I did because I will remember that kiss for the rest of my life. This is awkward because I'm supposed to be here to help and support you, not distract you. The respectable thing would be to resign."

"What will that serve? I need you here. You would be miserable if you left without completing your job. Meg, we are grown-up women. It happened and I am glad. For me, it felt right."

I stared, speechless. "It did?"

"You know very well it did. Furthermore, I cannot promise it will not happen again, if you will let me. But I will try very hard to restrain myself." A smile creased her lips.

Restrain yourself? From kissing me? This can't be happening. I must've been hit by lightning. "I…uh…"

"Meg, who is going to say anything? Please remember, my marriage is no more. *Fini.* Mario used me for his career. It was never about love. I thought maybe it was, once, but I was wrong." She stood up and walked to the piano, then turned to face me. "Perhaps I am confused by too many emotions. It is so confusing. It does not feel wrong when two people have desire and want to be close. Your kiss filled me with passion in my heart. I miss that from my life."

She was right; what was I so freaked out about? It was a kiss. We hadn't committed a crime.

Ellis, you're a lesbian, you just kissed the woman of your dreams, get a freakin' grip.

I moved to her side and took her hands. Kissing her palm, I said, "I'm sorry I'm acting like such an idiot."

"I think more like a ragamuffin," she said, and pressed her soft lips against my forehead.

Rehearsal started late. It was fortunate for Stefan, because he arrived even later. The rehearsal room was hot and humid from the rain, and a new storm threatened. I sat contentedly on the sidelines watching the action and watching Nicole. Today her style looked almost Cheshire Cat-ish. Her movements were fluid and upon careful inspection revealed an impish grin lurking just below the surface. It fascinated me. Her voice sounded even more lush and alluring. Maybe the humidity was better for the voice.

The third act was complex for the principals and the chorus because of the difficult stage directions. Lars stopped frequently, redirecting and scolding people. When he halted the action to work on the dance sequence, Nicole came over and sat next to me.

"How're you holding up?" I handed her a towel because perspiration glistened on her face and arms.

"I survive." I took the towel and reached in the cooler for some orange juice. She looked a little warm and rosy.

"Can you take a little break? You've been at this for over two hours."

She squeezed my arm and smiled. The touch was brief but meaningful. Nicole had missed very few opportunities to lay a hand on me in some manner all afternoon. Innocent and casual, they all had the same effect of reconnecting our bodies. In spite of my best efforts, each touch elicited a small throb.

My brain worked diligently to keep me focused and on task, but inside, deep inside, yearning grew in tsunami waves, crashing against my resolve.

When we finally were able to leave, the sun had moved far to the west illuminating more threatening clouds. Lars pulled Nicole aside, and I nodded to her and went to the car. It was stifling. I opened both doors and turned on the air conditioner, then stood outside and waited. When Nicole reappeared, she looked flushed. As she moved closer to the car, I would have sworn she was staggering.

"Nicole?" I stepped toward her and she reached for me.

"So dizzy…" I spun her into the front seat and squatted beside the car. "That was odd."

"Okay, we're going home, you need to rest." I drove quickly up the hill toward the air-conditioned house, hoping the cool air would help. It was undoubtedly the heat, humidity, altitude, and some dehydration. I had thought we were past the sinking spells, but evidently not.

I dropped everything by the door and supported her enough to get to her room. She flopped on the bed. "I am just a little weak."

"I know, but you're really flushed." I put the back of my fingers against her face and neck. She was overheated. "I'm going to turn on the shower. Do you think you can walk in there?"

"Yes, just give me a minute." She closed her eyes and rested while the water warmed sufficiently. A cold shower might have thrown her into shock. She managed to walk to the bathroom and leaned heavily against the vanity. "I must have overdone it a little." Her voice was weak.

"Can you manage while I get you something to drink?" My mind was racing between best- and worst-case scenarios. *Maybe I should dial 911.* I realized I had no idea where any paramedics were located. Santa Fe?

Nicole teetered a little pulling off her shirt, then

sat on the commode to get her balance.

It worried me. "Okay, I guess not yet. Want to go back to bed?"

"No, I really want to shower. I think I can do it, just help me get in there. I can sit on the bench."

I pulled her up while she stepped out of her shorts and panties, and I tried hard to focus on anything but her body. *Oh, Lord.* She stepped into the glass-walled shower and managed to sit back on the marble bench where the double showerheads gently rained tepid water on her.

"Don't move, I'll be right back." I hurried to the kitchen and threw ice in a glass along with some tea. I was terrified she'd get up and whack her head into shiny marble walls. Nice headline: "Stitches required for the face of the leading lady." *Wonderful.*

When I got back, she was not unconscious but simply sitting with the water cascading across her extremely lovely chest. I stood like a deer in headlights, completely forgetting I ever learned any manners. *Meg, stop it.*

She opened her eyes and caught me standing like the gobsmacked dolt I was, holding her glass. I must have looked idiotic because she actually laughed. "This feels wonderful, just like the rain this morning. Why do you not join me?"

"No!" I whirled around and put the glass on the vanity.

This sent her into fits of laughter. "Oh my, you are something. Maybe the most endearing soul I have ever met. Meg, dear Meg. Are you so embarrassed? I tease you but only in fun."

I turned and leaned back. She knew I was embarrassed and conflicted. "Nicole, please."

"I am sorry. I see the desire in your eyes and it makes me happy coming from a very attractive woman, you know."

This was not fair at all. How could she scare me and then start flirting? "Do you think you'll be okay?"

"Yes, I will be fine. You go, and as my penance, I will cook a nice supper, *n'est-ce pas?*"

I literally ran down the hall and out to the guesthouse. I got inside and slammed the door, leaning hard against it while my breathing and heart rate slowed and I could walk unaided. I needed a shower as well. Mine would be cold.

I had come perilously close to stripping my clothes off and getting in the shower with her to satisfy the fire consuming me. I had to think of something, because my resolve had nearly imploded not only from the beauty of her hot, wet body, but her invitation. Her words weren't said in jest, and we both knew it. She was as willing as I was eager.

It was wrong in so many ways. My will was disappearing like morning fog in the heat of the sun. This had moved at warp speed past the crush stage in only twenty-four hours.

I shivered under the cool water, my heart aching for her touch and the feel of her lips. The cry that escaped from my throat surprised me. I leaned against the wall and allowed the tension to drain. The fierce longing eventually abated, replaced by the memory of her smile. I wrapped myself in a towel and stretched out on the bed, dozing off almost instantly.

Act II Scene 7

When I awoke, it was almost dark. Then, unbidden, the events of the past twelve hours resurfaced in a mixture of confusion, guilt, and extreme pleasure. I processed them as logically as I could and repeated platitudes about being an adult and maintaining appropriate distance and intellectually acknowledging the fact that I was terribly attracted to the woman in the main house a mere few hundred feet away. *It's okay. You've had a crush on her for years and you were perfectly capable of functioning. There is no reason that it should be any different. Just maintain some distance and try to avoid any intimate situations.*

Then the other voice started. *Whom would it hurt to have a little summer fling, for heaven's sake? She's right: you are both adults, and besides, who would know? You both want it. Why in the hell are you resisting her?*

I got up and threw on some clean clothes, ran a comb through my hair, straightened my shoulders, and marched up the path to the house. In either case, hiding out was not the answer. As soon as I slid open the patio door, I could smell garlic. When I stepped into the kitchen, I found Nicole at the stove with two pots simmering. In the background, she was playing Handel's "Water Music" and she didn't hear me at first. I had to admit that I loved those occasional moments when I could observe her unnoticed.

The music soared majestically, and Nicole swayed in time as she stirred and tasted from each pot. This time she was wearing a long, sleeveless shift in rich jewel tones. Just below the tempting aroma of the food was the lingering bouquet of lily of the valley.

Her head rocked from side to side with the surges of the bassline in the music. There seemed little doubt that music stirred her soul deeply. In that moment I knew she was the most beautiful woman I'd ever seen, and I just wanted to savor this scene.

My reverie lasted only a short time before she stopped and turned toward me. Her face glowed with what looked like contentment. She wiped her hands on a towel. "Your timing is perfect. But how is it you always appear so quietly?"

"I was enjoying your reverie. You really love music, don't you?" Crimson rose up her neck.

"Now you know my secret—my only true love is music. It always has been, and it always will be."

"I think I always knew that. One has only to listen to you sing to know that your heart is in your work." I took a step closer. "Is there anything I can do to help you?"

She looked back at me with a very suggestive expression and winked. "Not right now, but you could set the table and pick out some wine."

I was happy to oblige her by doing a task, which kept me from getting too close. I brought several candles to the table and lit them just as Nicole brought two steaming plates with what looked like a stew. It smelled heavenly.

"I'll just get some ice water. Would you like some?" I asked.

"Yes, please."

Dinner was leisurely and pleasant, and we stuck to a conversation about the afternoon's rehearsal. She reminded me that the closer we got to the opening night, the more frequently tempers would flare. "You didn't know me well during my last visit, or maybe you are too polite to say anything. I managed to irritate the entire cast by insisting on more rehearsal. There's a good possibility I will do that again. I think the expression is 'forewarned is forearmed.'"

"Are you suggesting I wear a bulletproof vest or avoid you altogether?"

She laughed, spilling wine on her chin. "First, I do not own a weapon. And secondly, I would be terribly unhappy if you ever avoided me."

The levity of the moment was gone.

I paused to gather my thoughts before I spoke. "I guess there's still an elephant in the room."

"An elephant?"

"A subject no one wants to bring up or talk about."

Nicole looked down at her glass, then at me, "I think that is true. It feels not as comfortable between us…something unspoken?"

"I think we both know what it is. I just don't know what we can do about it." I pushed my empty plate aside, as if somehow that gesture would take away the temptation, or that Nicole could do anything to stop the way I felt.

Confusion colored her eyes. "Are you angry with me?"

"Of course not," I snapped.

She leaned back and looked at me. "I think you sound angry. I do not know what made you unhappy."

I tried a deep breath. "Nicole, I'm trying really hard to maintain a respectful and professional relationship."

"The anger in your voice sounds as though I'm doing something evil to prevent you from doing your job." Now, her voice sounded tense and angry.

"That's not it at all. I'm sorry, it's a little tense. It's just that I think we're close to crossing a boundary—"

"Whose boundary?"

"Well, I don't know, exactly, but an employer/employee kind of thing."

"Really? Because I did not exactly hire you." She grabbed the plates and jumped up, heading for the kitchen.

Oh boy, between a rock and hard place again. "I wasn't trying to pick a fight, I'm just really trying hard to be considerate."

"Correct me if I am wrong, I believe I asked you if you wanted to kiss me *not* if you would be considerate."

"You're right. I just thought that since you were married—"

"We discussed this. I am legally separated. Never mind. Evidently I was reading something that is not there." Her voice sounded tight and hurt, and I didn't know what to do.

"Nicole, you didn't read anything incorrectly." It hurt my heart to feel her pull away.

She shut off the water and turned to face me. "Just answer one question. I believed you were attracted to me. Was I wrong?"

My heart was pounding in my chest and my mouth was so dry I could barely swallow. "Will you sit down so we can talk?"

"I do not want to sit down. I want an answer."

Oh, yeah. She was angry. "No. You were not wrong."

Her hands were on her hips and her eyes narrowed. It was all I could do to keep from bolting out the door. *Take your medicine, Ellis. You opened this topic.* My pulse was now a Gatling gun.

Finally, she threw the dish towel in the sink and returned to the table. "I am listening."

I poured more wine for each of us and took a deep breath. Cards-on-the-table time; she'd shown me her cards, now it was my turn. No more bluffing.

"Nicole, I've probably been sending mixed signals and I'm sorry. I wasn't doing it on purpose. It's just that I'm frightened."

"Of me?" She pressed her hand to her chest.

"No, let me finish. I was attracted to you when we worked together the last time. When they offered me this job I thought I'd died and gone to heaven because I could see you every day and quietly carry on my secret crush. No one would be the wiser." I drank a swallow of the wine and watched her face.

She still looked skeptical, but I continued my earnest yet pitiful confession. "I didn't realize we would become as close to one another as we have, and when you asked me about my other 'secret…'" I laughed mirthlessly. "About my voice. And then you freed me, allowed me to feel that joy again. I was so ecstatically happy and so grateful to you. And then, we kissed. That kiss unlocked the door to the feelings I've been holding tightly inside for so long." I swallowed hard and took a deep breath. All in, now. "Yes, I'm desperately attracted to you and I can hardly stand it.

It's just that we're both a little off balance emotionally, and I don't want to take advantage of that situation. Do you understand what I'm trying to say?"

"I hear your logical explanation and it makes perfect sense, but we are talking about matters of the heart, desires, physical yearnings. Can you not see they are very different things? You cannot take advantage of me unless I wish that."

"I know they're different, and I understand how easy it is for people who are mutually attracted to jump into a physical relationship. I'm just not sure I could do that...and then say goodbye to you in two months."

There. I said it, and it was true.

Her expression softened. "I see. Because I teased you, it was a silly game and you did not take my feelings as serious."

"Nicole, I know you are not unkind, I'm just not sure what you think we can have in two months. What do you want from me?"

"Is it so hard to believe that I have feelings for you? I have felt the electricity between us for a long time but feared that you may have been involved in a relationship with someone else. Your kiss touched my heart as well, and I have thought of little else. I do not know what this means, I only know that it feels like desire. I want more of this feeling. My body wants more."

I swallowed hard. I didn't know what to say to her. There was an intense, begging ache in my pelvis. There were no other arguments. She had feelings for me, the same as I had for her. At least I thought that's what she was saying.

She smiled sweetly. "Meg, we need not do anything if it makes you this uncomfortable. I enjoy your company and humor. I like to be close physically and feel your body near me. I love the way you watch me when I work. Maybe it is just you are not used to having anyone touch you as much as I do, but I am unable to help it."

"Oh, Nicole, I feel the same way. I love being with you and having you brush up against me or touch my arm. It fills me. God help me, it makes me want you so badly."

She smiled sadly and shook her head. "Then why are we arguing?"

Damned if I knew. We wanted the same thing, and I was digging my damn heels in the ground.

She waited for my reply and I simply shook my head.

"Meg, when you were betrayed by your girlfriend, that was the same time you had your surgery and lost your voice, yes?"

I nodded.

"You were scared to ever sing again, yes? But you did."

I looked up at her as I sensed where she was going with this.

"Maybe it is possible you are afraid to love again?"

※ ※ ※ ※

I spooned coffee grounds into the basket, added water and turned it on. I hoisted myself onto the counter while I waited—impatiently. Sleeping had been fitful at best. Nicole had sent me off to bed while she cleaned the kitchen. She probably knew I could beat myself up better than she could, and of course she was right. I tossed, turned, and argued. The voices played both sides of the argument, eventually concluding that her simple assertion bore more truth than I cared to admit. I couldn't, wouldn't sing because I was afraid it would hurt me. Fear paralyzed me.

When she gently led me to the opportunity to use my voice again, I overcame my fear and triumphed.

Presented with the opportunity of a lifetime to share a relationship with a beautiful woman who was ready and willing, I was scared of being hurt. Now she was offering to lead me past this fear.

You've been dreaming about this chance. Which would hurt worse: to walk away and never know, or to enjoy every minute you have? Damn, Ellis, this is your moment.

Nicole came out about twenty minutes later looking like she had slept poorly as well.

"Good morning. How are you feeling?"

She stood at the end of the counter. "I am all right." For the first time, Nicole looked restrained.

I put down my cup, moved closer, and opened my arms. She slid in and put her arms around my waist as though she did it every day. I pulled her close and held her, rubbing her back. "I did a lot of thinking last night, mostly about what you said about me being hurt by Bekka and being afraid. I think you're right. I was afraid to sing for fear of pain, and you helped with that." I leaned back a little to see the glistening blue eyes looking back at me. "Maybe you would consider helping me again…if I promised to double the foot massages?"

"That is what I prayed you would tell me." She hugged me tighter and my senses filled with her. "First, I think we will sing, *mon amie*."

Nicole sat at the piano when I brought the coffee.

"Carl will be here in an hour, and if you're comfortable, you could sing with us."

I handed her a cup. "I'm not sure I'm ready for that, but we'll see." Stranger things had happened. She started with her usual scales, and I sat next to her on the piano bench comfortably and sipped my coffee. Soon it was my turn, and surprisingly after the first set of scales my voice began to assume a comfort level. We sang together slowly and gently at first, then increasing the range and volume.

"I'd like you to stand if you will, and we'll work a little on your breath control. Start with the 'ah' sound up then down. Do the same with 'e.'" I followed her directions as she moved up the keyboard in half steps, singing along with me.

The vocal tone was growing in intensity as well as volume, and I was extremely pleased. She was singing an octave higher and our voices blended in a very pleasant harmony. I was singing a duet with *the* Nicole Bernard.

"Now I want you to sing five notes, and when you get to the top, hold it as long as you can."

I did as she asked. Near the end, the volume faded rapidly. So much for not practicing for two years.

"Good. Again, and this time I am going to push on your abdomen. Don't let me push you over."

I started again, and she placed her fist in my solar plexus and began to push. I leaned into her and the volume of my voice increased. It was startling, and I stopped singing.

"*Très bien*, it is still there. You must remember where your voice comes from and stop focusing on your throat, because it is fine. Maybe sometimes during the day you could work on your breathing, just to remind your body how to do it. Let's try some songs."

She opened the score and flipped to a scene in the first act. "Start here with Alfredo's toast."

It was his famous opening aria "Libiamo"—let us drink with a beautiful cup. It was a familiar and fun aria, but not one I had ever thought to sing. I read over her shoulder and stumbled over the Italian pronunciation but kept on singing. She sang the second stanza and the parts for the chorus. Before I knew it, the hour was over.

"It was amazing and so much fun. I hardly know what to say, and I certainly can't begin to thank you. Words are just inadequate."

She grinned impishly. "It is fun for me, as well. I like to teach. I especially like to teach you, you have a lovely voice. It is too bad that you were not able to follow that dream." She stood and squeezed my hand. "I am going to run to the washroom and then change my clothes before Carl gets here. Do you think you're ready to sing with us?"

"I'm not sure, but if you need me to help to do a scene, I'll try."

She left, and I sat down at the piano and put my hands on the keyboard. It had been years since I played. I felt a little sad about losing two years' worth of enjoyment because I was afraid. Music had always been important to me...until I shut the door. Was I willing to do the same thing with this relationship, however fleeting?

※※※※

When we got to rehearsal, Lars wanted to redo part of the dramatic third act finale. He'd worked with the designer and changed the set design so that the bed was facing another direction. In theory, it looked more workable, especially since Nicole would then be facing the side on which the chorus made a brief appearance.

Nicole was amenable but Stefan was being a little petulant. Lars gently convinced him that it would make him look better, and then they started the scene. Nicole seemed stronger in her part. She and Carl had worked on it, and it showed. As I listened, I conceitedly thought that I sounded better than Stefan did. Maybe it was just because singing those beautiful lyrics to Nicole about love felt very real to me. I wasn't acting.

Germont missed a cue, the chorus was behind on the tempo, and the wall behind the bed leaned precariously. Lars yelled, then threw his clipboard at his assistant. I took the opportunity to take Nicole her water bottle as the crew straightened the set. Nicole's fingers purposely stroked my hand when she took the bottle. I nodded in acknowledgment. She returned to her marked position near the bed, and I couldn't help noticing how well her jeans fit her trim figure.

I took the opportunity to go outside for a few minutes to get some sun and fresh air. I found a place to sit not too far from the door and pulled out my cell phone. I had been extremely neglectful, and there were several messages waiting for me—two from my mother, one from Lena, and one from Liz. I knew my mom was at work and Lena seldom answered her phone when she was working with the horses, so I called Liz.

"Well, hi there, PA to the stars."

"Hi Liz, sorry I've been so neglectful. How have

you been?"

"Keeping out of mischief, mostly. I've been dying to hear about your job. Have they offered you a chance to run the company?"

Yeah, like that would happen. "No, but I really do have some news. Nicole and I had a conversation about my singing, and she actually remembered my voice. I couldn't believe it. Long story short, she said that she was willing to work with me if I wanted to, so we started doing some exercises and guess what? I didn't lose my voice. It's still there, and not too shabby if I do say so myself."

"Meg, that's incredible. What a wonderful surprise. I'll bet you're thrilled."

"I really am. We practice every morning, and it's getting stronger. She's even let me sing along with her when she rehearses, and I think we sound pretty good together."

"What did your mom say? I'm guessing she cried."

"I haven't had a chance to tell her yet, been really busy getting ready for the opening. I haven't been home for a few weeks. I wanted to tell them in person."

"Do you think you'll be going to Lena and Brenda's party?"

"I'm not sure yet. We don't open until the following weekend, so it could be super busy or not at all. I'll have to find out."

"Do you have the dates for the performances yet?"

"Not in my head, but I'm sure they're on the website. I hope you can come. It should be a really good production, and of course Nicole is spectacular."

"I wouldn't miss it, but I'll be leaving on vacation for a couple of weeks. My sister invited me to her cabin in Colorado—I'll email the dates. I've got to run. Take care, Meg."

"Have a great time. Bye, Liz."

I put the phone away and listened to the music from the rehearsal room. I zeroed in on Nicole's voice. As usual, the hairs on my neck stood up and a warm glow rolled over me. Something felt different. When this rehearsal was over, I was going home with that voice and the woman who possessed it. I was feeling a little smug about the fact that I had managed to go all day without having a libido attack. I managed to work efficiently and professionally without succumbing to overpowering lust. Yet.

The afternoon sun grew less intense as the evening approached. The clouds from earlier had dissipated and the electric blue sky was the perfect background to the soaring silhouette of the main pavilion, the curving roof lines resembling sails in a full wind. I walked through the parking lot until I felt the need to get back.

Nicole was sitting in back watching as Lars worked with Stefan. She smiled as I approached.

"Are you finished?" I said, sitting behind her and leaning as close as I dared. Her perfume, warmed by her body heat, drifted up and begged me to move closer. I rested my arm on the back of her chair, my fingers scarcely brushing her shoulder.

Not the place or time, Ellis.

"I think maybe yes, but I am not sure. I would like to rest and then I would like to eat something. The wonderful breakfast, I am afraid, has burned off."

I laughed. The wonderful breakfast of which she spoke was soft-boiled eggs. "What are you in the mood for?"

She looked over her shoulder and chuckled. In a loud whisper, she said, "A giant hamburger."

I covered my mouth and nodded. "Okay." I sat back a few inches and watched her head move with the music and the muscles under the skin of her neck change slowly with the angle of her head. Small delicate ears adorned with single gold hoops framed her gentle face. I wanted to touch her skin so badly.

Nothing could be more wonderful than to watch her lovely face, whether at rest, or when she was laughing, or concentrating, or, best of all, singing. Her face was rapturous when she lost herself in her music.

The assistant director came over. "Ms. Bernard, you may leave if you wish. The rest of the rehearsal will be with the chorus."

"*Merci*, I will see you tomorrow then." She turned to me as he left. "I want to get out of here."

We made our escape, and I stowed the music and cooler in the back seat. "Do you want to go home first?"

"No, I'm hungry. Please take me to get a wonderful hamburger." She buckled her seat belt with an air of finality.

"Well, one of the best is the Rio Chama steakhouse in Santa Fe. It's usually crowded, but we might be early enough. If it's too busy, there are a couple of other joints."

"Great. I never eat hamburgers unless I am here, then it just feels like I should. And you, do you like them?"

"I admit I eat them more often than I should when I'm out. I don't make them at home. They don't taste as good. Do you eat the New Mexico green chiles?"

"Oh yes. I must have the chile and the cheese."

Well, okay then. Sounds like something she is very sure of liking.

We found a parking spot a couple of blocks off Old Santa Fe Trail, just south of the plaza. "Do you mind walking a little bit? It's right back there."

"I don't mind. I feel like I have been sitting too much. I will get a soggy bottom, no?"

"I don't think so. I think you have a sexy bottom."

She laughed and began to sashay down the street, flaunting it comically. "*Merci beaucoup, mon amie.*"

I went up to sign us in. "The host said there was a thirty-minute wait for a table, and would we like to wait at the bar."

Nicole pouted. "Maybe we can eat on the patio?"

"Certainly," the host said when asked, and escorted us to a nice umbrella-covered table near the bar. I noticed him looking at Nicole, trying to remember why she looked vaguely familiar. She was hard to place with her casually mussed hair, jeans, and sleeveless top. I said nothing.

Two wings of the building and two high walls overgrown with vines and overhung by large pine trees sheltered the square patio. It was cooler than out on the street, and very intimate. Nicole asked me to order, and we each had a margarita.

"Meg, do you think your parents will come to the opera?"

"Sure, they wouldn't miss it. They probably already have tickets. I'm not the only Bernard fan in the house."

"*Merde*, I should have spoken sooner. I thought it would be nice if they could come to the Sunday performance."

"I can check and find out. Why Sunday, when the opening is Thursday night?"

"Opening night will be crazy, and I think my parents will come for the weekend. I haven't heard for sure, but I suspect they are in New York already."

"Your parents are coming to the show?" A cold lump formed just beneath my breastbone.

"Well, yes, they always come to at least one performance. Sometimes they stay longer."

"Your parents are coming to stay with you?" My heart was in overdrive and my brain raced to keep up. Where would they be staying, and what was I going to do? I'd go home. Yeah, no need to hang around if her mom was there. The show would be running. She wouldn't need me to hang around, and I'd just make myself scarce anyway. No reason I'd need to spend a lot of time with her parents.

"Meg. Meg? Are you listening?" Nicole's voice intruded.

"What? No, sorry. I was just—"

"You're pale, what's wrong?"

"Nothing." *Oh shit. Busted again.*

"Meg, your hands are shaking. What on earth is going on?"

"Your parents and my parents at the opera at the same time, don't you think it will be a little awkward?" I said with what sounded like a squeaky voice.

"We will be working, but I thought we could all have dinner at the house beforehand. That would be nice, no? My parents do not know many people here and it would be nice for them to have someone to talk to other than opera employees."

I heard words coming out of her mouth but they

were coming too fast to make sense. Both of our parents in the same house, the house I shared with their daughter, the daughter who was getting divorced but they didn't know that. *Holy buckets of batshit. Breathe, just take a deep breath, and try to focus on what she's saying.*

Nicole shook my arm. "Have you been struck mute? What is happening?"

"I'm sorry, just had a little brain fart. I was overwhelmed by the thought of meeting your parents and then mine and the opera...it just took me by surprise."

She laughed. "You're nervous."

A merciful deity sent our food at that exact moment. "Hey, look at this, will you? A green chile cheeseburger fit for a queen, complete with sweet potato fries."

All conversation ended as we began to eat. The petite and lovely hellion across the table wasted no time attacking a very large, juicy burger that necessitated the use of both of her hands. I stopped between bites just to watch the complete abandon with which she consumed her meal.

Nicole seemed to take her life in large bites as well, with a big appetite and full appreciation. My heart clenched and I desperately wanted to lean over and kiss the mouth wet with chile, beef, and cheese. She looked up at that moment and must have seen my yearning. She paused briefly and watched me. I wiped my own face and picked up my drink. She did the same, and reached out to clink my glass. What had just passed between us? I felt fluttering in my chest and a warm glow spread out from my core. My face felt hot and my breathing shallow. I couldn't tear my eyes away—and she knew it.

Act II Scene 8

The sun set while we finished our meal, and after we were both full and tired. I was grateful to walk slowly back to the car. Neither of us wanted to revisit the parent scenario just yet.

A warm breeze riffled the trees and the crickets began their serenade. The tourists had gone and the Santa Fe streets featured very old adobe homes lining the narrow street. A warm glow emanated from the little windows, and the hum of the swamp coolers accompanied the crickets.

Nicole put her hand through my arm and interlaced her soft fingers with mine. It felt right and very comfortable. "This was lovely, but you didn't have to pay."

"I wanted to," I said.

"Thank you."

I leaned over to unlock the passenger door, and she moved a little closer so when I straightened up she was inches from me, her hand tightly holding mine.

"I would like to kiss you again, if you let me." She was looking at me the same way she had her meal. I moved a little closer. Her soft lips brushed mine and her warm breath teased me. I pressed forward and her mouth covered mine just like the recently consumed meal. I was next.

The groan must have come from me as I felt an aching fullness in my lower abdomen. I could taste the salt from the fries, the lime from the margarita, the chile, and then her tongue swept across my lip. I surrendered to her begging lips. I leaned her back against the car and pressed my pelvis into hers. She whimpered and pulled her head back. "Not here."

I drove as quickly as I could, but not nearly as fast as I wanted. I could hear her breathing and feel her soft fingers stroking my inner thigh. My mind raced with warnings and what-ifs, but the overriding urge came from the center of my body and soul. I needed to connect with Nicole on the most primal level of my being.

"You must believe me now, that I am not playing a game with you. I am very serious," she said in a sultry beckoning.

"I believe you, and I feel the same way. Very soon, there will be no going back. We're stepping off the cliff, Nicole."

"If you are holding my hand, I will jump." Visions of Thelma and Louise flashed across my mind screen. I took a deep breath, and everything began to tingle. *Don't hyperventilate, dork.*

The garage door closed and we went into her house. There was an air of expectation and a little uncertainty that permeated everything. She followed me to the kitchen and unpacked the cooler. In the bright lights, our faces flushed and our desire was palpable.

"Would you like a glass of wine?" she said.

"Definitely. Are you as nervous as I am?" My palms were sweaty and trembling.

She nodded her head and laughed lightly. "This

is silly, no? One minute there is so much passion, then we are two scared children."

I dried my hands and took the glass she offered and saw how dark her eyes were. "Oh, the passion is growing. I just don't want to rush. I want to share every second with you and not miss a thing."

Nicole reached over and trailed her cool fingers along the side of my face. "Is it of desire or love that you speak?"

I put down my glass and ran my palms along her arms until I took both hands. "I don't know. It comes from my heart and moves me closer to you as though my body was in a force field. I am powerless to stop it, unless you say no." We were inches apart, and her eyes were filled with the same longing.

"Will you stay here with me, or do you want me to come to you?" she whispered.

Those words caused my breath to catch in a gasp. I wanted nothing more. "Oh yes, come to me when you're ready. But first sit with me and drink your wine. We have all night."

We went outside to the patio and sat together on the glider. The moon had set and the velvet black sky erupted in sparkling lights of different sizes. I pulled Nicole close and we kissed again and again. The kisses grew longer and deeper. I savored each taste of her as it fueled the fire inside. It was like a first date with all the excitement and newness. She purred as I kissed below her ear and down the front of her throat.

"Please, don't stop." She growled and slid her hand down my chest.

"I couldn't if I wanted to." I pulled her hand to my lips and kissed each fingertip, finally drawing one into my mouth. She groaned and wove her other hand into my hair, pulling me to her and seizing my mouth with her own, thrilling me with her fierce intensity. I succumbed to the desire and lost myself in her seductive kiss.

I had a sudden idea and stood up. "The hot tub. Come with me. I want to be rid of restrictive clothing, both yours and mine." We ran down the faintly lit path to the walled-off deck. I charged up the four steps and folded open the cover. The control panel shimmered with a blue light, and I quickly located and switched on the jets. The eerie glow from the panel and the walk lights made the area look like a stage. I kissed her gently. "Will you come with me?"

She nodded slowly and pulled her shirt off in one move. I followed her lead. We stepped out of our shorts at the same time and stood looking at each other's bodies with shyness and wonder.

"My God, you take my breath away. If it's possible, you're even more beautiful in this light." I took her hand and stepped into the warm, bubbling water, pulling her next to me. When our bodies touched for the first time, it shot honest-to-God electrical shocks through me. At first, we wrapped our arms as tightly as possible and held on. I felt her heart thudding against my ribs and her hot breath caressing my ear. Our slippery skin glided and touched.

We each explored the soft contours with our hands and relished the sensations of the warm bubbling waters surrounding us.

"This feels exquisite to be touching you and feel your hands on me. It is better than I imagined," she said softly.

I touched her face and placed slow, gentle kisses on her cheeks, eyelids, forehead, nose, chin, and finally her swollen lips. I trembled with anticipation and raw need. I ached for her.

She stroked my sides and back as she teased her tongue into my waiting lips. The aching pain in my core came from molten desire, and only one thing could quench the fire. She held me firmly with her hand in my hair and slid one hand to my breast, gently cupping it.

I was a prisoner of her powerful kisses, and surrendered easily as she pulled me closer.

Our bodies slid against one another as hips pressed and glided together, creating a wet kind of friction. I moved my hands to her rounded ass and pulled her hard against me. Desire rapidly morphed into need.

I whimpered. "I'm so close…I can't take much more."

"Try to wait. I want to take you in your bed," she said hoarsely, then kissed me hard.

She moved me to the edge of the hot tub to climb out but I pulled her in for another kiss, afraid I couldn't wait. She gave willingly.

We snatched up our clothing and I switched off the jets. I dropped everything trying to get my keys out of one of my pockets while Nicole nibbled on my neck.

Once inside, I reached for a light switch.

"It is much cooler in here." Nicole shivered, and her erect nipples were testament to the temperature.

I pulled her close and kissed her neck. "I think you'll warm up again."

She arched her back, pushing against me. "I think so." Her mouth was on mine.

I took her hand and led her toward the bedroom.

She closed the door and I turned down the bed. I lit the large pillar candle on the dresser. The light danced across the vigas in the ceiling. I looked at Nicole standing in the doorway looking radiant and self-satisfied.

"You're enjoying this gradual seduction, aren't you?"

"You have no idea." She drew her hand slowly down across the front of her body.

She reached out for me and I pulled her to the bed, sitting beside her and trailing my fingers down her arm. I trembled with anticipation. "Nicole, I feel like I'm in a dream and I never want to wake up." I watched her body respond to my touch and felt the heat rise in my own. I caressed the smooth skin on her belly. "If you have any second thoughts, please tell me, because I'm so aroused right now."

"My only regret is that I waited so long. When I woke in your arms after Mario left, I wanted you. At that moment, I felt safe and loved. I remembered the joy of a woman's body." She kissed my hand. "The softness of the skin." Her fingers were under my breast. "The taste of her skin." My nipple reacted to her tongue.

She pushed herself back on the bed and stretched out, opening her arms and legs, begging. "Please make love to me and show me your feelings."

My heart threatened to explode out of my chest. Carnal need consumed me along with an exquisite desire to please her. I rolled next to her, trembling. "I will do everything you want and more. Guide me with your desires. Tell me how to please you." I bent over her and kissed her stomach, then trailed light kisses across her body.

Nicole embraced me and pulled me to her mouth.

I leaned on one elbow as I ran my tongue across her lips while I encircled her breast with my fingers.

"Yes, squeeze me hard and then kiss me."

I captured her mouth as I caressed then squeezed her nipple. The guttural sound assured me that I had achieved my goal. Our kisses became hungrier and she guided my hands along her hot skin. Gently and slowly, I made my way to her begging vulva. Her grip on my neck tightened as I brought her close with my mouth, then slowed.

"Please, Meg, now. Now…*ah, mon Dieu.*"

I carefully kissed, caressed, and probed her intimately as her body trembled, jumped then arched sharply as spasms rippled through her. I held her tight as she trembled.

I moved up her body, kissed her temple, and whispered in her ear, "Your body is so alive and responsive."

She pulled me on top of her and held me as her breathing slowed. Our mouths sought each other. We kissed deeply, unhurriedly, as her hands caressed my chest, neck, and ass. I moved against her, straddling her leg. The grunting was involuntary as the inferno incinerated within me.

"It is my turn to pleasure you, *amoureuse*. Let me love you." She rolled me onto my back and settled her hot body between my legs. Her searing kisses covered my face and neck as she moved to my throat. Her hand found the aching nipples, suckling one as she squeezed the other. The shock waves surged into a demanding desire. My body quivered with need.

My hips thrust against her, begging for relief. "Oh God, please."

At last I felt her delicate hand slide down my

belly and she deftly stroked me to the edge of sanity, drew me back with soft kisses, then sent me crashing to the rocks as my desperate, throbbing body exploded with fire and intense pleasure.

I screamed her name as my entire body seized in spasm, then lay rigid and motionless with aftershocks.

Nicole slid her body on top of me, stroking my face with her fingers and kissing me sweetly. Our musky scent drifted around us. "You are pleased, then?"

I laughed hard and returned her kiss. "Dear Nicole, I have never been more pleased in my life. Unbelievable."

In the candlelight, her eyes shimmered and gazed warmly at me. "You are a wonderful lover, do you know that?" She sucked on my lower lip. "And your strong body wants to be pleasured, it thrills."

I shook my head. "Not me, us. It was a dream for so long, now you're here. Suddenly it's a reality. All I want is to fill you with joy."

Her lips curved and she answered me. "You do."

I felt the kindling crackle as it ignited deep inside and pulled her into my arms.

"Nicole, you are so intuitive and sensual, and you seem so natural making love to a woman. Who was your first?"

She pulled back and sat up against the headboard. I rolled my head into her lap. Her fingers felt warm on my shoulders as she traced circles with her thumb.

"Lily was my first girlfriend. We knew each other since we started school. We shared everything and I loved her very much. When we were caught kissing in her room, we were separated by our horrified parents.

"They sent me away to boarding school. *Ma mère* was not so angry, but oh, *mon père* was furious. I feared him and decided I must follow his wishes. There were many boys to date, but you know, it is not the same."

I put my arm around her waist and held her, kissing the soft skin of her stomach.

"Later, there was an older woman who taught voice, and also other things. I did not love her, but did as she instructed and learned much. When I began singing professionally, well, my agent arranged for me to meet prominent people to help my career—mostly men. It was not always pleasant, but expected. Then I met Mario. He was young and romantic. He treated me very well, but now I think maybe it was his agent matchmaking."

She slid down into my arms and cuddled under my chin. "With you, I believed it was just for me."

I kissed her forehead. "It was just for you and only you."

We dozed and made love again. The new fire seemed inextinguishable.

Act II Scene 9

When the first light shone through the window, the realization of what was and what had been dawned just like the sun: warm and bright. The beautiful naked body of Nicole Bernard was curled beside me. *Holy Mother of God.* I dared not move for fear she'd vanish. Soft snoring rumbled against my shoulder and her arm draped limply on my chest. The faint smell of shampoo and the chemicals from the hot tub mingled with the scent of our love. I felt intoxicated by the rush of memories and drifted back to sleep.

I woke when Nicole crawled back into bed and reclaimed the cold spot, and I was glad to have her back next to me. Her kiss was cool and tender. "Mmm, you taste yummy and minty. I'm jealous."

"I'll wait," she whispered.

I hopped out of bed and made a dash to the bathroom. As soon as I was relieved and refreshed, I hurried back to bed. Nicole was still there and looking sexy as hell. I pulled up the covers and slid close to her warm, waiting body. She put her arms around me as I nuzzled her neck, promising to ravish her slowly and carefully.

"I want desperately to be ravished by you, but first we need to talk about parents."

The whoosh was the sound of the air leaking out of my punctured balloon. "Huh?"

"You are bothered by the idea and I am not sure why. Maybe you do not want to meet my family, perhaps?"

A vision of a large family gathering with a million questions about Nicole and me formed in my mind. I rolled up on one elbow in order to restrain the lascivious desires. "No, that's not it, really. It's just that…oh, how can I say this? Well, won't they think it's strange that I'm living here and my family is visiting and, well, Mario isn't here? I mean, I just think there'll be a lot of awkward questions."

She tipped my chin down and smiled. "You are so adorable and such a worrier." Then she kissed the end of my nose. "You see, I think, it will be wonderful for my family to meet some nice people to share the opera with and tell us how wonderful it was and how happy they are to be all together."

"And this is why everyone in the world loves you." I pulled her close to me and kissed her. She responded enthusiastically and pushed her knee deftly between my legs with the same effect as striking a flint to tinder.

"So, you will ask your parents to come Sunday and I will call and get tickets, *bien*?" she said as she began fondling me.

"*Bien*. But Nicole, I'm out to my parents and they know how pathetically smitten I was about you, I'm afraid."

"Out?" She looked up from her work.

"They know I'm gay."

"This is good." Her hands rose, emphasizing her comment.

"I'm just guessing your parents may not be so understanding." I gasped as she intensified her exploration.

"Of what?"

"Nicole...stop a minute...they think you're still married. Don't you think they'll suspect something if I'm living here?"

"Of course not, why would they? Is that what is worrying you, *ma petite*?" She stopped her oral assault on my breasts. Briefly.

"Yes!" I knew this battle was all but lost.

"You know, it occurs to me that I am forty years old now, and my parents, they do not control me. I will just try very hard not to kiss you too much, okay?"

I groaned loudly and rolled back.

She must have assumed victory because she took full advantage of my weakened state, reigniting the inferno and fueling it with her bold frontal attack.

※ ※ ※ ※

Coffee in hand, remembering what Nicole showed me, I ran the scales on the piano. Fatigue weighed on me and a longer shower might have helped, but to be honest, I couldn't wait to see her again. Snippets of our first night flitted across my mind like bold highway billboards. It seemed a little like previews to a great love story or steamy tell-all. Didn't matter, I felt great. I may have been legally drunk on passion. The touch, taste, and feel of Nicole branded me as hers. Just remembering her mouth on me spiked my pulse rate. The woman could kiss.

My left brain screamed over the lush violins in my right brain. *Attention: There is an important production opening soon from the Santa Fe Opera with the renowned Nicole Bernard.*

It's time to get back in the game. This is about her career, not your horny ass.

I sang a bit more and the conversation about "the parents" snuck back. Hell, she wasn't worried, and my parents, well, they'd probably be amused. They'd never think it was serious, but I knew they'd love her. And then there were her parents. That could be tricky, and nothing I could prepare for or rehearse.

The note was a *D*, but I hit something sour. I tried again but stopped when I heard a giggle. In the doorway stood my exquisite lover. I froze. She was wearing simple shorts and a tank top. She was radiant.

"Good morning."

Her greeting was more personal. "Lover," she murmured, kissing and caressing the back of my neck. "You are ready so quickly. I am sorry you had to wait for me."

You bet I'm ready. The groaning sound came from me. "I had to hurry, I'm hungry." I pulled her to sit next to me.

"Would you like me to get you something?"

"Oh, you already have." I brazenly nibbled her ear and turned her face to capture the mouth I craved. It took a nanosecond for her body to respond to my entreaty. Zero to sixty in three seconds. I held her face and feasted on the gateway to ecstasy. *Need air.*

Nicole smiled, her face flushed. "I thought you said you were hungry."

"I was. I am. More, please."

She pushed me back. "*Ma chérie*, we must work. Please. There is a full rehearsal, and today we have the orchestra for the first time. I need to be ready, and you may be surprised to know I did not get too much sleep because of my insatiable lover."

"Me, insatiable? Ha."

She kissed me sweetly and put my hands on the keyboard.

I knew this was a big deal. The orchestra didn't even show up until a couple of weeks before the show, and with five productions ready to open and needing time to coordinate their music, we wouldn't have the time we were accustomed to having, no extra time for figuring out the next line. More importantly, the conductor would be in charge.

Nicole abbreviated her warm-up but asked me to run through a couple of the difficult scenes. We started with the second act scene with Germont, Alfredo's father. It is an important moment when Violetta unselfishly gives up the only person she ever loved so Alfredo's sister can marry without humiliation.

I could stumble through Germont's part so she would feel a little more comfortable with her aria. Heck fire, I'd humiliate myself anywhere for this woman, so why was I worried about her parents? We reviewed each part and she wanted to begin with his request that she leave Alfredo.

After moving the furniture out of the way, we walked through the scene. Germont implores her and at first she refuses, and then gives in. The music is beautiful even without accompaniment. The lyrics helped me to understand Germont's motives and Nicole sang with affecting innocence. Two or three times we harmonized and it gave me a thrill to my toes to look into her eyes and share something about which we were both so passionate.

She sang, "Embrace me like a daughter," and clung to me. I held her, briefly forgetting we were rehearsing. Soon the scene ended and she smiled broadly.

"You are a wonderful rehearsal partner, and I think your voice sounds stronger already."

"You have no idea how much that means to me. I really enjoy singing again, especially with you."

Neither of us moved. I wasn't sure what she was thinking but I suddenly felt flushed and a little dizzy. My pulse crept up and my breathing was shallow.

"Nicole…"

"No, please, we must not. I want your touch on my skin and your lips, but it is *très impossible*."

"When? Tell me when."

"After rehearsal, my love, I promise. We must leave right away or I will not be able to go." She hurried from the room and I deflated quickly.

Ellis, come on. Have a little respect for her priorities and don't blow this.

I sat hard on the ottoman, trying to recover. This was going to be a challenge—for both of us.

༄༄༄༄

The pavilion buzzed with activity, the sounds of carpenters, crew, lighting, and a full complement of musicians. It was exhilarating. I insisted Nicole eat before we left and reminded her that I would be off stage right with water. She gave me a quick hug and trotted up to the stage. I wondered if this was what mothers endured on the first day of school, watching a kid go for the first time. I felt proud, scared, and terribly invested in this woman.

The orchestra members were busy with instruments, music, and rearranging the chairs in the pit, but they all stopped when Nicole came over to greet them. Some were familiar, some weren't, but all of them were pleased that she made the effort. I watched with a new appreciation of her professional and personal skills.

The past few weeks had been an education about the life of a professional singer. It was easy to idolize her or any other prominent figure in the spotlight, but most people never thought about fights with husbands, physical ailments, cravings, or an inconvenient affair of the heart. Whatever happened between us, our lives would never be the same.

I picked up the cooler and the music bag and marched myself closer to the stage. I took a seat on the aisle and waited to see how they'd start. A few minutes after ten, Lars came on stage accompanied by Ernesto Ricci, a well-known conductor and no stranger to Santa Fe. I had met him while I was an apprentice.

"Ladies and gentlemen, I am pleased to introduce Maestro Ernesto Ricci to those of you who may not know him. He and his fine orchestra will be conducting this rehearsal, which will be a complete runthrough. I'll be taking notes and we will meet together after the rehearsal to discuss them. Please remember this is the first time for the orchestra to work with you, and I expect your full cooperation."

"Thank you, Lars. I'm honored to return to this beautiful venue with such talented people. I'm particularly glad that once again I can work with the lovely and gifted Madame Bernard." He bowed to her. "The talented members of this orchestra have practiced hard to give you their best. Without further ado, we will begin in approximately ten minutes."

I could feel butterflies just as if I were going to be performing. There really is nothing like the immediacy of live theater. Everyone is nervous and excited and the air is filled with electrical energy. I took my things and went up the steps to the wings at stage right, which is actually the left side from the audience perspective. I had to find an area that was inconspicuous but also available in case Nicole needed to find me. As soon as I found one of the stage crew, I explained that I was Ms. Bernard's personal assistant and needed to be close by during the rehearsal. He directed me to a small shelf along the wall where I could put my things. It was close enough to the stage that I could see without being visible to the audience. He pointed to a stack of folding chairs and suggested I bring one over.

The bulk of the stage directions came from the opposite side with a stage manager perched near the light board. Scene changes, lighting changes, and costume changes all originated from that area. Fortunately, the way the director had staged it, the few times Nicole would exit or enter the stage would be on the side opposite the board—my side. It seemed like a good time to check the cooler to see if I could get her something to drink before we started.

"Six water bottles, three orange juice, and four energy bars," I muttered to myself, then felt a hand on my waist that was both familiar and exciting. I turned slowly. "Hi there, beautiful," I whispered.

"Is this where you will be?"

"I think so." I handed her a juice bottle. "I'll try to keep an eye on you, in case you start looking dry."

"Thank you. I will like that you are watching me." She winked and finished the juice.

"Don't start something you can't finish," I said.

She offered her most seductive smile. "Oh, I will

finish, have no fear."

A crew member interrupted us to show her entrance. She handed me the empty bottle and squeezed my hand as she left to make her entrance. The fluttering started again, this time a little lower in my body.

※※※※

The first act went smoothly considering the number of people on stage, and Nicole sailed through effortlessly as though she'd done this a hundred times before—which she hadn't. Her confidence, as usual, buoyed up the rest of the cast, including Stefan. Being on stage with a full orchestra to back him kicked his performance up a notch. I knew I was smiling and couldn't help myself; the pieces we'd worked on for weeks we're coming together and it was thrilling.

As they finished the first act, I grabbed a water bottle and hurried around to the rear of the set, where I knew Nicole would exit while they changed the scenery. She was perspiring heavily, and I was glad that I had remembered a towel. I doused one end of it with water and handed it to her. I didn't comment, as I wasn't sure whether she had completely finished the scene in her head.

She drank quickly and wiped her face and neck with the damp towel. After a few deep breaths, she leaned against the wall and looked at me. Nicole was there, not Violetta. "How was it?"

"Good. Smooth and crisp. Everyone stayed with the conductor and even Stefan sounded good. You, of course, were brilliant."

"Yes, but they pay you to say that." We both laughed until we heard the music for the second act.

She hurried out and I resumed my post, because this act would be important. Nicole had very little time to rehearse this with the new actor playing Germont. I listened carefully. This guy was good, very commanding with a nice baritone voice that complemented Nicole's soprano.

There was a short break between the second and third acts due to a far more complicated set change. Nicole and I took the opportunity to go outside and walk around. I insisted she eat one of the energy bars and have more juice, but overall I was impressed with her stamina.

"Would you do me a favor?" she said as we found a bench in the shade and sat down. "For the last act, would you sit in the back of the house and listen carefully?"

"Sure, is there a problem?"

"No, but I must sing more softly for part of it and want to be sure that I will be heard back there." She slipped off her shoes and stretched out on the bench.

"I understand. I think you'll be fine." I looked down at her and smiled. "I'll bet I owe you more than one foot massage, don't I?"

"I think you may owe me much more than a massage."

With the various technical difficulties changing sets, it was almost three o'clock when they started the final act. I gathered up our things and moved to the back of the pavilion as Nicole had asked. I was tired and couldn't imagine how she must be feeling, although, if memory served me, the adrenaline of performing helped while just sitting and watching was kind of nerve-racking.

Even from so far away, Nicole had intensity about her voice that enabled her to project. Part of it was her ability to inhabit the character, which kept her audience with her. Only once did her voice drop, and it was during the exchange with her maid, Annina, which was probably because she was facing upstage.

The final lines were sung by Alfredo: "She is gone, oh grief." I wiped my eyes and sniffled—the ending always got me. It was just a matter of waiting and watching as Lars went from one performer to another making comments. As soon as he finished speaking to Nicole, she began scanning the house, and I assumed she was ready to go. She joined me in the last row and took the water bottle I handed her.

"What did you think?"

"You made me cry again."

She turned and looked surprised when she saw my reddened eyes and snotty nose. "We sing this every day and it still makes you sad. That is so sweet."

"There was only one time when I had trouble hearing you, your conversation with Annina, and I think it was because you turned up stage. Otherwise, your voice carried beautifully. I'm not sure if it works the same with the full house, which I'm sure you'll have."

"Thank you. Oh, that reminds me, my mother will be arriving on Friday with my grandmother. It seems my father must remain in New York because of a business meeting with some other bankers. He will come to the show later in the summer. Therefore, I asked Greta for four tickets for Sunday. Have you spoken to your parents yet?"

Whoops. Friday? So soon. "No, I haven't called yet, but I will this afternoon. Are you ready to leave?"

"Almost. Someone from wardrobe has to give me a time for a final fitting and I think it will be later today. I hope so, because I really want to rest for a while. This was exhausting."

"You were great. This was strenuous work and you held up well, don't you think?"

"Yes, I think it must be because I have a wonderful assistant who takes such good care of me." She growled a little. "Now I would like to go home and be taken care of."

Her words created stirrings low in my pelvis. "Okay, you wait here while I run down and ask what time you have to be back."

I returned quickly. "They're really jammed up with some problems, so Louise said you could come back tomorrow morning, if that's all right."

I gathered up the cooler, the bag, and the diva before making a beeline to the car. We were home in a matter of minutes, and in the house even faster.

"What do you need to do first?"

"I'm starving, but first I need a shower. Do we have anything quick to eat?"

"You go ahead, I'll find something. Wait, there's something I forgot." I caught up to her at the steps and gave her a kiss. "I've been waiting to do that all day."

She smiled tenderly and put her palm against my cheek. "Me too. I will hurry." She disappeared down the hall and my heart squeezed a little from her touch. The day had been very productive and I was grateful there had been no problems, but at this moment I was thrilled we were back in the privacy of her house with no anticipated interruptions.

After scrounging through the refrigerator, I came up with some cold chicken, a hardboiled egg, romaine lettuce, a tomato, and some blue cheese. A little French bread, along with some strawberries, should do the trick. There was also a chilled bottle of white wine, but I thought it might be best to wait on that.

After preparing the salad, I divided it between two plates and set the table. I was just pouring the iced tea when Nicole reappeared in my favorite red caftan looking refreshed and hungry. "Much better."

"All ready for Madame. Please join me."

"How have I managed all these years without you?" Her eyes twinkled with mischief as she strolled toward me looking very seductive. I put down the iced tea glasses and waited for a sign that our evening could be an irreverent exploration of newfound joy.

My breathing halted as she slipped her arms around my neck and covered my lips with the most exquisite kiss in the world. I reached around to pull her even closer, reveling in the fact that our bodies fit together so seamlessly. Her minty fresh tongue teased my lips apart and explored brazenly as I lost feeling in my legs.

The dormant spark in my pelvis came to life, and I felt myself falling into a fiery abyss. At the last second, she broke away. "And I've been waiting all day to do that. It's only a preview. First I need to eat and then I want to play."

I grabbed the edge of the table. "Uh-huh, yes, dinner. All ready, but I'm not sure I have the strength to lift a fork."

"Would you like me to feed you?" she said, purring.

Now I was sure I was going to faint. "You are so unfair." I sat down—or should say I collapsed—into the chair.

Nicole attacked her meal. "This is wonderful. What a perfect idea."

We talked a little about the rehearsal and laughed at some of the usual mistakes made with the first major run-through. The chorus bumped into each other constantly, Stefan missed a couple of key cues, and at one point a gust of wind blew through the large opening at the rear of the stage, knocking things over. When we finished, Nicole insisted on cleaning up while I called my parents.

"Hi, Mom, it's your lost daughter. I know, it's been way too long, and I apologize. Listen, have you and Dad got tickets for *La Traviata* yet? I figured you would, but listen. Nicole would like you both to be her guest on Sunday because her parents will be in town and she would like to have dinner with you before the performance."

I covered the mouthpiece. "She's talking to my dad."

Nicole leaned over, dishcloth in hand, and kissed me again.

"What? Okay, yes, I'm sure you can sell them. In fact, I think Liz might be interested. I will send her a note when I know the details. Absolutely, I'm looking forward to it. Yes, she wants to meet you, too. I will, I love you, too."

"Are they going to come?" Nicole sounded just as excited as my mother.

"Yes. They're thrilled that you even asked them, and my mom insists on bringing something for dinner."

She squealed with delight and I shuddered.

"Oh *chérie*, I know this makes you nervous, but it will be all right, trust me. Why don't you run along and shower? I need to make some phone calls anyway, and I will come find you."

This last was said with more than a hint of promise.

I ran my hand down the back of the silk caftan to caress her lovely derriere I'd been ogling all day. "I can't wait," I said, and disappeared out the back door.

Act II Scene 10

A cold shower might be appropriate, but tonight there was no more holding back. It was still late afternoon and the temperature was in the high eighties with no breeze. I quickly stripped out of my hot clothing and felt my skin tingle with the cool air and the memory of her touch. The only thing more exciting might be her desire for me. It was a heady elixir, and the combination literally intoxicated me to the point that the only thing I wanted was that magical release.

The shower felt good, and as I lathered my hair and soaped the rest of my body, the rekindled fire surged through me. Even though it had only been twenty-four hours, I ached for her touch and her taste. This incredible woman was more than I ever thought I deserved. I quivered just thinking about her.

The contents of the closet seemed Spartan. Now I wished I'd brought more clothes. And better clothes. Especially now that her family was coming and my family was coming. Oh, Lord. But how could I have anticipated a few weeks ago that the job I took would be so involved and so enjoyable? I picked out a clean T-shirt and shorts, reminding myself to do laundry soon, and walked to the living room. Looking out the window to the main house, I hoped to see her on her way down the walk. Not yet. She probably had things to do.

Seriously, though, was there anything more important than continuing the play we'd set in motion? As soon as I sat down, I remembered I hadn't combed my hair. *Where has your mind gone, Ellis?* I tried to comb the thick wavy mass into some sort of style and realized that I was long overdue for another haircut. Then I remembered Nicole's fingers in my hair and how good that felt. Maybe it could wait another week or so. As an afterthought, I added a spritz of cologne. "I'm ready for my close-up, Ms. Bernard."

A fleeting thought about Pearson made me feel guilty, and I pulled out my cell phone to check with my neighbor. I'd left her plenty of money but still felt bad that I hadn't been in contact. I should probably find out if she might be interested in seeing the opera. We'd never discussed it. I wasn't even sure she liked music. Humph.

One task completed, I thought I might as well contact Lena and find out about her barbecue. I'd waited deliberately because I was playing with the idea of inviting Nicole. I wasn't sure how she'd like the idea of a ranch barbecue with a gang of lesbian cowgirls. However, she'd surprised me at every turn. Maybe she'd enjoy it.

It was amusing to think about the stereotype that I had created of Nicole compared to the actual woman. I was incredulous when I thought about her initial attraction. I never in a thousand years would have expected that she had been with other women. So much for gaydar.

A mellow feeling came over me as I stretched out on the couch. It almost felt as though all of the angst from the last few years just dissipated. This new job challenged me and provided an enjoyable adventure. It not only allowed me to be back in the theater, I also had the chance to offer some support and help to one of the brightest stars in the opera world. The real perquisite was a summer romance with a woman whom I idolized for years.

Even now, the thought—the mere thought!—of her sensuous lips set me ablaze. I closed my eyes just for a moment and could instantly visualize Nicole standing at the kitchen sink in her red caftan. Her words of promise echoed in all four chambers of my heart with a delicious resonance. The gentle beating lulled me into a state of deep relaxation.

A clicking sound woke me from a deep sleep. I listened again and it was the resetting of the motor in the swamp cooler. I stumbled through the dark into the kitchen. The clock on the microwave said eleven fifteen. Wow, I must've been more tired than I thought. But where was Nicole? I checked both bedrooms and they were empty. In order to find my shoes, I had to turn on a light. Then I began to worry. I hoped she was all right and wondered why she just hadn't called me if she'd changed her mind. Fear began to ramp up as I jogged up the path to the main house. There were no lights on except the one over the kitchen sink. I let myself in and walked through the house listening for any unusual sounds. An uncharacteristic panic lurked in the back of my mind.

There were no sounds and nothing out of place. Without knocking I pushed open her bedroom door, holding my breath. Faint moonlight outlined a red-clad form curled up on the bed. As I came closer, I could hear her characteristically soft snoring. I slid down on one knee and started breathing again with great relief. My heart was still jackhammering in my chest. *She's okay.* I wanted to touch her face to feel further reassured, but resisted. *Thank you, God.*

After regaining the use of my legs, I carefully covered her with the bedspread and crept out of her room. The locks were secure on both the front door and the garage door, so I switched off the light and went back to the guesthouse. Relief that nothing was wrong overshadowed my disappointed libido.

We were in the final stretch for the show and everyone was tired and on edge. We both needed a good night's sleep. This week would be the grand opening starting with *The Marriage of Figaro* and continuing with *Madama Butterfly*. There was no performance on the Fourth of July, and then the following Thursday *La Traviata* would premier. I prayed that it would be a successful opening and, more importantly, that we would all survive the "family dinner" and the Sunday performance.

Once each of the five of the operas had opened, they would begin a revolving schedule each week until the end of August. Realistically, I knew I should just plan to not see much of Nicole for the next week or so. Even thinking of that hurt my heart, but there was no point in setting unrealistic expectations.

Your job, Ellis, is to help this woman give the best performance of her life. You are not being paid to lust after her like a horny teenager.

"Oh, shut up."

When I walked into the kitchen the next morning, the lady of the house was fully dressed, humming, and stirring a skillet full of eggs. One big ker-thump and my heart started beating again.

"Good morning."

"*Bonjour, amie.*" She waved the spatula. "I am preparing a wonderful breakfast to make up for passing out and abandoning you. Is it in your heart to forgive me?"

"I fell asleep, too. I didn't wake up until after eleven and came looking for you. I was a little worried until I found you sound asleep, and then I was just relieved."

She pushed the skillet to a cooler burner and turned off the gas. After wiping her hands on a dishtowel, she walked over and put her arms around my waist. Even at this early stage, we drew tremendous comfort from each other's arms. It felt so natural and so comfortable. Her cheek felt warm and soft against mine, and I kissed her neck.

"Dear Meg, I think we have some busy days ahead."

"I know we do, and I don't want to distract you from this really important performance. As soon as things settle down, we'll have plenty of time together. If you want."

She turned her face and looked at me. "I do want, very much. Tell me, how did one so young become so wise?"

I chuckled. "I'm not sure it's wisdom. I was just taught that patience is a virtue." Her eyes were looking into mine with an inexpressible kindness and affection. I made a silent vow to do whatever I could to make sure I would always find that look waiting for me.

We kissed for the sheer joy of the connection, her lips communicating even more than her eyes. I would have happily remained standing in her arms all day—but it would not be this day.

☙☙❧❧

The first stop was wardrobe. I dropped her at the door and went to look for Greta. I promised to pick up the tickets, check on transportation for her mother, turn in my time sheet, and find out the details for the opening gala events. Nicole needed to make some public appearances. These were special events for the patrons who for years had been the financial mainstay of the opera company. I hoped they'd excuse me from attending, if for no other reason than I needed to get some new clothes, a haircut, and some Pearson time. Nicole and I had already discussed it, and she begrudgingly agreed that my time was better spent taking care of my personal needs, and that she would stick religiously to the eating plan while I was away.

All but one of the costumes were nearly ready, but the red wig didn't work so we needed to wait for some adjustments. I plied her with water, and we headed to the rehearsal room to meet with Carl, Stefan, and Lars. On the way over, Nicole told me the gossip—that by leaving early yesterday, we'd missed a big dust-up between Stefan and Henry, the new Germont. Hence, we had a new rehearsal. Lars wanted Nicole present to balance the male egos and to add her opinion. In her place, her understudy would be with the chorus working Act Three.

Three hours later and with a growing headache behind my eyes, Lars mercifully dismissed us. He called for a quick run-through of the first two acts at six, which gave us a couple hours to regroup. Nicole looked tired, and without asking, I drove home.

"Iced tea?" I said, pulling out the pitcher.

"*Merci.*" We stayed in the kitchen, opting for the counter.

"There's some fruit salad, or would you rather have an early dinner?" I examined the shelves for the third time, hoping for different results. I needed to shop.

"Both. I'm hungry."

We munched and swilled iced tea for a while and replayed the scene from rehearsal. It had ended amicably with a few changes. Nicole had some awesome diplomacy skills. I needed to pay attention.

"I thought I'd run to the store while you rest, if that's okay?"

"Good idea. It will be busy the next couple of days. First, I will give you money." We had agreed she would pay unless there were personal items I needed.

After digging for her wallet in her purse, she handed me two fifty-dollar bills. "Will this be enough?"

"More than enough, considering all the events you need to attend."

"Ah, sweet mercy." She groaned, dropping her forehead to the counter. "Those are the worst part. You are sure you do not want to go with me?" she said, popping her head back up.

"I didn't think you'd need me with all the staff that will be showing you off."

She smiled. "True, but…what if I wanted to show you off?"

"Not happening! You have some duties to attend to and I need to stay in the background and man the home front."

Her expression morphed into a pout.

"Oh, come on. Your adoring public needs you, and your adoring assistant will wait patiently."

Nicole reached across for my hand, stroked it with her thumb, and said, "Is it sometimes hard to be patient? For me it becomes harder, I think."

"Yes, it is hard." I felt the lump swelling in my throat, but this wasn't the time for my earnest professions of desire. "We'll have time, we will. Tomorrow night and Saturday are the main events, and there's nothing scheduled for Sunday. I was wondering... well, some good friends of mine throw an annual Fourth of July barbecue at their ranch. If you were interested, we could do that."

Her eyes lit up and grew large with pure delight. "A real ranch? With horses and lots of cattle?"

I laughed out loud. "Yes to horses, not cattle. It's a working ranch, so it's not fancy. Just good food and some old friends, most of whom have never heard of you."

Nicole clapped her hands and jumped off the stool, throwing her arms around my neck. "Yes, please take me to a barbecue."

"Yes, ma'am. If that would make you happy, we'll go."

☙ ❧

As I expected, everything spiraled up: activity, schedules, and tempers. When Nicole and I finished vocalizing on Friday morning I cautiously asked, "Since you will be going to Santa Fe a little later with some of the cast, I thought it might be a good time for me to go home and take care of some business and bring some better clothes back. Like we talked about."

At first, she said nothing, then began to put away the music. "I guess I am pretty selfish. I have not thought about the fact you have another life and other responsibilities."

She leaned over and ran her fingers through my hair slowly. "Of course I will miss you quite a lot. When will you come back?"

I knew there was another cocktail party Saturday before the opening. "Probably late tomorrow. Will you stay after the party and watch the show?"

"No, I will see it another time. I would rather just have a quiet evening after all the business."

"Perfect. I'll be back by then and you can tell me all about it. Then Sunday afternoon I'll take you out to the ranch." I stood up and started to get my things together.

"Meg, will you at least kiss me before you go?"

My innards flip-flopped and I returned to her, still seated at the piano bench, and pulled her to her feet and into my arms. "That is a request I will never deny you." I crushed her lips with all the passion swirling within me. I tried without words to express the intense care and desire I felt for the astonishing woman who had opened the carefully locked corner of my heart.

Her arms tightened around me and she returned the kiss with gusto, eliciting an ecstasy I had only experienced once in my life...and only from her lips. God, this woman knew how to kiss. I began to waver about leaving, until she pulled free and pushed me away.

"Go, *mon amie,* and return quickly."

Act II Scene 11

I parked in front of my apartment building. Everything looked the same except that I hadn't been there for almost four weeks. Hard to believe, and yet everything in my world was now tilted on its axis. I pulled the laundry bag from the back seat and climbed to the second floor of the once familiar building.

I moved in after Bekka and I split in order to get as far away from her as possible. It was a modest one-bedroom unit in a small building with easy access to shopping. My school district was only a few miles away but far enough that I was not likely to run into students.

As I passed Mrs. Cochran's apartment, I could hear Pearson mewing. I went to my apartment first and threw in a load of wash before I went over to see him. I told her that he was perfectly fine staying in my apartment, but she insisted on bringing him over to hers, citing loneliness. I'm guessing it was hers, not his.

After making some polite conversation with her, I took Pearson back to my apartment for a little while. It was probably unfair, because I would only be home for less than twenty-four hours. My kitty understood when I explained to him that I needed to pay some bills, do some laundry, make some phone calls, and take a good look at my wardrobe. This meant that I would be talking to him constantly, which he appreciated.

Not surprising, the wardrobe of the school nurse is less than stylish and borders on functional. Almost everything I own has to be washable in hot water since the little beings I care for are vectors of disease.

I found a Diet Coke in the refrigerator and sat on the couch with Pearson. He was winding between my ankles the whole time I unpacked, and now sat rubbing his head against my shoulder.

"I missed you too, buddy, but I'm sure Mrs. Cochran has been very attentive." In my view, he looked a little heftier. "See, the thing is I have a new job with this really nice lady, and she wants me to stay with her because I think she likes me as much as you do. Besides which, I am her emotional prisoner. Do you know what that means?"

I took a swallow of soda and Nicole's image appeared before me. The ride home and away from her had been brutal. On at least two occasions, I almost turned the car around. It was silly and I knew it, but there was nothing I could do about these feelings. Nicole and I had been together constantly for over a month; we worked together, rode together, ate together, laughed together, and, on one magnificent occasion, made love together.

Leaving her house for even twenty-four hours felt a little like torture, and I fought valiantly to keep tears at bay. "Pearson, do you think I'm silly? I mean is it possible that I'm falling in love again?" He had found a comfortable spot on my lap and was purring loudly. "You're right, it probably is too soon. I have to tell you, though, she makes me very happy, and I'm pretty sure she likes me. And I'll tell you something else if you promise not to breathe a word of it. Nicole

Bernard has magic lips. That's right. I have never met anyone that can disable a person with just a kiss, but she can."

A glow started deep inside, and I had a picture in my mind of the heart light that Neil Diamond sang about. Nicole could touch that part of me so easily.

Stop mooning over her and get something done. You'll be back there before you know it, and you need to finish a few things first. Ellis, get moving.

I pulled out my cell phone dutifully and punched in Lena's number.

"Hi, girlfriend. How's it going?" she drawled. "Did the boss lady give you permission to use the phone?" I could hear her chuckling.

"I escaped. Actually, I'm at home doing some laundry and a few chores. The reason I called was to ask you if it would be okay for me to bring Nicole to the barbecue."

"Of course, why would you even ask? So does this mean your relationship's a little more serious?"

I didn't know how much to say at this point. "Nicole and I get along really well, and…it's been terribly busy so I thought we could both use a day off. I'm not sure how many horse ranches she visits on the opera circuit."

"Well, I for one think it's a great idea. Brenda will be thrilled. We even planned a little fireworks display, which so far we'll be able to do. Of course, the county fire marshal could change his mind anytime."

"That sounds like fun. Do you want us to bring anything?"

"We'll have beer and wine along with food. If you guys want something special, bring it along. Do you think she'd like to ride?"

"Gosh, I don't know. But I'll ask her."

"It'll be great to see you and Nicole. I'm glad you called, Meg." We hung up.

"Okay, Pearson, let's get some work done. Where are my boots?"

※※※※

By early Saturday afternoon, I was getting antsy. The bills were paid, emails answered, and I'd packed so many clothes Nicole might be afraid I was staying forever. I just wasn't sure what I might need for the next couple of weeks in terms of dressy duds. I knew what to wear for the barbecue, I knew what to wear for the performances, and I even knew what I needed to wear for Nicole.

I knocked on Mrs. Cochran's door at three with Pearson in my arms.

"Oh, I'm glad you're back. I missed you, Pearson." Mrs. Cochran was a spry eighty-two-year-old widow with a big heart and few friends. We had become friends of necessity and helped one another frequently.

"You have no idea how much I appreciate your taking care of my boy." I handed her some more money along with my cat. "I'll check back, and you know you can call me anytime."

I put two bags in the back of the car and jumped in. Seat belt fastened, music playing. "Nicole Bernard, ready or not, here I come." The CD blasted and I sang along with it—for the first time. I was singing out loud. I had no illusion about quitting my job or changing careers, but the complete joy that filled me was indescribable. Being able to make music was a gift, and I felt incredibly grateful.

Of course, singing aloud reminded me of the first lesson with Nicole and her gentle patience. If I didn't watch myself, I could fall very hard for this wonderful woman. I needed to remind myself that she would only be here for eight more weeks. That sounded like a long time, but I knew when that last day came it would have gone by in a whisper.

I pulled into her driveway and sighed; it actually was like coming home. With my bags under both arms, I struggled to open the front door. I knew it was still early because the champagne reception ran from three to six. The house was deadly quiet, and I stood for just a moment breathing in the essence of what was there—her scent and energy. Before going out to the guesthouse, I walked down the main hall to the master bedroom, half hoping, I guess, that she might be there.

The door was wide open, the bed made, and there were two or three outfits lying on top of it. I picked up one and just held it. Nicole must have had difficulty choosing. I could smell her perfume and, without thinking, began to hang the dresses up. I wanted everything to be nice when she got home.

Back to reality, Ellis. Stop acting weird and moonstruck. Geez.

I made short work of putting my clothes away and tidying up my place. The living room looked all right, but I was hoping to make it a little more, I don't know, romantic. Looking through the cupboards revealed several more candles and a fancy tablecloth that might hide the functional Mission-style wooden table. I had brought back a bottle of champagne in case Nicole was not already sick of it from her social engagements. That went into the refrigerator.

The activity of the preparation sent me to the shower. The temperature outside was in the low nineties and I found some loose cotton shorts and a tank top to wear. My place was finally all set, and I decided to head up to the main house and scrounge up something for supper. I was sure the opening gala would be a food fest, but there was no harm in fixing a few things to keep on hand. My mom had really tried, but I didn't catch on to the whole recipe/measuring thing. Cooking is not my forte, but there are a few standards I can fall back on, one of which is pasta salad. Really, pasta, dressing, and some chopped vegetables. Easy peasy.

It turned out so well that I even baked some pre-cut Tollhouse cookies. For the first time since I moved in, I felt comfortable enough to use the rather expensive CD player in the kitchen. My growing new relationship with music caused me to bring some different CDs—vocal CDs—with me on this trip. I chose one by Sarah Vaughan. I'd had it for years because it contained her classics. By the third cut, I was really into it and even trying a little harmony with the vegetable chopping.

On my hundredth trip to the refrigerator, I took out a partially full bottle of white wine. What the heck? After turning up the volume, I finished singing "Someone To Watch Over Me" and started "Our Love Is Here To Stay" when I felt a hand on my shoulder.

I jumped, and Nicole laughed. "Would you like to dance?"

She must have been behind me for a while, though I never heard a thing. She looked beautiful. Her hair, makeup, and perfectly beautiful lavender dress radiated diva.

"I'd love to." I wiped my hands and pulled her into my arms, swaying to the lush sounds of the Los Angeles Philharmonic. With her heels, we were the same height. She had one hand on the back of my neck and the other resting in my palm. We circled the large kitchen and I moved her to the living room. The song was brief, but we continued to move slowly until the next one began.

She kissed my neck and whispered, "I am glad you are home."

"So am I." I pulled her closer as I basked in the warmth, scent, and feel of her body. "It does feel like home with you," I said softly.

The CD ended.

"You look stunning, Nicole. How were your appearances?"

"Thank you. They were fine, but I must change. And may I have some wine, too?"

I floated back to the kitchen as she headed for her room, pulling off her jewelry. Now my day was perfect. Damn, I loved holding her.

The pasta salad was finished with the addition of a few black olives. I poured wine for each of us and Nicole reappeared in her red-caftan-esque glory. Dazzling. She took the wine and looked at the bowl I had on the counter.

"That looks yummy. Is it just for you?"

As if I could deny her anything. "No, I made it in case you needed something to eat."

"I am hungry. These PR things are so busy with introductions and pictures I never get to eat much."

That worried me a little. "Sit down and let's eat, then." I served up two bowls and sat down with her.

"So everything went well?"

"Yes, tonight's performance was a complete sellout."

Nicole described the events of the past thirty hours as I watched her face, her animated hands, and her twinkling eyes. As usual, she attacked the food with gusto. She would make any cook happy.

When I refilled her wineglass, she leaned back and looked at me. "Please tell me what you did, because I missed you."

"Not much. I washed clothes, played with my cat, paid some bills, and thought about you. Oh yes, and I checked with my friend Lena. She was thrilled that I wanted to bring you to the barbecue and they're planning some fireworks. Oh, and she wanted to know if you'd be interested in horseback riding."

The twelve-year-old in Nicole lit up. "Oh yes! I would love that. I have never ridden a horse. How wonderful." She got up and walked around behind me, nuzzling my neck. "I am very glad you are here." Her breasts pressed against my back and both hands slipped under my tank top, rubbing my back while she kissed my neck.

I sat up and arched my back as my middle ignited instantly. Her lips were inflammatory on their own until her hand slid around me and caressed my searing breasts. Toast. I was toast. I couldn't speak because I couldn't breathe.

"I think maybe you missed me a little."

"Oh, dear God, yes."

Her hands were cool and I was not.

Between nibbles and the ministrations of her tongue, she managed to say, "Do you have plans tonight?"

"I sure hope so, because I'm in so much trouble right now."

"Do you think you would be all right for a little while if I have to make some calls?"

"I don't know." I was moaning audibly. "But I'll try."

"I'll hurry and meet you in your house," she said, and pressed her lips to mine with what I would describe as urgency.

※ ※ ※ ※

The sun's last rays were shining in the window when I heard footsteps on the walk. The kitchen clock suggested it had been over two hours. I'd been lost in a new novel and was surprised it had been so long.

"May I come in?"

I sat up and smiled. "You don't really expect me to say no, do you?" I stood up and moved closer.

"A thousand pardons for my tardiness. I had to make many phone calls, when all I wanted was to be here with you." Her arms encircled my waist and the scent of lilies of the valley transported me instantly. Our lips met tentatively and my body came alive as though I reconnected to my source of power.

I took her hands and pulled her over to the couch. "Come to me," I whispered. She wasted no time draping herself comfortably across my lap. "This feels familiar," I said, kissing her cheek and biting her ear lobe.

"Yes, I like being in your arms and being so close." Her head fell back, exposing her neck, and I couldn't resist the notch at the base of her throat. My kiss elicited a deep whimper that stoked the fire between my legs. I leaned her back a little farther and ran my hands along her side to her breast. The silk was cool and soft under my fingers, but the thin fabric could not disguise the heat of her skin or her taut nipples.

Nicole pulled my head up and captured my mouth in an excoriating kiss. Her tongue was everywhere and her mouth was demanding. Things moved very quickly, and I soon found myself on my back with Nicole on top with a leg on each side of my hips. She pulled the caftan over her head, leaving her naked and breathless.

"You have no idea how much you are turning me on right now," I said, giving over complete control.

She kissed me again and began tugging at my shirt. I sat up just enough to have it yanked over my head and our mouths collided with a strange kind of savagery that I never expected. Without breaking the kiss I was suddenly on my back again with her hands on each shoulder. I was panting as we both broke the kiss and came up for air. She jumped up and began pulling my shorts off.

My heart thundered in my chest as she stretched her body out on top of me and shoved one leg between mine. With one deep hungry kiss, her mouth moved down to one breast. My nipple caught between her lips and her teeth, and I felt a sharp pain that traveled like a shot to my exploding core that was pinned beneath hers. I cried out which only seemed to excite her more.

Her frenzy was exhilarating and a little frightening. I had never seen this part of her, this wild untamed animal, but I was hers completely. I closed my eyes and there were spots dancing before them. My hips thrust repeatedly against her and she responded with equal force.

"Oh fuck!" I screamed as everything exploded and my muscles vibrated with spasms.

Then everything stopped. There was stillness except for our heavy breathing.

Nicole stood up, looking horrified. She began to cry and ran from the room.

My brain was whirling as the throbbing subsided. I tried to breathe and to stop the trembling in my hands. Why did she run off? I couldn't even stand up yet.

"Nicole?" Nothing. "Nicole, are you all right?" I tried to sit up but was still a little dizzy. I finally managed to get safely to my feet, and I hurried down the hall to the bedroom. She lay facedown on my pillow, sobbing.

I carefully approached her. "Are you okay? What just happened?" She continued to cry. "Nicole, please."

Finally it eased. "I do not know, I was suddenly so very angry."

"Yeah, I got that. Is it me? Have I done something to upset you?"

"No, it is not you. I must leave. This was wrong. I should not have…" She rolled over and got up.

"Wait, please help me understand…" But she was out the door.

I stood naked at my front door, watching her run up the walk with the red caftan trailing from her hand, feeling as though a truck had run over me.

ACT II SCENE 12

I got dressed and sat staring out the window. Dejection was not a new feeling, but guilt and self-doubt gnawed at the corners of my confidence. *You knew this was a mistake. You never should have gotten involved with her. You're an assistant and you'll never be any more than that. But why was she so angry?*

Tears stung my eyes, and I pulled my knees up and wrapped my arms around them. I began to rock back and forth as I allowed the hurt to invade. I should have known. It was far too soon to think of attraction as anything more than a summer romance. Besides, it could hardly be considered a romance after only two encounters. Not even, really. One and a half. My chest hurt when I thought about the tenderness that we had shared the first time. I knew it wasn't my imagination. Nicole told me she had feelings. So what had just happened? I deserved to know that.

I washed my face and slipped on my sandals. If I'd done something wrong she could fire me, but dammit, she should tell me to my face. The fear morphed into indignant anger.

The house was quiet as I closed the patio door. When I passed through the kitchen, I could see her on the living room sofa, just like the last time I found her curled up there. She saw me as I walked in and didn't move. I took a deep breath.

"I think we need to talk. I really want to understand what just happened." I sat down in a chair across from her.

"*Je suis désolée*, I am impulsive and so I was so unfair to you."

"Nicole, tell me what the hell just happened."

"It is not important. I behaved badly."

I could feel the anger bubbling just below the surface. Not important? What the hell did that mean? "It's important to me," I said, sounding much harsher than I intended.

"Please, trust me, and please know it was not you."

"What? Somehow, that doesn't help. I was the one who didn't want to start anything and you're the one who said you had feelings. Now you tell me that it's not important. What am I supposed to believe?"

"*Ma chère*, I mean what I tell you, it is just that—"

"Just what?"

She had both hands folded in tight fists in front of her mouth and all I wanted to do was shake her. Instead, I jumped up and stormed out to the kitchen. I paced back and forth for several minutes, then reached for the refrigerator and snatched the bottle of wine from earlier. I grabbed an empty glass from the counter and poured a generous serving. My hands shook as I downed the first swallow. It was déjà vu. Once again, I was the one betrayed. "Goddamnit!"

I couldn't stay still. I paced, then I took the wine with me into the den. I sat down at the piano. The singing, the first embrace, was it all a lie? I don't know how long I sat there before she came out.

"Meg, it was because of Mario. He called me."

I looked up to see her standing in the doorway,

pale and very serious.

"He was angry because the lawyer told him he was not allowed to come here. He wanted to know why and threatened to make a lawsuit if I prevented him from coming to the opening performance. I did not know what to do, so I told him yes."

I stared in complete disbelief. What else could possibly happen? Now it would be my parents, her mother, her grandmother, her husband, and me—her lover. This had all the makings of a French comedy. I just didn't see the humor.

Her face was pleading. "Please understand, when I came to you it was with desire, and the passion I felt suddenly turned to rage and all I could think was about why Mario would do this to me. I shared everything with him. His career would never be if I did not help him every day, and he humiliates me." She stroked my fingers. "I was not fair to you and you did not deserve it. Can you ever forgive me?" Her voice wavered.

"Nicole, I understand how much he has hurt you. It's wrong. I was not upset because you were angry and aggressive, I was upset because you ran off without talking to me. If you had just told me this instead of running away, I would have understood. When you bolted up and ran out of the house without a word, I thought it was entirely my fault—"

"*Mais non*, nothing could be further from the truth. It is with you that I feel safe. Always I am safe with you, Meg. But I believed I hurt you."

"This isn't easy, is it? I think we're both overtired, and you have another big day tomorrow. You need rest. Do you want to stay here, or do you want to come with me?"

"If you forgive me, I would like to sleep in your arms tonight."

I set the wineglass down and said, "Then please stay with me."

※ ※ ※ ※

Nicole and I turned down the bed together without further comment. We were both drained, and I didn't want to get into a conversation about Mario. Not tonight.

I deliberated about whether I should leave my T-shirt on since I normally slept in the nude, but I wasn't sure how she felt now. When Nicole pulled her caftan off, I did the same.

"I want to feel your skin when you hold me," she said simply.

Her skin was warm and soft against my body, and I folded my arms around her and moved as close as possible. "Nothing could make me happier than to have you so close. I'm sorry there was a misunderstanding, and I wish it would never happen again. Sadly, it probably will. We're still learning each other. Please remember, Nicole, no matter what, you can always talk to me. Always. Even if I get angry, I won't leave."

My fingers tingled as she kissed them, and the overpowering desire to kiss her neck drew me to her. I placed a gentle kiss behind her ear and fought back the urge to make love to her. She held my hand tight to her breast and her breathing slowed.

My own eyelids were heavy from the emotional roller coaster and it dragged me under quickly. It may have been a minute, an hour, or even more. I might have remained that way but for the gentle pressure on my cheek and my neck. It felt tender and gradually I surfaced when something soft pressed on my lips. As my other senses awakened, I was aware that Nicole had turned and was facing me, her arms around me, our bodies completely touching, skin on skin. Her face was only a breath away. I could feel soft puffs of air with each exhalation, and the sweetness of her delicate kisses.

The sensation that I was melting into her was delicious. I wanted nothing more than to touch her. Everywhere. My palm trailed up her back lightly, finding tiny hairs on her soft skin at the base of her skull. I touched the delicate bones in the back of her neck and the curve of her shoulder blade while she continued to saturate my lips with her kisses.

I paused to explore the small of her back and the curve of her bottom, and then slid her leg on top of mine in order to learn the back of her thigh and the small hollow behind her knee. To free my other hand, I rolled onto my back, pulling her with me.

The weight of her body on mine further connected us. Now, I was able to stroke her entire body with my hands. There was a narrow valley between the muscles on either side of her spine. Below the delicate skin, I could feel the ribs along her side right up to where the tissue became soft beside her breasts. Her narrow waist fanned out slightly to her hips and strong muscles curved to her thighs. Was there anything softer or sweeter than a woman's skin?

I was home, my heart was full, and I could have died happily at that moment. The small kisses were lasting longer, and I pulled her hips closer with both my hands. Her arms were under my shoulders holding on tightly, and she continued to escalate the delicate assault on my mouth. It was teasing, tender, and incredibly sensuous, and every nerve in my body reacted to what was happening.

The muscles in my lower abdomen relaxed completely as the blood flow to the area increased. I spread my legs, hoping for the pressure of her body between them, and when I did the tip of her tongue penetrated my lips, causing my back to arch. I moved my hands lower, pushing us even closer together, and she moaned into my mouth.

With deepening kisses we crushed together slowly and deliberately. The fire had re-ignited and was consuming me. Nicole's body was damp and trembling. I slowly rolled her onto her back and stretched her arms above her head. Her eyes were dark and her breathing shallow. Her lips parted and I ran my tongue across her lower lip before capturing her mouth completely as she sucked my tongue forcefully.

I knelt between her legs, pushing them aside with no resistance. I deliberately moved my mouth to her throat and then her chest. I sucked both breasts individually until her hips bucked and her hands grasped the headboard. I used my lips, my tongue, and my teeth to mark her breasts, stomach, and abdomen.

After a long slow march, I pushed her knees up as she begged. She was ready when my mouth captured her for the final time. Her cry echoed in the large room.

When her muscles relaxed, her tears began. I moved to her side and embraced her shaking body.

We lay together quietly, renewing our raw and tenuous connection. She stroked my arm as she lay curled into my shoulder. "I believe you may have forgiven me," she said, and I could feel the smile.

"You could say that. I was hoping I communicated a little more than that."

"Oh, but you did, and I am very grateful because I am not sure I deserve it."

"You were angry and I didn't understand what was going on." I kissed her damp cheek, tasting the salty tears. "Can I ask you something?"

Her expression became quite serious. "Of course."

"Well, I don't consider myself particularly naïve. I mean, I have done a fair share of kissing in my life." She smiled. "But I have to tell you, I have never, ever met anyone who could compare to you when it comes to the things you do with your mouth. Seriously, where did you learn to kiss like that?"

Nicole laughed aloud, and it was a very welcome sound. "You must remember that I am a professional and I have kissed a good many people, both men and women, in the course of my career. Some of them were very, very good and some of them just dreadful."

"C'mon. I don't think you do that kind of kissing during any opera or the show would run even longer than four hours."

"It is true. When I kiss on stage, it is much more brief, but for you I...I wanted it to be different. I want you to believe me when I tell you of my feelings. My English does not always tell you the words of my heart. I want to show you that I care for you." She sat up a little and leaned on one elbow, cupping my face in her hand. "This is new to me as well and it is very special. I want to tell you some things." The sound of her voice grew more serious.

"Every day you are here for me—to help me, to anticipate my needs, to keep me safe, and to make me laugh. Do you understand that no one has ever done that before? When it became obvious that we shared special feelings, I could not trust so soon. You were gentle and kind and patient. I admit I am not always so gentle or kind."

I started to interrupt but she put her fingers on my lips. "No, it is true, and before the show is over, I am sure that I will make you angry again. It is not because I want to and I will try to be careful. If you think that I am mean or unkind, tell me. Do not shut me out the same way I did to you. It was stupid and unfair of me, and you deserve better. We both do."

I pulled her close and kissed her forehead. "I understand."

Then she showed me what she felt she could not express.

Act II Scene 13

First, it was only soft breath against my cheek. I gradually became aware of the warm body nestled beside me. I didn't move but waited until my senses were more fully alert. It was then that I noticed Nicole's soft body and her hand around my waist. I sighed with contentment.

After more leisurely and sensuous lovemaking, we managed a few hours of sleep. I marveled at how every single touch, embrace, and kiss were as different as the moods. I believed I would never grow tired of touching and caressing her body. It was only with great willpower that I was able to resist in this moment.

However, watching her sleep was delicious. Her long lashes graced her cheeks and her softly parted lips were full and calling to me, begging me to taste them. She stirred and let out a huge breath while her hand moved up to my chest.

We lay wrapped in each other's arms as I watched the sunlight gradually brighten the bedroom. Eventually, she began to wake. Unable to resist, I pressed my lips to her forehead. She stretched then shifted her body until she was half on top of me, which allowed me to wrap both arms around her.

"Do you think we could just stay this way all day?" I asked.

"It feels good, *oui?*"

"It feels perfect. You fit me like a glove."

She chuckled softly. "And sometimes I think the fingers move inside the glove."

We both started laughing. "And does the glove enjoy that?"

"Oh, very much. I think, sometimes, the more fingers the better it feels."

We shook with giggles as we both tried to think of something even cleverer.

"Would you describe yourself as a long white opera glove? Or are you more like a soft leather work glove?"

By now, she was laughing so hard tears were running down her face. "I think it would depend on the occasion."

The jocularity continued for several minutes, and I was thinking how nice it was to begin my day laughing with a lovely woman beside me. It had been far too long, and it felt good.

Nicole ran off to get ready and I jumped in the shower. She was excited about the barbecue but wanted to spend some time rehearsing first. She had asked Carl to come by at eleven and wanted to vocalize before that.

I stayed in the shower enjoying the hot water and reviewing recent events. The thought of Mario returning made me uncomfortable, and I wondered what else she might have told him in her anger. But it was her decision. My feeling was that his appearance was all about making himself look good. He had no interest in Nicole's performance. I did.

If he came for the publicity, fine. If he came to get back in her bed...I didn't know. I couldn't prevent it, so the thought scared me a little. *Ellis, get a grip. Think about the way that you both made love. That wasn't casual sex. If you want this to work, you have to act the part. This is not the time to waffle on your feelings.*

Right. I put on some khaki shorts and my favorite red short-sleeved shirt. It made me feel special and more attractive.

※ ※ ※ ※

The morning flew by, and soon we were saying goodbye to Carl. Nicole and I had spent an hour warming up, and I was astonished by how far she could push my voice and how much better it sounded. Our daily singing was wind in my sails. I floated through the rest of the day with new confidence. I left her to work on her arias while I got some things ready for the afternoon.

The new directions from Lars changed the interpretation of the songs, and I think made them more poignant. Monday would be another complete rehearsal with the orchestra. I was impressed with how much progress the company had made in the last week. Everything seemed to be coming together.

Nicole was in an exceptionally good mood, and I was glad. She had been so upset the night before about the argument with Mario that I was afraid it might hang over us all day. She was flitting about, alternately singing and making silly comments about what to wear to the ranch. Maybe she was just excited about doing something that wasn't work related. I could understand that. Truth was, I was looking forward to it as well. I hadn't seen most of these women since the last barbecue, and we always had a good time.

This year would be different. I would be bringing someone with me. I was afraid to use the term "date" and I certainly wouldn't refer to her as my summer fling. If I was honest, I would simply introduce her as the finest lover I had ever known. I laughed out loud thinking of how absurd that would sound.

"What's so funny?"

Startled again by her stealthy entrance. "Oh, nothing. I was just thinking about the barbecue and how much fun it will be."

"I am very excited about it. Tell me, what did you tell your friend about me?"

Damn, did I make that lover comment out loud? "She knows that I'm working for you and I'd told her that we were…good friends."

She crooked one eyebrow. "Good friends? You did not tell her I was your glove?"

I imploded in a puddle of laughter. When I could finally speak, I said, "No, I didn't mention that. Is that something you'd like me to announce to the group when we arrive?"

She struck a rather seductive pose and tilted her head to one side. "I think you must decide how much you want to say." Her expression changed rapidly to serious and she walked over to me. She put both hands on my chest and I wrapped my arms around her waist, waiting. "Meg, I did not think. For your friends, maybe you want to be professional so they do not know. Please tell me."

"You are just the sweetest thing that ever lived. I would like nothing better than to put up a billboard telling the world how happy I am. However, I think for the next couple of weeks we need to be a little bit careful because of the show. We are both still employees of the Santa Fe Opera and I don't want anything to distract from this incredible production."

"Did you say that most of these friends are not familiar with me?"

"That's true, but I don't know who they talk to and I'd like to protect you a little."

"Then you would like me to behave myself?"

I kissed her forehead. "I would like you to have an incredibly enjoyable day and do whatever makes you comfortable."

"Hmm, then maybe we could make love with one another all afternoon. How would that be?"

My knees buckled. "We could, if that's what you wanted, but we might miss the fireworks."

Her smile grew wicked as I felt her hand slide down inside my shorts until I gasped. "Maybe not all the fireworks."

My cell phone started vibrating in my hip pocket. She didn't move as I reached for it.

"Hello? Oh, hi, Mom." I grabbed her wrist while she giggled. "No, this fine, I have a minute." I shook my head but Nicole just continued her manual exercise.

"Great, I'm sure Nicole would love an angel food cake with fresh raspberries." I could hardly breathe.

Nicole grinned, nodded her head, and pushed me back against the wall.

"That really isn't necessary," I said, glowering at her. "Yes, that's very sweet of Dad to offer the champagne. I'm sure everyone would like that. Of course it's appropriate for an opening." My body betrayed my conscience and responded fully to Nicole's groping.

That seemed to be some kind of a cue for her to intensify her efforts, and my body began to react independently of my already weak willpower. My mother was describing the dress she bought, my father's new tie, and how excited she was about meeting Nicole, while her daughter's hips were moving as if she had Saint Vitus dance.

I let go of Nicole's wrist in order to clasp my hand across my mouth to keep from making lewd noises.

"Listen, Mom, I really have to hang up. Okay, bye."

And not a minute too soon. The muscle spasms brought by my orgasm almost dropped me, but Nicole held me tight against the wall.

My breathing slowed and I shook my head. "You are a mean, mean person. You are sneaky and wicked."

She only laughed. "I cannot help myself. You are so easy to arouse, and it gives me such pleasure. Besides, no matter what you say, your body tells me the truth."

I couldn't deny it.

"You win, you evil temptress. Then let's get ready. We have to leave in less than an hour."

It was true, my body reacted like Pavlov's dogs to her touch, and it took only minutes to bring me to a very satisfying climax. How lucky could one dog get?

ACT II SCENE 14

The small duffel bag held the few things I would need for the evening. I changed out of my shorts for obvious reasons, grabbed some patriotic boxers, and pulled on a pair of comfortable jeans. I had my boots in the bag in case I wanted to go riding, and added a pair of socks. As an afterthought, I threw in some black cargo shorts. A hooded sweatshirt was the only other thing I could think to bring.

I put the bag by the door, made one last sweep, and remembered the wine I had bought for Brenda. I sat on the end of the couch and looked around as my mind willingly jumped back to the little scene in the kitchen. I couldn't help but start laughing when I thought about the beautiful, professional Nicole Bernard with her hand jammed between my legs. Bit by bit, she was dismantling the fancy image I had carried for years.

She was so much more than a cardboard cutout. Her sense of humor was wicked and she was incredibly sensitive. Nicole was fragile and she was wildly sexual. Still, there was so much I wanted to learn about her.

I locked up the guesthouse and ran up to the main house, anxious to see her after being separated for twenty-eight minutes. I found her in the master bedroom pulling clothes out of her closet. I stood in the doorway shaking my head. "Madame, we will be attending a small casual barbecue on a working horse ranch. I don't think you need to put so much effort into your wardrobe."

She turned, surprised by my voice. "*Chérie*, it is important that I do not embarrass you in front of your friends." Her smile was full of promise and mischief.

"But, *chérie*, after that little stunt you pulled earlier, I have no more self-esteem. You have ruined me."

She fell back on the bed laughing hysterically, then sat up. "You are not angry. I made your body so happy."

"You embarrassed me in front of my mother, and don't forget, your mother is coming in less than a week. Perhaps we will even the score." I edged closer to the bed with my hands out in front of me, fully intent on tickling her.

She edged back farther on the bed. "Don't you dare."

I crawled up the foot of the bed. "Or you'll do what?"

She squealed with delight as I trapped her beneath my body. The laughing eyes turned darker as she panned down the length of my body. "I like you in those blue jeans." She reached up and put both hands on my breasts. "I also like your very squeezable soft breasts."

I knelt above her, recognizing how perilously close I was to ruining another outfit, and quickly decided to abort this attempt at intimidation. I kissed her and quickly rolled off the bed, howling, "Get thee behind me, Satan."

She found me in the kitchen a few moments later. She hefted a large purse packed with everything she thought she'd need. "I do so love to torment you," she said, smirking.

I put my arm around her shoulders, "There is no one I would rather have torment me and we will have plenty of time to play, so let's go." She turned and kissed me soundly. All I could do was smile.

After stopping for gas, we drove south and east around Santa Fe toward Pecos. It wasn't that far, but skirting Santa Fe is what took the time.

"Tell me about your friends," Nicole said, tucking her leg under her and readjusting her seat belt.

"I'm not sure who all will be here for sure. Lena and Brenda own the place and have for several years. I knew Lena in high school, and then we both went to Eastern New Mexico University. She majored in veterinary medicine and I majored in nursing with a minor in voice. Brenda transferred in sophomore year and the two of them hooked up. It just seems like I've known them forever.

"I didn't see much of them while I was apprenticing for the opera company. But they never really took a liking to Bekka, so maybe that was why."

"You do not like to talk about her, do you? Is it still so painful?"

I glanced over. Her expression was sincere and interested.

"Well, it was until I spilled the story to you. Some of that anger is gone. Mostly it's embarrassing. It seemed like everyone knew she was cheating except me."

"You seemed very happy when I knew you. What was it that attracted you so?"

I had to think. It felt like a long time ago, but it really wasn't. "I think at first I was a little intimidated by her. She was bigger than life and had a commanding presence. Everyone on the stage crew liked her.

When she started flirting with me, I was thrilled. She was so strong and sure of herself that I never doubted that she could do anything. From the beginning, Bekka made all the decisions. I think my bout with cancer was the first time in her life that she couldn't control everything. She hated the fact that I was in pain and constantly nauseated. To be honest, I wasn't terribly attractive, since I spent a lot of time crying or vomiting. The first few years were good, though. We traveled, entertained, and lived as though there was no tomorrow. Damn near wasn't."

"We are not so lucky with lovers, are we? But your friends, they have been together a very long time, *n'est-ce pas*? I wonder why it is that some couples have love that triumphs over obstacles and others are defeated by them."

We drove in silence for a few minutes, pondering that notion. It seemed true. Lena and Brenda's relationship had weathered personal and professional ups and downs over the years, and those travails had only strengthened their bond. Every time I got together with them, they seemed to be more comfortable with one another, which always made it hugely comfortable for me. They were like family, and I was secretly thrilled to be able to introduce Nicole to such great friends.

Without saying anything, Nicole reached over and took my hand, interlaced her fingers, and just held it.

I turned off the state road onto their long driveway and wound through the hills to the small valley containing their ranch. It was a sheltered spot with a good-sized stream meandering through it. There were two large pastures with the paddock in the middle. A wooden bridge traversed the stream from the road and opened into a large graded area in front of the house. Already, there were half a dozen cars parked there. The barn was on the north side and the garage and storage sheds on the south. Behind the house, a huge covered patio overlooked much of the valley and the pastures. It was a perfect spot to lounge reading a book or to entertain friends.

"This is absolutely amazing. Look at all these buildings. It seems like many people should be living here."

"Just two, I'm afraid, along with a selection of dogs and cats. All set?" Nicole nodded.

We carried our bags to the front door just as Brenda opened it. "Welcome." She embraced me warmly and turned with their hand out to Nicole. "You must be Nicole, please come in. My name is Brenda Vargas, and we're delighted you could join us."

"I am so pleased to have been asked. You have a beautiful home." Nicole smiled most beautifully.

Brenda escorted us through their house that was essentially a very large one-story log home. There was a gigantic field stone fireplace on one wall of the living room that opened through to the family room and kitchen. On the other side of the living room was a hallway to the bedrooms and baths. The western wall was mostly windows and patio doors that opened onto the large patio. The view was spectacular, especially at sunset. Handcrafted wooden fences surrounded the large pastures and the enclosures near the house. On her free days, Brenda had put a lot of time into her flowerbeds because everything looked perfect.

A dozen women welcomed us as soon as we got outside. Most of the guests were sitting or standing around the bar and the built-in cooktop counter, which was covered with a number of appetizers and snacks.

Country music echoed from the hidden speakers around the backyard.

"Somebody pinch me, is that Meg Ellis?" Laughter erupted, and one by one I was passed around and greeted with hugs, kisses, and more than a few wisecracks. Brenda and Nicole just stood enjoying my embarrassment.

"All right, you guys, time to play nice. I'd like to introduce you to a good friend, Nicole Bernard." I put my arm around her shoulders in a very primitive but subtle indication of my connection. My friends were fun but could also be a little coarse. This wasn't the time for it. "I will let each of them introduce themselves, but first let's get a drink," I said to Nicole.

Lena came out of the house with a tray of glasses and set them on the bar. "Meg! Hey girl, it's good to see you." She wrapped me in a bear hug, then turned to Nicole and said, "And I am glad to meet you, Nicole. I guess you've been keeping our little school nurse from running the streets this summer, and we're very grateful."

"Thank you for including me. Meg speaks very highly of both you and Brenda."

Lena winked. "I'll tell you the real story later. Can I get you each something to drink?"

With beer in hand, we visited with most of the women before I pulled Nicole aside. "Would you like a little tour of the place?"

"Yes, please." She put down her still full glass. I never thought to ask if she even liked beer, and she didn't say a word when Lena handed it to her.

I took her through the house and pointed out the many unique touches that they had added to make this home special. We ended up in the kitchen, where Brenda was dishing up some guacamole.

"Lena just went out to the barn and said to tell you that if Nicole was interested in a little riding to meet her out there."

Nicole's eyes lit up. "Oh, I would love that."

All I could do was smile. "Let's go."

As we followed the path to the barn, Nicole took my arm. "It is okay if I do this?"

I kissed her cheek. "This is your day to do as you please."

Lena was waiting with several horses saddled. She asked Nicole a few questions and then led her over a sorrel mare with white socks. "Chelsea is everyone's favorite beginner horse." I stepped back as Lena instructed Nicole in Horsemanship 101. When she was ready, Nicole bent a leg and Lena hoisted her into the saddle effortlessly. The look on Nicole's face was sheer unadulterated joy.

"Look at me! I'm riding a horse."

Lena and I both laughed. She looked adorable, but the horse wasn't moving. Lena adjusted both stirrups and tightened the cinch. With equal patience, she led Nicole around the ring two or three times giving pointers. Finally, she handed her the reins and directed her on what to do.

Anticipating this momentous occasion, I had brought my camera and started taking pictures. If I ever wanted to retire with a great deal of money,

I could sell these pictures to the tabloids. This was pretty scandalous. Well, actually, the raunchy scene in our kitchen earlier might have been a little more scandalous.

After about forty-five minutes, Nicole was done. I watched with amusement as Lena lifted Nicole down to the ground. Lena just nodded her head as Nicole spoke animatedly. Clearly, she had enjoyed herself and I had enjoyed watching her. Her jeans fit her like an expensive pair of gloves and I chuckled. She had selected a pale blue sleeveless shirt with white stripes and the *pièce de résistance*: bright red leather western boots. When I turned around, I found half the women on the patio were standing to watch. I was not the only one admiring her.

I edged closer and heard her thanking Lena profusely. She turned when she saw me and beamed. Soon we were walking arm in arm back to the house.

"That was so much fun," Nicole gushed. "I would love to come again and learn more. Why did you not ride?"

"I have in the past, I just didn't feel like it today. But I'm glad you enjoyed yourself."

We each got something to drink after I asked what she wanted. The winner was lemonade. And then we found a large chaise lounge on which to sit. Nicole sat on the foot of the lounge until she finished her lemonade and then managed to scoot between my legs until she was leaning against my chest. I felt proud and more than a little titillated. We were not the only couple being demonstrative, I noticed. The afternoon was winding down and the barbecue was smoking with all manner of specially prepared items. The guests were relaxed and happy.

The strong westerly breezes through the mountains had kept the temperature pleasant for most of the day, and as evening came both the wind and the high temperatures diminished. We sat with a small group of women, most of whom I'd known for years, and the conversation moved from politics, to history, to social networking. Nicole seemed quiet but attentive, and I was perfectly content to sit with her and share our connectedness.

Just before dinner, Nicole asked if we could take a walk. We followed a path between the two pastures to a small grove of trees near the rear of the property. Verdant green underbrush and bushes provided a screen of stillness, with sounds of distant crickets and an occasional dove calling her mate. We found ourselves alone in a natural chapel.

"Thank you so much for bringing me here. This has been the most delightful afternoon. I cannot remember when I ever felt this relaxed, and your friends are wonderful to me."

"I'm glad. It's exactly what I wanted for someone working as hard as you for the last few weeks. You deserved a real break." We stopped under a trimmed blue spruce.

She draped one arm across my shoulder and with the other hand stroked my face but said nothing. The look in her eye said it all, and I leaned forward to claim the kiss that was waiting for me. The electric circuit tripped as our bodies pressed close. Short, grabbing kisses interspersed with deep probing ones, and quickly the arousal I'd held in check was consuming me.

"Do you know why I wanted to go for a walk with you?" she said breathlessly.

I muttered something unintelligible into her neck.

She smiled and whispered in my ear, "Because I desperately wanted you to kiss me hard and make love to me."

I gulped lovingly and quite unromantically. "Now? Out here?"

"Are you embarrassed? Or perhaps you are not feeling as aroused as I am."

"Nicole, are you nuts? I'm quite sure that I am even more turned on, but how do you—"

She was already unbuttoning her blouse. "I think it will not take very long." She smiled again and pulled me behind the large tree where a woodsy darkness engulfed us. Once our mouths re-engaged, my rational brain short-circuited and my hands became slaves to Nicole's demanding needs.

An old-fashioned ranch triangle clanged loudly, summoning the guests to dinner. We pulled ourselves together and leisurely strolled back flushed, heaving, and hand in hand from our secret hideaway like two guilty teenagers. Nicole laughed loudly as she periodically groped my ass. The high color on her cheeks told the tale to anyone who cared to look, and they did.

Lena and Brenda had done this event for years, and it had become a drill. Three picnic tables sat end to end, covered with red, white, and blue tablecloths, and decorated with small flags. As each guest piled their plates with corn, chicken, ribs, burgers, potato salad, coleslaw, and cornbread, we took seats in rows facing each other.

I once again marveled at the appetite of the petite woman across from me. I was halfway through my meal when she went back for seconds, and when she returned she took a seat on the bench next to me. The beer and the wine had tempered the conversation to a more relaxed and more humorous level. One by one people started telling stories about past barbecues, each one funnier than the last.

Over the years, there had been some incredibly amusing incidents including riding mishaps, volleyball injuries, cheating girlfriends, as well as a number of people ending up in the swimming pool. At one of these stories Nicole turned to me. "They have a swimming pool as well?"

"Yes, behind that low building over there."

Her eyes lit up and the mischief returned. She whispered, "Does anyone ever go skinny-dipping?"

I had almost forgotten, but three years ago a small group did sneak off after dinner and did just that. I nodded.

She moved her hand to the top of my thigh and inched her way up. "Do you think they would let us do it again?"

I squirmed a little while my face flushed. "I think you'd have to ask." I wasn't sure how comfortable I felt about Nicole being naked with this pack of wolves.

Lena banged her beer can on the table. "Can I have your attention please? I have an announcement. My beautiful wife was generous enough to get us a karaoke machine." Shouts and applause erupted. "While I get the fireworks ready, please pick up one of the songbooks, find a favorite song, and entertain us with your talent."

We all made our way to the other end of the patio while Brenda and two volunteers cleaned up.

One by one, drunk or sober, some of my oldest friends marched up to the microphone to surprise us. Some of them were quite good, and several were downright funny.

"Come on, Meg. Why don't you two sing us something?"

Nicole looked over her shoulder and whispered, "Shall we?"

I suddenly caught a case of the stammers and couldn't seem to vocalize anything helpful.

She didn't push it but waited until I nodded. We skimmed the songbook, picked a number, and quickly strategized.

When the music started, Nicole took the lead. "Somewhere over the rainbow..." Her light coloratura floated across the patio without the microphone. She started very softly, and within a minute you could've heard a pin drop. I stood beside her watching the animated lyrics on the screen feeling my heart squeeze in my chest for the lyrical beauty I was hearing.

We'd spent weeks singing and rehearsing, but I'd never heard her sing something contemporary. Nicole completely captured the mood of the song, and it transported me to a farmhouse in Kansas. After she sang the first chorus, I joined her with a rather mediocre harmony, but since we'd been practicing together we knew how to blend our voices. When she sang the next verse, she stood facing me looking directly into my eyes, and when she finished there was a brief silence and then thunderous applause.

Everyone was on their feet crowding around us with congratulations and thanks. Nicole beamed, and

I was ecstatic. My only disappointment was the fact that my friend Liz had been out of town and unable to come to the barbecue. I would have really enjoyed having her here to meet Nicole and hear me sing.

The outdoors speakers erupted with sounds of John Philip Sousa followed by the cracks and pops of the fireworks show. We all went out into the yard to watch in wonder. Lena had selected an area far from the house and the stable, to avoid scaring the horses. Most of the display was relatively quiet, without whistling or other high-pitched sounds or even any loud explosions. Visually they were spectacular. It was a short display, and everyone was singing along with the world-famous Marches as we all drifted back to the patio.

We were among the last and right behind Tracey and Amy when Nicole said, "Let's go find the pool."

"Did you ask Lena?"

"Yes. She laughed at me and said to have fun."

Amy overheard us. "Hey, are you guys going skinny-dipping?"

"I guess we are now," I said, turning toward the pool area.

Nicole squealed, grabbed my hand, and off we went.

"Can we join you?"

Over her shoulder, Nicole yelled, "Sure."

When we got there, no lights were visible except the solar path lights and the sliver of a new moon. It took all four of us to fold back the solar cover, whispering as if this were a state secret. The moon reflected off the surface of the water. Suddenly tight jeans and shirts felt constrictive.

On opposite sides of the pool, Nicole and I

stripped down as Tracey and Amy were doing the same thing on the other side. I couldn't see them but I could hear the giggling. One by one, we jumped or slid into the water, eliciting stifled shrieks. Laughing and splashing consumed several minutes until Nicole spotted a beach ball. We tossed it around for a while until the other couple lost interest. Apparently, we all had the same idea because soon we were on opposite sides of the shallow end and all that anyone could hear now was whispering and gentle splashing.

It came as no surprise to me when Nicole swam up behind me, encircling my waist with her body pressed against my back. "Are you enjoying yourself?" I asked softly.

"More than I ever thought. I cannot remember when I have had so much fun." Both hands were on my breasts, gently massaging them. "I like to be without clothes, *n'est-ce pas*?"

"I noticed." I was beginning to realize that it was probably not just immodesty, but Nicole might actually consider herself a naturalist. There would be no arguments from me, although I tended to be more conventional. I pulled her around in front of me and ran my hands from her shoulders to her lovely derriere, pulling her close to me. "I like everything about your body, watching it move, touching it, kissing it, biting it, and feeling the way it presses against my own." With each example, I demonstrated.

The water was refreshing and enhanced the sensations we were experiencing. Like magnets, our mouths drew together repeatedly. Nicole's kisses were full and rich, each one filling me with contentment.

The escalating passion dampened when two, and then three, and finally six other people discovered our secret. Although the area was dark and quite secluded, I selfishly wanted Nicole to myself and encouraged her to leave with me. Reluctantly, we got out of the pool and grabbed our clothes. I pulled her around to the front door of the house where we could sneak into the bathroom unnoticed.

Grabbing a towel, I covered myself and retrieved both of our bags from the bedroom. The extra change of clothes had been a good idea, because pulling on a pair of jeans while damp was not a comfortable endeavor. Getting dressed, however, took a little longer than usual because, evidently, neither one of us was finished kissing.

"I am sorry to be such a pest, but you make me greedy," Nicole said, holding my face tightly.

"I know." I pushed her against the bathroom door. "If we don't get out of here soon, these clothes will be back on the floor. We need to go outside." I groaned, wishing I could just drag her into the bedroom, which I probably could do without anyone batting an eye. Good Lord, I *was* a horny teenager. One would think I never had sex before in my life and now I couldn't get enough.

She captured my mouth again and said, "We could go out to the car."

"No, that's where I put my foot down. I'd sooner go back in the woods than to try and squeeze into the back seat of a car."

She laughed. "You are probably right. Can we go back in the woods?"

"My God, woman, are you serious?"

Her grip on my hair and her tongue in my mouth told me wordlessly that she was completely serious and that there would be no further discussion.

I embraced her and kissed her as tenderly as I could manage. "Let's join the others for a little while, enjoy a glass of wine, and then we'll take a walk. Deal?"

Nicole put on her best pout, although her eyes were twinkling. "As you wish."

I put both bags by the front door and took her hand. "Try to be a lady, will ya?"

She erupted with laughter as we joined the group at the bar. It took several minutes before somebody noticed that we both had wet hair. Teasing and rude comments ensued, while I raised one eyebrow and nodded, as if to say, "See?"

≋≋≋≋

One glass of wine did the trick, and by eleven we were hugging our hosts goodbye with promises of getting together again soon. Lena made Nicole promise to come for another riding lesson. Nicole agreed if they would join us for dinner one night.

The ride home was comfortable and quiet. Nicole held my hand and hummed softly to herself. I couldn't remember the last time I had enjoyed myself like that. Nicole filled my heart and showed me a new kind of joy.

As we turned north toward Tesuque, a cold chill interrupted my reverie. Tomorrow was the beginning of a big week: the opening of *La Traviata*, the meeting of both of our families, and the reappearance of Mario De Luca.

Act II Scene 15

The technical rehearsal was a chance for the crew to make sure all of the cues were correct, all of the set pieces worked, and the props were on hand. We were using the main stage and had only three hours to get everything right. There was another production waiting to do the same thing in the afternoon, and, of course, there was a performance that evening.

Everyone was on edge, and I tried very hard to stay out of the way by clinging to my little shelf space near the wall. I had my score open and was ready to make notes if anything changed, and to make sure Nicole didn't forget anything.

The temperatures were already in the eighties, and if the flushed faces were any indication, the cast and crew were overheated. Nicole was a seasoned trouper and had performed all over the world in less than ideal conditions. She was careful of her voice and managed her physical activities with ease. An atypical singer, Nicole didn't feel comfortable standing in one place singing—never had been. The multiple levels on the stage kept her moving and she never missed a beat. Stefan flubbed a couple of lines and became frustrated, while Nicole never lost her temper.

There were only a few instances where Nicole actually came offstage, and I managed to be there every time with water or juice and a towel. She stayed focused and we didn't talk. I understood. It was the way it had to be in order to maintain concentration.

Our morning did not start in the usual fashion, which was entirely my fault. I suggested she sleep in her room because we both needed rest, and after the day of temptation we'd had, I wasn't sure we would sleep if we were together. As a result, she was up early and had already finished vocalizing by the time I came in, which surprised me. The coffee was made and she was in the shower. When she appeared, there was a quick kiss and a "good morning," and she wanted to go. The playful nymphet from twenty-four hours before was gone. At first I thought she was angry because I didn't sleep with her, and then I realized that Nicole Bernard was in full production mode.

By twelve thirty, Lars called it a wrap. We had to clear out for the next cast but agreed to meet in the rehearsal hall at one thirty for notes.

"Are you all set?" I asked as Nicole joined me outside.

"Yes, I think so. Louise sent me a note about one of the costumes, so I will need to see her later today."

I made a note. "How about we go home for some lunch?"

She simply nodded and took the towel I handed her.

As soon as we were in the house, she headed for her room. "I'm going to take a quick shower, and I'll be right out."

I went out to the kitchen and put out the pasta salad. It was weird because we had essentially gone about twelve hours without any contact or even much communication. I felt a little pathetic, but I missed her. God, it was like withdrawal.

The table was set and I was just pouring the iced tea when she returned.

"I feel so much better. I was just drenched. That looks wonderful." She sat down at the table.

"How do you think the rehearsal went?" I said, not asking what I really wanted to know.

She wiped her lips with the napkin. "Fairly well. I think the technical aspects were fine, but I am concerned about Stefan. He is too nervous and forgets things. I think this afternoon we will have to work together some more."

"You're probably right. It's a good thing he's working with you and not someone else."

"Why?"

"You're very patient with him. Other actors are sometimes less kind, shall we say."

She continued to eat, the worried look remaining on her face. After I cleared the dishes, I had to ask. "Nicole, is everything all right?"

"What do you mean?" A look of genuine surprise covered her face.

"You just feel a little distant and I wanted to make sure you're not angry with me."

"Why would I be angry with you?"

"I don't know. I just wanted to check." Now I really felt pathetic.

She got up and walked over, smiled, and gave me a brief kiss and a pat on the cheek. "I have too much on my mind, and we should get going."

The afternoon rehearsal focused more on details of the scenes. Lars worked with the principals, and the accompanist worked through the large chorus scenes.

I slipped out after a few minutes to take a message to Louise in costumes and used the opportunity to make a phone call.

"Hey, Lena, it's Meg. I wanted to thank you for another incredible party. Every year you seem to outdo yourself."

"Thank you. It was fun, and we loved seeing everyone. I'm glad you had a good time, and I have to tell you, Nicole is really hot."

"She enjoyed herself, too. I've not seen her that relaxed and silly since we started working." It was true, and the memory warmed me.

"No question about the fact she enjoys your company. Man, you two were something else."

"Like I said, she was just having a good time."

"Are you trying to tell me there's nothing between you two? C'mon, Ellis. I've known you for too long and there's definitely some chemistry goin' on there."

"You wouldn't think that if you saw her today."

"What do you mean?"

"She's all business today. She's barely said ten words to me." It stung when I spoke the words aloud.

"Really, I'm surprised. I thought you two were headed for a very hot night," Lena said very sincerely.

"Not so much. I thought it would be better if she got a good night's sleep so she stayed up at the house."

"Meg, tell me, what's going on between you two? It looked to me like first love."

I knew better than to think we were anything like subtle. "I don't know. In all honesty, I think I might be a rebound girl. After all, she's legally separated from a bad situation and I think she's just playing for our team somewhat spitefully or out of need. Don't get me wrong, it's been incredible. Nicole is an amazing woman and we've gone places I never dreamed of, but that will likely be over in a couple of months."

"That's too bad, because she's a fantastic woman and you guys are good together. You should have heard the gossip after you left. There were some choice comments made by some of our more lecherous friends."

"I'm sure there were. I saw the way they were looking at her, and I understand why. She's all that and more. If circumstances were a little different…I don't know. She's made me do some serious thinking."

"Meg, never say never. If this is what you want, go for it. I'm no expert, but clearly she has feelings for you as well."

"Not today. As I said, she's all business right now and I'm her personal assistant."

"Hey, she has a job to do. Hang in there, tiger. She's worth it."

"Thanks again, and we'll get together soon, I promise." Maybe she was right. After hearing her words, I felt rather melodramatic. This show opened whether or not Nicole and I were flirting or fussing. Nicole was focused on her job, and it was time I did the same.

༄༅༅༅

Tuesday was not unlike Monday, except that it was a dress rehearsal. Nicole remained aloof and focused. She worked with Carl in the morning creating her part like the true artist she was. I remained attentive but in the background. This was when my assistance would prove its worth.

She had been somewhat resistant when I insisted on checking her blood sugar twice a day. It was clear to me that her energy expenditures had doubled and it would be in everyone's best interests to head off any problems. Eventually she conceded.

It had been almost forty-eight hours without her usual affection—not that I was counting—and I missed it. For several weeks, there had rarely been an opportunity when we were in close proximity that she didn't touch, hug, or kiss me. To be fair, she wasn't being affectionate with anyone else, either. Nicole had a laser focus and spent every free minute paging through the score.

We didn't get home until after eight and we were both exhausted. Lars had dinner brought in so we wouldn't have to stop. By the time he finished with his notes, he had thanked everyone and sent them home with instructions to rest, hydrate, and not abuse their voices.

"I could really use a glass of wine. How about you?" I asked, going to the refrigerator.

"Oh yes, that would be perfect, and maybe we could sit outside for a while."

We took our glasses out to the patio and stretched out, I in a lounge chair and Nicole on the glider, to watch the moonrise. "Meg, would you do me a favor?"

Such a question. "You know I will."

"I have not slept so well. Will you let me stay with you tonight?"

My heart did a backflip. "I…I thought you wanted to be alone so you could rest. It wasn't that I didn't want you, please know that."

"It is hard for me, Meg. I want to be with you very much. However, when we are together there is no sleep. It is not your fault I have poor self-control."

"Nicole, I've missed you." I could hear my voice crack and felt the lump in my throat.

"I know, *ma petite*, it is hard for me as well. I thought it would help me to focus on my work and yet still you are on my mind all the time. I see you everywhere and want very much for your hands to be touching me."

"Me too. But we may as well get used to it since we'll have company soon."

She dropped her head back against the glider. "*Mon Dieu, ma mère.*"

And your ex-husband.

"They will only stay a short time, because they are expected in San Francisco to visit my aunt."

"Do you think it would be easier if I went home for those few days?"

"Hell no!"

I laughed. Nicole seldom cursed like that.

"It will be okay, I am sure. I will just feel better if you are nearby. They will like you, I know, and we all will have some fun," she said.

"The most important thing is opening night. We have to focus on that."

"I know. You are right."

I crossed over to the glider and sat beside her, putting her legs across my lap. "Are you worried about it, the opening?" I began massaging her feet.

"No, not too much. Stefan is nervous and that can affect the others, but I think it will be all right."

There was something else, so I waited.

"That feels very good. I forgot our deal."

"Yeah, I owe you a few."

After a minute or two she opened her eyes and looked at me very seriously. "It's Mario. I am very afraid he will make a scene. He has a bad temper and he feels that I have humiliated him. If I try to keep him away, he will be vengeful."

"You don't have to see him. I'm sure he will just make a big entrance and leave." At least, that's what I hoped.

She looked skeptical. "Yes, that would be good."

"I won't leave your side."

"Promise me."

"I do. You will be safe. You only need to sing like an angel and give the audience a wonderful show."

She smiled weakly. "Will you make love with me?"

I reached for her hands and we descended the path to my guesthouse. My heart filled with joy as she awaited my touches. I took great care to undress her with tender words and gentle touches. Her arms opened to my embrace and our lips touched in a long-awaited reunion.

I made love to her with a reverence I had seldom felt. Her beautiful body was a sacred place in which I longed to dwell for a long time. The soft whimpers from her lips were the instructions I needed in order to please her.

Her climax was slow and deep, and she clung to me, her final kisses filled with tenderness and gratitude. My heart swelled to bursting as I wrapped her in my arms and we drifted off to sleep.

This woman brought me a joy that was hard to describe. We shared without motive, or selfishness. Every intimate moment moved us to a deeper level of connection. I didn't want to utter the word *commitment*. I felt as though we were consciously moving closer to the edge of something very serious and unbelievably wonderful. I had times of sheer delirious joy and happiness. Nicole Bernard had everything I ever dreamed I could want in a woman.

There were little pieces of me that had never seen the light of day, but with her I felt a willingness to be completely open physically, mentally, and emotionally. I wanted her to touch every piece of me. There was nothing I would withhold or deny her.

All I wanted in return was for her to teach me, teach me how to love, teach me to be generous and giving. Teach me to soar with her.

I woke to find she had gone. I felt a little sad but glad we were able to enjoy uninterrupted sleep.

She was finishing her yoga when I found her on her balcony wearing some lacy black panties. Only lacy black panties. Her back was to me as she moved through the poses. I watched in silence, admiring the graceful way she moved, every gesture measured and precise.

I backed away and went to start breakfast. Today would need to be low stress. *Maybe we should take a ride or just get out of the house for a while. She can decide.*

Since it was after eight, I called the office.

"Hi, Thad. Is Greta in yet?"

"No, she had to make a stop in Santa Fe this morning. Are you psyched for the opening?"

"We're ready. I think Nicole will be brilliant. Tell me something. What kind of security do you have around here?"

"Well, we have a company that monitors the property twenty-four seven and we have volunteers to help on performance nights. What were you concerned about?"

"I just wondered about backstage access. Can anybody get backstage?"

"The stage crew usually monitors that pretty carefully. What's up, Meg?" Thad sounded concerned.

I might as well say something. "Well, originally Nicole asked that her husband not attend the opening night performance. Then she relented, because he threatened to make a stink. She's a little worried about him making an appearance, and I think it would be better if she had no distractions."

"Let me check with Greta when she comes in. I'm sure there are some kind of plans for this kind of thing. Thanks for letting us know early. I'm really glad you're keeping an eye on her."

I smiled. *Eye on her.* Hell, there was very little I hadn't had on her. *Nasty. You are just nasty, Ellis.* "I appreciate it, Thad."

"Meg, can I ask you a personal question?"

"Sure."

"I've been hearing rumors about you and Nicole being very 'chummy' and wondered if there was any truth to the gossip."

Fuck. "Thad, Nicole and I work very closely and spend a lot of time together. Being her personal assistant—"

"Meg, I would never say anything, you know that. I was just being nosy, forgive me."

"I think it's best everyone focus on the opening, right now. Thanks, Thad. Talk to you later."

It shouldn't have come as a surprise. Summer liaisons happened all the time. That's how I met Bekka. I fell in love for the first time with the hottest member of the stage crew and we embarked on a whirlwind romance. There was a lot of sneaking around backstage, unused rehearsal rooms, utility closets. The environment was rife with drama. Like many good things, however, the relationship with the hot crewmember crashed because of my all-consuming post-op depression after the cancer.

Nicole appeared just before ten looking very relaxed. I decided not to say anything about my conversation with Thad. "Did you sleep well, Madame?"

Her sparkling smile should have been answer enough. "As a matter of fact, I did. You see, I was very relaxed and comfortable."

She strutted across the kitchen until we were standing nose to nose. "And what about you? How was your sleep?"

Her lips were brushing mine as she spoke. I couldn't focus because her eyes were so near, and the proximity gave me a little thrill. "I slept well because I was exhausted, also a little lonely."

Our breasts were touching as her lips continued to lightly brush mine, sending ripples down my spine. "That is so sad. Do you miss your pet so much? Pearson, yes? Maybe you would like to have him in your bed with you."

"You're right. Maybe it's Pearson I miss." I stood transfixed, unable to decide what she was doing.

She trailed her lips across my cheek to below my ear, as if she were uncertain where she wanted to plant them. Every nerve in my body was on high alert, and I could feel heat rising up my chest to my neck and ears. I could barely hear her soft words.

"You smell good."

I had to put my hand on the kitchen counter to steady myself. This was a new kind of torture, and I wasn't certain if I was experiencing pain or pleasure.

"Nicole?"

"Um-hm."

"Would you like some breakfast?" I said so weakly I could hardly recognize my own voice.

She trailed her tongue back to my lips with a deliberate intent.

"Yes."

"Okay, are you...are you going to kiss me anytime soon? Because I'm going a little crazy here."

Her laugh rippled up through her body as she put both hands on my face. "Of course I am."

I'm sure I didn't breathe for a couple of minutes as she thoroughly took me prisoner. I surrendered instantly. Moments like this I would happily give up breathing, eating, or sleeping.

Over the surprise French toast, I offered several options for the day, ignoring the most obvious one.

"Yes, I need to get out and get my mind away from this production. Maybe we could go shopping?"

"Would you like to go to Santa Fe? Or would you like to go down to Albuquerque?"

"Maybe we would go to Albuquerque today. I have not been there in years. We could walk around a little bit then maybe stop for dinner on the way home."

"Sure, an easy day with no stress."

※※※※

I parked in the public a lot just east of Old Town, and we followed the path to some of the local shops. We leisurely wandered through small boutiques, art galleries, and several requisite tourist stops. The heat was oppressive, and we slipped into the dark cool air of the church on the plaza. San Felipe de Niri, built in 1793, was the oldest building in the city, which was founded in 1706. The area had an old-world feel even though much had changed around it.

After walking around the square and visiting several shops, we paused as the sun began to dip behind the trees near the river. Nicole looked tired and I felt the same way.

"Are you ready to head back?"

"Yes. I think I could do with a nap."

"Deal. You can snooze in the car on the way to Santa Fe. We could stop and pick up a couple of hamburgers on the way home."

"That would be perfect. I don't mean to be a bore, I just feel so empty," she said.

"You're tired, I understand. It's been crazy but it will be over soon. Are you feeling nervous at all?"

"Not too much. I would like to sing a little in the morning and then I think I will be ready." She yawned.

It took a little maneuvering to get out of Albuquerque at that time of day, but soon we were on the highway headed north. It had been a comfortable day for both of us. I felt close and connected but without pressure. As we drove, her hand lay loosely draped across my leg, her eyes closed.

Moments like this I wanted to bottle, to enjoy this sweet liqueur one day when I was feeling lonely because she was gone. We still had weeks ahead, but I didn't want to fall into a state of complacency because I didn't want to miss a single memory. I would recount this summer to my grandchildren one day. Well, maybe.

I stopped briefly in Santa Fe at Blake's Lotaburger for their highly acclaimed green chile cheeseburgers. I snuck out of the car while she slept. She only stirred a little when I started the car and then drifted back to sleep.

She was nestled against the door with her leg tucked under her, and once again the sight of her sleeping caused butterflies in my chest. I allowed myself to fantasize a little about what it would be like to be with Nicole not just for a few months, but also for years.

Could I give up everything to travel with her and be her real personal assistant wherever she went? Where would we live? Would we be legally married somewhere and have children? Would our families understand this? How would it feel to give up my career, or could I still do some kind of work to maintain some dignity?

And Nicole—could she love me enough to want me and be willing to share her life? She was a wonderful, mercurial woman who astounded me at every turn, but I couldn't honestly say whether it was infatuation or true love. I only knew I wanted to be with her in every possible sense of the word.

She woke suddenly when I turned into the garage, oriented herself, and then noticed the sack of food.

"I guess I conked out. I am so sorry. I must be a terrible companion."

I grabbed the food bag. "*Au contraire*, you are a delightful companion asleep or awake."

She bumped me with her shoulder. "You are just being too kind."

"I first thought we could eat outside, but it's too hot," I said as I put the food on the table.

"Wouldn't it be nice to have a pool like your friends do?"

"Well, you do have a hot tub."

"That's the problem. It's hot." She grinned.

"I can turn the temperature down and take the cover off. It might be comfortable in a little while."

❧❧❧❧

I reluctantly slipped out of Nicole's bed early and made my way down to the guesthouse. The whole notion about the hot tub became a moot point after we finished eating. For some unknown reason, we ended up in a very intense discussion about her character, Violetta Valery.

In her interpretation, the woman who lived as a courtesan was the only character capable of unconditional love. The fact that she gave up Alfredo so that his sister could marry allowed her to triumph over her happiness.

I'd argued that the reason she gave him up was that she knew she was dying and thought he'd be better off without her. We both agreed that the end of the scene, when she gives him the locket with her picture and says to give it to the woman he will find to love, marked her last selfless gesture. She says to him, "Tell her I did this for you."

We continued that conversation as we cleaned up the kitchen, locked up the house, stripped naked, and crawled into her bed together. The kisses and caresses were warm and welcome, and both of us drifted off to sleep quickly. I only woke up once and snuck into the bathroom. Coming back into the bedroom, I stopped suddenly to look at her sleeping. Again. I couldn't imagine ever getting tired of looking at her like this, and when I crawled back under the sheets and moved close to her, I held my breath. I was afraid when I slipped my arm around her that she would be able to feel the pounding in my chest. Resisting the urge to caress her pained me.

In the morning, showered and dressed, I finally allowed myself to think about the opening night. In the past I had attended opening night for several operas, and there was an absolute adrenaline high for every one of them—even when I wasn't performing. Nicole was going to be brilliant. Her voice was so well suited to this role and she looked breathtakingly beautiful.

On impulse, I pulled out my cell phone and dialed home. "Hi, Mom. Are you in the middle of something or can you talk?"

"Hi, honey, what a lovely surprise. Your dad just left for work and I was making a sandwich."

"I just wanted to talk a minute. I feel neglectful since I haven't called you very much. I'm looking forward to seeing you both on Sunday."

"We're both so excited, but isn't tonight your opening?"

"Yes, that's partially why I'm up so early. Couldn't sleep."

"Are you worried, honey?"

"No, just excited. I think it'll be a wonderful production."

"I'm sure it will be. Ms. Bernard is very lucky to have you to help her."

"Well, it's been kind of mutual. I have a surprise for you. Nicole's teaching me to sing again." I sounded nervous.

"Oh Meg, that's wonderful! You can't imagine how happy that makes me." It thrilled her, as I knew it would. My mom wanted me to sing as much as I did. Maybe more. Performing had always been her dream but it never happened. The closest she ever came was the recitals her students gave.

"I know. I'm pretty excited. Mom, I was really afraid I might never be able to sing again and I know you and Dad were, too. Nicole has been so patient and kind. Well, it's not perfect yet, but I'm much more confident."

"Isn't that just the answer to a prayer? I mean, who would have thought after so many years that a wonderful singer would come along and…"

I could hear her voice crack with emotion.

"I know, I feel really lucky. Hey, we have a lot to do today. I'd better get up to the house. I love you, Mom."

"I love you too, sweetie. We'll be thinking about you, and please give Ms. Bernard our thanks."

I stuck the phone in my pocket and wiped my eyes with the back of my hand. *You have no idea how lucky I am, Mom.*

Once I got the hot tub recovered, I went in and started the coffee. Carl would be here at nine and I hoped for some very smooth rehearsal time. My ears perked up when I heard humming from down the hall. The lady was awake. I continued reading my email and answering a few until she was ready.

"*Bonjour, amie.* Is that coffee I smell?"

I stood up and received a warm hug and a kiss on both cheeks. "You are up so early. I looked everywhere for you." Her arms were loose around my neck.

"I wanted you to be able to sleep as long as possible, and I couldn't be trusted to just lie there and look at you." That was the truth.

Her chuckle rippled through my body. "I understand. I was awake even earlier to just watch you breathe. It was hard."

The butterflies took off and I hugged her close to me, enjoying the comfort and the warm scent of her skin. "There are the croissants that we bought in Old Town and some raspberry jam if you'd like, or I can cook some eggs."

"Oh yes, the croissants. I nearly forgot."

※ ※ ※ ※

Her session with Carl lasted over two hours, and I helped a couple of times when she felt she needed me. I was reading in the living room when he left, and watched as Nicole grabbed a water bottle and began to pace. I didn't say anything because she just looked like she was thinking about something.

"Meg, is there anything I am forgetting?"

"I don't think so. It wouldn't hurt for us to run over to wardrobe a little bit later just to be sure everything is okay. You're scheduled for makeup at seven. Is there anything you want me to do?"

She continued to pace and then stopped. "Would you think I was crazy if I would ask you to massage my feet again?"

"Of course not, but would you like a regular massage? I can call and schedule one."

"Could you do it and we would not have to go anywhere?"

"Yes, I guess. It would depend on what kind of a massage you were looking for." I wasn't sure if she wanted her muscles relaxed or she wanted something else, and I didn't want to misread that.

She walked over and stood in front of me looking very serious. "For a little while, I would like very much not to think about the opera at all. I would like to clear my mind. I tried yoga this morning but was not able to quiet my mind. But, you can always make me forget my troubles. Please?"

"Whatever will make you feel relaxed, I will gladly oblige," I said while a trip hammer kicked into high gear and a flush spread instantly to my extremities. I stood up, took her outstretched hand, and followed her to the bedroom.

She started to unbutton her shirt and looked over at me. "Do you ever feel uncomfortable that I am so forward with you?"

"Not really uncomfortable. Surprised, I guess. Look, Nicole, as you pointed out we're both adults and I think it's pretty obvious how aroused I get just being in the same room with you. The only reason I'm so restrained is out of respect for your position here. If our paths had crossed under different circumstances, I'm not sure I would be able to maintain self-control." I walked closer to her and touched her face with my palms. "Feel free to loosely interpret 'personal assistant' in any way you choose."

"Thank you, dear and personal assistant. I would greatly enjoy some of your massage mastery."

I stood by admiringly as she removed her clothes and stretched out on the bed while the ambient temperature in the room rose. I went into the bathroom to wash my hands, check my libido, and retrieve her bottle of lotion.

Some serious concentration was required. I diligently covered every surface of her body with the lightly scented lotion, allowing my fingers to study every curve and sinew with not only my hands but also my eyes. My own body thrummed with exhilaration as my hands caressed her warm, flushed tissues.

Her groans and sighs controlled not only my movements but also my pulse and blood pressure. I took special care with her hands and feet, because of their sensitivity.

When I gently rolled her onto her back, her open eyes were dark and unfocused. Her breathing was ragged. "Kiss me there," she whispered. I bent over her and carefully, deliberately, unleashed my lips and tongue to finish the mission.

Delirious with joy—every motion, every breath, every sweet taste of her transported me to a higher plane. My own body rippled with little electrical currents as she reached a pleasurable crescendo.

We lay together breathing heavily, her with exhaustion and me with need. In a very hoarse voice, I heard her say, "Take your clothes off now."

It was a struggle to stand on rubbery legs, but it took only a minute to step out of my shorts and yank my tank top free. She opened her arms to me and the heat of our bodies collided. We moved together slowly as first her hands and then her mouth claimed me. I could no longer think. My core melted and my brain was close to exploding. Her hands were everywhere and my breathing became deeper and more difficult to control. Sensations of raw carnal pleasure overwhelmed my cognition.

I heard my voice crying out over and over, helpless with sexual bombardment and desperate need for relief. My hips jerked, my back arched, and my breasts throbbed. When I could no longer stand it, she dragged me over the edge of resistance and I cried out her name.

Covered with wetness, hers and mine, I willingly succumbed, blowing out the air of delicious defeat.

She stroked my damp forehead. "You know, I am not thinking too much about work right now."

Act III Scene 1

I'll be back in a few minutes and find you in the dressing room."

"All right. Meg, please stay close even if I seem to be ignoring you. I am sometimes not present because of the part. It will help me to know you are there."

"I will be, promise. However, even if you're not fully there, take the water when I give it to you. Break a leg."

She kissed me quickly but hard and got out of the car. I drove down the hill and parked. As I walked backstage, I replayed the afternoon antics. We were both nervous. Turns out, an afternoon in bed was surprisingly relaxing. We talked about silly things, like childhood memories and first pets.

Somewhere earlier Thad had sent me a text message that there would be a new security guard just to keep an eye out for Mario. He wished us luck and said he would see us later. I didn't mention this to Nicole; she had enough on her mind. It wasn't realistic to think Mario De Luca would fly out here to make an ass of himself. However, it wasn't my job to make assumptions or to figure him out. It was my job to make sure that Nicole Bernard was healthy, happy, and ready to give the performance of her life.

For the occasion, I wore black slacks and a lightweight black shirt. Hopefully, I wouldn't die of heat prostration, but I wanted to be invisible moving around in the wings. Nicole would have a few moments between scenes and a longer break during the Act Two intermission, and I intended to be prepared if she needed my help. I made sure there would be a chair in the area of her exits and entrances, and it became my post.

By eight thirty, the house was nearly half-full. Many of the audience members had come as early as six o'clock to tailgate. A tradition of longstanding, theatergoers would bring elaborate picnic dinners, candelabras, and dine alfresco before the show. It was a sight to see as people assembled in groups as small as two people or as large as eight, dining on a couple of beach chairs in the parking lot, or even full tables and chairs adorned with tablecloths and crystal.

The pavilion sat on a broad mesa overlooking the Sangre de Cristo Mountains to the east and the spectacular sunsets to the west. Although designed as an outdoor venue, the pavilion was covered with swooping roof panels with side baffles to protect it from wind. The acoustics were world class, and each patron had a small screen for the Electronic Libretto System on the seat in front of them. The only element that wasn't wholly controlled by a state-of-the-art system was the lighting; turning off the "house lights" effectively meant waiting for dusk to darken enough to create a theatrical environment. Though that meant later start times in the summer, the opportunity to witness the exquisite backdrop created by the waning sunlight against the mountains was worth driving home after midnight.

I wandered downstairs for the last time and listened to the hum of excited voices preparing for that spectacle known as "opening night." Nicole was dressed in an elegant cardinal red satin strapless ball gown with a rhinestone belt. Her auburn wig adorned with curls and her makeup was perfect; she was the quintessential Violetta Valery. She was singing scales as she paced back and forth. *Break a leg, dear lady,* I wished silently and headed back upstairs. I wished the same to each of the cast members that I met along the way.

 I took my seat and waited as the orchestra tuned up. I peeked around the corner and watched as the audience members filled in their seats. The eclectic attendees were dressed in a wide array of fashion from ultra-casual to ultra-dressy and everything in between. The Santa Fe Opera had fans from every lifestyle. The number of young patrons was especially heartening.

 At last, the conductor made his entrance from under the stage, and the house stilled instantly. Behind the open stage, the sun was setting when the first cords from the overture sounded. I had goose bumps of anticipation. The chorus filed on stage singing and soon from upstage, Nicole Bernard made her spectacular entrance. Every eye was on her. From that moment on the show was hers.

 The first act flew by with only the tiniest missteps. No one would have guessed. I was waiting when Nicole exited and handed her the water bottle as I carefully dabbed at her perspiring forehead and neck. She sat quietly catching her breath as I knelt beside her.

 Immediately one of the women from costumes appeared to help her change into her Act Two dress, which was far more casual. They also swapped out her wig for something less showy.

 As soon as the set was complete, the conductor

began the music. She squeezed my hand briefly and made her entrance.

The second and third acts went perfectly, and Nicole was as strong as I had ever seen her. The set change from the party scene to her cold, bleak room took a little longer, which gave her a moment to prepare for the solemn mood of the fourth act.

Nicole had elected to go without the wig, just wearing her hair short and combed back. Someone from makeup applied a pale foundation and some dark shadows for her eyes. Appropriate, I thought, for a woman's final farewell. She stood barefoot in only a white nightgown on a darkened stage with one spotlight. Many who had played the part insisted on stylish hair and makeup even for a death scene. Not Nicole.

Nicole was an actor, and she took this part very seriously.

When the final lines faded and Violetta lay sprawled on the bed in Alfredo's arms, the house erupted in applause.

I watched with tears in my eyes until the lights dimmed and she finally stood up and ran offstage. She barely had time to catch her breath before joining the cast for the final bow, and there were two more curtain calls.

Backstage was crowded as I made my way through the stagehands and chorus to get downstairs, along with a few well-wishers who had gotten past security.

Once I reached the dressing room, I could see Lars, her fellow cast members, and the conductor congratulating Nicole. I chose an inconspicuous spot near the door and just waited. Thad and Greta found me on their way out.

"Margaret, wasn't that marvelous?" Greta gave me an unexpected hug.

Thad followed suit, gushing. "Omigod, she was incredible—totally awesome—and her voice is to die for. You must be so proud because she told me how much you've supported her. Meg, honest to God, she told me she didn't know what she would have done without you. For real!"

"You've done a great job, Margaret, and I'm very grateful for everything you've done for Nicole." Greta shook my hand again. "You both deserve to celebrate."

"Thank you. It was a terrific show, they pulled out all the stops."

They disappeared around the corner and I glanced into the dressing room. Nicole was still holding court and all I could do was grin like an idiot. I felt proud, happy, and enthralled.

The hair on the back of my neck prickled as I heard a familiar voice. I looked around and didn't see anyone until an attractive dark-haired man came around the corner. I looked for the security guard and didn't see him.

There was a brief moment of panic, and then I stepped towards the doorway.

"Mario, nice to see you." My voice quivered with nervousness.

"Ah yes, I have forgotten your name...the gay assistant, right?" He managed to keep a smile on his face, but his words held a snarky tone.

I bristled. "It's Meg. Can I help you with something?" Face-to-face, he was a good half foot taller than I was.

"Yes, I'm here to see my wife." The cocky grin made me nervous. Where in the hell was security?

"Mario," I said more softly. "She doesn't want to see you tonight. Maybe you could just leave quietly."

His face clouded and his genial expression disappeared. "How dare you? I don't think it's any of your business. This is a private matter." Spittle jetted from his mouth, and he moved closer.

I looked around quickly. Where the fuck was the security guard? "She agreed to let you come to the opening, so please be respectful and don't make a scene." I edged closer to the doorway, blocking it.

"Who do you think you are to tell me what to do? Get out of my way." He wasn't that big, but he was angry.

"Please leave. Don't make me call security." Before I knew what happened, he shoved me roughly into the wall where I collided with a fire extinguisher. I fell to the floor and looked up as a very tall man grabbed Mario by the arm and spun him around.

"You'll need to leave, mister," he said, the threat evident. Mario yelped a little as he was escorted down the hall.

Thad appeared along with someone from costumes who helped me to my feet. Thad said, a little too loudly, "My God, you're bleeding!" That brought several other people with towels and advice.

"I'm okay, it's just a little cut." Resistance was futile, and soon I was hustled to a first aid area where a paramedic cleaned the area above my right eyebrow and applied a couple of Steri-Strips.

"It could use a few stitches. You might want to go to the emergency room, especially since it's on your face."

"Oh, I agree. It looks horrible. Maybe you need an X-ray," Thad said nervously.

I looked in the mirror. It wasn't too bad, and I needed to get back to Nicole.

By the time I reached the dressing room, it had cleared out except for two or three people. Nicole had changed into street clothes and removed most of her makeup. She looked in the mirror, saw me in the reflection, and spun around.

"What happened?" Her voice was high, her alarm evident.

"It's nothing. I hit my head on the fire extinguisher. Are you ready to go?"

Hopefully, it was clear I did not want to talk about it, but I knew she wouldn't let it go.

I picked up her bag along with my things. Nicole said goodnight to people we passed and thanked them as we exited the building.

"Are you sure you are all right? Because one of the regular patrons invited us for a glass of champagne in the parking lot. Would you like to do that, or should we go home?" Nicole asked.

"Sure, I'm fine. Why don't you go ahead? I'll get the car and meet you."

She looked uncertain, then said, "They are waiting near the picnic tables."

"I'll find you. It's okay, you go." I smiled, hoping I looked better than I felt. My head was pounding and the last thing I wanted to do was socialize, but I reasoned that if I took my time getting the car she might already be done with her champagne and maybe we could go home.

My neck muscles were tight and my guts in a knot. I was still angry with myself that I hadn't used better judgment and found the security guard first thing. I was embarrassed that I got hurt. And I was furious with Mario, the arrogant prick. But in the greater scheme, I reasoned, the outcome was the important part—Nicole didn't see him.

I felt no need to rush to join the line of cars waiting to exit the parking lot. A lovely *joie de vivre* permeated the atmosphere; happy patrons were taking their time and savoring the evening. The rear lot had a side road, and I swerved around to reach the main lot without too much hassle. Parking the car on the west side of the lot, I checked the mirror on the visor and tried to pull my hair across my forehead to cover the cut. *Put on your game face, Ellis.*

Nicole spotted me immediately and reached out her hand. "Oh, here she is. Meg, join us, please. Eleanor, this is my wonderful assistant Meg Ellis. I don't know how I would've done this without her help."

One of the men handed me a champagne glass, and Nicole clinked hers to mine and beamed at me. Her warm expression salved my injured pride and throbbing head.

"Thank you. I deserve no credit for your brilliance." And with that, everyone started applauding.

It was a lovefest that Nicole richly deserved. I quietly took a seat behind her, hoping to stay out of further conversation.

The stall strategy didn't work exactly as I had hoped. Nicole had finished her glass of champagne and was now enjoying her second. I understood fully that the adrenaline rush of the performance would take a while to wear off. Six people were sitting comfortably around a folding picnic table, none younger than forty, all hanging on her every word. Nicole mesmerized them with her anecdotes.

The table glittered with champagne glasses, a candelabrum, and silver plates covered with appetizers. Stars shone brilliantly overhead, and the warm, dry air cooled to a comfortable temperature. The mesa overlooked the dark desert and the glow of Santa Fe lights seemed distant.

It was after midnight by the time we got home, and Nicole was still riding an adrenaline high from the evening. She chattered about her nervousness, the exhilaration after the first aria, and her fear when Stefan almost forgot his lines.

We both stood in the kitchen, I rinsing some glasses and Nicole scrounging in the refrigerator. She finally settled for a bottle of water and stopped when I turned to face her. I wasn't sure what it looked like in the glaring kitchen light.

"*Mon Dieu*, let me see your face," she demanded, touching my cheek gently. "There's so much blood. I had no idea, why didn't you tell me? Sit down and let me clean your face."

"It was an accident. I'm all right." In truth, I hadn't even gotten a good look at my appearance and was embarrassed that I joined the post-performance party looking like a defeated prizefighter.

"No, you're not. Already the bruising is near your eye and there is blood in your hair and on your shirt." She pulled one of the kitchen stools to the sink and pointed. With a clean dish towel, she patiently washed the area around the injury, including my hair and my neck.

"Ouch!" I squealed. The area was more tender than I thought.

She was ringing the towel and looking at me.

"There is something you are not telling me."

"It's nothing, and it's all over. No harm done." I avoided her intent stare.

She lifted my chin and held it. "Meg, you have never lied to me, and I can see it in your eyes something is very wrong."

"I don't want you to be upset, promise?" She nodded. "I had a little run-in with Mario. He wanted to come into the dressing room and I asked him not to. He tried to push me out of the way and I fell and hit my face against the fire extinguisher. The security guard showed up and escorted him from the building. That's all."

Those pale blue eyes turned very dark as she set her jaw. She picked up the closest thing at hand—her water bottle—and hurled it at the wall, cursing.

"The bastard! It is not enough that he humiliates me and ruins my life, now he attacks you. I will kill him!"

"Nicole." She wasn't listening. "Nicole, listen to me. It's all over and he's gone." I took one of her fisted hands and carefully brought it to my lips. "It's okay."

She was shaking with anger. I waited until her breathing slowed and then pulled her a little closer so I could put my arms around her waist. Her body was rigid, but I held on. Eventually, she rested both hands on my shoulders.

"We both knew this would be a possibility and it could have been much worse. Nobody saw him do it and I'm sure he was gone before he could make any noise. Let's not allow Mario to ruin this beautiful night. Please."

Nicole rested her chin on the top of my head. "Oh, my dear Meg, what have I dragged you into?"

"You haven't dragged me into anything. I'm here because that's my job, and I'm in your arms because it's the only place I want to be."

Her lips pressed against my forehead and I could feel the teardrop on my face. I had no idea what she was feeling at that moment, but I refused to let go of her.

I tucked my head under her chin and rubbed her back gently. "You were brilliant tonight, and even after I saw dozens of rehearsals you still took my breath away and reached into my heart. I'm not the only one who loved you tonight. A thousand hearts were broken, all at one time. And when we wake up tomorrow, it will be a new day and your family will be here to share your joy."

Pulling back a little, she stroked my face with the backs of her fingers and looked into my eyes with a mixture of wonder and tenderness.

"Stay with me tonight so I'm not alone and I do not worry."

Act III Scene 2

"Stupid. A registered nurse who doesn't have the sense to use ice on an injury. How dumb can anybody get? Look at you." I leaned closer to the bathroom mirror to get a better look at the large bruise on the right side of my face. "That's going to be tough to hide," I muttered.

I looked in the medicine cabinet hoping to find some acetaminophen for my persistent headache. The throbbing pain was the only reason that I'd left Nicole's warm bed so early. I quietly closed the bedroom door and headed to the kitchen to make a strong pot of coffee. Nicole hadn't mentioned what time she expected her mother, but I wanted to be ready. Looking around at the recently cleaned house, I had to admit with great relief that Maria did a spectacular job and everything was sparkling.

I headed down to the guesthouse to get ready. No matter how nice the house looked, when the disfigured personal assistant came in she would look like the loser in a bar brawl. The other scenario was that the diva had an uncontrollable temper and had smacked me. She did have quite a temper, as I had witnessed.

Nice first impression for the family, Ellis. Classy, ya know?

The warm shower felt good on some surprisingly sore muscles in my shoulder and neck. I was careful to keep the water off the Steri-Strips so they wouldn't come loose. Señor De Luca had shoved me harder than I thought because new bruises on my shoulder and right leg were just starting to make their presence known. I suppose the adrenaline had kept me from noticing. His words echoed in my head. I didn't know how long I could keep his nasty accusations from her. And I didn't know with whom he may have shared his opinion.

Covering the bruises necessitated some longer shorts and a baggier T-shirt. I didn't have foundation makeup and rarely used eye makeup, so I wasn't quite sure how I could hide this. Hopefully, Nicole could help.

She was waiting in the kitchen when I returned to the house and just stared at me when I came in.

"Do you think I will be arrested for assaulting you?" She said seriously, but her eyes twinkled.

"I wouldn't dream of pressing charges, because I enjoy being assaulted by you." I proved my point by soundly kissing her. To her credit, she didn't resist and responded readily.

"You know, not only is your voice getting better," she practically purred. "Your lips are stronger." We both started to laugh, each having our images of what strong lips could do.

Her thumb stroked my cheek as she shook her head. "Does it hurt so much?"

"No. I was foolish and forgot to put ice on it, so the bruise got larger. I'm afraid it looks worse than it is, and I'm going to be embarrassed when I see your family."

"I think I can help cover it. Oh, I got a phone call earlier. Their flight is delayed and they will not arrive until mid-afternoon."

"I'll let Thad know so he can check the arrivals," I said, retrieving my cell phone. Thad was on speed dial by now.

Nicole busied herself with eggs and cheese while I toasted some bagels. As I waited for the bagels, I watched her move about the kitchen. Her jeans fit like a glove, a short T-shirt teased, and her lovely feet were bare. It took very little imagination to remember the beautiful curves on her naked body as she slept. My heart felt fluttery again, as it did whenever I realized how lucky I was to be enjoying whatever kind of relationship we had.

My heart was on my sleeve, but I wasn't sure about Nicole's feelings. I knew she was fond of me and appreciated what I did for her. And I didn't think either one of us would question the intense physical passion we shared. Sex with Nicole was unlike anything I had ever experienced in my life. Every time I thought that it couldn't get any better, I was wrong. We both acted as students and teachers. The result was immensely satisfying.

No matter how passionate the lovemaking, neither of us shared the kind of endearments that might indicate a deeper relationship. Even the idea of taking it to that level seemed impossible because of the various obstacles we both faced. After this contract was complete, Nicole had projects in New York and in Europe. If Mario continued to fight the divorce, he might drag me into it.

I had at least two more years on my contract with the school district. Even if I didn't, my income was not enough to travel, especially with the lingering medical bills. And yet both of us continued to push the boundary on how much we were willing to share, at least physically.

This was a bizarre situation to be sure.

She served up the plates and I added the buttered bagels. I brought the orange juice and coffee to the table and we sat down together.

"Do you want to know one of the things I like the very best?" she said.

"Tell me."

"I very much enjoy starting every day having breakfast with you. It makes me extremely happy."

"Now that you mention it, it's one of my favorites, too."

"Is there another?" She grinned.

"Oh, many others. The one I enjoy a little more is holding you in my arms when we sleep." I reached out my hand.

Her eyes welled up a little and she reached across the table. "We are very fortunate that our lives have come together at this moment."

Short of blurting the feelings that threatened to explode out of my chest, I didn't know what else to say. I squeezed her hand and then kissed her palm.

"Lars wants us to meet at eleven for some minor changes," she said, then laughed. "Minor for me, perhaps, but not so much for Stefan." We both laughed as she described some of his bloopers.

"What would you like to do about dinner tonight? I have no idea what your family might enjoy."

"I thought about that and remembered how much they enjoyed the New Mexican meal they had on the last visit. I was told there was a very good place to get New Mexican food over in Tesuque."

"I know the place you mean. I can't think of the name of it, but I'll look it up. If you call in an order, I'll be happy to go pick it up a little later."

She turned off the water and folded the dish towel. "I think I may have to keep you on my payroll forever," she said and curled one on arm around my neck, pulling me hard against her open lips.

✦✦✦✦

It was nearly four when I got back to the house with aluminum pans of heavenly smelling enchiladas, tamales, refried beans, and some wonderful sides including guacamole and salsa. I stuck both pans in the oven and the sides in the refrigerator. I had also purchased some Corona beer, more wine, and some stuff for margaritas.

Nicole was busy rearranging the two guest rooms and I ran down to my place to change my clothes. I could not believe how nervous I was about meeting her mother and grandmother.

Settle down, cowgirl. It's not as if you're going to ask for her hand in marriage, for heaven's sake. You work for the woman. They don't have to like you.

After arguing with myself for twenty minutes, I selected a long-sleeved peasant blouse and some boxy cotton shorts. I changed out my gold hoop earrings for some unusual long beaded ones that I bought at an art show two years ago. I fussed with my hair—without luck—and cursed about not getting a haircut. *Deep breath.* A little mascara and eyeliner was the best I could manage. Nicole had promised something to cover the bruise that ran down from my temple to my cheekbone.

I could hear my mother's voice echoing from the past: "That's a nice outfit, honey, you look really pretty. You know if you just used a little bit of lipstick…"

The memory made me smile. Mom so wanted a sweet girly girl.

Nicole was in her room getting ready when I walked in. She turned around and smiled. "You look wonderful, not anything like a ragamuffin. Come with me and I will cover that bruise." We went into her bathroom and she took out a tube of makeup that was greenish in color and began dabbing it on carefully with a sponge. *Green? I sure hope she knows what she's doing.*

"There, that's better. Not perfect, but certainly less obvious."

I looked in the mirror, surprised at how well it covered. And, it didn't look green at all.

"Thanks. Now least I don't feel like such a freak."

"You are no freak, you were wounded in the line of duty." She kissed my nose.

I followed her into the bedroom. "Nicole, speaking of duty, what are you going to tell your mom about Mario and why he's not here?"

She walked over, sat on the edge of the bed, and crossed her legs. "I will tell her the truth. I just…it was too hard on the phone. It is interesting that she was supportive when she thought I had found someone to settle down with, but she never really liked Mario very much. I think she will not be too disappointed."

What I wanted to ask her was whether she would say anything to her mother about me. Maybe there was not much to tell. I guess I would have to wait and see. Her cell phone interrupted.

"Yes? Hello, Thad. Wonderful. We'll be waiting, thank you so much for calling."

"They're on the way?" I asked. Nerves were starting. I swallowed a lump threatening to choke me.

"They just passed through Santa Fe and should be here soon. Do you think it would be appropriate to ask Thad to stay for dinner? He has spent nearly the whole afternoon driving and waiting, and I'm so glad we didn't have to do it." Nicole changed her blouse for the second time, teasing me with her body.

"I think that's a very nice idea. He's been very helpful to me as well. Do you think I should make some margaritas?"

"That's a wonderful idea. My grandmother loves them."

She does, huh? "I wasn't sure when I bought the stuff, but I figured we'd use it sometime."

"Meg, I am very excited for you to meet my mother. I think you will like her and I know she will like you." The red sleeveless blouse won.

Man, I hope she does.

The limes were sliced, the salt poured, and the first batch of margaritas was in the freezer. I had just decided that the chips and guacamole could probably wait when I heard the car door slam. Showtime.

When I got to the door, Nicole had already reached the car and had her mother in a warm embrace. They hugged, kissed, and then assisted her petite *grand-mère* out of the back seat. Both women looked very much alike, with high cheekbones and oval faces. However, her mother was quite tall, maybe five foot nine, with dark brown hair pulled back. With a nice figure and a stylish navy pantsuit, her mother created a classy picture.

By comparison, her grandmother looked like a pixie. When she took off her sunglasses, she had the same peacock blue eyes that Nicole did. The silver-white curls glistened in the sunlight like a crown. She laughed easily and was very agile, even with her ornate cane.

I hurried down to help Thad with several pieces of luggage, but Nicole grabbed my arm.

"Mother, *grand-mère*, I would like to introduce you to Margaret Ellis, my assistant and my indispensable friend." She repeated the same thing in French to her grandmother. I assumed.

I reached out my hand to her grandmother first and then her mother. "*Bienvenue.*"

Her mother smiled. "*Ah, parlez-vous francais?*"

"*Un peu,*" I said with a terrible accent. and everyone laughed. *Swell.*

Thad and I followed everyone into the house with a number of suitcases that caused me more than a little worry. I began to wonder about Nicole's comment and just how long "a short time" really was.

An hour later we were all settled around the patio table with margaritas and nachos. Nicole had directed the room assignments and luggage placement and helped her family settle. Thad and I assembled the margaritas while he regaled me with stories of his adventures at the airport. It was never easy to just drive in and pick someone up, and this was no exception.

Her mother had made the trip several times, and they were flying from New York so it wasn't an international flight, but there were still delays getting the luggage together. Thad did this regularly and the responsibility didn't upset him. Thad thrived on chaos. Since he'd had an hour to talk to Nicole Bernard's mother, Thad had loaded up with scads of personal trivia. He probably now knew more about Nicole than I did.

"I nearly forgot!" Thad jumped up and headed inside. "The reviews, they're in my briefcase."

Nicole and I just looked at each other. I never even thought about the fact there would be print reviews already. But of course there would be, as several members of the media were at the dress rehearsal and two of them did quick interviews with Nicole. I guess I figured they wouldn't come out until the Sunday edition.

Either Nicole or her mother translated most of our conversation for Nicole's grandmother. Nicole had whispered to me that her grandmother understood some English but only spoke a few words.

Her grandmother's eyes, on the other hand, needed no interpretation, because on more than one occasion I found her watching me carefully. It was a little disconcerting because her gaze was so intent.

Thad returned with two or three pieces of paper and handed them to Nicole. "Read the one from the *New York Times*, it was wonderful."

Nicole read aloud as her mother translated. I watched with amusement as Nicole's voice got higher and her cheeks colored. Pleasure glowed on her face, as did my pride. Our eyes met once in shared communication, and all I could do was smile.

Thad regaled the guests with glowing reports about the show and I snuck inside to refill the glasses.

The evening temperatures dropped and we all enjoyed a leisurely supper with stories and camaraderie. Thad made his excuses right after dinner and I walked him to the door. "Thank you so much for inviting me to stay. This was so much fun, and I think Nicole's family is wonderful. Don't you just love her to pieces?"

"Yes, indeed. They're each delightful, and I'm glad you could stay. It would have been hard for Nicole to make that trip to the airport, and I know she was thrilled by the reviews."

He started to leave, then turned back and hugged me tightly. "Thanks again, Meg."

I went back to the kitchen and started to clean up. This wasn't the time for a third (fourth!) wheel, and I wanted Nicole to have time with her family. Shortly, the remaining dishes were cleared, rinsed, and put in the dishwasher, the leftover food wrapped up and refrigerated, and the small amount of leftover margarita mix—I drank.

Nicole came into the house with her grandmother. "*Grandmère* is worn out and ready for bed. I'm going to get her tucked in and I wondered if you'd mind sitting with my mother."

"Sure. Would your mom like coffee or something?"

"A good idea, why don't you ask her?"

Just then her grandmother said something, and Nicole smiled. "She would like to give you a hug."

I walked closer and the little woman put her arms around my neck and kissed me on the cheek. "*Bonne nuit, chérie.*"

"*Bonne nuit.*"

They walked down the hall and I felt a little glow. What a sweet gesture, and gratifying. I hurried outside and found her mom sitting on the glider.

"Madame Bernard, would you care for some coffee or tea?"

She looked up and smiled. "Why, thank you. Some tea would be lovely, but please, call me Catherine. I think you prefer Meg, is that correct?"

"Yes. Let me start the water and I'll come back and talk with you."

Cups, tea bags, milk, and sugar, but I couldn't find any lemon. I set the teakettle on the stove and returned to the patio.

"Nicole tells us that she has been very pleased with this new opera production. From the reviews, it sounds like it will be wonderful."

"I think you'll enjoy it. The music alone is worth it. Of course, Nicole is the jewel in the crown of this show. Her talent and hard work have brought the entire cast up to a new level. Lars, her director, seems to have a unique ability to bring about her best."

Her mother was smiling. "You sound like her biggest fan."

I knew I was blushing, but I didn't care. "I may be, not only because I enjoy her singing but because I've had the opportunity to see how hard she works."

Nicole joined us and sat beside her mother on the glider.

"*Grandmère* began to doze as soon as her head hit the pillow. This has been a very long day for her. What were you two discussing?"

"Meg was just telling me that you have done such a wonderful job and why she is your biggest fan." Catherine smiled as she made the comment.

Nicole flashed me a stifled grin. "Believe me, it was a joint effort. I think I have never had a role that made me be on stage so much, and it would be impossible without help."

Her mother reached over and took Nicole's hand lovingly. "I'm very proud of you, my darling, and cannot wait to see you perform. Maybe you would like to tell me about why you needed a personal assistant when your husband should be here."

Okay, that's my cue. "Why don't I get the tea?"

"You don't need to leave," Nicole said.

"The water's ready, I'll be right back."

Shit. I didn't think this was going to happen so quickly. I took my time steeping the tea and brought the tray out to the small table near the glider. Nicole seemed calm as she described Mario's refusal to come to New Mexico this summer because of other obligations.

"He came last year, though," her mother said.

Nicole looked up at me, took a deep breath, and continued. "His other obligation is twenty-two years old and a college student."

Okay, that should clarify everything. Her mother took the tea I offered without a word. There was no disguising the set of her jaw because it was identical to Nicole's. I handed Nicole a cup and then I sat down quietly. I squirmed, they sipped, and the only sound was crickets for several minutes. *Awkward.*

Her mother looked at Nicole and then at me. More quiet. "Have you tried to discuss this with him?"

Nicole fussed with her teacup. "Yes, he came out here and surprised me several weeks ago. I told him I knew about the other woman. He lied about it and we had a rather awful fight. He finally told me he would not give her up, and I made him leave."

After another long silence, her mother responded. "My darling, I am so sorry but not surprised. Sadly, I do not think this is the first time."

Nicole's head snapped up at that comment. "What? He told me it was the only one."

"I have no proof, but there were rumors when you were both in Paris. Your father became angry and wanted to hire someone. Have you spoken to a lawyer?"

"Yes. I contacted my agent and she has made arrangements."

"So. There is no more reconciliation then."

"I think no. I hope not," Nicole said and turned away. Her voice quavered. She told me this would be hard for her, but there was little I could do.

"You hope not, what does that mean?" her mother asked.

I could see her shoulders droop. "He was at the performance last night."

"Did you speak to him?" The shock in her mother's voice was unmistakable.

"No, I did not see him."

"How…" Her mother looked directly at me. I didn't say a word but looked at Nicole for some help. Nothing. "Your face…was there a confrontation?" Her mother formed it as a question, but there was nothing equivocal in her tone. She had guessed correctly.

Nicole, please say something.

"Yes. He came backstage looking for me and shoved Meg when she asked him to leave. Her face was injured trying to protect me." Her voice cracked.

"Your father is going to be very unhappy." She turned to me. "Meg, I am sorry you had to be involved in this sordid family business. Nicole, I think I will retire for the evening. Thank you both for a delicious meal." She put her teacup on the tray and walked briskly into the house.

We sat in silence for a few moments.

"Well, that went well, don't you think?" I managed to say with a modicum of fake cheerfulness.

Nicole scowled at me. "I'm not sure. She seemed

upset but I am not sure why. Either because Mario is a jerk or because you were injured. I think she will say something tomorrow. She probably wants to call my father first."

I started putting our cups back on the tray. "It's been a long day, and everyone is tired."

Nicole followed me in and helped me finish up in the kitchen.

"Meg, I cannot thank you enough for everything you did today—and every day. You were very gracious to my family and made them feel welcome." She leaned her head against mine.

"I wanted to do it. I think it's important they enjoy their visit with you, and it's a special bonus if they like me."

"I think they will like you because I like you. In time, I think they will understand that." She moved closer to me and put her hands on my waist.

I moved back a little. "I don't think you should do that."

"Why?"

"I just don't think it's a good idea." I felt uncomfortable thinking about either her mom or grandmother walking into the kitchen.

She laughed. "So are you going to run off to the guesthouse and make me come looking for you?"

"I think we should just cool it tonight. You need to be here in case they want something."

The famous Nicole pout reappeared. "And what about me? What if I need something?"

Why did she always do this to me? "Nicole, don't do that. You know I'm right."

She leaned forward and whispered, "You could sneak up on my balcony."

"No means no."

※※※※

It was the first time I had to make coffee in the guesthouse, but I wanted to leave the Bernard women to themselves. They weren't here to see me, and I knew they had things to discuss with Nicole.

My little kitchen was empty. I scrounged around and found some melba toast in the cupboard and a protein bar in my backpack. *You know, you could always take yourself out to breakfast. You're not a prisoner here.*

I looked out the front window to see if anyone was outside. They weren't. After pacing for a few minutes, I brought my coffee into the living room and settled in with a book. Maybe this would be like a day off. I could even go to my apartment.

I heard a knock at the door and looked up to see Nicole poke her head in. "Are you up?"

"Hi, come in." Her greeting alone raised my heart rate. *Stupid, betraying body.*

"I wasn't sure where you were. I thought we would all have breakfast together."

"I just thought you needed time with your family. Or needed to talk."

She moved my feet and sat next to me. "You are right, we did. I just missed you." She stroked my bruised face and shook her head. "Are you okay?"

I kissed her forehead. "I'm fine. I missed you too, but it's clear your mom wanted to talk to you."

"Believe me, she has. My father called me at dawn because she called him last night. He's very angry, not with me but with Mario. My mother must have told him Mario was violent because he wanted me to order security."

"Nicole, I'm sure Mario was on the first plane out of here. He was undoubtedly embarrassed when they escorted him out of the building."

"I know. Will you come up and join us?"

"Don't you think they would enjoy talking with you alone? Maybe you could do something special with them. I thought I might run back to my apartment."

She sat up a little straighter. "Are you upset with me for some reason?"

"No, not at all. They didn't travel all this way to see me. This is for you, Nicole. Besides, we will all be together tomorrow for dinner."

Oh. My. God. The epic family gathering. I had been in denial.

Humor, pathos, and Gallic drama.

Her eyes looked sad as she put her arms around me, pulling me close. I stroked her hair and kissed her temple, inhaling her shampoo and savoring the touch of her skin. "I'll be back tonight. Enjoy your family, and I'll see you all a little later."

Her lips were on me for one of her take-no-prisoners kisses. My body surrendered as I pulled her closer with one hand on the back of her neck. It was fast, hard, and intense. We separated, chests heaving, knowing we had to stop right then or there would be no stopping.

"*Au revoir.*" And she was gone.

Yowza, what just happened? No question, I am hopelessly addicted to those kisses. My hands shook and heart pounded as electrical surges pulsed through my body.

Act III Scene 3

The house was quiet when I returned Saturday evening and Nicole's car was gone. There was a piece of paper stuck to the front of the refrigerator.

Meg: We're having dinner with Lars and his wife, not sure when we'll be home. —N

I took the note down and smiled, feeling just a little silly. I loved her handwriting. I folded the note, put it in my pocket, and proceeded to forage in the refrigerator. There was plenty of food left from the night before, so I prepared a plateful to take down to the guesthouse. I stuck two bottles of beer in my backpack and carried it all down with me after leaving a few lights on. I didn't want our guests to come home stumbling in the dark.

As the food heated in the microwave, I changed into something cooler. Boxers and a tank top would suffice since I wasn't entertaining. I stood looking out the window with mixed feelings. Relief, because I didn't have to go along for another uncomfortable social event. And sad, because I missed being with Nicole. Our continuous state of togetherness created a strong connection.

The little time in my apartment with Pearson helped. At first, my cat acted aloof and distant. It was punishment for leaving him. I tried numerous tricks to lure him to me. Even canned tuna didn't perk him up. There wasn't much I could do if he continued to sulk. I didn't think the Goddards would appreciate having a pet in their guesthouse, but if he didn't snap out of it I might have to ask.

A small TV in the kitchen provided a brief distraction, and I sat at the counter watching a baseball game as I ate my dinner.

Like a loyal watchdog, I continued to check the main house from my living room. I gave up around nine thirty, rinsed my dish, and took my book to the bedroom. Two chapters tired me and I switched off the light. It was dark, and I was surprisingly lonesome.

Remember, Ellis, tomorrow is the great family get together with your parents. You're going to need some sleep.

≈≈≈≈≈

The sails flapped in the breeze and the sailboat listed portside as it crested another wave. I stood at the helm wrapped in the arms of the most beautiful woman in the world. The spray from the salty waves breaking over the bow covered us as we hungrily explored each other, mouths firmly attached and hands grabbing at each other's clothes. My body was on fire. Cool fingers trailed from my shoulder down my back. I moaned softly, suddenly aware that the fingers were not part of a dream.

I sat up with my heart thudding against my ribcage and a cold sweat on my forehead. As soon as my eyes adjusted, I realized I was not alone.

"I am so sorry, *mon amour*."

"Holy fuck! You scared the crap out of me." I flopped back on the pillow as my heart continued to pound.

"I only wanted to surprise you, not give you a heart attack." She kissed me gently.

"Yes," I said, panting. "Surprise…that you did…wow." My breathing slowed.

"You are not so glad to see me, I think."

"No, I just wasn't expecting you."

She stroked the damp hair off my forehead gently. "Would you like me to go?"

"No, I want you to stay—what time is it?"

"Almost midnight."

Now fully awake, my heart had resumed its normal rhythm. "Did you have a nice day?"

Nicole moved a little closer and slipped one bare leg across my hips. "Can we talk about it tomorrow?"

Her warm soft body loomed over me, dimly lit by starlight. The heat of her ignited the barely glowing fire within me. My head fell back as her soft lips began the destruction of my resolve. I lost control of my muscles as my body began to move with her slowly and rhythmically. My breasts tingled to the touch of her tongue and teeth as muscle contractions throbbed between my legs.

I reached for her and she pushed my arms above my head, capturing my mouth with a fiery kiss. I was incapable of anything but surrender and opened everything to her, begging for relief of the aching need I felt. She teased me to the brink repeatedly until I could stand it no longer. My body exploded, sounds tearing from my throat. My legs squeezed hard against her.

Her hands, no longer cool, caressed my breast and she murmured into my ear of pleasure and joy and desire. I felt lightheaded and delirious as though a catapult had just flung me into outer space and then dropped me back to earth.

My body continued to quiver wherever she touched me. I pulled her close and kissed her hard, I needed to connect again, to be inside her, and feel her heat.

She obliged to me willingly, and I felt as though my hands reached into her heart.

We awoke an hour later still wrapped tightly with our arms and legs intertwined. In the stillness, I could feel both hearts beating against my chest, hers and mine. It was the closest I had ever felt to another human being in my life, as though we were one.

Her gorgeous eyes twinkled at me. "That was incredible."

"Nicole, I have no words to describe where you took me and can't begin to tell you how I feel."

She put her finger on my lips. "You need not tell me, I was there with you. I am with you."

"How is it possible…" Her kiss, gentle on my lips, silenced me.

"I should go. If I stay there will be no more sleep."

I pulled her back for another kiss. "I don't want to let you go."

She stood up as I held onto her hand, "Nicole, I—"

"Say no more, mon *coeur*."

She disappeared before sunrise and I lay sleepless, savoring the ecstasy.

The Bernard women sat around the table as I entered. Newspaper articles, photographs, and breakfast pastries littered the table.

"*Bonjour*, Meg," said Nicole, looking very chipper.

"Good morning, ladies. How is everyone this morning?" I thought that sounded pretty friendly and neutral. I moved directly to the coffee pot, poured a cup, and then joined them.

Catherine pulled out a chair beside her and I sat down. "We were just trying to get Nicole caught up on news from home, nothing very interesting, I'm afraid. How about you, did you sleep well?"

I almost aspirated my coffee. "Yes, very well, thank you. I must have been more tired than I thought."

Nicole made herself busy with a croissant and her mother tipped her head to one side and said, "You must have had a busy day yesterday. We were sorry you couldn't join us. Did you have to work?"

"No, I needed to catch up on a few things at my apartment in Santa Fe."

"You don't work in the summer?" her mother asked

"Not usually. I work as a school nurse for the Santa Fe school system. I usually have a few months off during the summer, except for this year."

I tried stuffing my mouth as a deterrent, but it didn't work.

"Working with children must be very interesting and gratifying. What made you decide on that particular job?"

I noticed that Nicole was keeping *grand-mère* in

the conversation by translating. Perspiration started forming in the middle of my back.

"Well, I enjoyed my pediatric rotation because the kids were so resilient. After I graduated, I worked in the pediatric intensive care unit for a short time, but that was just too painful. I decided I wanted to work with a healthier population. School nursing is a little less stressful, with better hours and summers off." I hoped that was the end of the inquisition.

Nicole reached over as though she were reading my mind and put her calming hand on my back. "The Santa Fe Opera Company chose Meg especially because she had a nursing background and she was one of their apprentices for two years. She has a wonderful voice."

"That's very interesting, and a good combination, I suppose, but why did they think you needed a nurse?"

Crap on a cracker. She didn't tell her mother about her blood sugar problem. I'll just bet this is going to be a new session of "ask the nurse." I think it's time for another cup of coffee.

There were half a dozen French phrases bandied about, none of which I could understand. Then I heard Nicole explaining.

"You remember last year when I had trouble with a couple of fainting spells? It turned out to be related to low blood sugar or something. Anyway, somebody decided that it would be better to have someone check my blood sugar and keep an eye on me."

That sounded reasonable to me, so I went back in and sat down. The look on Catherine's face told me that she wasn't completely satisfied with that explanation. "Meg, what does this mean? Is it dangerous?"

I looked at Nicole, and she nodded for me to continue.

"It's not dangerous. Many people have trouble with blood sugar being too high or too low. We just needed to create a schedule to make sure she got what she needed to balance with her activity level. It's worked out well, and she's had no major problems." I didn't think it was necessary to mention the couple of minor fainting spells. I turned to Nicole and said, "If you want to warm up, maybe we should start soon."

She understood what I was saying and took it a step further. "You are, of course, right. I forget sometimes I have to sing tonight. Let me change my clothes and maybe we could take a short run before vocalizing."

I wasn't quite sure what the "short run" was all about but went along with it. "Okay, I'll change my shoes and meet you out front."

"Mother, please enjoy the fruit and tea. We will be back shortly to sing a little for you." She kissed her mother and we both left.

"What was this run about?" I said as we jogged down the road.

"I just wanted to talk to you for a minute. I am sorry you had to explain being my nurse. I have not talked to her for a long time, and when I did, I did not want to alarm her."

"It's not a problem. It just felt a little awkward. I mean, she's your mother. Of course she's going to be worried."

"You were wonderful. I'm sure she's much more

comfortable."

"And what were you and your grandmother conspiring about?"

"She's just curious about you."

I stopped, breathing hard. "What do you mean, curious?"

She punched my arm and laughed. "She just likes you. That is all."

We ran a bit farther on the dirt road to the hill above the subdivision. The morning had been sunny so far, but the western horizon was dappled with amassing cumulus clouds. I hadn't heard the weather forecast but hoped it wouldn't be rain. We started to walk back, and for just a minute, she reached over and took my hand.

"I thought about your suggestions yesterday and you are right. I called the catering company that works with the Opera. They were very reasonable, so I ordered a light supper for five o'clock. They will come and set it up then come back and clean up afterward. It would be too busy for everyone to try to cook and clean up."

"Wonderful. I was worried that you'd overextend yourself and be tired tonight. I was also going to suggest we head over to the theater around seven so you have time to concentrate."

"You read my mind."

She put her arm around my waist and hugged me as we started up her driveway.

"Will you sing with me today?"

"I don't know if that's—"

"Please?"

"Okay, a little."

We both took some time to freshen up and drink

some water. I joined Nicole and we did some scales to get started. We sat together on the piano bench hip to hip and read off the score. She picked some random selections and I sang whatever part was necessary. Even when she was working at half voice, the silkiness of her tone enveloped me and caused me to shiver.

Our two guests moved into the den and sat quietly, listening. When I looked at their faces, there was no mistaking the love and pride they both felt.

After being afraid for so long, I looked forward to the opportunity to sing with Nicole each day. It was like coming into the sunshine after a long illness. Who wouldn't give their eyeteeth to sit beside Nicole Bernard and sing scales?

※ ※ ※ ※

In the early afternoon, we all reassembled after some delicious naps. For our Sunday afternoon supper, I chose the print sundress and sandals, knowing it would make my mother happy. I brushed my hair back and used a little product to make it look as though I'd made the effort.

The bruising was either less noticeable or I had gotten used to it, but I still wanted to put a little of that green makeup on to avoid alarming my parents. Like Nicole, I didn't want to have that conversation on the phone. As soon as I was dressed, I snuck up to Nicole's room and entered from her balcony—just like a secret lover or something. Well, I guess that's exactly what I was.

She graciously applied the green stuff as I tried to untie the sash on her robe.

"Stop it and hold still."

"I can't help myself. You have such beautiful skin, and I just have to touch it."

"No, you don't."

"Yes, I do." My fingers slipped inside the robe to her breast.

"Meg!" she whispered loudly and continued with the makeup.

The velvet softness awakened my senses as I lightly ran my fingers between her breasts. I pulled her robe apart enough to see the incredible curves and taught nipples.

"You take my breath away," I murmured.

She finished by stroking the makeup with her fingertips and staring into my eyes with unguarded pleasure.

"Kiss me and then leave quickly," she said very softly.

I pulled her close and kissed the corner of her mouth, enveloped her lower lip, assaulted her open lips, and left the way I came.

※※※※

The iron knocker on the front door announced my parents' arrival. I greeted them both warmly and listened as they both complimented my appearance and then expressed their concern about my bruised face. I minimized it and escorted them into the kitchen where my mother could put away the dessert and my father could chill the two bottles of champagne he brought. They looked around the house with great appreciation as much for the extravagant decorating as they did that their little girl had a nice place to stay. I showed them around briefly until Nicole came out.

She looked breathtaking.

Her hair was styled, her makeup was tasteful, and the emerald green and cerulean blue dress made her eyes look electric. This beautiful creature would be the death of me.

"Nicole, I would like to present my parents, Robert and Beth Ellis. Mom and Dad, I'm pretty sure you recognize our hostess, Nicole Bernard."

"I am so pleased to finally meet both of you, so I can tell you how much I appreciate your wonderful daughter."

The mutual admiration society continued as we walked out to the patio. As soon as I reached the patio door, I heard the front door knocker.

It took me a while to show the caterers where everything was in the kitchen. We had to look to find the leaf for the dining room table, but as soon as we did they assured me they could handle it. When I joined everyone on the patio, the happy little group exchanging stories stunned me. It was like the old home week or something. I simply stood there and watched in disbelief as my mother and Nicole's mother were engaged in an intense discussion while my father and Nicole were talking with her grandmother. What had I been so concerned about? They sure as heck didn't need me hanging around.

I edged up behind Nicole. "The caterers are here and are setting up. They said everything would be ready in about a half an hour. Do you think I should open the champagne now?"

"No, I think we can wait a little bit. Everything seems to be fine. Your parents are delightful."

As promised, the woman from the catering

company waved to me from the door. They had done a beautiful job, the table was set, and there were fresh flowers as a centerpiece. The different entrees Nicole had ordered were prepared and in chafing dishes on the large granite island. It looked just like a photo shoot from *Food & Wine Magazine.* I thanked her and she promised they would return around seven to clean up. They would lock the door and leave the key in the mailbox if no one was here.

"Folks, dinner is served," I announced from the doorway.

My dad helped Nicole's grandmother to her feet as the two mothers started indoors. Nicole and I followed everyone, bringing up the rear.

"Are you feeling more comfortable?"

"Yes, I don't even need to be here," I said, smiling.

"Oh, yes you do, my wicked little friend," she said and made a healthy grab of my ass.

"Hey!"

"Payback, my dear."

Our guests were milling around the bountiful buffet, oohing and aahing. Even Nicole looked pleased. They had lightly grilled chicken breasts, cheesy potato puffs, a gorgeous seafood salad, fresh fruit, hot rolls, and a platter of raw vegetables. They even set out Mom's angel food cake.

As each filled a plate, I poured the champagne and set it on the table next to the water glasses.

Though the dining room was ready, the glorious weather beckoned us to eat outside. My mother and Catherine were sitting together, then my dad, with *Grandmère* beside Nicole and me.

When I sat down, my father asked if he could say

grace, and everyone nodded appreciatively. We joined hands and my dad said a simple grace. For a moment, I could feel a kind of energy running through all of us; it tingled in my hands. He finished, and Nicole squeezed my hand.

Everyone thanked Nicole for this gracious celebration, and we toasted with champagne.

My parents were querying Catherine about Nicole's extraordinary musical gift while *Grandmère* was engaged in a busy conversation with Nicole. She spoke rapidly, and I couldn't understand her dialect.

"What is your grandmother so busy discussing?"

"First, she was raving about the food, and she just now said she thought you had beautiful breasts."

I choked on a potato puff. "She did not."

"Yes, she did. She thought you looked like a passionate young woman and very pretty."

I just stared at her and then her grandmother, who was smiling at me. "Does she know what you just told me?"

"Her hearing is excellent, and she understands quite a bit of English."

I turned back and whispered, "I am so embarrassed I could die."

"Don't be. Later, I will tell you an interesting story about my grandmother."

When I looked up again, both women were looking at me with an identical twinkle in their eyes, as though it were an inside joke.

"Meg, your mother tells me you had quite a promising vocal career," Catherine said.

Oh God. Kill me now. "I think that might be an exaggeration, plus, the surgery derailed that idea. Would anyone like more champagne?"

"Well, we heard you sing this morning and your voice is quite lovely."

"Oh honey, we'd love to hear you sing. Could you and Nicole do something for us?" Mom asked.

Once again, my idol came to my rescue. "I would be happy to some other time, but unfortunately, we must leave early to get ready for the performance," Nicole said.

"Of course. I understand. How silly of me. Nicole, we're so looking forward to this. It's such a beautiful opera, and you are so gracious to get us all tickets," my mother said.

"It is the least I can do for your kind support." Nicole smiled warmly at my parents.

I started to clear the table so we could have dessert, and as I leaned between my father and Nicole's grandmother, she patted my ass. I almost dropped the dinner plates as she whispered something to Nicole, which made them both giggle. I knew my face was scarlet. Who gets groped by an eighty-five-year-old Frenchwoman?

The angel food cake with fresh raspberries and whipped cream was a huge success, and my mother was pleased to contribute. When I looked at the kitchen clock, it was almost seven.

"I think we better get ready to go. I still need to change my clothes," I said.

Nicole cleared her throat. "As much as I hate to do this, we have quite a lot to do before the show. Mr. Ellis, I am grateful for your offer to take my family over to the theater, and you are all welcome to come back here after the show for champagne."

There were things I wanted to ask Nicole about the secret conversations with her mother. Not to mention her eagle-eyed grandmother, but now wasn't the time. Opening night had been spectacular, but there were a dozen more performances to go and each one had to be special. I put on my personal assistant hat so that Nicole could transform herself into Violetta Valery.

I dropped her off and went to park the car. Nicole sang in the morning, rested in the afternoon, and ate a modest supper. She barely touched the champagne, and I felt confident she was ready to go.

Wardrobe and makeup took the normal amount of time, and by eight thirty I left to go to my post. I walked outside for a little while just to get some exercise and checked to make sure the families found their seats. Nicole had secured some excellent seats in the orchestra section, and I could see the foursome about ten rows back in the center. I moved backstage feeling incredibly grateful for friends, family, and the enchanting Nicole. The first cords of the overture sounded.

Act III Scene 4

When I pulled the car into the garage, my dad's car was already parked at the side of the driveway. They greeted Nicole with applause and embraces, which she truly deserved. The performance was much smoother and more polished; her voice held up well and her acting was even more intense.

My dad sounded like a schoolboy. "Nicole, I have seen dozens of Violettas in my lifetime, but you gave the most honest and nuanced perspective. And your vocal prowess is exquisite. Thank you so very much." He reached out and kissed her hand, and I wanted to cry. I'd never seen my dad so enthralled in my life.

"We're not going to stay because we both have to work tomorrow, but this was the most enjoyable evening. Nicole, thank you again for being so gracious and for all you've done for our Meg." My mom's voice cracked as she finished, and I hugged her. Then Nicole hugged her and started a round-robin of hugging. I walked my parents to the car.

"I love you guys, and I'm so glad we could all get together," I said as the car doors closed.

"Keep up the good work, Meggie. This was a perfect evening." My dad waved.

I waved back as they drove off, feeling a little sad. I wished I hadn't been so self-conscious, because the night would've been perfect if they'd heard me sing. Maybe another time.

When I came into the kitchen, Nicole and her mother were talking as they set out some cups.

"We were about to have some tea. Come and join us," Nicole said. "*Grandmère* went to bed."

"While you two wait for the tea, I'm going to change my clothes," Catherine said.

Nicole hoisted herself onto the kitchen counter next to me. "How do you think the show went?"

"I thought it ran a little smoother. You seemed more comfortable, and the scenes with Stefan were more believable."

"I thought so, too. It was good. I am pleased that everyone enjoyed it."

I turned to stand in front of her and put both hands on her legs. "Forgive me for being repetitious, but I thought you were amazing tonight. The more you do this the better you get, and your upper range poured out as smooth as aged brandy."

She smiled and put her palm on my cheek. "I never tire when you tell me, because I believe you and I think you would tell me the truth."

The sound of slippers sent me to the stovetop to remove the teakettle and look busy.

We sat around the table as Nicole and her mother dissected the show a little bit. Her mother loved the performance and had several interesting observations about some of the scenes. She knew her business.

"I'm so proud of you, darling. Many would rest on their laurels, but you continue to grow as an actor. I am also pleased that this ugly incident with Mario is not interfering. It could have been detrimental to your performance." She sipped her tea. "You seemed to take it in stride. Perhaps it was easier for you because you have support."

This comment caught my attention, but I continued sipping my tea.

"*Merci, Maman.* You know how much I value your opinion."

"Tell me, do you think some of the credit belongs to Meg?"

Uh-oh.

"A great deal of the credit goes to Meg." *Oh no, she has that look.* "Without her, I am not sure I would have been able to do this alone."

"Your grandmother seems to think you two are very close." The comment sounded barbed.

Nicole looked at me with a kind of discerning expression. "I think that is true. We have worked through a very difficult situation and every moment I felt supported. Meg has never told me what to do or what not to do. She simply stood behind me and gave me her strength." She reached across the table and put her hand on top of mine, then looked at her mother. "I do not remember ever having a friend who is as loyal and nonjudgmental."

"You are very fortunate, then. Those are the characteristics of a close friend." Her mother glanced at me with a half smile. "And you, Meg, do you think what my daughter has just told me is true?"

"I think your daughter is very kind to me."

"Perhaps you'll tell me how you feel about my daughter."

If there is a God, the earth will open and swallow me up right now.

"Mother, please…"

"It's okay, that's only fair." I put down my cup and clasped my hands together to keep them steady.

"Madame Bernard, I worked with Nicole several years ago and she inspired me to be the best singer I could be. If it hadn't been for the cancer surgery, who knows? Maybe I would be in New York today, singing." I knew my voice sounded tight. "But I quit. I never sang again until a few weeks ago, when once again Nicole inspired me, encouraged me, and helped me to find my voice."

The unbidden tears rolled down my cheeks and I couldn't stop them. "Your daughter is not only an extraordinary musician and actor, she is one of the most amazing women I have ever met. It has been the greatest joy of my life to be able to work for her and with her. There is nothing I wouldn't do for her."

"Your impassioned words are a balm to a mother's heart. And all the more when Nicole's grandmother suspects there might be, shall we say, a casual physical relationship?"

I did know what to say. Nicole did.

"It is true that Meg and I share a physical attraction for one another, Mother. And I would happily tell the world and be open about it. However, it has been Meg's desire to protect my name and the reputation of the opera company during this busy season. With my separation from Mario and his intolerable behavior, I...we, don't want negative publicity. Or any publicity."

There was a huge pause, which allowed me to exhale.

"I understand, and I agree with Meg. I would continue to urge discretion and patience until this matter is legally concluded. Nicole, you have been hurt and may be more vulnerable than usual." She stood. "I think I will retire as well. We will be leaving tomorrow afternoon, but I hope to come again and see you both."

She took her cup to the sink, then turned. "Oh, and I won't be discussing this with your father just yet. Sleep well."

Nicole and I stared at each other, slack-jawed.

"What just happened?"

"I am not sure, but I think it was good. I forgot to mention that my mother is rather protective of me. Well, they all are."

"Your grandmother thought we were fooling around. Where did she get that?"

"I didn't say a word, I swear."

"Does she have magical powers or something? Oh, and another thing, were you aware that she grabbed my ass after dinner?"

"What? No, she didn't."

"Yes, she did, while I was clearing the table."

Nicole started giggling and then I started, and pretty soon we were both hysterical.

"We'd better step outside before we wake somebody up," I said.

I turned off the lights and we went over and sat on the glider. Nicole slipped her hand through my arm as we rocked back and forth.

"This has been another one of the happiest days of my life," I said. "Starting around midnight."

She squeezed my hand, stroked it with her thumb, and then leaned her head on my shoulder. "It has for me as well." She looked up at me. "Do you know, I think it is easier for me to sing when I'm surrounded by people who love me."

I kissed her forehead. "That makes sense, but you're always surrounded by people who love you."

"Not like family."

I knew what she meant.

"Tell me about your grandmother."

She laughed, then groaned. "Near the end of World War II, my grandmother met a young man on his way to the front. He was scared and wanted someone who would be waiting for him. For some reason, he touched my grandmother's heart and she agreed to marry him. They were together only three days before he left for the front, and three months later she received word that he died. She was pregnant with my mother and had no choice but to raise her singlehandedly. Fortunately, she met another young widow who also had a child. Together, they raised their children.

"Many years later, when I returned home from boarding school, my mother finally told me the whole story. While I was away at school, the woman passed away after living with my grandmother for over forty years as lovers. I always knew her as Aunt Cici."

"Your grandmother is a lesbian?"

"Yes."

"Unbelievable." I couldn't quite believe it, but then everything made sense.

"Maybe you understand a little more about me?"

"I'm sure I will as soon as I can absorb all this."

We rocked in silence for a long while, each of us with our thoughts.

"Can I ask you something?" I asked.

"Always."

"Do you believe you're a lesbian?"

"I'm surprised you have to ask."

"I'm serious. You've lived much of your life as a straight woman, right up until a few weeks ago."

"Meg, a name doesn't tell me who I can love

or who I will be attracted to. What difference does it make?"

Her comment stung me, as though she trivialized my question.

"It doesn't make a difference, and maybe that's not my question."

"I see. You still do not know whether you can trust me."

"I promised myself I wouldn't have this conversation. I wanted to let our relationship unfold whichever way it went. If this is a summer romance or if you just need to express yourself because of frustration or anger...I thought it wouldn't matter. I would just be here for you."

"And what has changed for you?"

The feelings were coming back and it was hard to contain them. My chest felt tight and my throat constricted. "Tonight, when I told your mother how I felt, I realized I felt more for you than a summer romance or a casual sex partner."

"But you are not sure how I feel?"

I shook my head because I didn't trust my voice.

"Meg, I am torn in many directions right now. I am still angry with Mario. I am still preoccupied with the show. I was very worried about my parents' reaction to the divorce. And I do not know what my future will be like now."

The pain in my chest got worse instead of better. This was not the reassurance I hoped to hear. I needed to concentrate on her words and not lose control. I knew I was breathing too fast.

"Can you hear me?" She turned my face to her. "Every moment I spend with you is thrilling. You transport me to a safe, wonderful place. I told you the truth when I said that I had never enjoyed lovemaking until you awakened something in me, a desire I hid from everyone. There are times when I want you to touch me so badly I think I will die. But, is that enough to sustain us both? I am unsure of my future and what I could offer you. Do you understand?"

I nodded. "I think so." But I really didn't. My heart pounded and my gut ached, and my expression must have relayed it.

"I am not being clear. The happiness we share is something I cherish so deeply that I am afraid to utter the words. I have never had this kind of feeling about anyone and it is so new. I cannot know how to trust it. Can you understand? We have known each other for just a few weeks, and I want to know so much more. Can you be patient a few weeks more and let me know you better?"

"I will wait for weeks or months if there is a chance of being with you." It was not what I wanted to say. I wanted to beg her to trust me now. To be with me, now.

"Meg, trust my lips and trust my touch. They will never lie to you."

"I will." I had no choice. Her words told me nothing—no commitment, no promise. Did we have a relationship, or just some kind of affair?

Act III Scene 5

I started the coffee early since I hadn't slept much, surprised I was the first one up. I was more surprised when the first person to join me was *Grandmère*.

"*Bonjour.*"

"*Bonjour.*" I pointed to the coffee pot and she nodded. I brought the cup over to the table and went back for the sugar and cream.

We sat together enjoying the morning sun and the aroma of coffee. She smiled and pointed at me and said, "Glowing."

I nodded and said, "*Oui*, very happy."

"*Très bien.*" She nodded, looking very much like the cat that swallowed the canary. Either she had already spoken with Catherine or Nicole, or maybe the lady was a mind reader.

She reached over, patted my hand. "*Vive l'amour*," she said, and winked at me.

Catherine was the next to arrive, and poured herself some coffee. She kissed her mother and sat down. They had a few words, so I got up to retrieve the pastries. I passed them around as they both started grinning.

"My mother says she thinks you are glowing today."

"Well, tell her thank you."

"She knows what's going on—she and Nicole

spoke—and I just confirmed it for her." *Gulp.* "There is no need to be embarrassed. We're both very fond of you, and clearly Nicole is, too."

"Let me reassure you, Nicole and I talked after you retired and we both agree that it's far too soon to make any decisions. We have feelings for each other, but she has a job to do and so do I. We have time to think about it, and we will."

Catherine briefly explained what I'd said to her mother, and I knew she understood.

"That's probably very wise. My daughter can sometimes be impulsive, and as a result she has had relationships that are, shall we say, less than perfect. I can see in her eyes how much she trusts you, and I think you have integrity. She is precious to me, Meg."

"I respect that, Catherine, and I respect Nicole."

"Did someone call my name?"

"*Bonjour, chère fille*," Catherine said.

Nicole first hugged her grandmother and then her mother, then, surprisingly, me.

"Meg was just reassuring us that you both have agreed to be patient."

Fortunately, she resisted the smart-alecky response. "That is true."

We talked about their plans to visit relatives in California. Then, as often happens, they began to tell stories about Nicole growing up. I loved it and Nicole was mortified, especially the stories her grandmother told, which Catherine translated and obviously embellished.

We didn't finish our conversations until noon. Nicole pulled me aside and said, "Why don't we take them to the airport? Would you mind? It is a long drive but I would like a little more time."

"I think it's a great idea. I don't mind. Why don't you call Thad and let him know?"

Her mother was thrilled, and oddly, so was I. These women had grown on me and I was sorry they were leaving so soon, even though they would be back again later this summer.

Catherine insisted we just drop them off and not stay. I unloaded the luggage and asked the skycap to find Madame a wheelchair. The Albuquerque Sunport is a small regional airport, but I saw no reason for Catherine to have to juggle a carry-on in addition to helping her mother.

They disappeared into the terminal and Nicole stood on the sidewalk with her arms tight around her and tears in her eyes. I put my arm around her shoulders and urged her back to the car as a tall uniformed security guard approached us.

"Sometimes, my mother can make me so angry, and we have had some serious fights, other times she is the dearest person in the world to me. I was not sure how this visit would go, especially with the news about Mario. She was wonderful, *n'est-ce pas?*"

"I like your mom very much and I'll admit I was nervous about meeting her. And your grandmother is just amazing. All the women in your family are pretty amazing."

She edged a little closer and put her head on my shoulder and rested her left arm on my thigh. "You made a very big impression, I think. Not only do they like you, they trust you. That is very unusual because my mother never trusted anybody I brought home."

I was beaming with pride. It could've gone so much differently. But, everyone got along well, and with *Grandmère's* astute observations, we were all able to talk about the elephant in the room. I was going to put off discussing our relationship further as long as possible. "Of course she can trust me. I'm a professional, you know."

There was a long silence followed by small talk and radio roulette. It was comfortable, and I looked forward to the time together in that big house, just the two of us.

"You know, I was thinking about the enormous amount of leftovers we have. Maybe your friends could join us for dinner."

"That's a great idea. We can pay them back a little and not have to cook. When would you like to do it?"

"I have a performance Wednesday, maybe Thursday or Friday?"

"They'd love it. Brenda works in Santa Fe, and Lena could just pick her up after work. I'll give them a call and we get home."

"It's nice to hear you say that. It does feel a little bit like home, *oui?*"

※ ※ ※ ※

The next few days flew by as each of us found new ways to relate to one another. Something had shifted in a major way. Nicole still performed brilliantly and I was still her attentive personal assistant. However, there was another current running just below the surface, and we both acted more openly but at the same time more cautiously.

I was glad that we talked about the powerful attraction between us, however it seemed as though shining a spotlight on it made us both more cautious and guarded. We'd lost some of the spontaneity we had when we treated it more like a game. I missed the secret "us" and the way we played together. But, every day I felt I loved her a little more.

On the upside, we were both more affectionate and took time for sharing. It just wasn't quite as exciting as the heart-attack moments when I would wake to find a beautiful woman beside me, whose hands were on me... Now, I expected it.

That said, there was no question that my feelings for her grew deeper and more genuine than the heady infatuation I felt earlier. Whenever I thought of her, a blanket of warmth and desire filled my heart until it felt it might burst.

You know, Ellis, you could do something about the spontaneity. Surprise her, mix it up a bit, do something unexpected.

With that thought in mind, I started to formulate a plan. We were expecting Lena and Brenda at six, and Nicole had run down to the rehearsal hall to meet with Lars and the choreographer. I stayed at the house to get the food out of the freezer and decide what else we needed, but that didn't take long. A large window of opportunity widened.

First, I rummaged through Nicole's bathroom for a few items. Next, I piled cushions from the patio furniture on the flat chaise lounge and covered it with a sheet. I pulled it closer to the more shaded side of the house and draped a king-sized sheet along the beamed patio cover to provide even more privacy. I retrieved the fancy Bose radio from inside with a couple of CDs.

Almost ready, I dragged a table a little closer and set out an ice bucket next to the flower bouquet from the dining room table.

When everything was ready, I hurried to the guesthouse, took a quick shower, and threw on the loosest shirt I could find.

Nicole arrived about twenty minutes later, looking tired and a little grumpy. She came out to the kitchen and began talking, then suddenly stopped, looking at me.

"Why are you dressed like that?"

"I just wanted to have a comfortable afternoon before our guests arrive." I smiled.

She lifted the hem of the shirt and looked at me wide-eyed. "You have nothing on under that shirt."

"I know. Come with me. Please." Pulling her hand, I led her out to the patio where soft music was playing and a breeze ruffled the crisp white sheet.

"Well this is lovely," she said, looking at everything. "Is this for our guests?"

"I thought you might enjoy a nice massage, and we don't have time to go anywhere." I opened the champagne and poured her a glass. "Why don't you sit there and enjoy your champagne while I start on your feet?"

She raised her eyebrows and pursed her lips. "Why not?"

I sat on the deck, slipped her sandals off, and poured some of her expensive lotion into my hand. Her eyes never left me. I rubbed the sides of her calf, alternating soft and strong strokes. When I reached her foot, I massaged each toe.

"You know you will spoil me," she said in a very sultry tone.

"That is my evil plan." I switched feet and could almost feel the tension leaving her. When I finished the other foot, I knelt in front of her and slowly began to unbutton her blouse. It slipped off her shoulders and I removed her bra, exposing her chest. I heard her gasp as I pulled her to her feet. Slowly removing her slacks and panties, I pointed to the chaise. She swallowed the remainder of her champagne and put the glass down, then leaned over and stretched out on her stomach. Her well-defined muscles slid beneath her soft skin, begging for my touch.

"This is incredible, Meg. I feel so decadent and naughty."

"I want you to feel relaxed and cared for." I sat beside her and began to massage her neck and shoulders. It was hot on the patio but there was enough of a breeze that it wasn't oppressive. I continued down her back, gently working the muscles.

"Oh, that feels wonderful." Her voice dropped and oozed relaxation. I moved down a little farther to her magnificent derriere and long legs. I was trying hard to focus on my movements and not how easy it would be to shift to a different kind of massage.

When I reached her feet, I asked her to turn over.

As I reached for the lotion, she said, "I think I might be more relaxed if you would take your shirt off and let me watch you."

"As you wish." I could've pulled the shirt over my head; however, I chose to unbutton it slowly. It hung just below my hips and had at least eight buttons. Nicole was lying on her back with her hands behind her head, her keen eyes fixed on me as she nibbled her lower lip.

The shirt slipped onto the deck and I sat down beside her, rubbed the lotion between my hands, and reached for her neck. Our faces were very close and I could see her dilated pupils. I massaged her neck and shoulders as she watched. When I took one arm, I brushed across her chest, eliciting a tiny gasp.

Her arms were soft and strong, her hands delicate. The skin surrendered to my touch. Her hand relaxed as I dug my thumbs into her palms, and she groaned. I was just finishing when the last of the Mozart symphonies concluded. The next CD was Beethoven.

I stood up and went over to retrieve the large basin with rose-scented water and a sponge.

"This is going to feel quite cool. Tell me if it's too much."

I trailed the large sponge, dripping with water, down each arm.

She shivered. "Oh, that feels so good."

I refilled the sponge and stroked her face and her hair, allowing the water to run free. With each stroke of the sponge along her hot skin, I could see goose bumps. Her breasts came alive with the cool water, and I trailed the sponge down her legs and back up her inner thighs.

I rolled her toward me and supported her with my left arm as I sponged her back down to her thighs.

By the time I finished, she was completely soaked and sexy as hell. Her eyes were still intently focused on me, her mouth open, lips parted, and she was breathing heavily. I reached over to the table for the towel and carefully dried every part of her.

I poured another glass of champagne and handed it to her. "Are you feeling better?" I said with a smile. I was standing naked as a jaybird in front of her, and more than a little self-conscious.

Her eyes were no longer fixed on mine because her penetrating gaze focused on my body, making me feel even more uncomfortable. Nicole enjoyed being naked; I lacked her uninhibitedness.

"I think I do not get enough time to admire your beautiful body, and I like it very much. Often we are in the dark and I must rely on my sense of touch, but this is so much better. Come closer."

My mouth was dry, and I knew my face flushed because the heat was much more intense than it had been a moment ago. It's okay being naked in bed with your lover or even those memorable moments with your gynecologist, but standing in broad daylight was just weird. Then, she touched my hip with her fingers.

"I'm so jealous of your wonderful figure, your soft hips, and your narrow waist and your breasts… They are luscious, like juicy ripe fruit."

She trailed her fingers to my sides and stroked my breasts lovingly. The tenderness in her eyes melted my heart and took away my embarrassment.

"Nicole, no one has ever said that to me. I've always been a little ashamed."

She pulled me closer, kissed my belly, and wrapped her arms around my hips. "But why? Your body is young and strong and oh so exquisite. It gives me pleasure just to look at you."

The fluttering in my chest began.

Nicole stood up and ran her hands across my face and down my neck. "You are too hot, I think. Please sit." She reached down for the sponge and wiped my face. "Now I will bathe you."

She squeezed the wet sponge over the top of my head and the water surged down my neck and back. The cooling sensation caused me to shiver when water trickled along my shoulders and back muscles, the tingling ricocheting down my spine. The next rush of water covered my face as rivulets made their way across and between my breasts to my belly and between my legs. I closed my eyes to experience every minuscule sensation.

The large sea sponge caressed my skin, and her skin brushed against mine repeatedly. I felt as though I were floating on the ocean caressed by small waves as the sun warmed me at the same time.

The next sensation was the towel patting me dry. Nicole cradled my face in her hands and tipped my face up, like angel wings, and kissed my lips. "Lie with me here in the sun and let me feel you."

We both stretched out on the chaise facing one another. She traced the features on my face with her fingertips and then slowly raked my hair back from my face several times.

"I like being with you. Everything about it feels right and good," I said and reached to her lower back to pull her closer. Our skin just barely touched and her eyes focused on mine with a sleepy contented gaze.

We lay together that way as the sun made its way across the patio. We touched each other, caressed, and whispered, with a sense of appreciation and wonder. No urgency.

※※※※

A tingling sensation in my left arm brought me fully awake. Nicole's cheek was on my shoulder with one arm and one leg across my body. The memories flooded back in and joy swelled my heart. I pressed my lips to the top of her head and inhaled her soft scent mingled with roses. I couldn't imagine being any happier; I had the greatest gift in my arms. I watched the dappled sunbeam dance across the covered patio and realized it was probably late afternoon. Very late. *Shit.*

"Nicole? I think we should get up," I whispered. "We have company coming...very soon."

Her eyes fluttered and her lips turned into a smile. Her palm rested on my cheek and she turned her soft lips up toward me. I craved her generous offer, her exquisite kiss—soft, sensuous, and long.

"Please, we have to get dressed. They're going to be here soon."

The Bernard pout. "Very well, but I am not finished kissing you."

"Neither am I, but we did invite people to join us for dinner, and while I don't think they'd object to sitting around naked, it would be polite to at least start dressed."

We both started to laugh, but honestly if I asked, Lena and Brenda would probably have no issue with a summer supper-*au-naturale.*

We straightened up the patio, and when we came into the house it was five thirty. I began dinner preparations as Nicole ran for the shower. There was no way I would wash away the taste of her on my lips. Thinking about our afternoon delight reaffirmed my idea of making a reservation at the 10,000 Waves Spa in Santa Fe to enjoy their soaking tubs, enclosed patios, and massage services for both of us. *Yes.*

At precisely five fifty-five, the door knocker sounded. These good friends epitomized punctuality. I greeted them both. We had the customary awe-inspired comments about the décor, design, and furnishings—and we were still in the living room. Nicole appeared at the top of the stairs looking even more stunning—if possible—than she had a half hour earlier. She wore a seafoam green fitted halter top with some equally fitted shorts. Her hair was wet and styled loosely, and she had on just a touch of makeup and some very rosy cheeks. Every time she entered a room, my pulse increased and I was captivated all over again.

She greeted Lena and Brenda warmly and effusively as long-lost friends. "I am thrilled you could join us on such short notice."

"It worked out perfectly. I had to go into Santa Fe anyway, so it was easy for both of us," Lena said, releasing Nicole from an enthusiastic hug.

After touring the house with Nicole, our guests assembled on the patio for cocktails and appetizers. I set the table up for some casual dining and was glad I left the radio for some background music. The early evening light cast a glow on the adobe walls making colors brighter and more vibrant. New Mexico's thinner atmosphere created a more reflective light that enhanced colors. It felt good to be serving people I cared so deeply for in such a beautiful environment.

"Just the other night we were sitting out here," Nicole said. "And I told Meg that I wished we had a swimming pool like yours." She reached over and stroked my arm and wrist as she spoke, something she had been doing all evening.

Brenda smiled and nodded. "You two started something that night, and after you left I think everybody got in that pool naked. It was quite a sight."

"I must say, the highlight for me was hearing you both sing. Meg, I can't remember the last time I heard you sing," Lena said, leaning forward. "You sounded good."

"I have to credit my coach. Nicole is so patient, and encouraging… Well, I'm grateful," I said, pleased with the compliment.

"Nicole, I'm sure this is rude, but would you be willing to give us a little sample from the opera?"

"I don't think Nicole—" I started to object.

"No, I don't mind, especially if you'll join me." She winked at me and I caved.

"Let me get this table cleared and I'll meet you guys in the den," I said.

Lena stayed to help me while Nicole and Brenda went into the house.

"You look really happy, my friend, and it's pretty clear that something's going on here."

"Lena, I wish I knew. We talked the other night for the first time about the fact that it's more than a little affair. We both admitted we had feelings for one another, but she couldn't commit to anything more."

"It's only been a short time. I'm sure the more she gets to know you the more surprised she'll be."

"That's the thing, Lena. In four weeks I'll have to start back to work. I'll still be able to work with her in the evenings, but we won't have as much time together."

She stopped loading the dishes into the dishwasher and looked at me. "Meg, have you thought about what you want? I mean, where do you think this relationship will go, realistically?"

I shut the water off and looked at her. I didn't know the answer to that. Neither one of us was in a position to quit our jobs. Maybe that's why we hadn't ventured into more planning. Where could it go? "I can't even think about details, I just want to be with her, and I don't know how."

"I guess you guys have some work to do. Don't get me wrong, you're my closest friend and more than anything I want to see you happy. Nicole is a beautiful woman and attracted to you. I just don't see you following her around the world as her assistant. You've got a life here, and I can't see her settling down in Santa Fe."

Her words cut me like ice-cold fingers tearing at my heart. The romantic teenager wanted it all, wanted to give up everything to be with the one she loved. The responsible adult recognized the reality—I'd really just started my career as a nurse and had deep roots in the community. Why would I jeopardize that on a summer fling?

I heard Nicole talking and laughing in the other room and a pain shot through my heart. I couldn't bear the thought of not being able to hear that laugh.

Don't get morose, Ellis. A few hours ago you were the happiest you've ever been in your life. How you could forget that and start awfulizing the worst-case scenario is amazing. Buck up, girlie. A beautiful woman is waiting for you.

Lena gave me a big hug. "Let's go have a little entertainment, all right?"

"Sure."

Nicole and I regaled our guests with part of the first act from *La Traviata*. I wasn't sure if Nicole felt obliged to do it, but Lena and Brenda loved it, and so did I. Every time she looked me in the eye and sang was a little piece of Christmas.

Nicole was comfortable, lively, and interesting as she interacted with two of my oldest friends. I could have done fine without the embarrassing questions about high school. After very little coaxing, Lena relayed the story of our history.

"You need to understand, Meg was an insufferable show-off in high school. Not only was she in the show choir, but she also worked on the yearbook and got trophies for swimming, track, and basketball. We had a bunch of classes together, and by the end of freshman year we were pretty tight. We stayed that way through high school, and when it came time for graduation we both opted to attend Eastern New Mexico University."

Nicole and I were still sitting on the piano bench, and she held onto my arm and hand but listened with rapt attention. I knew what came next.

"Being so far away from home, I convinced Meg that it was the perfect opportunity for some innocent experimentation." Lena waggled her eyebrows. "We tried smoking—hated it. Tried smoking dope, same thing. Drinking was much more fun, but that led us down a twisty path to sex."

Lena was enjoying this far too much.

"Let me interject here," I said. "We used to talk about guys and girls we thought were cool, we even double-dated with some geeky guys. So, let's cut to the chase. Lena was my first lover. We had fun figuring it all out, but ultimately it didn't work and decided we were much better friends. It was about the same time that we met Brenda and suddenly I was history. I have no regrets. I now have two fabulous friends who are perfect together."

"Thanks for giving her up so gallantly, Meg, because she's made me incredibly happy," Brenda said.

They kissed each other and Nicole grabbed my hand. I looked over to see her smiling with tears in her eyes. She excused herself and left the room quickly. The three of us just looked at each other.

"Is she okay?" Lena asked. "I didn't think that would bother her."

"Oh, I'm sure it didn't," I said, although I couldn't imagine what happened.

"Baby, it's pretty late. We better get going," Brenda said.

"Right. We should probably say thank you to Nicole. Should we wait?"

"No, I'm sure it's okay. I'm really glad you could make it, and I'll tell her what you said."

I had no idea what was going on. I rarely saw Nicole when she wasn't one hundred percent in control. Lena and Brenda waved as they drove away, and I went back to the house to find Nicole.

I found her sitting on the side of the tub in her bathroom. Her expression was unreadable, but it was clear she had been crying.

"They had to leave but wanted me to thank you," I said.

She nodded.

"Is there anything I can do?"

Nicole carefully wiped under each eye with a tissue, pulled her shoulders back a little bit, and shook her head.

I leaned my hip against the sink and rearranged the various bottles of perfume, makeup, and other mysterious potions. The conversation about Lena and me played through my head. What could we have possibly said that sent Nicole running from the room? I couldn't imagine it had anything to do with short-term experimentation fourteen years earlier.

After several painful minutes, I said, "Well, I

guess I'll go work in the kitchen." She said nothing, so I left.

I knew better than to think that a few short weeks or even a few short years would grant me the kind of wisdom I needed to anticipate or understand the workings of another's mind. Nicole Bernard was as much a mystery to me today as she was almost two months ago. She was both mercurial and very sensitive.

The last time she had gone wonky on me was when she and Mario fought. *Jeez, what if he had called? She wouldn't have to tell me—I mean, it's her business. That would sure explain it, but I hope not.*

After I straightened up the patio table and chairs, I wiped down all the surfaces and then stretched out on one of the lounge chairs. The CD player was still playing a recording of *Madama Butterfly* made by the Metropolitan Opera many years ago.

I felt a smile forming as I remembered the performance. I was only twelve and I wore a new dress. It was my first opera and I was a hormonal preteen. The exotic sets and the exquisite costumes were the most beautiful things I'd ever seen. Everything about the production was magical to me, and I think the beautiful Cio-Cio-San was my first real girl crush. Her sudden death marked the teen me early as a romantic.

That defining moment inspired me to study music, something my parents had been trying to get me to do for years. They tried with ballet lessons, which were nothing more than comical. We graduated to the piano and then to voice. When I saw that performance, I knew I would sing opera.

For a stubborn, moody teenager, I was lucky to have parents who were supportive and patient. They had enjoyed the time together the previous week and I knew how much it meant to them to see me re-engaging with the music.

The intrusive sound of my cell phone interrupted my reverie. "Hello? Hi, Dad, I was just thinking about you guys."

"Meg, honey, your mom has been in an accident. They're taking her to the University ER." His voice broke.

I sat up. "What? When did that happen?"

"About twenty minutes ago. They just called me and I'm on my way to the hospital. Please come as soon as you can."

"Okay, yes I will. See you soon." I couldn't catch my breath and my hands were trembling. *Please, no. Not Mom.*

I ran into the house and found Nicole in the kitchen. "I just got a call from my father. My mom was in a car accident coming back from a concert. He's on his way to the hospital, and I told him I'd meet him there." My brain raced with a thousand worst-case scenarios.

"Do you want me to go with you?"

"No, I don't know how long I'll be there, and you have a show tomorrow night." I couldn't think about anything else right now. "I have to go."

"Meg, please be careful and call me when you find out something."

Act III Scene 6

The University of New Mexico Hospital and Clinics sat in the center of a huge campus. During nurses' training, I had done some of my rotations there and it had grown larger since then. I parked in the new structure and hurried to the emergency room. The large waiting room crawled with Friday night specials. It was nearly midnight and it would get busier in a couple of hours when the bars closed.

My dad was standing near the desk, looking down the hallway.

"Dad, I'm sorry it took so long for me to get here. Traffic was awful."

He wrapped his arms around me and hugged me tight, "I'm just glad you're here, kiddo. They just took Mom down to X-ray. She seems to be all right but banged up. I talked to her for a minute before the doctor saw her."

"What happened?"

"There was a recital for some of her students tonight and she was just coming home. While crossing Carlisle, a car ran the light and hit her broadside. It spun her around and a car going southbound clipped the rear of her car."

My brain was having trouble listening to his words as I visualized my mother thrown around in the car. On the drive down, I had envisioned every worst-case scenario and best-case scenario at least twice. My professional brain focused on the logistics of what she might need. The daughter part of my brain was twelve years old and terrified of losing her.

I had horrifying moments thinking about arriving too late and not being able to say goodbye to her. And my poor dad, he depended on her so much. It would be devastating for him to lose her.

"She'll be okay, Dad. Mom is strong." I said the words and prayed that they would be true. His arm stayed around my shoulders and he simply nodded.

"Are you Mr. Ellis?" A young resident appeared in the doorway. He looked like Doogie Howser, with long hair and some baby stubble on his chin. He also looked tired.

"I'm Doctor Lombard. Your wife is on the way back from X-ray, but I just wanted to let you know that she's okay. There's a hairline fracture of her left humerus, and she has spasms in the muscles of her neck. There are some superficial cuts from broken glass and a lot of bruising. There was no loss of consciousness, but I think we'd like to keep her overnight to be sure there are no other injuries."

"Can we see her now?" I asked.

"It'll be a couple of minutes. I'll send the nurse out to get you."

"Thank you, Doctor." My dad shook the kid's hand.

"Dad, that's good news. Mom is going to be sore for a while because those neck spasms are like whiplash. She'll need some help to get around."

His eyes welled up as he reached for his handkerchief. "I'm so glad you're here, kitten. I don't know what I'd do if anything happened to your mom."

"I know. Me, neither."

"Do you folks want to follow me back?" I looked up and saw a cute young woman in maroon scrubs motioning us to the trauma room. She looked even younger than the doctor did.

"After you see her, someone needs to go to admitting to fill out the paperwork."

She stopped in front of a partitioned area in the large trauma room. At least five other accident victims were being managed.

We passed one gurney that was empty except for a bloody paper sheet, soiled dressings, ripped packaging. On the floor was the cutaway clothing. The air crackled with electricity and rushed voices issued commands.

Parts of my training came back. I remembered trauma medicine as an intense experience. Some people thrive on the adrenaline it produces while others become overwhelmed by the stress. I enjoyed the challenge at the time but realized I couldn't maintain that level of intensity.

My mom would remember none of this, fortunately. She was dozing when we slipped beside her bed. My dad took her hand and kissed her cheek. There were several fresh bruises along the side of her cheek along with several small cuts. A sling held her left arm in place, and there was an ice pack on her head.

"Hi, Mom," I said softly, taking her other hand gently

"Meg, darling, you didn't need to come down here. I'll be all right." Her words were slow.

"Of course I did. I had to make sure they were taking good care of you."

Her smile was genuine but weary.

"Honey, did the doctors talk to you about your injuries?" my dad said.

"Yes, they told me they wanted me to stay overnight. I just don't think that's necessary. I'd rather be home in my bed."

"I know, Mom, it's just that you were hit pretty hard and they want to make sure there's no delayed reaction. It will be a lot safer. We don't want to have to bring you back," I said.

My dad went to admitting and I stayed with my mother until it was time to go upstairs. She shared a double room with an elderly woman. My dad joined us, and we hovered over my mother's bed until she kicked us out.

"I love you, Mom."

"I love you too, honey. Now you get some sleep. Don't you have to work tomorrow?"

"I'm going to stay with Dad tonight and we'll see how soon they let you come home. Don't you worry about me. I want you to rest and call the nurse if anything changes."

We were able to pick Mom up early the next afternoon. Her bruises were a little more vivid the next day and she moved very slowly because of all the sore muscles. I had spent the morning rearranging the living room to make it more patient-friendly. My dad and I both agreed that she shouldn't have to climb stairs for a few days.

Over pizza, we finally began to talk about the great time they had with Nicole and her family. They raved about the opera. It suddenly dawned on me that I got so caught up in worry and urgency that I hadn't even called Nicole to let her know my mom was okay. I would have been furious if the tables were turned. I looked at my watch; it was after seven. She would already be in wardrobe or makeup. Maybe later.

My mother was looking at me intently, as if waiting for an answer.

"I'm sorry. What?" I said.

"I asked how you and Nicole were getting along."

Good question. "Fine, I think it's been kind of chaotic lately. Lars made a few changes in the show that called for a little more rehearsal. Plus, Nicole can be such a perfectionist. She worries whenever there's a change." *Or is it me that's worried about change?*

My dad cleared the table while my mom and I sat and drank tea.

"Honey, it certainly seems like you and Nicole are forming a very close relationship. Is it any more than that?"

Crap. How is it that mothers know that stuff? I moved the placemat back and forth nervously. "I don't honestly know and it's a little frustrating. I've tried hard to maintain a professional distance because I work for her. There's been a lot of flirting and there is certainly an attraction—for both of us. I'm just worried that she's rebounding from an unhappy relationship. Even if she does have an interest, I just don't know if there's a way that either of us can manage a relationship right now. I start school soon, and she'll be leaving shortly after that."

Mom focused on her teacup, which usually meant she wasn't telling me something. "Yes. Well, you do have demanding careers…"

"Mom, is there something you're not saying?"

"Honey, Nicole is a lovely woman and you know how much we all admire her. I remember how you had such a crush on her when you met her, it's just—"

"It's just what? You think it's still some schoolgirl crush?" I said, feeling suddenly defensive.

She reached over and covered my hand. "Sweetheart, I don't want to see you get hurt again. After Bekka, you had a terrible time. Your dad and I were so worried."

"That was different. Besides, we don't have a real relationship, it's just…I don't know what it is."

"Do you love her?"

My head snapped up and I looked at her. She was completely serious.

"I honestly don't know. When we're together sometimes, I can't imagine being any happier, and in the next minute, she can be very cool and aloof and I feel like I'm imagining things. I do know that I have never felt these kinds of feelings ever in my life. They're powerful and unrelenting."

"You'll know, and so will she. I think you need to give this more time and consideration," she said.

"Thanks, Mom. I will. Meanwhile, you look like you're ready to fall asleep in that chair. Let's get you tucked in."

"On one condition. Right after breakfast, I want you to go back to work. Promise?"

"Promise." I gave her a gentle hug and kiss, grateful that I was able to do so.

Act III Scene 7

The dashboard clock said a little before noon when I got back to Nicole's house. Time just got away from me. I planned to have breakfast with my parents but then I needed to help my mother to wash up and get safely back to the couch. For my dad's sake, I wrote down some instructions about medications and bandages. He protested, saying he could remember, which normally he could. Today he couldn't because he was worried.

Again, I had forgotten to call Nicole. I justified it thinking I would be there soon enough.

As soon as I walked in, I could hear the piano and Nicole's voice lighting up the house. I put my backpack on the floor and went out to the den. She didn't look up, so I stood in the doorway and watched. Her voice captured the emotional line from her scene in the second act as she sang with her eyes closed. Her expressive face conveyed such intense emotion it was a pity that most of the audience was unable to see it.

Abruptly, she stopped and looked up, again sensing my presence before I made it known.

"You surprised me."

"I didn't want to interrupt."

The look of pleasure and surprise on her face changed in front of my eyes. The look became something else, something darker. She looked down and played a few random notes.

"Your mother, she is all right?" she said quietly.

"Yes, she's pretty banged up and has a fracture in her arm. They kept her overnight and we brought her home yesterday afternoon."

No response.

"Nicole, I'm sorry I didn't call. It was hectic and confusing...I meant to."

There was a tense silence, and then she slammed the lid down on the keyboard, surprising me.

"I was worried." Her eyes were teary and very dark. She had both hands on top of the piano. "All I asked was that you call." Anger edged her voice.

"I know. I'm sorry. We were just so worried I didn't think—"

"You didn't think. How was I to know that you did not have an accident?" A tear ran down her face.

"Nicole, I was upset and worried. It was wrong not to call you and let you know everything was all right. If I were in your place I would be just as angry. I don't know what more I can say."

She stood up, brushed past me into the kitchen, and began pulling things from the refrigerator.

Sonofabitch. "Do you want me to leave?"

She closed the refrigerated door, and I could see the tears in her eyes. She simply shook her head.

"What's wrong? You were upset about something when I left, and obviously whatever it was is still bothering you," I said.

Her arms clasped tightly around herself as she rocked back on the refrigerator door. She looked like a tightly wound spring, but I wasn't sure what boiled beneath the surface. Was it anger, fear, frustration, or something completely different? I needed to buy some time. "I'm going to the washroom and I'll be right back. Maybe we could just talk a little bit?"

A few moments later I stood looking in the bathroom mirror unable to decide what to do. I splashed cool water on my face and neck while I tried to figure out how to approach this. If she was angry because I didn't call—well, I deserved it. If something else was going on it was important to find out now. Although there was no reason on earth she'd have to tell me unless she wanted to.

This was hard stuff. When I found her sitting at the piano just now, it steered me to a special place—beyond words—and reminded me that the strong feelings I experienced were simply because I cared for her so deeply.

I took a deep breath and started back down the hall. I found her in the living room. There were two bottles of water on the table, signaling to me that at least we were going to talk.

I sat down at one end of the sofa and faced her. "Do you want to tell me what's going on? Because I hate feeling that you're angry at me."

"I have so many feelings right now, but I think it is not so much anger as it is fear. When there was no word from you, I thought something might have happened, and then all day Saturday, nothing. I felt perhaps you forgot or that it didn't matter."

"That's not true—"

She put a hand up. "Let me finish. I must tell you all at once, or I may not be able. On Friday night when your friend Lena was telling us about how you two met and how, well, that you were lovers, I was so moved. Your friends love you very much, and they love each other for so many years. It made me sad."

Nicole stood up to retrieve tissues as tears rolled

down her cheeks. I was confused but had to let her finish.

"I have worked very hard for my career and it has been good, but I think your friends are happier. They are so comfortable together and I can see their love. When I looked at you, I could see that it might be possible for you to love me like that. I could see a day in the future to tell people how we met so many years before."

My heart ached watching her describe something that she felt was so elusive. Her voice choked up as she continued. "Then I did not hear from you and I was afraid that I would never feel that closeness again."

She stood up and paced in front of the fireplace, just where she stood when I met with her more than eight weeks earlier.

Her voice softened. "I went to the theater Saturday. I prepared as I always do, and everything was the same except for one thing." She looked up at me. "I kept looking for you. I put the cooler in the chair the way you always do and when I would come off stage I would be excited thinking about the pride on your face as you waited for me. But you were not there.

"I sometimes feel I do not deserve a relationship, because when you are not here I get angry, and when you are here I am not sure how to be with you. Maybe this is why my husband left to be with another woman. Maybe it is just not possible."

Her body began to shake as she sobbed harder. I understood what she meant, and I didn't have words to fix it. "Nicole, please let me hold you."

She came over and curled up next to me so I could hold her. I stroked her hair and inhaled her now familiar scent. Her body shook with sadness. Her words pounded in my brain.

"I think I understand, and I'm so sorry that I wasn't there. I broke my promise and I let you down. I wish I could promise you right now that I will never do that again. I can't. It was my mother, I had no choice. Except that I should've called and I promise you I won't leave you not knowing again. It's cruel. We have to be able to share or we have nothing."

"I know. I must use the washroom." She stood and walked out of the living room.

I finished the bottle of water and took it to the kitchen. The refrigerator held no answers and very little food, and I had started making a grocery list when Nicole returned.

"Would you like some lunch?"

"I think I am not too hungry and I need to review my music." She passed me and went to the den.

After Nicole declined my offer, we just moved around each other in uncomfortable silence. I didn't know what else to say, and clearly the issues were not completely resolved.

I thought part of it might be the difficulty communicating complicated intense emotions or conflicted feelings in two languages. I don't think I could have done it. So, I figured she might need more time. Nevertheless, I felt heaviness in my chest. The comfortable familiarity was absent. I didn't even attempt to touch her because she was avoiding contact.

I watched carefully for signs of the first thaw. I needed to talk and wanted to share with her how frightened I'd been and how much I wish she'd gone with me. It was moments like this when I wished I had someone with whom to confide and share my feelings.

For me, that confidant was Nicole. Her soft words and gentle touch could have reassured me. I needed her touch, but I had broken her trust and she needed time. The afternoon passed into evening and Nicole started cooking supper. I had spent the afternoon doing laundry for her and myself, so maybe this was her pitching in. It wasn't as though we weren't talking. It's just that we weren't saying anything, and it was driving me crazy.

Over coffee, Nicole outlined her schedule for the week. There would be more rehearsal for some additional changes. She had scheduled several interviews, two of which were Monday morning. She asked me if I wanted to attend any of the other performances, to which I readily agreed. Then came the moment I dreaded.

"I do not know what makes me be so tired, but I think I should get some sleep," she said.

Fearing the worst, I said, "Then I guess I should go down to the guesthouse." She didn't argue.

I picked up the basket of clean laundry. "Goodnight, Nicole. I hope you sleep well."

"*Bonsoir.*"

Sadness burned in my throat. I walked slowly down the path, illuminated by moonlight. I felt disconnected and very alone. What I needed most right now was the warmth of her body near me. I was scared that the chasm we allowed to crack open might remain forever, and that would break my heart.

It was busywork and I knew it, still I put the laundry away, rearranged my drawers, turned the TV on, turned it off, and paced around the living room. My throat was still tight and my shoulders were tense. All I needed to do was let go but I was afraid the tears would consume me.

You might as well face the facts, Ellis, this little faux pas of yours hurt her. The lady was depending on you and you let her down. You already got a glimpse of how she reacts when she finds out people aren't dependable.

The pillow I was clutching to my chest became a projectile when I hurled it across the room. I knew it was my fault, but I didn't know what else I could do to make up for it. Dammit, how could she not understand? It was my mother! The guesthouse suddenly felt too small and I went outside.

A light breeze carrying the sounds of the crickets and the distant yipping of the coyotes were the only sounds on a beautiful summer night. The lights were out in the main house and I wandered back up to the patio, hoping that I would find her waiting for me.

It was empty. I sat on the end of the chaise with both elbows on my knees. There had to be something I could do. I wasn't willing to give up without a fight, but I also didn't want to aggravate the already tense situation.

I flopped back on the chaise, staring at the blue-black canopy over me. The moon upstaged most of the stars, but the vastness of the New Mexico sky was still breathtaking. The ageless beauty of the night sky was somewhat reassuring. I thought about how many millennia human beings looked into the firmament for answers just as I was doing. How many lovers, how many tortured souls, how many frightened children, had looked up thinking that an answer lay among those stars, or with a personal version of the universal life force? I wasn't alone, not really.

My mom had told me to trust that the relationship would grow if it was meant to, and that all we needed to do was continue to talk. Nicole didn't seem to want a talk right now. My silent prayer was that she knew my feelings in her heart, and trusted them.

※ ※ ※ ※

Having slept poorly, I welcomed the opportunity to enjoy a hot shower and a cup of coffee. I was pleasantly surprised to find a beautiful coffee cake on the counter. Just as I was about to cut it, Nicole appeared looking fresh but not well rested.

"Good morning," I said, sounding much more chipper than I was. "Act as if," the saying goes.

"*Bonjour*," Nicole said and walked over to me. She hesitated briefly and kissed my cheek. "I see you found the coffee cake. It is beautiful, yes?"

"Did you make it?"

Her unexpected laugh sounded like a delicate crystal wind chime. "*Mais non*, I cannot bake."

She poured coffee as I cut up the pastry and served it. "Did you sleep well? I know you were very tired."

"For a little bit. Then I would toss and turn too much." She sipped her coffee, watching me over the rim of her cup. "And you? How was your sleep?"

"I'm not sure I slept at all. I was very restless and uncomfortable."

"Perhaps you have things in your mind," she said, a gentle salvo.

"That's true, too many things that worry me."

"I understand. The worries, they seem so much larger in the dark."

"That's certainly true. Larger than reality, I'm sure."

"Yes, in the daytime they do not seem so big anymore."

Her eyes softened around the corners, and the small furrow between her brows diminished. I could feel some of the muscles in my shoulders relax. There was a small crack of light shining in the darkness.

We sat down at the table for a few minutes to eat, and I felt as though some of the tension dissipated.

"I should sing a little bit to warm up. Do you think you would like to sing?"

"I'd like that very much."

Once we completed the scales and warm-up exercises, Nicole chose several sections of the opera to work on and I sang parts where needed. We sat together on the piano bench, but the connection we made was through our voices blending and harmonizing. Soon I realized that the lines we were singing were becoming more emotional and delivered with greater feeling.

It was amazing, because I felt as though we were sharing feelings without discussing particulars. Her eyes locked on mine as she sang various sections from a wonderful love story, and I responded in kind. We connected again—tenuously, but still connected—and some of the icy cold parts inside of me began to warm.

We sang for over an hour and finally stopped. There was nothing more to say but my heart continued to broadcast.

"I am happy you came back to me," she said.

"It's where I want to be." And I meant it.

Her hand was resting lightly on my arm and a flood of warmth flowed through my body. *You need to make this move. It's up to you now.*

I leaned close enough to kiss the corner of her

mouth, and whispered, "It has been so hard for me without you."

She closed her eyes and squeezed my arm. "I am so sorry, *ma chérie*, I pushed you away. It was wrong, and it hurt me too."

Her lips brushed mine and I felt her breath on my cheek. I leaned my cheek against hers and closed my eyes to feel her nearness. Her fingers touched my hair and I wanted to bury myself in her. The smell of her skin was as soothing to me as my grandmother's kitchen on a winter morning. Nicole filled me and warmed my heart.

"You forgive me," she said.

"Always." I touched my lips to hers with a promise. She took my lips softly with hers, and my heart rejoiced with the sweetness of her kiss.

❦❦❦❦

Greta had scheduled a small rehearsal room for the interviews. Nicole was adamant that no one come to her home or ask questions about her personal relationships. The only acceptable topics would be the current production, her schedule, or music-related questions. It surprised me a little when Greta took me aside and told me that Nicole had the same rules the last time she was here. When it came to public information, Nicole was an intensely private person. I got the message.

The first interview was for the *Taos News*. Taos was a beautiful, small, northern New Mexico town that was popular with tourists and skiers, and had an excellent reputation with artists.

The young woman seemed knowledgeable about opera and had done her homework on Nicole's repertoire. Nicole's modest but brightly colored dress was a good contrast against the drab walls of the rehearsal studio. The photographer also snapped a few shots just outside the door with a background of cholla, chamisa, and the startling blue sky, which contrasted beautifully. He agreed to send copies to her agent, and I made a mental note to ask for one of the outdoor shots. I hung back out of the way, hoping they would think I was one of the regular staff. Talking to a personal assistant might be a little too tempting.

The next magazine interview lasted a bit longer and focused on her unique interest in acting. After several minutes, I took the opportunity to go for a walk.

When they finished, Nicole approached me. "Mr. Wells would like to buy lunch. Would you come?"

"No, you go ahead, and I'll meet you back here for rehearsal."

She touched my hand briefly and then left with the reporter. I watched them walk to his car with the briefest feeling of possessiveness. He was young, handsome, and very knowledgeable about opera.

I chose to go back to the house and make lunch. It would be a chance to talk to my parents and have a little time to think.

The house felt unusually quiet as I made a peanut butter sandwich. I tried to imagine what it would be like to live with Nicole all the time, to build a life together. Would her mood swings become an impediment, or would I learn to read them better? Beyond the drama and the passion were the quiet moments we spent just talking. Nicole was both intelligent and inquisitive. Her interests reached far beyond her musical career and her passion for history was almost as intense. She taught me so many things about European history. Her interest in American history astounded me. More than once, I had to do an Internet search to answer some of her questions about my own country. We seemed to share similar political leanings and we had just barely scratched the surface on the subject of religion.

Cell phone in hand, I made my way out to the patio to call my folks. I happened to gaze up at Nicole's balcony, six narrow steps above me. At the top, a chair faced the lower patio and it held one of her robes. Curious. I wondered if she had been sitting out last night. Was she watching me? Were we both looking for each other because of mutual need? I'd never know.

"Hi, Dad, how's it going?" I listened while he described Mom's restless night and sore muscles. He reported that she was eating fairly well but was less and less willing to walk around because of her stiff joints and fatigue.

"That's pretty normal after a car accident, don't be too worried. As long as she doesn't have a fever and isn't sleeping all the time, it's probably all right to let her rest. Do you have an appointment with her doctor?"

He sounded a little better than he had on Sunday. I would have to try to find some time to get down there. Maybe I should take Nicole; it would certainly cheer my mother up.

"You know you can always call me, Dad. Hug Mom for me. Bye."

I looked at my watch and realized that the rehearsal would be starting shortly. Music bag in hand, I headed out to the rehearsal hall.

Nicole was talking with Stefan, and it looked like this rehearsal was primarily for the principals. Most of the chorus was involved with other productions. She waved to me and I took a chair behind the accompanist.

Lars worked patiently with Stefan. I thought he had improved, but evidently Lars wanted something he wasn't getting. Of course, my eyes were mostly on Nicole. She worked masterfully with every detail. Even a tiny error would elicit some terse French expletives.

Even as I sat in an impersonal rehearsal room, the walls fell away. I saw Violetta Valery, the frail courtesan, fighting against the conventions of society and a fatal illness to find a little happiness. It wasn't words, lyrics, or even notes coming from her, but a plaintive cry to be heard. With every effort, she became even more believable.

Sometime later in the afternoon, my phone started to vibrate. Fearing news from home, I slipped outside to answer.

"Hi, Liz. How're you doing?"

"I'm okay, but I just got back and heard your mom was in the hospital."

"She was in a car accident and got pretty banged up but she's fine. She's at home."

"I called them to see if I could come over and pick up the tickets they offered me. Your dad said it was fine, but I didn't want to intrude if she wasn't feeling well."

"I think she'd be happy to see you, and I'm really glad you're going to take their tickets. When will you be seeing the show?"

"A week from Friday. One of the teachers I work with was interested and it turns out she's a big fan of

Ms. Bernard, so it will be fun. How are things going with you?"

Good question. "It changes from day to day. I enjoy being up here again and Nicole has been wonderful. I've learned a lot. We've only had to do one or two shows a week, but starting August first that will increase to several times a week until the end of the month."

"When does your school term start?" Liz asked.

"The kids will start on August twenty-second, but we will have orientation and meetings around the sixteenth."

"How is that going to work, with two jobs?"

"I think it will be okay. School gets out early enough for me to get back up here in plenty of time. The commute isn't that bad, either—it's only another twenty minutes."

"Well if something comes up, let me know and maybe I can sub for you."

"Did they cut your hours?" I realized I had been so self-absorbed all summer I hadn't even asked what one of my closest friends was doing.

"Oh gosh, I guess we haven't talked. They cut my position, as well as two other nurses in the district. I may do some temp work or go to one of the contract companies," she said somewhat flippantly.

"I'm sorry, Liz. That sucks."

"You know, I was getting kind of tired of the politics and thinking about a change anyway. It was probably for the best, but I hope I find something soon. I hate to ask, but do you think we'll have a chance to meet Ms. Bernard?"

"Oh, I'm sure we can arrange something because she enjoys meeting folks after the performance and getting their feedback."

"I'm excited to see her. And you."

"Me too. Hey, the rehearsal's breaking up so I better go. Give my mom a hug for me, will you?"

The rehearsal room was nearly empty, and Lars waved to me as he left. I was surprised to see Nicole speaking with a woman I hadn't seen before. Gesturing elaborately, the woman stood quite tall with thick raven hair. Her chic outfit and jewelry made me doubt she was an employee. I hadn't seen her before.

I stood and watched from the door for several minutes as they carried on a very animated conversation. There was a familiarity about the way they talked and laughed, frequently touching one another. It wasn't hard to believe that Nicole had friends here. After all, she'd been out here on several occasions.

They began to walk to the door with their arms wrapped around each other making promises to get together for lunch.

"Nicole, I would love to but this week is just crazy. Next week, lunch for sure. I'll call you Monday to set it up."

"It is wonderful to see you, Marjorie, and I look forward to lunch. *Adieu.*" Nicole waved from the end of the sidewalk as her friend walked away.

I went over the piano and picked up her things. Being irritated surprised me a little. I had friends, no reason to think Nicole shouldn't have friends. I turned my head and looked over my shoulder. It was getting much harder to ignore the feelings I had for Nicole. The infatuation I felt a few weeks earlier had evolved gradually into the deep, warm feelings of love. Maybe it was friendship love, maybe it was idol worship, but I guessed it was the real thing.

With Bekka, my emotions were youthful, exuberant, and fluid. This was different. My earlier experience of working with Nicole distilled and fermented into something rich and complex. The fluttering in my chest started as it always did when I thought about her. Then followed the dreaded cold sensations, thinking about her leaving in a few weeks. I took a deep breath and grabbed the cooler.

You knew where this was going, Ellis, and three months was all you had. You know it and she knows it. Don't waste the time you have.

"All set. Are you ready to go?" I said.

Nicole was positively glowing, which didn't make it any easier for me to act casually.

"Yes, I cannot wait to get home and tell you all about what happened. It was amazing. I am not sure I even know how to describe it." Her face beamed with excitement.

She grabbed my arm and stopped me in my tracks.

"Stefan had one of those moments where everything became clear to him, and so did I!"

Oh, God.

※ ※ ※ ※

Nicole continued the excited twittering about whatever had happened, and clearly I wouldn't have the opportunity to ask about the mysterious woman in the immediate future. I closed the garage door and we went into the house. I proceeded to start my normal routine of unpacking things, getting something to drink, and sitting down to talk.

She was far too excited for that. "Meg, please. I must tell you what is in my heart. It is important."

"Okay." Her plea was earnest and urgent.

"Come sit with me," she said, pulling me into the living room. "I want you to listen to me."

I could not resist her solemnity and intensity. "I will. I want to know what happened." *Wouldn't it be great if after that I could tell you how I felt, how much you mean to me?*

"Today when Stefan was singing about Alfredo's unrequited love, he became Alfredo for a little while. I could see the passion in his eyes, and I could understand how much he suffered because he was not able to tell Violetta of his love. I watched him change before my eyes and what happened was that his beautiful blue eyes became your eyes. It was your beautiful brown eyes that I was looking into when I sang to him. Do you understand?"

No. I had no clue. I shook my head.

Her voice cracked and she took both my hands. "It was you I wanted to be singing to. It is you that I want to tell of my love."

My brain was racing far too fast to process those words. "You, I want to love." Her eyes were clear and focused, and if I didn't understand the words, I understood her look. *Answer her, you stupid shit.*

"You...you want to tell me of your love?" *Oh, that was stellar, very impressive.*

"Yes, I do, very much. I think you care for me as well and I don't want to play anymore. I want you with me in the morning and at night and all the time. I want to have you touch me and caress me because you are always near. Please tell me that I am not wrong, that you do love me in return."

All the noise in my head cleared away and all I could see was Nicole's adoring eyes looking into mine.

"I hardly know what to say. I think I've always loved you, but it wasn't the right time. I dream of you, Nicole. I ache for you when you're not near, and I ache when you are because it's not near enough."

"It took me so long to understand, and I am sorry because I know you were confused," she said.

"Nicole, I love you. I hope you are saying the same thing because I feel like my heart will burst if you don't." I was trembling with excitement and fear. Was this happening?

"Oh, *mon amour*, this is new to me. My heart is so full of love for you I have trouble finding words... *Je t'aime, je t'adore.*"

Her hands shook when she placed them on either side of my neck and pulled me slowly to her waiting lips. We kissed deeply and slowly. I closed my eyes and melted under the sweet caress of her lips. Each of her kisses sent waves of longing rippling through my gut. I burned with desire and a fierce love I had never experienced.

"I want you so desperately right now—"

The feelings we had both held back burst forth in a fury. Fire from within was consuming my body and I wanted to devour her just to ease the hunger.

"Meg, love me now...please."

Our kisses became the conflagration that threatened to consume us both. My need grew and she pulled at me. I pushed her shirt over her head and my ravenous mouth seized her breast. She gasped.

"Oh, please, touch me and hurry. I need you to be inside me," she whispered hoarsely as she straddled me.

A flurry of clothes-pulling, ravenous kisses, clutching hands, and ragged breaths combined with guttural moaning.

Nicole was begging, her hips bucking wildly as she struggled against my hips. She looked wild and beautiful, and I took her at first gently and then hard. She fisted both hands in my hair and crashed through the barrier. She yelled, falling backward and pulling me with her.

"No. Do not move your hand, not yet," she said, gasping loudly.

I didn't. I stayed connected, believing I held her soul. I pulled her up with my other arm and hugged her tightly. "I love the way you feel and the way you move with me."

She opened her eyes and they were wild with desire. She smiled and began to rock her hips again.

I captured her mouth as she opened, drawing her in. She willingly rolled onto her back, inviting me to continue. It was slower and more deliberate as I worked my way down her slick belly, but she was wet and ready.

In between moans, groans, and expletives, Nicole managed to utter a few words. "Promise…you'll never…stop…"

My reply was to bite her inner thigh sweetly.

"Ouch!"

She pulled me up, kissed me hard, and then drew my lower lip between her teeth.

"I am so sorry I wasted so many years being unsatisfied," she said as she stroked my face and ran her fingers through my damp hair. "You seem to always know what my body wants, and it gives me such great pleasure."

Our bodies were heaving for more air, and I smiled at her. "I practice all day long. I watch you

move and breathe and sing. All the while, in my mind, I'm caressing your body with my hands and my mouth and kissing you everywhere. I pray for the time you will invite me to your bed and give yourself over to me completely, to love you as no one has ever done."
I opened my mouth to savor her neck.

"I am so lucky to have you in my life." She thrust her head back for me.

My heart was so full at that moment the pressure almost scared me. Every nerve pulsed wildly. "Pinch me."

"What?"

"Pinch me so that I know I'm not dreaming," I said breathlessly.

There was only a moment to see the impish glint in her eye before I felt a sharp pain shoot through my breast directly to its target between my legs.

My muscles contracted defensively, and the ripples flooded my body with arousal. "Okay, okay, I'm not dreaming." I pulled her hand to my mouth and kissed the palm. "I love you, Nicole."

"I love you too, very much."

Our lips met softly and our bodies fused in a kind of promise. I felt her tongue slide softly to my ear. "Come to bed with me," she said, groaning.

"Bed?"

She giggled. "You thought I was finished making love? *Mais non, chérie.*"

Now, I'm not one to complain when a woman I have fantasized about begs me to come to her bed because she wants to make love. I have also learned my lesson when I ask someone to pinch me, although… it was oddly titillating. I needed a quick trip to the bathroom and Nicole took the opportunity to run to the kitchen.

I folded back the bedding and made myself comfortable on a half dozen pillows. When I looked up, Nicole was juggling a wine bottle, glasses, and a platter of food. Naked. I had to laugh. "You aren't finished, are you? Do you intend to handcuff me to the bed until fall?"

"No, silly. I am quite sure you will stay of your own free will. I just thought we needed to keep our strength up."

She set the plate on the bed while she opened the wine bottle. It was a tasty platter with grapes, strawberries, thick slices of cheese, and some pieces of chicken. I took the glass she handed me.

Her glass held high, she said, "I would like to make a toast to the most wonderful woman whom I have ever met."

I could feel my eyes tearing as we drank. She picked up a strawberry and held it to my lips. "Sweet Meg, I want to apologize because I have been so moody and difficult. It is not my wish to confuse you. Please trust my heart."

"I don't think you know how much that means to me and how I've longed for some sign that it was not just a summer flirtation to you. If it had to be just for fun, I would've taken that just to be near you. To have you love me is scary and wonderful and more than I deserve."

Nicole took my glass and put it and hers on the table. She moved the platter to the floor. "I think our picnic will have to wait a little while because there is more I need you to know from me. I can show you, and I think you will believe me."

ACT III SCENE 8

My head swirled with freshly minted endorphins and my legs were still a little weak. I watched happily as Nicole cooked breakfast. The kitchen looked the same with the sun beaming through the skylights and the smell of coffee and bacon. Everything looked the same and yet everything was different. My world had shifted a hundred and eighty degrees in the span of twenty-four hours.

All of my awkwardness, silliness, and secret fantasies over the last several weeks had magically transformed. All of the worry and doubt, all of the weeks Nicole and I flirted, teased, worked, and even argued, and then something wonderful happened—we clicked. I couldn't imagine my life without her now. Pretty amazing.

"Come and sit down," she said, serving the plates.

"Can we talk a little bit?"

"Of course, *chérie*, about anything you choose."

"I would like to talk a little bit about our schedules, but first I need to tell you how lovely you look this morning. I mean you always do, but you seem to be more radiant this morning."

"Darling, I am more radiant and I have good reason to be. I have never been happier."

My heart swelled hearing the words and seeing the look in her eyes. "I do love you so. Therefore, after breakfast, I'll print out my work schedule for the year so we can start making plans. Does your agent have a schedule for you that can be emailed?"

"I am sure she does. Would you like me to call her?"

"I just thought we could put our schedules side by side and find how often we can be together."

The Bernard pout. "Are you sure you don't want to just run away and live with me?"

"Oh boy, do I. However, I signed a contract for the school year. It's only until May. I'm sorry. I wish I didn't have this obligation, trust me."

"I know. You told me." She smiled as she said it, but the smile never reached her eyes. We needed to talk about both of our calendars in detail. Bottom line—we had some serious obligations in the short term. It created some tough hurdles for two people now living on raw desire, carnal lust, and volatile emotions. I wanted to put everything aside for hours, days, and weeks to absorb every nuance of the woman I loved. Hell, I wanted to sweep everything off the table and make love to her spread out in front of me, begging.

New love is so heady and consuming, but there were some practical concerns. I agreed to stay with her through August and commute to the schools. Nicole would check to see when her schedule might permit return visits to stay with me, and I would fly to see her on my breaks.

Even though she resisted the idea of using technology, I convinced her that we could communicate several times a day by phone, text, instant message, and video. Nicole hated the demands of technology, and even cried when she thought she would not be able to talk with me if she couldn't master the techniques. I assured her we would practice for the next few weeks. For now, we were together.

"After you call your agent, why don't you go ahead and start vocalizing and I'll clean up the kitchen?"

We both carried our dishes to the sink, and I started rinsing as she stood beside me rubbing my back with her head on my shoulder. "I think I will never grow tired of the feel of you near me. Your wonderful body is strong and very soft." She followed up her comments by moving her hands to my belly. My breath caught in my throat when she caressed my breast with her soft fingers, and I could feel my vision darken. Her touch created a Pavlovian arousal in my body. My pulse sped up and my muscles contracted in anticipation.

"Go and make your phone call," I said, squeaking out the plea. A couple of more minutes of foreplay and I knew we'd be back in the bedroom or on the floor. I leaned both arms on the sink as my pulse slowed.

Who can ever be ready when a dream comes true? For so long after my breakup with Bekka, I haphazardly drifted through life, but always I could return to the happy moments in that first summer when Nicole occupied my thoughts and fantasies. Now those same fantasies that sustained me through the hard times had become my reality.

The sounds of the piano brought me around. I looked up as a cloud scooted overhead, blocking the sun through the skylight. This house, this time, and this woman created my new universe. It was an endless gift.

The music was beautiful and the lyrics were German. I walked into the den and stood behind her to see the score. The new music had come via USPS Priority two days earlier: *Ariadne auf Naxos* by Richard Strauss. The music seemed vaguely familiar. I stood silently behind her, feeling her intense energy, and my hands settled on her small shoulders.

"Do you like this piece?" she said, turning a few pages farther.

"Yes, it seems familiar. What's it for?"

"I have a gala concert in New York in October and must sing some new songs. Then I will perform this opera in Paris in the spring."

Paris in the spring. I couldn't imagine anything more romantic. I made a mental note to check my schedule for spring break, hoping that it would coincide. I looked down at her dainty hands on the keyboard and listened as she effortlessly sang the rather challenging aria. Standing so close to her, I could almost feel the musical notes she was singing dance around inside of me, enhancing the already fluttery feeling. I whispered a silent prayer and kissed the side of her neck. "You sound beautiful. Keep singing, and I'll work on the schedules."

She turned sideways and offered her lips. "Another kiss before you go."

≈≈≈≈

Things amped up around the house as we both adapted to our new roles. There was a new energy inhabiting the body of the mercurial opera singer. She was more like a giddy teenager, and it was all I could do to encourage restraint when we were in public. I think she would have gladly taken out a full-page ad complete with pictures. Even though I felt the same way, I still believed it was in both our interests to maintain a low profile as long as she was performing here and I was working for her. The call from her agent brought relief to both of us. Mario would accept the terms Nicole offered. He would not contest the divorce. News of her separation and divorce was not public yet, and it seemed to me we were courting disaster to announce that she was now banging her personal assistant. I cringed just thinking about what the tabloids would do to her. The school district would not be much kinder.

The August schedule rotated *La Traviata* every couple of days and required some adjustments to maintain Nicole's voice and stamina. We were lucky to have the scheduled breaks and supplements, and had prevented any more low-sugar episodes. I began to wonder how much of the disorder related to the stress she had experienced with Mario. Nicole seemed happy and I was ecstatic. Our days were busy, and the nights beyond my wildest dreams.

I labored over her schedule and mine, finding only limited overlaps where we could be together. At times, I just hated thinking about the physical withdrawal but had to push away those feelings. The moments we had together were more special because of the urgency and fear. I continued to rationalize that even an hour with Nicole was better than the alternative.

<hr />

"This is too hard. I cannot do it!"

The water bottle flew past my head and she ran

from the room.

"Nicole, please…" I clutched my head with both hands. We had been working every day using both computers to practice instant messaging and then video chat applications. At first, Nicole enjoyed the prospect, but at the same time she fought the technology. The time zone differences were a challenge. We worked slowly, but it was one step forward two steps back. I was frustrated and she was worse. I knew I was pushing her too hard, but we only had a couple of weeks before the end of the season.

She agreed to stay in Santa Fe another week so we could get our plans finalized, but had to be in New York by the second week in September. I could feel the anxiety start to bubble up just thinking about her departure. I spent hours reading over my work contract looking for some kind of a loophole. Being rash would only hurt me in the end. If I burned a bridge with the school system, it might be a big mistake.

I had no guarantees that this impetuous romance would last, and clearly Nicole didn't worry about it. Why should she? Her future was secure. Every week her agent sent new requests for her to perform somewhere in the world or do another recording or talk show.

Sometimes I felt completely insane to consider taking a risk like this. When I was with her, even just in the same room, I felt completely captivated by the power of her love.

My God, Ellis, you have gone from being a wimpy little girl to a complete head case. All you could think about was this woman and now she's begging you to run away with her. What exactly do you want? It's time to put on your big girl panties and make an effing deci-

sion. Are you gonna grab the brass ring or not?

Crap. Okay, truth time: I'm scared. Yes, I want this to work more than anything else. I'm afraid I can't do this long-distance relationship either, especially if she's not able to handle the technology.

My water bottle was empty, and I stood up and took a deep breath. I walked down the hallway and found her in her room lying on the bed.

"Are you all right?"

She rolled over on her back and looked at me. Her eyes were a little puffy but she smiled weakly and reached out her hand. "I am sorry, I just feel so stupid."

I took her hand and sat beside her. "I'm sorry, too, because I feel like I've been pushing you too hard. You're not stupid. This is hard stuff." I stroked her wrist with my other hand. "I'm scared about not being able to communicate with you whenever I want."

"But we can use the cell phone, *n'est-ce pas*?"

"Of course. It's just that I want to be able to see you, and that will require the video." I could feel her tense when I said that. I leaned over and kissed her forehead. "Let's not worry about that now. We still have time, and I want to enjoy every precious moment I have with you."

She pulled me down beside her and tucked her face close to mine. "*Je t'aime*," she whispered as she slipped her hand under my shirt, rubbing my back as I felt my heart constrict.

※ ※ ※ ※

Time was moving too rapidly even as I tried hard to stay focused on the moment to memorize every detail. Nicole was able to settle down and was soon pretty adept at using the videoconferencing feature. I was feeling more positive by the time the Friday performance arrived when Liz would bring her guest to the performance.

I poured some coffee for both of us as Nicole came in from the patio. She had chosen to do her yoga out there while I watched from the den. I never tired of watching her move. Her years of yoga had toned her body, and she had a precise economy of movement that was fluid and delicate.

"*Merci*, my darling." She took the proffered cup.

Her face flushed from the exertion and my fingers instinctively reached to connect while I kissed her forehead. "I thought you should know that watching you stretch is an incredible turn-on."

She grinned lasciviously. "I am shocked. You must be some kind of pervert."

"Exactly. You may not be safe with me." I reached my hand around to squeeze her ass as I ran the tip of my tongue along her lower lip.

She shivered involuntarily. "Do not start something you may not be able to finish," she said, grabbing the waistband of my shorts.

"I would never dream of doing that." I moved one leg between hers as I backed her against the counter. Her resistance was nonexistent, and she leaned her head back, inviting me to sample the soft skin of her neck.

She giggled a little and said mockingly, "Oh, please be gentle with me."

My laugh started us both off in fits of giggling. We continued moving against each other as she teased me with a variety of animal noises, dramatic groans, and expletives. I could hardly keep my mind on business, but fortunately my body knew how to respond without direction.

My cell phone interrupted again as we sat giggling on the kitchen floor. "Hello? Oh, hi, Liz. Yes, we're looking forward to it. Absolutely, but let me ask her." I disengaged Nicole's hand from my breast and tried my best to sound serious. "My friend Liz would like to know if she and her friend could meet you after the performance."

She looked up at me with the eyes reminiscent of a feral cat and nodded. "I look forward to it. Please tell her hello."

Her mouth moved rapidly to the breast left unattended by her hand. I almost yelped. "No problem, Liz. Nicole wants to meet you." I was sure the gasp was audible as a rapacious beast was abusing some very sensitive tissue.

"Me too. I'll be glad to see you and we can talk more then. Okay, you take care. Bye." I managed to get my cell phone up on the counter just in time. "Hey! What happened to 'be gentle with me'?" She was not listening.

※ ※ ※ ※

The Friday performance was one of the best I'd seen so far. Without taking credit, I had to guess that Nicole's increased stamina and new outlook on life had greatly enhanced her performance. Now, in addition to her skill and a great vocal gift, she had a new kind of freedom on stage. If possible, her movements were more fluid and her singing more effortless. I was doubly thrilled that one of my best friends was present to witness this.

As soon as the performance ended, I hurried to the agreed-upon meeting place to escort them backstage. While I waited, I listened to the gushing comments as the audience filed out. The glowing reviews were nothing compared to the individual comments from seasoned operagoers. Most of the audience were season ticket holders and had been for many years. Throughout that time, they had attended a large variety of operas including many world premieres of new works. Nevertheless, there were old standards like *La Traviata* that were always included each season.

"Meg, oh, that was so beautiful." Liz greeted me with a hug. She was beaming with excitement even as her ruined mascara testified to her reaction to the tragic opera.

"I'm so glad you liked it," I said, returning the hug. "I'm Meg Ellis." I reached out to her friend.

"Oh, I'm so sorry," Liz said. "Meg, this is Sandy Lopez. We work together."

"It's nice to meet you, Meg. I've heard so much about you." Sandy smiled and casually placed her arm around Liz's shoulders. *Well, I guess we do have some news.*

"Follow me and we'll go meet Nicole," I said.

Backstage was still bustling with cast and crew scrambling to break down the set because Saturday's production would be a new one. Nicole had already changed and was saying goodbye to some well-wishers.

"Nicole, I'd like to introduce you to my friend Liz and her friend Sandy."

She stood and graciously shook hands with both. "I am so pleased to meet you. Would you like to sit down?" She looked at me. "Maybe your friends would like to come back to the house for a glass of wine?"

The delighted surprise on their faces answered the question.

I helped Nicole gather her things, provided instructions on where to meet us, and led the way out to the cars. As soon as we got to my car, Nicole kissed me hard. "What did you think of the performance tonight?"

"It was electric. I've never seen you like that."

"I know. It felt so different, so alive. I did not do anything different, it just felt so right. It is a very good thing your friends were there tonight." She squeezed my hand. "*Je t'adore, chérie.*"

Once back at the house, Nicole excused herself to change her clothes while I provided a brief tour and opened a nice bottle of pinot. Nicole returned in my favorite red silk caftan, causing me to flush instantly. I'm sure Liz noticed but said nothing. We went out and sat on the patio to enjoy the warm night and the breeze.

"Meg tells me that you worked together before," Nicole said.

"Yes, we started working for the school district at the same time. In that first year, we got to be really good friends, but it was only recently that Meg convinced me to go with her to see an opera. I was hooked." Liz glanced over at me and smiled. "My gosh, it was nothing compared to what we saw tonight. I don't think I'll be able to sleep."

"It pleases me to know that you enjoyed it so much. It is my hope with every performance that someone will be as touched as you are."

"Oh, Ms. Bernard, it was beyond my wildest expectations." Liz was gushing now.

Nicole reached across the table and squeezed her hand. "Please call me Nicole. It is not so formal at home." As she drew her hand back, she ran her fingers across the back of my hand, a gesture that did not go unnoticed.

I poured more wine as we continued small talk about opera and school nursing. "Liz, did you have any luck finding a job?" I asked.

"Not really. I've got my name at the two agencies, but you know how it is this late in the season. They've got most of their positions filled."

"Maybe you could take Meg's job so she would not have to go to work," Nicole said, then winked at me.

I could almost feel my jaw hit the table. Nicole was looking at me with a very quizzical expression and a sweet smile. She nonchalantly drummed her fingertips on the table. "What? You did not think about this? It is so obvious."

Why hadn't I thought of that, indeed? Without thinking, I reached across the table and pulled Nicole's face close enough to kiss. "You're a genius! Liz, would you be interested in taking over my contract this year?"

Her face lit up. "Seriously? Do you think they'd let me do that?"

"I don't see why not. I'll just tell them that I need to move out of state. I mean, you're fully credentialed with the state, you have experience with the district, why the heck not?" The excitement was building inside of me just like the imminent eruption of a volcano. She could even take over my apartment if she wanted.

In minutes, thousands of new ideas formed along with new possibilities and new hopes. I could barely contain my excitement and I held Nicole's hand to keep from floating out of my chair.

Liz and I began to talk about various options in rapid-fire bursts, punctuated by comments from Sandy. It was clear from Nicole's expression that she did not fully follow the conversation, but I would fill her in later. By the end of the evening, we both agreed that I would contact the Santa Fe school district while Liz checked her options about the house she was renting.

Liz and Sandy both thanked Nicole for a wonderful experience and promised to continue their opera education. Liz hugged me tight with tears in her eyes. "I'm so happy for you, and I'm so grateful for your friendship and your help. This could be amazing—for both of us, but I will miss you terribly."

"Me too. But we'll stay in touch, I promise," I said. Sadness and joy battled for attention.

Nicole had already put things away, and by the time I turned out the lights and locked up the house, she was waiting for me. I closed the bedroom door and looked at her. The only lighting was two track lights above the bed. The dark green walls were a stark contrast to her lovely skin and blond hair. Her eyes fixed on me and I could feel my knees grow weaker.

The soft gray sheet draped just above her waist, and I mindlessly undressed as she watched me with both expectation and desire. My insides turned to jelly and I felt my heart pounding behind my breastbone. I could never have dreamed this and would never dare wish it. The woman I loved was waiting for me to fulfill our destiny.

In a matter of days, the promise of love we made

became manifest. There were many details to sort out, but somewhere in my soul I found a sense of peace. I stood quavering on a precipice of happiness beyond my wildest dreams.

As if reading my mind, Nicole smiled knowingly and nodded. "Yes, *ma chérie,* it is true. We will be together. I could not be happier."

My legs threatened to buckle as I walked to the bed. I lifted the sheet and slid in beside her, helpless to prevent the tears of joy streaming down my cheeks. "I love you, Nicole."

"You are trembling, my darling. What is wrong?" She pulled me close and stroked my face gently.

"I never dreamed...I think it's happening, though. Our dream is coming true. We're going to have the chance to be together. Do you still want me? Do you still want me to go with you? Please be honest."

"Oh, Meg, even more than I can tell you. I do not want to be separated from you for even a day. We will travel and make love and you will sing. Yes, you will have your dream, I promise you. There are people in New York who will help you. I do not understand the details you and your friend were saying but I believe what your eyes tell me. *Je t'aime, beaucoup.*" Her lips brushed mine and I could no longer control the trembling excitement. Tears covered our faces as our lips sealed our fate and our hearts pounded against one another.

If You Liked This Book?

Reviews help a new author get discovered and if you have enjoyed this book, please do the author the honor of posting a review on Goodreads, Amazon, Barnes & Noble or anywhere you purchased the book. Or perhaps share a posting on your social media sites or spread the word to your friends.

About the Author

Barrett Magill is a Golden Crown Literary Society Award Finalist who published six novels in four years starting in 2011 including: Damaged in Service, Defying Gravity; Dispatched with Cause; Deliver Us From Evil; Balefire; and Flights of Fancy before she joined Sapphire Books Publishing family in 2016.

Her YA entitled The Dreamcatcher was released January 15, 2017. Balefire was re-released in June of 2017 and her next novel, Highland Dew released in April 2018. The Audible version of Highland Dew was released in June of 2018.

With the New addition—Destiny's Child, Book Five in the Damaged series—released in July 2019, Sapphire Books re-released the original Damaged series eBooks one book per month March through June at deeply discounted prices.

Barrett is a member of the Western Women Writers of New Mexico, the Land of Enchantment Romance Authors, Romance Writers of America, Golden Crown Literary Society, Sisters in Crime, and the Petroglyph Guild.

After retiring from a busy nursing career, she moved west. Now, Barrett enjoys the inspiring mountain views from two acres of prairie in New Mexico's high desert. Her devoted pack includes a hyper border collie mix, and a sweet young blue eyed husky mix.

CHECK OUT BARRETT'S OTHER BOOKS

The Dreamcatcher - ISBN - 978-1-943353-67-5

High school is rarely easy, especially for a tall, somewhat gangly Native American girl. Add a sprinkle of shyness, a dash of athletic prowess, an above-average IQ, and some bizarre history that places her in the guardianship of her aunt. Then normal high school life is only an illusion.

Kai Tiva faces an uphill struggle until she runs into Riley Beth James, the extroverted class cutie, at the principal's office. Riley shows up for a newspaper interview, while Kai is summoned for punching out a classmate.

Riley is the attractive girl-next-door-type whom everyone likes. Though a fairly good student, an emerging choral star, and wildly popular, she knows she'll never live up to her older sister. She makes up for it with bravery, kindness, and a brash can-do attitude.

Their odd matchup is strengthened by curiosity, compassion, humor, and all the drama of typical teenage life. But their experiences go beyond the normal teen angst; theirs is compounded by a curious attraction to each other, and an emerging, insidious danger related to the mysterious death of Kai's father.

Their emerging friendship is tested as they navigate this risky challenge. But the powerful bond forged between them has existed through past lives. The outcome this time will affect the next generation of Kai's people.

Balefire – ISBN – 978-1-943353-91-0

Silke Dyson is a free-spirited artist and teacher struggling with a vision impairment as a result of a physical altercation. Kirin Foster is a pragmatic Type A writer for a travel magazine with great opportunities for travel, and a growing restlessness.

Their lives intersect at thirty-thousand feet during a tropical storm. With plans lost in the ensuing confusion, they form an unlikely friendship. The relationship strengthens in the warm tropical sunshine of the Belizean Cayes.

To their surprise, they discover a real connection with backgrounds in Milwaukee. Back home they continue an easy rapport with common interests and mutual friends.

Sometimes a random spark of kindness or caring can kindle a small flame. With patience and serendipity, a small flame can grow into a balefire—a beacon of hope to guide a pair of lost soul's home.

Highland Dew – ISBN – 978-1-948232-11-1

Bryce Andrews, west coast sales director for Global Distillers and Distribution, is tired of the corporate hamster wheel. She needs a change.

A craft whisky trade show offers her inspiration and

a chance to revisit Scotland and the majestic scenery of the Speyside region—best known for the "Whisky Trail." Bryce and her coworker, Reggie Ballard, need to find a wholly original whisky for their international distribution division by visiting a number of small distillers.

A blind curve, a dangling sign, and weed-choked driveway draw Bryce directly into a truly unique opportunity. She discovers a struggling family, a shuttered distillery, and a spitfire of a daughter called home to care for her confused father.

Fiona McDougall—the only child and heir to the MacDougall & Son legacy, had her career teaching in Edinburgh curtailed by fate…or serendipity.

When the stars finally align, the two women work together to resurrect a dream for themselves and the family business—if they can weather the storms of unscrupulous business practices in the competitive whisky market.

Other Books by Sapphire Authors

Last First Kiss: A Passport to Love Romance – ISBN – 978-1-948232-95-1

Alessia Cavalii is a rising star in the competitive international wine scene, and one of only twenty-six female master sommeliers in the world. Her home is a renovated winery on the windswept coast of Italy, she has a career she loves, and she is finally free of a toxic relationship. But Alessia is hiding a dangerous secret— one that could, in a second, shatter the life she's built. Parker Haven is a captain in the U.S. Army and stationed at the NATO military camp near Salerno. An investigator with the Military Police, she's pulled in to help solve a string of murders in the city and finds herself inexplicably drawn into Alessia's world. As the intrigue surrounding the case—and the alluring Alessia—spins more and more out of control, Parker realizes she may have to choose between her military career and the woman she's falling for. Do we ever truly know the people we love?

A storm's brewing on the horizon. Can Addie and Greyson weather it, or will it blow them over?

Blueprint for Romance: A Garriety Romance – ISBN – 978-1-948232-71-5

After the death of her husband, Dylan Lake's ability to trust in others is shattered. Her life is thrust into turmoil between caring for Emma, her seven-year old handicapped child, and working hard to make ends meet. Dylan doesn't have time to pursue a romantic relationship. Finding that one special person only happens in dreams. When fate keeps throwing Dylan and Kat together, Dylan finds her attraction to Kat something she can't ignore. Will her trust issues stop her from letting Kat into her and Emma's life? Leaving her old job and moving halfway across the country were the scariest things Kat Anderson had ever done. Starting a new life and career takes priority over any foolish notion of a fairy-tale future of romance and love. Kat's attraction to Dylan is time taken away from building a new business. Can Kat juggle love and duty to find her Happy Ever After? Welcome back to Garriety, the town with an open heart, and home to some of the quirky and warm characters from Add Romance and Mix. Join Kat and Dylan on their quest for true romance with a little help from Kat's sister Briley and her family, along with a host of new characters.

To Be Loved – ISBN – 978-1-948232-79-1

A dead body, women and kids in peril, treachery at every turn—no problem for the close-knit sexagenarian friends of the Silver Series, Dory, Robby, Jill and Charlene! When a calm evening walk leads Dory to suspect bad news is happening right next door in her placid neighborhood, and when a waif comes under Jill's wing, routine life takes a vacation. And when a corpse points toward a suspect who's far from virginal in character, and seems to link to the waif and the bad news, well! All bets are off. The women rally to defeat evil and correct injustice, helped with a generous serving of karma from a very unexpected source. Along the way, they work with and for the police, sometimes in—ah, unorthodox—ways. But what are a few more gray hairs to law enforcement when the cause of justice is advanced? They encounter smugglers in the devil's oldest crime, street-smart kids wiser than their years, maids in distress, and unlikely allies in Skid Row. But the persistent four also marshal the vengeance of the angels, through their own.

Bobbi and Soul – ISBN – 978-1-948232-41-8

Bobbi Webster wants nothing more than to be the best family practice doctor for her home town in rural Oregon. To accomplish that, she's enrolled in a two-year fellowship in rural medicine at Valley View Medical Center in Colorado. Sparks fly when Bobbi meets the Reverend Erin O'Rouke, a petite, feisty priest who meddles in the treatment of Bobbi's patients. To make matters worse, Bobbi wants nothing to do with any religion, much less the woman she dubs, The Elf.

Erin serves as vicar at a small church where a few parishioners have stipulated that she must be celibate, reflecting their "love the sinner, hate the sin" tactic. After she clashes with Erin, Bobbi recognizes how a recent breakup of an abusive relationship has falsely colored her perception of Erin's world and work. Likewise, when Erin understands how Bobbi's emotional wounds make her vulnerable, her natural empathy moves her closer to Bobbi.

They find themselves drawn to each other, but how can Bobbi and Erin overcome so many obstacles to find love?

Faithful Valor – ISBN – 978-1-948232-85-2

Sometimes danger isn't found on a battleground—it's sitting at your front door. Nic Caldwell is back Stateside, working the job she was supposed to have before her most recent deployment, and living her best life at home. At least she thought she would be, except her PTSD is always in the background, dragging her back to her tour in Afghanistan. As she struggles to control her demons privately, her public life with Claire is almost picture perfect. However, a picture can't show everything hiding just under the surface.

Claire Monroe has the love of her life back in one piece—almost. She's trying to help Nic adjust to her new normal both physically and emotionally while also going back to school and raising their daughter, Grace. With all the difficulties Nic's re-entry poses along with the new challenges of being an adult student, she wonders how she can guide them back to their old life while building a new one for herself.

Cece Ramirez has decided that the Army has served its purpose and she is ready for a new chapter in her professional and personal life. Retiring from active duty and moving on to a new role as a police officer on a college campus, she realizes that she's traded camo, discipline, and rifles for book bags, bikes, and rowdy post-adolescents. While she and the students at Cal State Monterey Bay might be the same age, their pasts are vastly different, and the transition from soldier to college cop may not be as smooth as she hopes. When a chance encounter at a near-base shopette challenges

Nic's authority and leaves her and her family in potential peril, Cece and Claire must pull together to back Nic up in peacetime, and right at home.

www.ingramcontent.com/pod-product-compliance
Lightning Source LLC
LaVergne TN
LVHW040038080526
838202LV00045B/3382